THE ROGUE ELF OF URLAS

SONGS OF SHADOW TRILOGY

J. T. WILLIAMS

To my time as a Paramedic.
I've seen death, I've seen new life, and I've been beside
souls at all points in the journey we all embark upon with
our first breath.
To those I saved and those I could not.

Death is not the enemy. It is but the equalizer of mortals.
Live while you have a choice. Embrace those you care for.
Love with all your heart and mind for it is but a short,
sweet time we have on this planet.
... make the most of it.

The World of the Dwemhar

If you would like to know about new releases, specials on other books, and get insider information before anyone else, head to my website and join my mailing list!

www.authorjtwilliams.com

STORMBORN SAGA
Stormborn
Mage Soul
Elf Bane
Stormborn Saga Trilogy
Ranger's Fury (Ranger Trilogy #1)
Black Moon (Ranger's Revenge #2)
Aieclo (Ranger's Revenge #3)
Epochs (Clockmaster's Shroud #1)
Shards of Etha (Clockmaster's Shroud #2)
Shadow Cry (Clockmaster's Shroud #3)

HALF-ELF CHRONICLES
Half-Bloods Rising
Seer of Lost Sands
Shadow of the Orc Star
Necromancer's Curse
Wrath of the Half-Elves
The Last Dwemhar

ROGUES OF MAGIC
Rogues of Magic Trilogy

LOST TALES OF THE REALMS
Ranger's Folly (Ranger's Revenge Trilogy Prequel)
The Dwarven Guardian
A Stranger's Quest
Wizard Trials

All books listed here are within the same world. For further information, please head to my website!

www.authorjtwilliams.com

FOREWORD

If you're new to the world of the Dwemhar and my epic fantasy world, welcome! You're getting the first three books of my bestselling Half-Elf Chronicles series and you're in for a wild ride. From the icy Glacial Seas and the secrets of the ancient races of old, to the southern deserts where demons haunt the sands, and eventually the Riverlands of lower Taria and the war against the Clan of Ur, you will not expect the story you're about to read. If you're a veteran of my world, you'll love the bonus material I've included after each book!

May the gods of the North watch over you,

-J.T. Williams

HALF-BLOODS RISING

HALF-ELF CHRONICLES BOOK 1

Updated 3rd Edition

THE URLAS WOODLANDS

He tasted the tinge of blood in his mouth. Kealin spat and moved his elven blade into an angle behind him. His master called this a guarded stance. He studied his adversary, watching his breathing, his footwork, his subtle movements, and his slight nuances that hinted at his next moves. His opponent moved forward and spun, slashing low before jumping into the air. The blade swung toward his head. He dodged it, sidestepping to the left before kicking his opponent's knee. He moved his hand along his hilt, spinning the blade to strike, only to parry another blow meant for his shoulder. The shadowy form of an elven warrior recoiled, and now it took a guarded stance.

Gravel sliding under his feet as he shifted his weight, Kealin ran forward. His opponent, taken by surprise in his agility, faltered. He struck him twice. His bare chest was chilled by the night air, but the half-elf did not mind. His blood was hot, and he was eager to fight.

Two more opponents, greater in size than the first, rushed him. He jumped, slashing one across the chest. The second one was more determined, but through a series of careful parries, he too fell. Now another one approached. This one was larger, and the half-elf knew he must be ready.

All around him, the trees of the great elven woodlands were alive with the songs of night. A faint glow of the moon was on large green leaves that rustled with a strong wind. The larger man was upon him. He worked to disengage, moving to the left, but the swordsman moved with him. He had played fair until now. His master would be happy with his work so far, but he was not one to rely on mere teachings.

He reached behind his back, drawing a second blade, and rushed his opponent. He struck repeatedly with the first blade. With a careful twist of wrist, he forced the man's sword upward. He locked the man's blade high. A split moment later, he buried the second sword deep in his stomach.

He smiled as the man fell to the ground.

"Kealin, your skill with two blades is exceptional. If only you could do such tasks without two blades. I am impressed but cannot approve of this. Your brother will not approve of such either."

The voice was that of Blade Master Rukes, and his own tone was less than approving.

"Then you can tell Taslun of my folly," Kealin replied.

"There is no need, little brother."

Kealin turned to see his brother approaching the

arena grounds. The collapsed forms of the phantoms he had faced vanished in a flash of sand. His brother approached just as the last one was blown away in the winds.

"The Urlas Blades use one sword, not two."

Taslun was the epitome of what the Urlas Woodlands wished to produce in a swordsman. Fearsome in many regards, he was also tall and slender. At all times, he had a long curved blade strapped to his back. He had spent many years learning his craft, and the lineage of their father was with him. He had pointed ears and blond hair he kept long down his back.

"I cannot expect a brother of mine to have such disregard for order."

"Then be sure Calak knows so he will not disappoint you. He is closer to you in blood; the elf side of him is strong. I must make up for that as I see I must."

"What you must do is come home now. Master Rukes is done with your disappointing practice."

Rukes confirmed his brother's words. "Tomorrow, young one. We will further your sword work."

Kealin bowed to his master and followed Taslun away.

They walked in silence from the arena. Under towering pine trees and beside the pools of the great lake, they passed over the white stone bridges that connected the cobblestone paths running around the entire lake. This was the Urlas Woodlands. A grand woods an entire world away from troubled lands. They were on the edge of this place. A large sea encircled their lands, but none normally left their shores. They were all safe here. It was an enchanted realm that only those of elven blood could find and dwell within. It was also a purist elf domain, but his family was allowed admittance. His father was a renowned Blade, the sacred elven swordsmen skilled in their blade work learned over hundreds of years. His father had earned his place in Urlas from fighting in wars long ago. But when he came, he brought his wife, a human.

Kealin was the younger brother to Taslun, and older brother to Calak, who teetered between his stalwart eldest brother and Kealin when it came to his own desires. Taslun was a step from joining the Blades of Urlas. He was just awaiting his final trials and the christening of the Blades.

Calak was hastily coming up and was like his brother Kealin in every way, but still not of the skill that he had obtained. In fact, Kealin was on track to surpass that of Taslun, but he believed he could never serve as a Blade of Urlas. His blood was not elven enough; he, like his sister, Alri, had taken after their mother. It wasn't like they didn't look like the other elves, but the council had deemed their blood not as pronounced. Alri was lucky in some regard. She was a mage, and fortunately for her, the mages did not have the same standards as the Blades. She, like their mother, was under the direction of High Archon Oaur, and was trained in many forms of spell craft. Though she was the youngest, she was not the type to be ignored.

"Father has called us home early; otherwise we would have tested your skill with dual blades against my own."

Kealin shook his head. "Why must we do that? Do you not believe your skill to be enough? We have ended that duel in a draw every time."

"I would like to show you what it means to be a real swordsman. You cannot claim a draw when a duel turns into you rolling around on the ground like an animal, kicking dirt in my eyes."

"But that is a duel in honor you speak of. In combat, it would be warranted. You can train for duels. I expect to use my skill for more than that."

"That would only be by the blessing of Master Rukes, which you will never get using two blades. Perhaps he will look over your half-elf blood if you will simply embrace his teachings."

Taslun spoke to him like their father, and that annoyed him.

"I do not disregard his teachings; only, I feel that they can be added to. The confines of the Blades restrict our actions."

"You cannot add to the traditions of our ancestors. One day, you will understand what I say."

Kealin stopped. "And one day you will all understand that I do not stand for our ancestors as you do. You and I are the same. Half-bloods. But you were deemed 'pure' by the council while I was deemed less."

Taslun turned. "I don't care if you stand as I do, but it is time we stop bickering as we do every day. We have no control over the council. Besides, there is news Father brings that I do not feel is the kind we want. I saw them packing earlier; he and Mother are preparing to leave."

They followed the path up into the mountains and

to a wooden structure built into the trees. It had stone lining the lower level, with wooden walls reaching up around a massive white tree. Their house itself was built into the tree, with interlinking platforms and structures that rose up in small towers, blending into the foliage above.

Calak sat cross-legged on a bench, looking outward beside Alri, who turned to see them. Their sister twirled her hair between two fingers and blew a loose strand out of her face.

"You are back," she said. "How did it go?"

"Taslun is most displeased," Kealin replied.

Taslun said nothing but smirked and shook his head.

"Children," a voice said. It was abrupt, and frankly, not the tone he preferred to hear.

Kealin turned to see their father and mother approaching from the upper alcoves. His father was in the silver armor of their people, and their mother held her wooden staff in the crook of her arm. She smiled at them.

"Come up here," their father said.

They followed in turn, with Calak approaching Kealin. He punched him in the shoulder.

"Two blades, again?"

"Yes."

"You know you are not supposed to do that."

Kealin glared at him, and he chuckled.

"Did you win?"

"Of course."

Calak smiled, and Kealin did the same.

Following each other up a wooden stairwell, they

joined their parents along an open-air balcony. The sights of the woodlands and the lights from other dwellings were easy to see from atop their own home. The dark woods contrasted to the starlit sky where fairies fluttering in the upper boughs of the trees looked at first like falling stars if you did not expect them leaping from branch to branch. Even far away from the other elves, they could hear flutes playing on the wind.

Kealin took a seat with the others. A large dinner was prepared but set only for four. As Kealin and his siblings stared, waiting, their father spoke.

"We are leaving and we depart tonight."

"Leaving?" said Calak. "Where to and why can we not come? It is so sudden. Where is the enemy? No one else prepares."

"They do. A great host is assembled but it has been mostly in secret. Our world is safe, children. But others are not so well. The gods of the northern world are faltering in their war against those we call the Itsu, the malevolent southern gods. Though the Itsu cannot enter these realms themselves, their actions are felt. We of magic are threatened, and we must respond.

"They have called all elves to the lands for a great war. The gods are in need of our skill. Shaman Iouir has foreseen greater misfortune striking the lands soon. The one called Kel has sought us Blades, in particular. We, with others, go to the calling of the gods."

"Then I will prepare my blade and leave with you," said Taslun.

"I forbid it."

"But I am trained as a Blad—"

"You are still a pupil in need of further training and more summers behind you. Until the Blade Master decrees, you are not to depart these lands, nor will any of you others. Kealin, that means you, as well."

His father focused his eyes on him and Kealin inhaled, nodding.

"Of course, Father," he replied.

Kealin respected his father more than he let on to the others, and his father's trust and respect meant much to him. It was one of the few things that did.

"Mother, why must you go? You are not an elf," Alri said.

"I know what I am, Alri. But I am trained as an Archon Mage; my powers will be needed. I have lived safely here for many years, and my life has been extended beyond that of normal length many, many times. I have been blessed by the elves, and I must repay that debt."

Alri did not seem convinced or calmed by their mother's words. She was red in the face and sniffled.

"Your mother and I regret this happening, but know that you are kept well in the Urlas Woodlands. Trouble will not befall you here. Rest, eat, and train yourselves, for the time may come when the bloodshed requires you to take part, but we hope that is not for many more moons."

They said little else other than goodbyes before departing. Shared hugs and swift kisses on the cheek followed. Kealin went to his father.

"Do well and be safe."

"We will, for all of you." He looked down on him

and then placed his arms around him. "I know you do not respect the ways of the elves, and I do not hold that fact against you, but remember that to use your blade for no reason but to kill makes you as the enemy yourself— senseless. Use your mind, son. It will not fail you, even if your blade does. That is the difference between you and your brother Taslun." He paused, "Remember that you must resist the path your sword will crave. I have done greater deeds with my blade sheathed than drawn."

"I will draw blood when it is necessary."

"Spoken as a Blade, son."

His father patted him on the back, and Kealin followed the others to the southern gate.

The southern gate was a sheer stone near the edge of the great elven lake known as Eldmer. A large gathering was already present on the shores.

Their parents left them, joining many others boarding silver wooden vessels destined for the southern lands.

The four siblings stood off to the side, away from the others. Their half-blood status had forced them to the fringes of society. It angered Kealin at first as he had aged, but now he embraced it. They were to be silent, as a custom, as the southern gate opened. Of course, he had no plan to.

Flutes began to play a sweet melody, and a loud horn called. The sheer stone wall split down the center and opened. It was through a lighted cave the elven host would pass, arriving into the other realm and to the world of danger, where they were called. Once through the passage of rock, they would emerge through a portal taking them much farther south than if they had simply sailed out of the bay. From their exiting of the Urlas realm, they could cut across the grand seas in great time. As the ships began to leave the docks, Kealin figured it was a good time.

"For the realms of Urlas, serve us well, elves!"

There were immediate glances from the other elves of Urlas. This was a moment of silence, but Kealin had never understood a reason to solemnly look on without any expression. His parents turned and smiled to him.

The great host departed with banners of leaves upon a blue standard. The flutes continued to play their melody as the host began entering into the cave.

They watched as their parents departed the woodlands with many others heading across the seas to the land across the world. The stone doorway closed.

Kealin spat on the ground and turned away from the others. In his mind, he felt that he would not see them for some time, and he trusted that to be true. He could see more than most with his mind, and it was what allowed him to use his blades as he did. It was not an elvish trait, and something he knew his older brother did not possess.

As they walked back, Taslun walked beside him. "Could you not resist talking out of turn?"

"Can I ever?"

That answer was sufficient, though it annoyed Taslun more.

KEALIN SLEPT WELL THAT NIGHT, even with the news

of his parents' departing. He awoke to a clamor downstairs, and to find Taslun restless, grumbling to himself. He was not so well.

He went downstairs to find his brother sitting in a chair, giving sharp glances to the corners of the room.

His brother grasped a bottle of wine and looked to him with the normal disappointing look that reminded him of their father when Kealin had done something wrong.

"What?" Kealin asked.

"I do not know," Taslun replied. "Perhaps you can explain to me why I am not good enough to answer the call to the grand gods of the North?"

"That is blasphemy, Brother. You heard our father. And why are you drinking? You don't drink."

"Yes, I heard him. But if it is as dire as it seems, then all Blades will be needed, and I should've been needed. This drink helps clear my mind."

"Do not bother, Kealin," Alri stated from the side of the room. "I have attempted to reason with him since before the dawn, and he will not listen."

"We go to the shaman today, little brother. We will have our answer to our questions!"

"And which question?" Kealin asked.

"The question of what we should do. Rotting here is not the answer."

Alri sighed. "I told him we were forbidden to leave. It seems with Father gone, he is not thinking clearly."

"Taslun is right," said Calak. "We need to do more. Don't you agree, Kealin?"

Kealin did not have an answer worth mentioning.

He wished for a cup of tea to wake up a bit more. Unlike Taslun and Calak, he could not just sleep well and wake up fresh, another curse of his less-than-elvish tendencies.

"It is early," he told them.

"Aye, Brother, but still late in my mind. Come."

Taslun, disheveled but walking, began out of the tree. Partially out of fear for his inebriated brother, he followed, with Alri and Calak trailed behind them.

The shaman Iouir could only be found at this hour. He lived atop one of the central mountains, and in general, it was impossible to find him except in the early morning. Much later into the day, he would be in a trance, one that he would not come out of for some time and, generally, never, if he did not wish to speak with you.

The central mountains sat near the Urlas Wood-lands headwaters, beside the sea, and not too far from their home. The shaman had a strange relationship with their family, and this was not the first time they had sought his wisdom.

In a single line, they ascended the mountain steps that rose up with intersecting platforms that were lit by multiple torches. Strange-looking wood and straw stat-ues, created by the shaman himself, greeted them every few paces.

Reaching the summit, there was a single hut with a steady trail of smoke rising up into the morning sky. A red cloth covered the door.

They parted the entryway cloth and took seats before a great carpet. Surrounded by a plume of white smoke was Shaman Iouir. He rarely opened his eyes, yet it was by some power he had greater sight than all of the other elves did. He had the ability to see beyond the mountain and hear unheard voices of the ethereal realms. Kealin had noticed long ago that the man was not an elf either, but he was shushed by his father when he pointed it out.

"The half-elf family has come seeking my wisdom, but I dare ask why, not that I need to know. I want to know what you will say your reasoning is."

Kealin looked to Taslun, who straightened his back to speak louder.

"Shaman Iouir, our parents have departed for distant lands. I worry for their well-being and seek your wisdom."

The shaman seemed to bow his head, and a slight grin split his lips. He reached beside him into a jar and tossed a handful of dust into a stack of wood before them. Flames leaped up, and Kealin recoiled back slightly from the blistering heat.

The fire grew in size and then began to change colors. Yellow, red, orange, blue, and then at last, a soft white.

"You ask a question that would be well to ask, but not what you wish to ask. Either it is the wine you are still filtering out of your mind, or you think you can deceive me. You wish to leave to help them and drag your younger siblings with you. That is short-sighted, young elf."

"I wish to do what I have trained for."

"And what is that, Taslun of the elves?"

The shaman had inhabited these lands for some

time, but there was not one person living who knew of whence he came from. He had lived nearby for longer than any elf knew, and considering elves lived until they were killed, or chose to die by their own hand, he was very old.

The elder brother thought for a while before answering. "To use my blade to uphold the elves and the reputation of those of Urlas."

"Then you would do well to listen to my knowledge, for it pertains to upholding your race."

The shaman shifted his hands around several pots in his vicinity. He mixed each of the materials in a large bowl in front of him before slowly pouring them into the fire. His voice changed as he spoke his wisdom, a custom of the shaman.

"Dey comes a time when yours father and mother need you, but I feel growing darkness is upon de Glacial Seas to our north. De elves of Urlas are needed by those of the northern gods, but it is the one dey call Dimn who needs you four. Yes, I see it will be by the horned ones you will be led. You must seek the horned ones out if you elves wish to be of use to de world. Look for de horns of the sea; dey will leads you."

An image came upon the smoke from the white fire. What appeared as ripples became evident as turbulent seas and a large tornado of ice growing in size. A great fire appeared, and the tornado became water and then steam and then smoke. Next came the image of a large creature swimming, a horn cresting the water. A moment later, a great wind came through the hut and swept the smoke upward and out.

They stared at Shaman Iouir, who now rocked back and forth with his eyes closed as he hummed to himself.

"That is it, then," said Taslun. "We must take to the Glacial Seas and search out these horned beasts."

"A word of caution to you who have been made wise," said the shaman. "Though you will know how you can help those you wish to, I did not say that it was a task that assures your own lives continue. It is a dark path if you wish to disobey your father's wishes, but one that is necessary in this time of the world, be it both for the good and the terrible. A shadow grows, threatening all, and your workings, though valiant, will not be yours alone."

The shaman began to hum before raising his hands. It was the signal that he was finished with speaking for now.

Kealin looked at Taslun as his brother ducked out of the hut. He followed after with haste.

"Is that it?" asked Kealin.

"Yes."

They began a slow descent down the mountain. Alri ran up beside Taslun. "Are we going?" she asked.

Taslun said nothing to her but started to walk faster.

"Of course we are going. We didn't climb the mountain for no reason," Calak said.

"Until our dear brother speaks, do not assume," Kealin advised. "Though I will not be staying behind. Even if it is against his wishes."

"For once, Kealin, I thank you for your stubbornness," Taslun said. He turned to the others. "But I cannot have you two going also. Alri, your arcane studies are important. I would rather you be safe here than out with us. Calak, though you train well with a sword, if the wars make it to our borders, you will need to watch out for Alri."

There was a short silence.

"Then I go with Kealin," Calak said.

"And I with Calak," Alri added. "You do not know how much help you may need."

"You are the youngest of us, Alri. I do not doubt your strength of heart, but I have three hundred years on you. Calak has one hundred."

"And I am not being left here," Alri said.

"Do none of you respect my wishes?" Taslun asked. "All the wisdom of years upon you, and you treat me as if you are mere children."

"Of course, we just have wishes too. Might I also say that you are going against the wish of our parents, and that is not something I do lightly myself. Now, when do we leave?" Kealin asked.

Taslun looked over each of them and sighed. It was clear he did not wish for all of them to go, but he knew them well enough to not try to prevent them.

"Soon. However, I wish for us to go speak with Master Rukes. Calak, go prepare one of the boats so we can traverse to the dwarven isles. It is there we will find a ship of size to navigate the Glacial Seas."

Calak nodded, and with him, Alri. Kealin and Taslun turned and headed toward the arena. The bay where they were to leave from took them from the enchanted realm too, but more directly and without a portal. Their realm sat within the far north and in icy seas. Their parents had gone with much fanfare and attention. They did not need or want that, and such small boats would likely not be missed.

Taslun and Kealin headed to the arena.

"I do not wish to endanger them," Taslun told him. "I wish you would stand by my desire to not allow them to go with us."

"We are family, even if we all debate, and I already use two blades in complete defiance of elven ways. I can easily defy my brother. Especially when his decision making is marred by a bit of early morning wine."

The two brothers shared a smile.

"I am with you, Brother, as are they. We will need all of our strength," Kealin said.

The two crossed into the arena and went to the far side. A steady plume of smoke rose into the sky from a stack just outside a stone hut. Master Rukes was garbed in a thick apron and lifted stones from a storage area outside into his smiting fire. They did not burn wood in the elven realm but used stones of the mountain that could burn and glow hot.

Master Rukes did not take time to stare at them as he went back into his hut. He emerged again with a black stone with red speckles. It was rushire ore. With a metallic tool, he stuck the raw piece of rushire deep into the burning hot coals.

"Master Rukes, do you have a moment?" Taslun asked.

"I have more than a moment." He stirred his coals and then withdrew the metal. In a rhythmic beating, he began hammering out what would become the blade of an elven sword. However, it would be many weeks of this process before the blade was finished. Rushire was drawn from the ground within the realms. It was unlike any metal used in the rest of the lands. Its use took a smithy of a certain regard, and Rukes was not only a blacksmith but an enchanter and crafter of magical items.

"What can I do for you two? Kealin is supposed to meet with me today for further training."

"He will not be," Taslun said.

Master Rukes looked up from his smiting and stared at them.

"You are the first to tell me this, that your brother will not be attending his training, yet you are the most stalwart in saying he must not miss a day."

"My siblings and I are leaving. We are needed in the Glacial Seas."

Kealin half expected their master to protest, to say something to dissuade them or to point out that they were not to leave. His reply was much simpler.

"What do you need?"

"Nothing beyond our blades. We wished only to let you know we will not stand idly by while our parents fight a war to protect us."

"Your parents go to stop a travesty from happening. They did not go with the Blades and archons across the lands to just fight a war, but to face a single enemy, in hopes of preventing further war."

Taslun walked around to a back room within the hut and reemerged with their blades and leather armor.

"You would do well to take also his extra blade," Master Rukes said.

Taslun looked at Kealin.They both donned their armor but said nothing.

Rukes snickered and smiled. "Your brother may not fight as we do, but he can handle himself well enough."

He looked at Kealin and then back to Master Rukes.

"I feel he should do as I and his brother train to do. We are doing this to protect our people; he must honor them and embrace the way of a Blade of the Urlas. But considering, if he wishes another blade—"

"I will do as my brother wants," Kealin interrupted.

Their master looked them each over and then went back into the room. He emerged a few moments later with another sword and set of leather armor.

"I admire your sudden dedication, Kealin. But I know it's not true no matter how much you claim it. Though he is less experienced, do not forget your brother Calak's blade. He does look up to each of you. Perhaps that can draw you to debate less and work together more."

Taslun nodded and then bowed. Kealin did so in turn. Their master bowed back.

"If you seek the Glacial Seas, know that no elven ship can take you. Those that your parents took will not return for some time."

"We head to the dwarven isles," said Taslun. "We can acquire a ship there."

"Careful, then. The city of Corson is one that has been amicable to us, but as you traverse the northern reaches, know that the sun is hidden this time of year.

Furthermore, you must watch out for one another, more so around those dwarves; it is a careful peace we have with them, and you will be beyond the blessings of the elven lands."

"Thank you, Master."

With that, they left the arena area and went back to their home. Kealin packed what little he wished to take with him, which was not much more than a thick coat and some travel meat. He walked near his sister's area and noticed her staff was gone. He quickly went to the doorway of their home and awaited Taslun. His brother had gone to find a map of the Glacial Seas. These seas were at the top of the world, and a place in legend to be barely traversable. The stories of maelstroms, beasts of the seas, and frigid waters were only some of the travesties that cursed those waters.

They met their siblings at the bay's edge. The vessel to take them across the waters to the dwarven islands was not much more than a fishing boat good for the shallows around the lands.

Alri stood on the bank as Calak gathered up ropes.

Taslun handed him his blade. "The master sends his luck to us."

"Well, I am glad the Blade Master approves," said Alri. "Archon Oaur does not approve."

It was then, behind the others, the elf Alri spoke of approached. He was a tall man, with a cloak of the woods upon him. Leaves, twigs, and other elements of nature made up his garb. He gripped a large piece of twisted wood as a staff.

"So it is true what your sister tells me. You are leaving."

"We must. The shaman speaks of darkness approaching a god of the North. We must go."

"Surely there are other elves who can do what you need doing? You four are young, innocent to the world, and I do not agree to Alri using her magic freely yet."

"Archon Oaur, I must go with them."

"And I told you before, I do not wish you to leave. You are safe here, with me."

Kealin walked between the archon and Alri. "She is leaving with us."

"Half-Elf Kealin, thank you for your presence on the edge of the Urlas Woodlands. Do you feel well knowing that you prevent your honorable father from living deeper within the realm? It is a sad existence to dwell on the edge of the sea. At least your mother has made a good mage for us of Urlas."

"I like the sea," Kealin replied. "What I do not like is a purist pushing his will upon my sister and his foul words speaking ill of my family."

"We are all half-elves," Taslun said.

The archon nodded. "Of course, just some are better than others. Very well, Kealin, I see your mother's stubbornness and tongue in you. Watch over your dear sister. I do not wish an ill happening upon her."

"She will be well," said Calak. "The best swordsmen in the realm protect her."

Kealin had still not backed down when the archon turn and left them at the waterside. He laughed to himself as he did.

"What was that, little brother? Do you wish to insult a master mage?"

Calak laughed. "He doesn't care who he insults. It is what makes him stronger than most."

Taslun gave Calak his armor and sword.

"Archon Oaur still sometimes points out that we are half-elven," Alri said. "It is why our family must live on the outskirts, and that we all know to be true."

"It makes no difference," Kealin said. "If we were around them who dwell within the realm, we would have to deal with them. I take no insult to it now. Though, I would like to once again gaze upon the lake from the high cliffs within the woods."

"Then let us protect these woods. With respect, those of Urlas will be more accepting to our status, and what they see as weakness will fade from their minds. Let us not tarry any longer. Into the boat."

The siblings filed into the small vessel, a carved-out wooden tree of massive size. It was with great pride the elves of Urlas were as simple as elves could be. Unlike those of the South who had grand cities, Urlas elves were closer to nature in every way, from their boats and clothing to the very homes they lived in. It was only deep in the woodlands that even a larger structure could be found, and that was only because the trees grew much taller there.

They paddled from the shoreline with ease as the four of them worked together to make headway. Kealin looked out across the water, paddle in hand; he drove it into the depths before pulling it toward him. The air was crisp, but he could taste the sea on his tongue. He had always felt at peace near the water.

"Did you find a map?" Kealin asked Taslun.

"Not one worth much. The lands of the North are locked away. I know the way to Corson, though. I've been there once."

2

THE SPICE RUNNER AND SEA DWARVES

I t took some time, but the mountains and the shoreline became a further distant sight. At first, there was thick fog, but passing out of their realm, it began to clear. Kealin looked back the way they had come and no longer saw any fog or mountains, only a wide open sea.

The island Corson was a place of intersecting cultures that, although close to the Urlas Woodlands, was not much more than a haven of travelers and criminals, for the most part. Most did not come this far north anymore.

In these regions, the dwarves once ruled much of the seas. The many islands were rich in minerals and fine ores, but that goodness and honesty had become degenerate, and it was more likely a dwarf would cut your throat than offer you something to purchase. Corson would not be the friendliest of places.

"So you have been here before?" Alri asked Taslun.

"Only once, and they attempted to rob our father."

"What happened afterward?"

"The fish ate well and there was a riot that chased us back to the boat."

Kealin scanned the distant shoreline, seeing buildings built on docks that ran all over the islands. The waves thundered against the coastline. Corson seemed to be one gigantic port, built on a foundation of wood and island rock that reached out over the ocean. It was darker here, and snowy. He looked out to see the sun just above the horizon.

"It is nearly night," Calak said.

"No," corrected Taslun, "it is only after noon. A trick of the eye in our realm. It is deep winter here, and though our realm is not too cold at all and has light, such is not the way here. When we crossed the waters, we passed into an unprotected realm. It was part of the reason why our parents did not wish us to leave. I assure you, our father would not approve of us going to this city, no matter the reason."

They guided their boat against a single dock that was open and tied the boat to a pole. A dwarf approached them, hobbling over other lines as he did.

"Elves. Great. Name and purpose here at Corson?"

Kealin spoke first. "Kealin, and with me, Alri, Calak, and Taslun. We are here to acquire a ship."

As he inscribed their names, his book glowed slightly, except for when he wrote the last one. It was then he looked up at Taslun.

"You've been here before," he said.

"I have. Long ago. Before my siblings had been born."

"I remember you. I was much younger then, and I do not feel I need to tell you to avoid what your father did."

"No."

"Good." He slammed the book shut. "If you are searching for a ship, a place called the *Spitting Crab Fish* is what you seek. It is up the road to the east, away from the docks. Beware, night is coming, and night is not a happy time in the islands."

The dwarf departed, and their path opened up. Kealin bound his cloak around him as they trudged up a snowy path onto a road capped with tall hills of snow. Most of the homes on the island seemed to have only their windows above the snowdrifts. Continuing on, there was a large multi-storied building on an isthmus of land. They went to it.

Written on a stone plank above the door were the words *Spitting Crab Fish*. A fishhook was off to the side and dark black in color. A stark contrast to the red paint all over the building. The smell in the air was like that of old fish. They heard a latch open a distance away, and a door fell down on the edge of the building before a rush of liquids came running out. It looked to be leftovers from the kitchen.

"This is it," said Taslun.

They pushed open the door and found a large dining hall with circular tables and not only a large bar running along the far edge of the wall but also multiple iron cooking pots.

The master of the building was a burly dwarf, much

taller than the rest, but still small by elven standards. He looked up happily at the arrival of guests but frowned as he noticed they were elves.

"If you are looking for accommodations, I suggest you find your way back out to your boat and go to the next frigid island. There is nothing for you here, elves."

"We have no issue with you, Master Dwarf. Only to be pointed toward one who can take us into the Glacial Seas."

There was an uproar of laughter. Around them, an assortment of dwarves, men, and others sheltering from the weather joked at the notion. Even the dwarf speaking to them was red and chuckling. He composed himself and made a motion with his hand to quiet the others.

"No issue is a good thing, elves. We do not wish for issues either. And we have some gifts from distant lands that assure such assurances."

The dwarf pointed to a statue, like a gargoyle of sorts, affixed above the bar and looking toward them with red eyes.

"A gift from the dwarves to any unwary trouble-maker. I believe only one person has been killed by it. Let's not make it more than that. Now, my name is Uris. Come and let me serve you. I will not allow a room, but I'm decent enough to offer food."

The four of them went to a nearby table and sat. A few moments later, the dwarf came with both bowls and spoons, as well as a large iron pot with a stewed fish menagerie to serve them. It was warm and full of herbs.

"Be thankful for the herbs you see. Our herbs took

an extra few trips before getting here. The ship that brought them is in for repairs. It seems he had a run-in with a bit of pirates, or so he claims."

From their side came a stranger with a belted sack hanging across his chest. It was a man with a short, scraggly beard that only just hung down the side of his face.

"Aye, if it wasn't pirates, it was some angry whale catchers, which are one and the same. I'm telling you, that bastard Rugag is behind it."

"And here is our bringer of spices," the dwarf said.

"The name is Vals, captain of the greatest vessel to sail the Glacial Seas."

"Greatest until the hull was ripped open and you took on water, barely limping into our docks. Aye, to be truthful, you crashed into the dock!"

"Very true, and I cannot deny I owe this man here a lot." He motioned to the dwarf.

"Yes, well, eat. All of you. My dealings with you, Vals, are only because of my kin who once sailed with you. By the way, you've been sleeping for so many days, I couldn't tell you, but I have it ready."

The dwarf went back behind the bar after serving the stew, and then returned with a parchment.

"Your repairs were costly. I'm assuming you do not have the money."

"Only have what you paid me for the spices."

The dwarf shrugged. "Well, perhaps you can rid our happy place of these elves. They are stinking up the place already. I gave 'em food. You can give 'em a ride. I need to get the table clear for Rugag. You may not like him, Vals, but he is a dwarf and, because of this, is our friend."

"Aye, pick some better friends." He turned to Taslun and Kealin, who were closest to him. "Names?"

"Taslun."

"Kealin."

"And what about you two?"

"Calak."

"Alri."

As Alri spoke, Vals seemed to become entranced.

"Dear dame, not only are you an elf but you must be one of the most beautiful I have ever seen. I had been entranced by elven beauty once before. It was long ago when I saw her, but her face has stuck with me. You remind me of her."

"Enough with the entrancing," said Kealin. "We need assistance."

The man turned toward him.

Taslun leaned in to the table. "You are well enough skilled to take us through the Glacial Seas?"

"Am I well-skilled? No, I'm a sick bastard of little skill who runs the gauntlet to deliver spices, wines, even coffee to the most desolate places of the world, for little pay, mind you, but for the thrill!I have a ship like no other, yes, the *Aela Sunrise*.

"I can do what is needed and of late, I work alone. Now I only have to watch out for myself. Part of the reason this Rugag doesn't like me. The only other cares I have are the animals that swim along my ship. I love the glacier sharks, in particular, but, too, the whales. Beautiful creatures and good friends."

"And why would a dwarf care for your love of sea life?" asked Kealin.

"Meredaas be blessed, do you not know what the dwarves do to them? They take them, kill 'em for the sport of it. Rugag collects the tusks of sea lions, narwhal horns, and any item from the sea he can use to adorn or fight with. He runs his own fleet of ships patrolling the waters, killing much more than is needed for oils and food. I know people must make a life here in the ice, but he does it for fun. One day, he will get his. If I could, I would sever his head from his body like he has done to countless of my friends of the sea."

The door swung open to the building, and a man in seal pelts with horned shoulders came in. With him, an entire band of dwarves, each with ice and snow on their beards, filed in.

"Very nice for you to arrive, Rugag," Uris shouted.

Rugag had a large sack with him. "More fish for you, Uris," he said in a deep tone. "Would've been better had we not been caught up with that damn Vals."

Vals recoiled down low upon the table with the others, careful to not show his face.

"Come, I will take you where you wish to go, but we need to leave."

Rugag began to shout again. "That damn Vals took out one of my masts this time. If I see him, I'm gonna kill him. Let him taste my dwarven trident. If he wants to stop our harvesting for the life-giving food, he can join our food. It makes no difference to me. I hear men can be tasty when cooked up right with a nice batch of carrots and shrimp. Do you think you could fix that up for us, Uris?"

Uris nodded. "Indeed I could, but the spices he brings are quite nice."

Kealin looked to the others as they all stood in unison. Vals was veiled and walked ahead of them. Kealin placed his hand on his hilt and began to walk.

"Damn elves aren't making it any better," Rugag said. "Next news will be they find us offensive for something. Go on, elf, go climb a tree. Chase your tree squirrels."

There was shared laughing among those at his table. Kealin turned, staring at them. "The only offense we take is having to listen to your raucous mouth this night."

The boisterous Rugag's smile turned to a glare. He drew his trident.

"Get out of here, elf."

"Put it away. You know not whom you speak to."

Taslun fell back from the others to grab Kealin from behind. "What are you doing? We do not need this."

He began to pull Kealin outside when the dwarves at the table stood and began toward them.

Alri and Calak were waiting with Vals when the group of them came out of the building.

Rugag held his trident, and now others held weapons too, forming a half circle around them as they were pushed toward the water's edge. The dwarves had been careful to block the path to the docks.

Kealin looked around, seeing the names of the ships and noticing Val's ship, *Aela Sunrise*, not too far away. Its lettering was crisp against fresh paint.

"We do not wish trouble," said Alri.

Kealin and Taslun stood beside each other. Calak was a few steps back, but all three had fallen into their stances. Their blades could be in hand in under a moment's need. There were sixteen dwarves before them. If they were skilled enough to fight, it was at least a fair fight by elven standards. A dead dwarf was not worth much but was something to smile about and to be encouraged in the lands beyond Urlas.

"We do not wish trouble ourselves," said Rugag. "But know we do not care for any at all beyond our people. I will let you live. Five elves. That is something to see."

Taslun released his grip, but Kealin kept his.

"We travel away from here and will not tarry any longer," Taslun said.

There were shared nods, and the dwarves parted the path toward the ships that had been recently repaired. Rugag's own ship was in the yard, and the fact his adversary's ship was just repaired had been completely ignored by the dense dwarf.

They began toward the *Aela Sunrise* at the moment when Rugag had noticed his mistake. At some point, not only had he missed Vals but, in his haste for warm food, he had ignored the direction they walked toward.

"Elves, why do you go toward that ship?" They continued toward the ship as the dwarves hastened their pace. "Come here."

They did not listen. Vals jumped to the ship and began cutting the dock lines. Rugag shouted loudly.

"Vals!"

Kealin drew his blade also and began cutting lines as the others made it onto the ship. The dwarves were following just behind. As Alri and Calak jumped aboard, they began to push off. The dwarves made it to the edge of the dock and, one by one, began to board until the fourth one missed and plunged into the water, starting a scene of shouting and screaming. Dwarves were not the best swimmers. Rugag did not make it onboard.

"Kill them!" he shouted from the shore through cupped hands. "Bring me Vals, dead or barely breathing, but bring me Vals!"

Taslun stepped forward as a dwarf drew a chained spike.

"It isn't personal, but we need the captain."

"No, it isn't," Taslun replied. In a motion, he drew his blade, rushing the dwarf. He was past him before his blade had cut through his neck. Kealin and Calak were upon the other two, and in quick slices, both fell dead. Alri looked at the last one who ran for the edge of the ship. He had thrown his fillet dagger as he ran, but it was a poor choice for fighting. The dwarf was almost to the railing when Alri brought forth her short staff. She made an entwining motion with her staff, and the man fell flat, caught in Alri's invisible snare. She dragged him back to the center of the ship.

Taslun and Kealin placed their swords on his neck.

"Tell your master to not hinder or assail this ship in any way ever again"—they each cut the tips of their blades into his cheeks—"or we will kill him and every dwarf under him."

The dwarf said nothing, but quivered. Alri used her staff as if she was shoveling trash from the ship, and dumped the man from the deck. He hit the water with a splash, and those on the shore began a hasty rescue with small fishing boats.

Vals worked to pull up one of the sails. The ship had been fitted to allow a single man to raise and lower the sails. He moved between masts, turning cranks and tying lines. If any would have asked to help, he would have refused it. This was his ship, and he knew her well. At last, they were making headway.

"Thank you!" said Vals.

"He is a poor life," said Taslun. "Not even worth killing."

"His kind has slowly killed all of my crew, leaving me to be by myself. My last man died a few weeks back. He was an elf, too, a good man. But enough of that. I have had much luck through the years. I expect it to change in time. Where are we to go? The Glacial Seas are quite expansive."

Taslun looked at Kealin. "Well, as to where exactly, it has been hidden from us. But we are to look for horned beasts to guide us."

"Horned beasts?"

"Whales, or maybe as you had said, a shark of some kind," said Kealin.

"Then I know where we must go," said Vals. "It is true fortune that has found us together."

As the ship made way, leaving the island behind, Vals went around the main masts and pulled a crystal out of the deck of the ship. He placed it in a metallic altar, and an image appeared in the air around them. It was a map.

"You see, most dwarves help me, as you can see with the gears to work my ship. This here was a gift of a different type. This ship is old and has been on the seas longer than myself. It is a relic in truth, from a race of seafarers beyond histories of songs I know."

Kealin looked up at the image. The contrast of glowing shapes with the backdrop of the starry night behind gave a somnolent feel to the air.

"What is this?" Taslun asked.

"It is a map, but not of parchment. It is one that shows the world as it is now."

The longer Kealin looked, the more he could see. The image was somehow above the lands. The clouds moved across the image, which even had the speckle of moonlight on the water. There were heavy clouds covering most of the map, except for where outlines of the islands were. Kealin could only imagine that this was how birds must see the lands from the clouds as they flew over.

Vals went to the map and pointed to an area to the east. "Here," he told them. "There is an island and the creatures I believe you seek. The creatures are called narwhals. Smart beasts, they are, but also prized to the types like Rugag. There are many narwhals in these waters, but some of the largest I have seen are here in this cove."

"Can they speak with us?"

"The question is whether you are able to listen, not

whether they can speak. All animals can speak if you can turn your mind to hear their voices."

Vals went to the helm and turned the ship due east. The winds cut across the bow as the sails adjusted to the change.

Kealin looked across the deck to see Calak standing by himself. He went to him.

"You are well, Brother?"

"I am," he responded in a hushed tone.

"You did well earlier. It was necessary, what we did. Do you understand?"

"I know. I had always believed war would come and we would fight then. That wasn't war."

"It is the same, Brother. Someone wished to do you harm, and you stopped them. That is what matters. If we were upon the battlefield, it would be the same—you against one with the thought in your mind of your next target before you have killed the first.

"Taslun is in love with the thoughts of our people, and I do dare tell you, in some ways, his belief is wiser. I do not wish to die, so I keep honor as a second-rank thought. I will survive."

Calak nodded. "I agree with that."

"Well, for now, you remain behind Taslun and me. I hope you will not be required to fight anymore. Watch over your sister."

"Always."

THE NIGHT PASSED UNEVENTFULLY, at first. Calak and

Alri slept, as did Taslun. Kealin remained awake, conversing with Vals.

"Yes, I have found the ocean provides all we need as people if only you show it the respect it deserves. I have survived storms I did not think survivable even with the blessing of Meredaas."

"I have only read of Meredaas," Kealin told him. "I understand he takes the form of a large fish."

"That is what I have seen in my dreams. I have dreamed frequently of the ocean. With my many days on it, I have never fallen out of love with the waters. However, I have had my misfortunes. I am constantly challenged to learn more, and I can tell you a curious wisdom is knowing that there is something new upon every rock and within every glacier. I run supplies, yes, but the adventure to have within these waters is unlike any upon the land."

It was then a sound came across the water. It was melodic and deep; the polar lights, glimmering above the waters, seemed to almost dance with the slow tones.

Vals smiled and closed his eyes. "My friends, I have not seen them in some time."

3

UPON THE AELA SUNRISE

The others did not immediately awaken. Kealin went to the side of the ship and looked over the edge. The water was breaking over something, and as he looked closer, he noticed a strange shape emerging from below the black depths.

"Embrace them. They come, for they know we seek them," Vals whispered.

Kealin continued to stare; from beneath the surface came their horns, long and silver, gleaming in the mix of starlight and moon above. Vals began a song.

"Starlight above us now we watch,
Sea-maids know what we do not,
Blessed souls amongst the ice,
Spiraled horns of magic thought."

THE OTHERS WERE AWAKENING. Joining Kealin, they watched as the pod began to emerge. There were at least eight narwhals following the ship as it continued sliding over the starlit waters. A ribbon of green appeared across the skies, splitting the lights already bending over the seas.

"Wura's presence," said Alri. "I have never seen the lights of the far north."

"A shame, but I am glad you see them now," Vals said. "The polar lights shine with the stars, and the glimmers above are a welcome friend most nights. Though I have never seen the god himself."

"Like Meredaas, I doubt he wishes to be seen by many," said Kealin.

Taslun looked to Vals. "How much longer until we reach the island?"

"Still some time. It will be midday when we get there. It is still before the new dawn now, but I expect you already know to not wait for the sun."

"How do you know the time, then?" asked Calak.

"The stars move in a way that I can watch for my favorite constellations. See there, my friend the seahorse."

Vals pointed upward just past one of the masts. Kealin could see the grouping of five stars and remembered from texts within the Urlas Woodlands of the creature Vals spoke of.

"I do not see it," said Taslun.

"You can't?" Alri said. "It is there. Its head and nose are the higher two stars; its body curves down the remaining three."

Taslun stared. "I see what you say, but I still do not. Perhaps stargazing is of more importance to archons than Blades."

Kealin could see it, and he went to Vals and pointed.

"So you gauge the passing of time by the position of the stars. So morning would be when?"

Vals nodded and pointed to the far horizon. "The bright star you see just coming up makes up the shell of the sea snail. Upon its full rise and nearing the setting of the sea horse, we will have morning. Though, no sun shall be had."

Kealin nodded but then decided to lie down himself. He had been up for some time now, and given the midday arrival at the island, he wished to rest.

TASLUN KICKED HIM. "LITTLE BROTHER, AWAKEN."

Kealin opened his eyes and sat up. Alri had made tea in a small kettle on a small stove of stone Vals had lit for them. A sweet aroma struck his senses.

Vals brought over a mug and poured a serving, handing it to Kealin.

"The sea snail is sitting, and now the penguin arises! It is midmorning! We have made good time!"

Kealin stood and joined Calak at the side of the ship. An island was now in view. Two massive glaciers were at either side of a sheer stone structure sitting as a lone tower on the isle.

All around them, the waters were alive with narwhals, their horns piercing out of the water and dancing in circular formations as the *Aela Sunrise* made its way to the shore.

"Yes! My friends are doing well," said Vals.

The ship came into a shallow harbor. A stone dock with an icy metal pole was the only place available to tie up, and one not normally used, except by Vals himself.

"Right, then," he said, throwing a rope over it. He exited the ship, followed by the others, and immediately they spotted a person emerging from the structure.

From afar, it appeared to be just a normal woman. If elven or human, Kealin could not decide, but as she drew closer, he knew it was neither. She was no one like he had met before.

In her eyes, he saw shifting blue. Her hair seemed to float with a soft glow upon it, and from the adornments of her body, he could make out shells of the sea.

"Valrin of the *Aela Sunrise*, it is good to see you. I understand from the seals that you took quite a blow with your ship while facing Rugag."

"Bastard pirate," Vals replied. "I gave him a scar, for sure. He had killed a few seals and took many fish. I did him some damage. But he will be back."

"Sadly, I do know," she replied.

Her eyes scanned over to Kealin, and she stared. He heard a whisper on his mind that he couldn't make out.

I do not understand.

But the woman just stared at him; a slight smile parted her lips. She turned to the others, looking them over in turn.

"Elves of the Urlas Woodlands. A rarer sight than most in the glacial waters of the North."

"You are right," said Taslun. "We come by the words of our shaman Iouir, seeking your narwhals as our guide to you."

"Then you are incorrect, for I have no narwhal to call my own. These creatures of the sea are my friends and are completely their own. The family who brought you in has taken incredible liking to you all. I doubt you will continue in the Glacial Seas without them near. A good occurrence; that confirms you mean no ill toward them."

"We do not."

"Then what can this sea-maid offer you? I have short time on land. I must return to the depths."

The woman began to walk toward the water as Taslun rushed to speak.

"A darkness approaches Dimn. We go to help the god."

She paused. "You seek a path to the sky temple, the birthplace of winds, past the maelstroms of protection. I cannot help you with that, for I am of the sea, of allegiance to Meredaas, sacred protector of the ocean realms. Dimn is of the winds. If darkness comes to the winds, then our world will falter. I had thought the poisons of ill were only to the south. I shall let Meredaas know myself."

She began into the water, her body changing form as the small amount of clothing she wore turned to scales like those of a fish and her legs melded together, forming a fin. She went into the surf, disappearing for a moment before arising again just at the water's edge.

"A mermaid?" asked Alri. "I never believed I would have a chance to meet one."

"Now you have, child of the woods," she said to them. "You seek the Isle of Knowledge, a place to the far north of here, nigh the top of the world. I know that Vals has a map of the old ones. I will mark it with a symbol. Do be wary of the Wight of the White Lands. That place of snow is not for the faint of spirit. A being dwells there now, and it is not one of the living such as are we."

With a turn, she went back under the water; the nearby narwhals turned and went out of the cove as the structure on the island faded from view in a thick fog. They were now alone on the shore.

Vals went to the ship and brought the map to view. The others followed. A single mark in the image of a fin appeared far north and beyond any other islands. There were dense clouds over the area.

"That water is treacherous. Storms brew. I have even heard of dragons that way. But they should not fear myself or this vessel, so that will play well to our journey."

"You do not fear this journey?" asked Kealin.

"It is an adventure, my friend. If there is risk to the sea and its creatures, and helping you four will assure the survival of my sea, then so be it. You have yourself a captain crazy enough to head to the far north!"

The ship was underway again. Leaving the waters of the island, they turned north. With the expanse of the starry sky above, Alri and Calak worked to make a meal from the stores of the ship, with a mix of stored meat and a jar of seaweed. Calak added spices from Vals' personal supplies, and after a little bit, they had a decent meal worked up.

They each had a bowl of the concoction.

"You elves cook well. I am surprised I cannot do business with you."

"Hidden realms make that difficult," said Kealin.

"True you are. But this is good. I am glad I took a journey with such experienced cooks. How old are all of you, anyway?"

"Older than you by a few lifetimes, and that is only our younger sister. She is two hundred."

"But she looks not much older than a young woman, no more than twenty years, by my guess."

"But she is two hundred," said Kealin. "It is the way of the elves."

Elves did not talk of age. There was no point when you were essentially immortal. It held very little value, and as such, that would be all Vals would be told.

"Well, I am forty-three in the years of men. I'm not old by any measure, but I am not young as I was when I first became a captain. Had my own adventures then," he paused and sighed, "Much has been lost in my life but now is not the time for this discussion. Perhaps, one day. I can say that I've fought that Rugag for longer than I care to admit."

THEY TRAVELED FOR SOME TIME. Many hours, in fact. As the fog rolled over the bow of the ship, the only light was the moon high above, casting a glow to the air. Vals began to look around.

He didn't say anything, but Kealin was unsettled by his erratic movements. Vals went to the helm and turned the ship to the right. He then ran to the aft of the ship and looked out. Taslun and Calak had noticed the change in direction and looked up from the reading that both had been engrossed in after finding that Vals kept a supply of books from his travels.

Vals returned to the helm; this time, he went right hard. Kealin looked as the ship passed through an arching glacier and then again, left. The crunching of ice at the bow of the ship sounded like a piece of wood being torn. Just as before, he went to the rear of the ship and looked out.

"What is it?" asked Taslun.

"We are being followed," Vals shouted. "I had thought it just a trick of floating ice, but we have caught a tail. There are not many in these waters, so we can assume who it is."

"Rugag," said Calak. "What must we do?"

"Lose him. Though I doubt it is his flagship, and so I doubt he is aboard. They have many ships. We will need to rid ourselves of our hunters or risk further issues."

"There is no chance he is simply seeking sea life?"

"No."

The ship was making good pace across the waters. Vals turned the ship back right, crunching through the ice with the metal of his reinforced bow. Their pace began to slow. The momentum of their passage was not as great as before, and Vals had to take a path less likely to be navigable. He flipped a lock below his foot and another crystal that lay hidden fell forward.

The ship began to grind to a halt, and they were rocked to the deck, losing footing from the jolt. All except Vals.

"Shield your eyes!" he said.

Kealin did so but still peered out. Vals twisted the crystal with his foot, and the ship began to glow from two planks at the rear of the ship and then up to the front. Back and forth the light went, until the center masts glowed brightly. He twisted the crystal and covered his own eyes.

Kealin could feel a rumbling beneath the ship and then what sounded like searing meat on an open fire. The sky around the boat flashed from a massive stream of fire shooting from the mast of the ship in a blast of arcane power. The ship jolted again, and the waves smacked against the ship, and the ice holding it cracked and fell away.

A gust came upon them, and Vals was at the helm again, the ship lurching forward. Kealin uncovered his eyes and went to the side of the ship. The *Aela Sunrise* had burned a path through the ice by power unknown or unseen before by any of the elves present.

They were headed toward a massive island, or glacier; from the distance they were at, it was hard to tell. Kealin looked back, as did Vals. A ship was still coming.

Up ahead, the blackness of the isle became evident, and its towering cliff face was sheer.

"That is a big glacier," Calak said.

Vals looked behind him and saw the deck of the following ship become alight.

"They are preparing to fire upon us. Brace yourselves!"

Kealin went to the rear of the ship as Vals began to make a turn around the dark isle. From the deck of the pursing ship, a light emerged, cast high into the sky and arching over the waters.

Vals turned and looked, shifting the ship to the left as far as his wheel would turn. The bolt turned downward. Kealin could see the iron tip as it flew over his head, just missing the center masts before splashing into the water, a chain hooked to it, whizzing in flight through the air.

"Down! Watch out for the tail!"

Kealin ducked just as the end of the chain slapped the deck, splintering the wood before ripping a chunk off the railing of the ship and following the bolt below. He looked back out to the ship, and Vals made another hard left. They passed beyond view of the ship, and the world became even darker.

He watched as the ship was veiled in a deep darkness and the wind died down. Vals had turned them into a passage in the glacier that was hidden unless you knew where it was, as he did.

He dropped two anchors and then joined Kealin at the aft of the ship.

"I had sheltered from a storm in this place before, but it was some time ago. I was going to go around the island and hope to lose them then, but I couldn't pass up this chance and this will work to lose them."

Kealin's siblings had joined them, and each watched out the opening in the cave. The ship rocked from the

occasional waves, the creak reverberating off the walls of
the cave, and the chill in the air was made worse by the
fear of being found.

A dim glow was on the black sea and the ship of
Rugag came into view. Vals pulled out a viewing scope
and twisted a crystal on its top. "I can see their faces," he
said. "They look, but they cannot find us. I believe we
are safe." He placed the scope back into a compartment
in the helm. "We will wait to be sure. Come, all of you. I
know you may find this of interest."

Vals went to the edge of the ship and laid down a
plank from the ship to the ice. There was a crunch as
two metal spikes bit into the ice to hold it in place.

He crossed the void and went to a sheer wall. The
others followed, doing as he did and careful of the edge.
He began to point up to the wall when it began to glow.

Runic symbols began to appear, and an image of the
islands appeared.

"Very strange," said Vals. "I was hoping to have
enough light to show you this, seeing as I had lightning
the night I came here before, but it seems it is not
needed."

"What is this place?" asked Alri.

"It was a cave with markings. I had thought they
might be elvish because they were not of the dwarves."

"It is elven," said Taslun, "but of a time long ago,
perhaps even before the dwarves. It may be before the
founding of the Urlas Woodlands, but I cannot be sure."

"It is an Edda of the gods. It tells how they took the
form of men at a time and of the creation of the worlds
and realms."

"The word 'Dimn,'" said Calak, "and here too, 'Wura.'"

"A remarkable find," said Taslun. "There seems to be lost knowledge in these icy regions."

"As I have said, the Glacial Seas hold many secrets. One could explore, I feel, for many lifetimes and not find what all it hides."

"They were not always frozen so. It is of interest, your work, Vals."

Vals laughed. "I'm but a spice runner for the islands, nothing more. Let us return to the ship. Perhaps we are safe to go."

Pulling the plank up, they each took hold of large guiding poles kept along the side of the deck. A more traditional method of moving through ice, they stabbed them into the walls of the cave.

Vals cranked the anchors up to their sailing position. The others grimaced and with significant strength and force, helped to push the ship out as Vals steadied the wheel. He looked out over the sea as he did. There was no sight of the pursuing ship, and as they raised the sails once again, they began back the way they had come to avoid another run-in.

"Do you not worry the rest of the fleet is near?" asked Kealin.

"They likely are," Vals replied, "but we cannot wait for them to be gone. They are a constant nuisance just as I work to be to them."

For a good while, their sailing was calm. Though

they had now turned back north, Vals checked the map and noticed they were headed for the spot marked by the mermaid. The clouds above were patchy but growing thicker.

Even so, Kealin looked up, spotting the stars. He noticed the seahorse reaching a high point in the sky. As the others slept, he lay down too.

"Kealin," Vals said.

He sat up.

"You sleep well. I cannot say for sure, but a foul stench is in the air. There is a sickness in the place we go to."

His eyes went back to the horizon, and he lay back down.

Does he not need sleep? I have not seen him lie down once.

His thoughts were chased as a hum began to fill the air, and he fell asleep to the words.

"I glance upon ye, darkening sea,
For with a yawn, I finally be,
Man of ocean, sailing fast,
Commander of the Aela's masts.

I wish to go where man don't find,
To aid the sea and all divine.
Help for the lost,
Risking life and limb,

Until I sink and no longer swim."

KEALIN AWOKE a few hours later on his own. The familiar awakening smell of tea filled his nostrils, but only Vals and Taslun were awake.

"It is the elven way," his brother said. "We do not dwell too much on the shifting of powers at the immediate, but it seems this new danger is enough to cause a stir to even us here in our remote lands."

Vals left the helm, locking the wheel in place and joining both him and Kealin.

"It is just strange to me that you would take such sudden concern for Dimn. I have never seen the god, but I had heard he was here. But in all my traveling, I had not seen the place you told me of."

Kealin had understood very little of Dimn besides the fact he was a god of the winds.

Vals sipped his tea. "A sea of maelstroms is not a friend to a boat like this."

"That is only legend," Taslun said. "I doubt it is true."

"What is only legend can be found to be true if you search long enough. At least, that is what I have found. I am interested to get to this next isle. An isle that is not on normal maps, especially."

"Kealin, did you sleep well?" Taslun asked him.

"Yes, as best I could given the rocking waves."

"Storms are brewing the further we go north," Vals

announced. "The others will be awake too soon enough.
The swells will get quite large, I am guessing."

"Do you ever sleep?" asked Taslun, noticing Vals
slurping down his tea.

"Sure. Just not when I am traveling. I am tied to this
ship in more ways than is seen. A blessing, I guess you
can call it. If it is at sail, then I am awake. An enchantment of sorts that the *Aela Sunrise* has. I do not tire
while at sea, but when in port, I may sleep five days
straight. I normally let the harbor master know wherever
it is I dock. They like it when I pay ahead for anchoring
before my polar-bear-like hibernation."

Vals went back to the helm just after setting down
his cup with the others. The ship was in rougher waters.
Taslun was staring off. He seemed to be thinking. He
looked down and then over to Kealin.

"Have you thought of Mother and Father?" Taslun
asked.

"Yes, I wonder of them."

"I had spoken with Vals; he saw an elven fleet in the
South before he returned to Corson, but he would have
been already north when our parents departed. He had
asked about us as a people; I think there is more to him
than he speaks, but I do not feel it is ill. It seems with
your recent conversations, you have made a friend. It
isn't like you."

Kealin smiled. "I guess it just took finding the right
friend. The sea is a uniting force that I have respected
for some time. It is rare a man would perform such a self-
less act as to protect the sea. I can respect him for it."

Taslun patted his back and embraced him. "You grow wiser, Brother. I respect you for it."

Kealin pushed off his brother's affection. "Enough, I may speak against the teachings of Master Rukes, but I am no fool to what is good sense." He smiled.

Calak and Alri were both up now, but they grasped ropes and wood. The seas had turned turbulent, and the ship was pitching and leaning as the swell increased.

"Hold on!" yelled Vals.

The ship rocked upward and then slammed back down. The horizon bounced as a flash of lightning illuminated the sea only long enough to see rolling black clouds above and a wave of rain overtake the ship.

"Take yourselves below deck!" he said to them.

Alri had been below a few times, and so had Calak. The cooking supplies and the tea were kept in storage there. As a wave of water struck the deck, rushing over the wood, they climbed one by one down into the bowel of the ship, the seawater pouring in above them. Kealin was the last one in and closed the wooden hatch.

"Does anyone else feel guilty leaving Vals up there?" asked Alri.

"He asked us to come down here," Calak replied, lighting one of the stored torches and walking around to light another to give some brightness to the dank surroundings.

"Yes, but what else would he do? Wait for one of us to be tossed overboard?"

"He respects us beyond what many men may even fathom," said Taslun. "Our love of trees may actually be less than his love of the sea. I have never seen such zeal in a man."

Kealin and Calak took a seat near a box as Alri and Taslun hung on to some overhanging ropes, looking up as the ship continued to quake back and forth.

The others seemed to drift into their own conversation, so Kealin spoke with Calak.

"Far from what we know, Brother?" he asked.

Calak shook his head. "Yes, but it is strange to see you not protesting our moves. I am not used to you going along with something. I'm used to the half-elf rebel Kealin."

"I'm still me. Do not worry your pure elven self." He teased.

"I've never understood that. I, too, think it is foolish to name you a half-elf and me a pure elf."

"It was decided when we were young by the Elders and only comes up when useful as a weapon against us." Kealin shook his head. "Taslun and you were deemed pure, for they sensed little of mother in you. I was more like mother, as was Alri. We may look the same, but it is the way our blood forms and the sense other elves have of it. The only true difference was what our people made it."

"I, at one time too wished to be a part of the others, but the older I became, the more I decided that it was not what made me. I would not allow some elf to tell me my standard. I rebel against Taslun because he holds it in such regard, but I do not wish you to do the same, Brother. My path is my own, and you must embrace yours. You wish to be a Blade Master as Master Rukes, and you should do it."

His brother nodded, but being younger and wishing to be as both Taslun and Kealin, he was torn.

The tossing of the ship had slowed, and now Alri and Taslun walked around, looking through stacked books that thankfully had not been soaked by the flow of seawater when they climbed down.

"He has quite a collection," said Alri. "I have seen at least three books speaking of elves before any of our time."

"I too have noticed; he has traveled far for some of these. The tongue is not elvish or dwarvish, or even a language of man. I do not know some of these writings," Taslun commented. "It is odd and wondrous all the same."

The covering above opened, and Vals stuck his head down.

"Everyone well? Come on back up. The clouds are still black, but the sea is not so rough."

They made their way back up to look out over a dark sea. Patchy clouds were above, with whistling wind blowing over the bow of the ship. Vals brought the map to view, and it appeared they were just over the spot that the mermaid had directed them to.

Large glaciers riddled their path, but still the *Aela Sunrise* pushed on. Breaking through tough ice was one success; avoiding the spiked bodies of a glacier to the hull of the ship was quite a different one.

Vals made a series of quick turns, with more than one ending with the splintering of wood and casted ice erupting over the side of the ship. They could see land coming up fast.

"You elves test my ship! I like it, and so does she!"

The wide-eyed captain spun the wheel, banking the ship to the left; it slid along the water, building up against the ice. The shoreline came suddenly with a crack and a thud. The ship rocked back to the left.

"Get the plank down!" he shouted.

Taslun and Alri tossed the wooden plank down and made their way to the icy ground. The path was still slick and precarious from the water and jagged glaciers roughed up by the ship. Kealin pointed for Calak to follow, and turned to Vals.

Vals nodded. "Go on, I will keep the ship well. I will keep a torch burning on the side to direct you back in fog and snow. Do not fear, I will not abandon you, no matter the cost."

Kealin nodded back and followed the others down.

Taslun and Alri were already a few feet from the shore. The winds tore across the lands that were barren with snow and rock as far as the night would allow them to see. Calak bundled himself in his coat as he went ahead.

Kealin checked his blade; the ice had kept its drawing from the ease he was used to. His brothers noticed what he did and followed suit, breaking the ice that held them sheathed. Alri took out her staff and blew into the tip. An orb of flames flickered alight, and she pointed it forward, a light source for their bleak journey.

4

BLEAKLANDS

They began across the open expanse, seeing little more than Alri's staff in front of them, the glowing orb pulsating as she worked to keep the spell controlled. Behind them, Kealin glanced to see the fading outline of the ship and then a burst of flame where Vals lit not one but two torches to light their way back.

The snow was coming sideways against them, and each walked with their elbows out and their heads down, attempting to force a path through the growing ice. None were wearing gloves, and so with tucked hands, they trudged. Alri was unknowingly lucky to be using her staff; the light that came off it gave her some warmth, but even that was chased away by the shifting winds.

They walked for a good while before they saw the dead trees of a once-grand forest. Behind them, the light from the *Aela Sunrise* was all but shrouded. There was a structure ahead, and as best any of them could guess, it was where they should head.

Passing through the crags of frozen trees, Kealin jumped as he saw something move within the crags, swooping with the winds and passing over them multiple times.

He drew his blade. "Brothers, to the sky."

Calak and Taslun both looked up, their own blades drawn as more of the figures swarmed above them, just over the screaming snowfall.

The creatures were opaque, with a dark fiery black center within their forms. It seemed that they could solidify and take the appearance as icy stone at will but most of them remained almost ethereal. They had no distinguishable arms or legs, only a gaping mouth and a bellowing sound that grew as they passed close, akin to a squelching cold gust, but not of the sound of wind at all. Taslun looked ahead.

"Lead us on, Alri. These creatures are staying high for now."

She gripped her staff with both hands; closing her eyes, she sought to increase her spell, and the magic flowed from her body into the staff. It glowed brighter, parting the snow, forcing it to swing around the orb of light she had created.

They drew closer to the structure, now taking a path between stone pillars that ran like a long hall all the way to the towering building.

The creatures above began to swarm over them. Twice, one came just over Kealin. He turned as one landed at the far end of the path they had taken. The specters began to pass in between them, slowing them one by one and separating their combined force.

"Faster! Into the doorway ahead!" Taslun ordered them.

Alri was in a dead sprint, as was Calak. Ahead of them, a large wooden door was beginning to open with their approach.

Kealin once again turned; the creatures were amassing and following their path. Another two had dropped between him and the way they were going. He stopped as the others went on. He slid his foot back sideways behind him and brought his blade in front of him.

Taslun looked, spotting his brother. "Kealin! Come now!"

The creature's mouth gaped toward the ground, and it let out a shrill that caused Kealin goosebumps. The creature formed a hand from its body and pointed a clawed finger at him. Kealin rushed forward, striking the creature, his elven blade glowing red as he cut into it.

He did not fear what he could kill, but the creature was not weakened, only stunned for a moment.

It grasped his blade, even as the elvish energies scorched its hand. Kealin ripped his blade from it and began to follow the others. He had garnered enough attention himself, and as Taslun ran toward him, he ran away from the entities.

The two creatures blocking his path rushed toward him; he sidestepped, grasping one of the pillars, and swung himself out of their path, slashing his blade at them from behind, and each seemed to shake from his strike, ceasing movement. The other creatures simply rushed over the two he had struck and, in a gust of snow and spectral energy, pursued him.

Taslun grabbed him as they met and pulled him toward the door. The creatures drew behind them. The shrill of their moans caused Kealin's neck to tighten. Falling into the open doorway, the creatures were repulsed as a blue fire erupted from the tower, connecting to all the stone pillars, creating an enchantment.

In an upward rush, the creatures fled the area. Taslun looked at his younger siblings, and Kealin drew in breaths rapidly. He smiled. Someone, or some power, had assisted them.

"Close enough to death, little brother?"

"Not death, just reassured life." Kealin laughed. "Strange creatures. I sense a fear they caused, greater than mere fear we conquer with our training as Blades."

"What were those?" asked Calak.

"Wights, or best I can guess," suggested Alri. "They haunt places of death, and this barren place is of that. I can feel necromantic energies. Archon Oaur told me of places like this. They are pilgrimage places for death mages, but at the same time, there are sources of wisdom beyond others here. The dead know much, sometimes more than what they did in life."

They turned to the doorway. A skeletal form stared back at them but did not attack.

Taslun stood with his sword in hand. "We mean you no harm. Did you protect us from the wights?"

It rattled its jaw, turning away from them, and began into the tower.

"Come on," he told the others.

Descending a long stairwell, Kealin felt a warmth compared to the outside world. Long-darkened torches lined the wall, with the occasional glowing stone affixed into the wall, lighting their path enough to where they were not bouncing off each other in the darkness.

There were the sounds of cracking and snapping bones around them. Other skeletons stood mindlessly by, staring. The one leading them seemed to crack his own jaw when he turned to let them know to follow.

Through twisting turns and into a large open room, they came to a large torch basin glowing with a blue fire. A walkway circled up to the top of the tower. The skeleton pointed and then stood back away from the path.

"This way," directed Taslun.

They began up. Kealin kept his blade pointed toward each skeletal form as they passed. He did not trust any of those within this place. Keeping an eye on those below, he followed the others as they snaked up the walkway.

An ominous sound began to echo around the room. A circular stone overhang seemed to vibrate with each tone of sound that filled the air.

"Is this music?" Alri questioned.

The sound became louder and the rhythm faster as they reached the top. The winds twisted through open alcoves surrounding the pillar in the center. All around them, they could see the grand expanse of white nothingness.

Taslun walked with Calak into the opening in the pillar.

"We come for wisdom," Taslun said.

Kealin followed with Alri and did not know what to make of the sight he saw in the wasteland of an island they had been sent to.

There was a massive organ, with keys of bone, and pipes blackened and sheer rising up from below the floor out of the top of the massive tower. A hunched figure bellowed over the keys. It continually pressed over the bones and arched its back with the swaying of the notes. It had no hands, but his arms moved over the keyboard just the same, each pressed down by power unseen. It was draped in tattered purple cloth, and its hair was black, gray, and straggled down its back.

It did not turn but spoke.

"Elves within my place of death? I am honored you would visit, but beware my wights. Outside the tower is a place of death beyond my protection, and they are hungry for souls to devour. Elves are known to be quite a wondrous snack to them. Eternal blood is sweet and satisfying."

The floor quaked and shook as the organ wailed, almost deafening to them. In a motion, the figure turned. A bony form stared at them.

"I know you did not risk yourselves for my wondrous notes of gloomy death, the cycle of life but a short one. Even as an elf. What do you seek of Vankou, Composer of the Songs of Eternity?"

Taslun stepped forward. "We are elves of the Urlas Woodlands. Dread falls upon the gods of the North, and darkness encroaches Dimn, God of the Winds. We seek to assist him in whatever it is he faces."

"And why would I care of Dimn or Kel or Wura or the goddess Etha? Just as much, the Itsu are of not my regard either. I am of death; my songs fill the ears of those in their moments of passing.

"If I am to be as I was, I would play my symphony for each of you, but I have had enough of death for at least ten thousand years. Do you not see you are upon a wasteland of ice? It is those gods who went to war with me in a case of holy vengeance. I once had a garden upon this rock, and now I have but ice and snow and winds."

Kealin stared at this person of death; in his mind, he began to see the creature moving upon the minds of each of them. He centered his thoughts on the figure and spoke. "Dis beast is not what we think. You will not game with us, Vankou."

The others turned and looked at him. Taslun stared. "What did you say?"

What Kealin could not tell was that his voice was not as before. In his thoughts to Vankou, he had tapped into a gift at this point he could only imagine.

Kealin looked at them, confused. "Dis is not a time for games from this beast. He will tells us what we seek."

Alri stuttered. "You sp-sp-spoke as the shaman does."

Vankou furled his cape and approached them. "I sense a darkness here and upon each of you. You fear my songs, but not for yourselves. Though that is what you should fear it for should you continue your path to Dimn. The world is changing."

The creature's eyes focused on Kealin, and though he did not move his bones, Kealin heard its voice.

Your gift is awakening and is one that will serve you well, but know my song is nigh for many. I cannot say who will hear my song, but know that even the gods of the North face desolation. That being said, you spoke to death as the ethereal do. Your mind knows much, and for that, your life will be one of sorrow, for happiness comes only with lack of complete knowledge in our lands.

Vankou looked to the others as Kealin stared at him, unsure of his words. He knew of no gift but only his own luck. He knew there was something within his mind, but he did not understand any awakening, or so the creature had called it.

The creature continued in its normal speech. "You seek Dimn, and I will tell you of knowledge long forgotten. The maelstroms of legend protect the island and the portal to the ethereal land of the god. It is for this reason that you must seek out the shells of Meredaas to gain entry and calm the storms.

"I can help you with this. I know of a place to obtain them. There is a hermit that dwells on a distant shore marked by a whirlwind of ice. He waits in prayer for his time of doom, but I will not give it to him. He is like me and doomed to hover between this world and the next. He will not give his keys to Dimn freely. Now, leave this place before I make you a member of my choir. The last elves who came upon my island have not left, and beware them yourselves. Remember, while you are within the walls of the tower, I offer my protection; beyond this place, they are free to devour what is upon their grounds."

The creature turned back to his organ and began to play a solemn tone, meticulously striking the keys and arching his back as before.

"We have what we need," Kealin said to the others.

"You are right, Brother, but what of your speech?" Taslun asked.

"If I knew, I would tell you. Let us get back to the *Aela Sunrise*. I have a feeling we have overstayed our time here."

Outside the windows, the wights were spinning atop the tower and howling. Taslun led them downward. Passing the large blue fire that rose as the sound of the Vankou's organ bellowed through the lower halls, they exited. The skeletons parted as the hurried party forced their way up the path leading to the doorway.

At the doorway, Taslun stopped and looked to the others. He lifted his hand to them. "Prepare yourselves, everyone. We make a run for the ship. We will not walk as we did before. The wights know of our presence, and they will try to divide us. Do not let them, and feel of no guilt to let them taste the power of the elves!" Taslun looked out and then back to his siblings. "Run!"

They all burst into a sprint, the colder gusts sweeping over them as they went down the pathway of pillars. The blue fire atop them stopped the advance of more than one wight already spotting them. The forms bounced off and upward, wailing as they did.

As they made their way onto open ground and the

tundra toward the ship, the entire host of wights began to pursue them. The sounds of the organ of Vankou still sounded; a horrible foreboding struck Kealin, and he glanced behind him.

The icy teeth of a wight greeted him and in turn he swung his blade, cracking the creature's skull. Alri lifted her staff above them, and an orb of light expanded over their party. The creatures drove themselves upon it, and it began to falter as the magic electrified their bodies.

"I cannot hold them!" she shouted.

"Keep running!" said Taslun. "We will not defeat them. We must get to the ship!"

Kealin looked ahead, spotting the torches in the snow flurries on the awaiting *Aela Sunrise*. He could see Vals moving frantically aboard, but he could not tell what the man was doing.

"We are nearly there! Faster!" shouted Taslun.

It was then a wight slammed into them from the side. Calak was hit and rolled; stunned, he was not moving. The wights swarmed him.

Kealin gripped his sword, swinging over his head at the wight nearest to him. His blade passed through its body, glowing red as it did. Upon striking its black core, it turned to a white color and was shredded apart by a sudden gusting wind. He ran toward Calak, who struggled to stand.

Taslun was now engaged as another group of wights swarmed him. Kealin pulled Calak to his feet and ran forward toward his other brother, slashing and stabbing at the wights.

"Slash deep, strike their cores, Calak."

But Calak had left his blade, a mistake of inexperience. He went back to get it, ducking as the specters flew down, grasping at him. The creatures amassed and once again went for the youngest brother. Alri shouted, running forward. Her staff hummed in her hand, its tip spewing out a burst of light, fracturing the forms of many wights and destroying others. Calak made it to his sword, gripped it tightly, turning to see another wight dissolved by his sister's magic.

Kealin and Taslun were each fighting their own wights, and two more of them had swung down behind Alri. They gripped her, pulling her upward. The other opened its mouth over her head, and a fume of black began to flow over her.

"Brothers!" Calak shouted.

Kealin saw his sister in the air and leaped up, slashing the one holding her. It turned to nothingness, and Alri fell. He swooped her up as Taslun smashed the other one away, his sword glowing bright red as the wight struggled to get away.

Kealin looked down at Alri, who shook her head and blinked rapidly.

"I am fine," she said.

Alri pushed his grip from her, and he set her down. She struggled to steady herself as she stood. She lifted her staff. Her hair furled and the snow near her melted as, in a flash, a blast of flames erupted off her, spreading out in all directions. The wights surrounding them recoiled, and Taslun directed everyone toward the ship again. Kealin pushed Calak as he stumbled up the plank in the ice. Vals reached down, grabbing at him.

"I've got you. Get everyone on the ship!"

Kealin grabbed Calak's sword just as he managed to stand back up. As one of the beasts swooped down towards the ship, he spun the elven blades and struck the creature across its jaw. It shattered, raining down pieces of ice.

The wights were unable to pursue them past the border of the isle, which became obvious as the creatures were dragged backward as they flew near the water.

Though she had claimed she was fine, Alri did not appear well. Her skin was blanched and sweat poured from her body even in the stark cold of the Glacial Seas. She stumbled toward the water's edge.

Kealin tossed Calak's blade back to him. He swooped up Alri before running up the plank to board the ship. Taslun came last, taking down two more wights before jumping aboard to join the others.

"All right, everyone is on board," Vals said.

He twisted a crystal on the side of the ship, and a wave of flames shot outward like before with the ice, but this time off the side of the ship. The wights were sent into a frenzy, fleeing back toward the tower.

He went to the helm, and the ship lurched away from the isle. Kealin held Alri in his arms. She wasn't awake, and he placed his ear to her chest. He did not wish his sister to be dead.

5

SHELLS OF MEREDAAS

His ear was pressed against her chest but couldn't hear anything. He began to weep but kept listening. Then, like a sunrise following a harsh winter night, he heard a sound, a thud against his ear, and he felt chills.

Alri began to breathe and opened her eyes. He looked down at her.

"Alri."

She cracked a slight smile and then opened her eyes further before taking hold of him and pulling herself up.

Taslun knelt down, helping to steady her. "What befell you?" he asked.

"I do not know, but I am still weak."

"The wights of some lands have the power to spread a sickness," said Vals. "We must hope you do not have that."

Kealin looked to Vals and then over to Calak. He stood, stomping over to Calak, grabbing him by his tunic.

"Do you not know to hold on to your weapon, Brother?" He pushed him against the edge of the boat. "You will not forget your blade again, will you? Must I stand beside you and assure you can draw it too, and teach you how to cut down your own enemies?"

Kealin looked into his eyes, and his younger brother stared back, breathing heavily and nodding. He then felt a hand on his own shoulder.

"Kealin. Enough."

Kealin let go of Calak and turned to Taslun. He stared at him, as did Calak.

"I, too, am annoyed," said Taslun, "but he is inexperienced. You may have made the same mistake yourself at his age."

"Doubtful. I should have two blades anyway; the way of the elves will get one of us killed soon."

He walked away from Taslun.

"You had a chance, Kealin! You did not have to wield but one blade, as has our father and the fathers before. Take your chance if you want; perhaps you would be better to have his blade than him?"

"No. We alone are responsible for our actions. He yet has time to improve."

He shifted his eyes back around to Calak. "I do not wish any of my siblings to die, and you are more capable than you showed yourself. Keep hold of your sword, Brother, or take yourself back to Urlas."

Kealin went toward the edge of the deck as Alri now stood watching him.

Vals looked over his elven companions and then went to Taslun. "Our next path?"

Taslun looked over to Kealin and then back to Calak before acknowledging Vals. "I, once again, do not know the place but only a clue. We were told to go to an isle marked by a tornado of ice. We search for a hermit."

Vals brought up his map and stared at it.

"I believe it here," he said, pointing at a spot further east of them. "But we go where not many sailors wish to go. It is a rumor of a place to most. The storms and tales of ice drakes make many fear those waters. I went once and had a run-in with a man of sorts, told me death would come to me if I ever returned."

"Truly?" asked Taslun.

"No." He smiled. "But even if he would have, he would not have been the first to threaten me, nor will he be the last. I do not fear death, for once I fear it, I am dead."

Vals went to the helm and wheeled the ship to an eastern path.

Kealin looked up at the still-starry sky and wished for sun. It had been such a long time since he felt warmth on his arms. He brushed his skin of the ice that had formed on his hair. Taslun and Alri were busy making tea, and Calak stood by himself, looking off the other side of the ship. Kealin thought to go to him when Calak turned and walked toward him first.

"You are right, Kealin."

"Of what?"

"To hold on to my sword. I will not fail you or Taslun again. I almost got Alri killed. You were right. You would do well with my sword compared to me, but I will not give it to you, for I, too, am a swordsman of the

Urlas Woodlands. I will rise to fight beside you and Taslun."

Taslun looked over, watching the exchange.

Kealin embraced Calak. "Very well, Brother. But know I will be beside you, and though I expect much, you are one of the few I will stand by if they falter. I cannot say that for others beyond this ship."

"But the way of the elves—" Calak paused. "You do not care for that."

Kealin smiled. "Yes, but you do. Embrace it. If you do not embrace it, you will be soulless in your zeal; blood lust alone is not enough. That is of our father's wisdom."

Taslun joined them.

"You tell our little brother of swordsmen of old, I see. You quoted one who knows more than most of our people of blade work."

"I quote what I have found to be true and makes sense and what our father has said. But of whom you speak, he, too, was not pure elf."

"Riakar was a swordsman of old, Calak. He came from the waters of a primordial sea, defeated the demons of old that swarmed the living realm at the birth of our people. He, too, fought with two blades. Kealin is much lower in his skill than Riakar." His tone changed to that of teasing.

"Aye, from the look of these thunderclouds ahead, it will not be blades we need to fear," said Vals.

They looked up, seeing in the far distance flashes of lightning streaking across the sky. The winds were beginning to cut across the bow of the ship in random gusts.

"Does this weather ever not turn from cold and clear to freezing and stormy?" asked Calak.

Vals laughed. "When in the Glacial Seas of the North, this is good weather! Pray you are never in bad weather in these waters."

The ship tossed from side to side and, as before in the previous storm, the thoughts of the ship's hold and the safety that might be came to mind. This time, however, they did not descend, at least not all at once. There were many rocks and glaciers in these parts, and Vals used their eyes as much as they could stand to help him in avoiding them.

It went on for some time, but then Taslun took Alri down below. She had begun to feel ill again. Calak and Kealin remained above and thus bounced between the two sides, watching and balancing in the torrential seas.

The ship arched upward, the horizon well below them. With great force, it fell downward, smacking the waves and throwing the two brothers to the deck.

"That was a hard one!" shouted Vals.

Kealin pulled himself back up. A glacier shifted in the waters and was running right for the ship's bow.

"Vals, to the right!"

He began pointing, and Vals nodded, rolling the wheel to direct the ship that way.

The scratching and rubbing of the ice beneath the ship was horrendous. Like cracking rocks and clashing steel. Kealin glanced at Calak, who just shook his head.

"Do not worry. This ship was made for these waters. It will take more than ice to destroy my beloved *Aela Sunrise!*"

The ship continued to toss, and Calak was thrown from one side to the next. Kealin ran along the railings and jumped to his brother as another swell struck the ship.

"Give me your hand!"

Calak reached for him, and Kealin grasped him by his gauntlet. The second wave tossed them up, throwing them onto their backs.

"No more, Brother. Head below. I will remain for now with Vals."

Calak shook his head and ran for the ladder, pulling the covering up before disappearing below.

Kealin went to the helm with Vals, who was in stance holding the wheel. The horizon bounced into view, and then the ship lurched down. They rode the back of the wave and then turned, curving up the next one.

The waves grew in size, the glaciers no longer a worry as much as the height the ship was being tossed.

"Take hold of the wheel with me, friend. My arms are tiring, and the seas are relentless!"

Kealin took hold of the spokes and worked to watch Vals as the waves passed under them. He could feel the tug of the rudder working to hold its course. The sails were still up, even with the twisting winds and slivers of ice striking them.

"We cannot risk lowering them. She will hold; we mustn't doubt her craftsmanship. If we do, we will not make it."

The wind howled, and the ship creaked and made cracking sounds. The lightning began to flash over and over, and Kealin looked as a wave appeared on the horizon, a growing massiveness beyond any that he had seen yet.

"W-w-hoa," Vals stuttered. He turned the wheel center and tapped Kealin's right hand.

"Hold it. We have no choice. Never have I seen one so big. I had wondered if this would be needed."

He went to the mast in the center, sliding on the deck as he did, and grabbed hold of one of the crystals.

Kealin struggled to hold it straight; bracing his feet, he gripped the wheel, but with every bit of the storm's energy working against him, he was not sure how much longer he could last.

"Vals!" he shouted.

But Vals was not coming back to him, not yet. The man twisted the crystal, and the masts became alight in gold. A sphere forming from the center of the ship encompassed the entire vessel, lifting it from the water and taking them over the edge of the wave.

The ship was flying. He was beyond amazed. He looked around and then to Vals. He loosened his grip on the wheel as Vals walked toward him.

"Very good. I did not wish to do this, but I had to."

At that time, the others came from below. Taslun looked around with his mouth open. "I heard the sea go silent and was sure my years had come to an end. What magic is this?"

"It is magic of a most important kind, for it saved us this night. But I had hoped not to use it. It makes the ship mostly inoperable for some time. Even after we return to the water, I will be able to do little more than steer. So I have only used it once, but that was a rather bored dragon, to say the least, and I got lucky it did not have the time to wait to fill its hungry belly!"

"How long will this last?" asked Kealin.

At that moment, the orb reabsorbed into the ship. They could see the night sky around them again, and in a slow descent, they went back toward the sea. The waves were still rough, but they had emerged on the lighter side of the storm.

"It varies," Vals said, "There are many secrets to this ship and even to me, elves, but that is perhaps a story for once our task is done." He winked.

Kealin gave the wheel over to Vals and went to Alri, who stood holding on to Taslun. "Are you well?"

"I am well. It just seems that whenever I try to do much with my mind, weakness strikes me suddenly, and I can do nothing."

"We must learn more of this sickness. Vals, do you know more of the wights or the sickness?"

He shook his head. "I am afraid I do not. I know of them, but that is all. I also do not know how an elf will progress with it, but I understand a normal man would already be dead. The sickness is quick, or so I had read once."

Taslun went to them both. "We must hope that Dimn can help when we reach him."

Though the sea had calmed, it was not without further surprises. Though it could only be steered, fate was with them, and the ship had gotten into an undersea current. The *Aela Sunrise* went around a large glacier, and as it came to twist around a large rock, the ship continued to turn.

"Small whirlpool," Vals told them.

He did not seem too worried as he turned into it and ran alongside the center. He caught enough momentum to pass out without an issue, and the ship drifted into another current.

"It was a small one."

He laughed a bit and then began a verse.

"Lo twisting seas shall pull us down,
You cannot go with a frown.
Turn ye ship and guide her true,
Keep on going to see her through!

Do not ye doubt the trueness spoke,
For it is known by the higher folk,
'Trust ye magic, o' seafaring man,
Or embrace your bones to the eternal land.'"

HIS LAUGHING at their near-mortal peril was not amusing to Taslun, who walked with Kealin to the front of the ship. In the distance, they could see a column rising. As they drew closer, the column appeared to shift and bend. The winds began rushing over them, and the *Aela Sunrise* drifted toward the west, keeping distance from the column. It shifted again, and the clouds above moved enough for moonlight to illuminate the twisting ice that made a constant shattering sound as the waters around it leaped up into its grasp.

"There is your tornado of ice you were looking for. Our landing is nigh, my friends."

As they came once again near the shore, Alri struggled to stand, feeling weak suddenly.

"Why do you not stay here, Sister?" suggested Taslun.

"I will not. I will be fine."

She forced herself up, pushing along the deck with her fingertips. She was too weak to stand.

"Alri. Please."

Alri looked to Taslun and to Kealin, who was at her side. "I need to help."

"Stay," said Kealin. "You will be safe on the *Aela Sunrise.*"

It was not by her own will but her lack of strength that she agreed. Vals went to the side of the ship and looked over.

"I can get no closer, but I feel we are close enough the ice should hold you here as the ship settles and refreezes. Let us hope that we do not need to leave quickly as last time."

"I hope not, too," said Kealin.

After embracing their sister, they each went over the side of the deck via the plank and began again across a barren icy landscape. Vals lit the torches as before, but they had no light to guide them, save the moon above. If any fortune could be noted, it would be that there was no storm, as before on the last isle.

As they crunched across the snowy field, they began to see large monolithic glowing stones. Each stood high into the air and seemed to release dust upward into the night sky.

"I have read of such stones," said Calak. "They draw magic and offer it to the winds to be scattered around the lands. They need darkness to draw from the arcane energies."

"Then they have plenty of what they need," said Taslun.

They came across another bay after walking for some time. To their right, the sight of the tornado of ice, and its screeching howl, became more evident and pressed upon them not to walk in that direction. But it was a single torchlight that could be seen in the far distance that urged them forward. Seeing as there was no other point to guide them and they were looking for a hermit by a tornado just like the one they saw, they continued on.

Drawing closer to the light, the storm off the bay swerved around them. Its dark clouds swirled over the hut, and the icy whirlwind spun snow toward them as they approached the house. It was a frightening sight to see, but the whirlwind held its position in an unnatural way. Clouds swirled above as if drawn to the very spot they now walked under.

The house was a stone hovel with a single window that glowed a yellow color in the dark night. From atop it, a single chimney came up made of larger circular stones, and around it grew a green grass, somehow alive in the frigid temperatures of the isle.

Taslun knocked on the door, but instead of an answer from the other side, the door opened. A figure in a gold hood stared out at them.

"Can I help you, good sirs, this frightfully cold night?"

The tornado seemed to slow and stop near the edge of the shoreline. The roar of its winds was horrendous.

"We have come to seek out your assistance in a trouble we have."

"Then you bring me trouble?" The voice became harsh. "You bastards of the earth, I cannot have you wrecking my home with your elven blood!" The voice then softened. "Come in, come out of the cold."

They followed the figure in, unsure if they were truly welcome or not. The inside of the hovel was plainly adorned. A bloody knife lay on a bare table, opposite a roaring fire that brought each of them much-needed warmth. Around the table was a white skin of some animal, and there was barely room for them as they huddled together. Kealin looked about and could see no fresh kills being prepared and was perplexed by the bright red blood on the blade. His hand was at the hilt of his sword, and he had no plans to remove it.

Looking around further, there were no chairs. Only the figure's bed that it sat on, looking out at them.

"What assistance can this lonely hermit offer elves of the woods?"

Taslun knelt down at its level. "We have been sent to

acquire a way to Dimn. A darkness encroaches the wind god, and we must assist him."

The figure did not move.

"We understand you have shells of a certain kind, capable of getting us through the storms that protect his land. Shells of Meredaas, God of the Sea."

The figure hummed a tune, much like the tune played by Vankou, and then stood.

"I do know of these shells. I have some. It is the ones that are pink. They do what you wish. The blue ones summon gods. I have both, as well as other shells. But can you do for me a task, a task I need assistance with?"

Before an answer was given, the figure's voice changed again.

"You need to give me a wretched rest, you flea-munching tree dwellers. How long must I remain awake in this torment of life? For three hundred, four hundred more years am I to be unable to leave, unable to do what I must to die? I am trapped by that wretched storm, in this wretched little wreck of a home, with these wretched tree dwellers!"

There was silence, and then it spoke again, softer like before.

"I am in need of assistance, as you kind elves wish to give me. I need a way out, a way to die, you see. I have a problem with that."

The figure stood and went to the table and the bloody knife. It picked up the bloody blade. Kealin's hand drew his sword partially out, ready to defend them.

"You see, when you insult the one called Vankou, you have problems. This is mine."

The figure took the blade and thrust it into the hood of his cape. A spray of blood came with each repeated strike as over and over it drove the blade into itself. But the figure did not stumble, did not fall. It stood just as before and set the blade on the table, a pool of blood forming around it.

The figure then reached to its cape, pushing back the veil. Kealin turned his eyes for a moment, for the sight was a hideous one. Where the figure's face should have been was a scarred mass of blood and tissue, the recent stabs scarring over between two eyes that by some power still could look out. Straggled gray hair hung down across the face, if one could call it a face.

"You will help me die, and I will give you the shells in payment."

The three brothers stood staring and not sure what to make of the arrangement given to them.

"How can you die if that did not kill you? We have but elven blades," said Calak.

"My death is a simple one," it told them. "This island has a place beneath the ground, a place where all can be explained. There is a demon there, placed by that one who plays the organ. It keeps death from me. If you can defeat the demon, I will give you the shells. It will not take much, for she can be deceived, if one can convince her that she is not being deceived."

"So the demon is a female? A human, an elf, a dwarf?"

"Just a demon," it replied.

"Where is this place?" asked Kealin.

"Beneath us."

The figure pointed down and then went to its bed, pushing it away, revealing a door in the floor of the hovel. The figure took a key and unlocked a large silver lock. The door opened with a clank on the floor.

"Down there you will find her. My temptation was always to try to win my death, but I could not. I could not do it. You must betray her to destroy her. So is what I have learned. Perhaps you three can." The figure jerked toward them, grabbing Taslun.

"Or perhaps you will die instead and be devoured by the hellish creature of fire!"

Kealin drew his blade and stabbed the figure.

It did nothing but look downward. A flow of blood ran down the elven blade.

"If only, good sir, that was enough."

The figure walked backward off the blade and backed up against the fire. "Please, go on and free me from my burden. My mind has been divided for some time in the madness of this place."

Taslun looked at the figure. "How can we know this is not some trap and that you will do what you say?"

"You do not, but what choice do you have if you wish to reach your goal? I seek death myself. What good does betraying you do for me?"

Taslun seemed convinced to Kealin, but Calak looked less than happy of their situation. Still, he pushed Taslun out of the way to go to the stairwell first himself. Kealin followed after him, and Taslun was the last.

As Kealin made it down to the lower level, he made out a grand beach. The waves came in off a blue shore, and across white sand scurried a crab into the surf. The sun was bright.

They walked together, each looking up at the sun and then across the expanse. Kealin looked around. "This is not real. What we are seeing is not right."

"I know," said Taslun. "It is the demon."

"She," corrected Calak. "But how will we find her here?"

Kealin turned and looked behind him. He drew his blade. A woman stood there. Her hair was long and dark; strands of it fell between her breasts. He could see her hips, but she wore a silver raiment across her waist that fell just above her knees. She walked toward them, a smile across her face.

He could see her eyes, scanning each of them. In his mind, he heard wails, but he centered his thoughts, staring at her. She seemed to be more than she appeared, but he could not see it, for it was shadowy and her image remained front in his mind.

"What are three of the most powerful race in the lands doing in my domain?" she asked. "What pleasures do you seek?"

"No pleasures," said Taslun. "We seek nothing."

The demon was not to be so easily tricked. "Taslun of the Urlas Woodlands, you cannot avoid conversation with such short words."

Calak stepped forward; he drew his sword and began toward her.

"Calak, the younger brother. You draw your blade so well, but dear Alri never stood a chance against the wights, and even now she is ill. How poor of you."

Calak stopped. "How do you—?"

"Your thoughts are mine, dear elf. Once more, what do you seek?" She looked to Kealin.

The wails returned, and her eyes began to burn in his mind. He lifted his head, looking down. He dropped his sword.

"I need not this blade," he said.

He then felt her gaze leave him. She now walked toward Taslun.

"What can I do for you?" She brushed his cheek with her hand.

"You can do nothing. I am not tricked by this."

Kealin looked to him but noticed he had begun to sweat.

"This is no trick, and you can remain here with me. No need to return to the bitter cold and the faceless man."

Taslun went to draw his blade, but her hand was upon his, and he began to waver even in his stance against her. Calak went to go beside her.

"I will throw you from this mount, demon!" he shouted. He went to her, but she raised her hand, and he paused, staring down into the sand.

He seemed afraid; his eyes widened, and he struggled to stand.

"What is it?" asked Kealin.

"A cliff, Brother. Do you not see it?"

He looked but saw nothing but the sand.

She reached into the sand and drew out a black stone. "Why not you taste the fruits of this land, Taslun? Just one taste."

Taslun looked down and smiled. "I am hungry, and it looks delicious."

Kealin looked to his brothers, Calak still worried he was to fall and now his elder brother who thought a stone to look like food.

"What is wrong? Do you not see this beach and that is a stone? Taslun, do not be fooled."

But Taslun was fooled.

"Brother, this is a berry, not a stone. Perhaps you should allow her to feed you."

Kealin turned to Calak, pushing him from his spot. He fell forward and screamed, striking the ground as Kealin knew he would. But he stood up, coughing not on sand, as Kealin saw, but black dirt.

"It was not a cliff," said Calak. "Where are we? What is this dark place?" He lifted his sword. "Taslun, it is a beast. I can see her now!"

Kealin looked around. This beach was not real, and that he knew. They had each seen what they loved. Calak, the mountains, himself, the ocean, but what of Taslun? How could he dissuade this mirage from his brother?

"Where are we, Taslun?" he shouted.

"We are in a place of wondrous glory, that an Urlas Blade would love, but this lovely woman wants to treat those of battle to a taste of her berries. Just a moment, little brother."

She was now near his lips with the black stone. It swirled with a black fire within, and Kealin stared into her from the side.

Do not.

The demon turned and looked to him.

You have power beyond what I could seek. My master must have known this. Why would he send you here? I will kill your brother; you cannot dissuade him.

Kealin looked to Taslun. His mouth was open, and she was teasing him with the berry. Calak had gained a fearful sight and a true one when he tested his mirage, or rather, was helped to test it.

Kealin turned. The ocean rushing up, he stepped into the water, and it faded to a black dust that spread out across the dark room lit by only torches that surrounded a great circle. He turned to see not a woman but a beast of white skin and tall black horns protruding from not only atop her head but the sides. Her clawed hand held the stone at Taslun's head, and his mouth was open.

He believes he is in a place of "wondrous glory, that an Urlas Woodlands Blade would love," Kealin thought to himself.

The demon interrupted his thought. *You know not what you think. Do not try it.*

But he would. His brother thought he was upon the field of battle; a battle maiden was to offer him a treat he would well deserve with his skill, but what if the enemy was not dead?

Kealin ran for his blade. Grasping it, he shouted, "Elf of Urlas, I am your enemy! Face me!"

His brother's gaze turned, and his blade was drawn.

"No!" the demon growled.

Taslun came upon him, his blade up, and Kealin

parried, throwing his brother to the side. He sidestepped
and ran upon him.

Taslun turned and looked at Kealin.

"I do not fear you, foul thing!"

The mirage had not faded, and his brother still
sought to fight him. He braced his blade against the
slashing sword meant for him and thought of how he
might change the mirage so as to throw out his brother.
He stepped forward, striking twice to throw Taslun
back. It was then he thought and shouted, "Calak, your
blade! Throw it to me!"

Calak did so, and Kealin caught it. In a fury, he
swung at his brother, swinging his blades as he did,
striking high and low at his brother's parries. With the
clanging of elven blades, he saw Taslun's gaze change,
and now he no longer fought. He recoiled and began
breathing fast.

"What trick is this, Kealin? Why do you fight me? I
was upon the war grounds, facing a—"

It seemed Taslun had been drawn out of his mirage
as well.

The demon stepped forward. She set her gaze upon
Kealin, and his forehead felt warm. The wails began
again, and he looked back at her.

*I know not my power, but this is my stand. I told you
I needed no blade. I can destroy you.*

The demon broke her stare, and a tear formed in her
eye. I cannot believe I fell for such a trick. I have been
deceived by my own master. You solved the riddle of the
mirages with little more than a simple distraction. My
master would not have done this for no reason. I have

tormented the faceless man for so long. Why now would he do this? I am betrayed to this fate and have been beaten by little more than you. It is over. I will fade, and he will die. Beware fate.

It was then the demon burst into a white fire. A wail bellowed through the cavern, and Kealin looked upon her form as she turned to dust and collapsed.

"Dis is de end for you," he said out loud.

Taslun stared at him. "You did it again."

"What?" he asked.

"Your voice, like the shaman. What happened?"

"I still don't know, but I could hear her thoughts. She said that her master betrayed her, but he had a reason. Her master was Vankou. He was whom I first did it with. She also said to 'beware fate.'"

"Force it from mind, Brother," Calak said.

Kealin handed Calak back his sword. "Thank you for this."

Taslun embraced him. "Thank you for stopping me from falling to its tricks. Those two blades are useful. But I do not know what to think of this power of yours. It is not elven; at least, not something I know of."

Calak laughed. "That is speaking of wisdom beyond, for our elder brother knows much."

"I do not know either, but it is of no concern now. Let us deliver the news to the man above. He will be pleased to know what has happened."

They went back to the stairwell and climbed up. They found the man lying on the ground, his bleeding face uncovered and his body partially in the fire and beginning to smoke as his hood and cape started to burn.

The blade from the table was in his neck, and a pool of blood covered the floor. On the table was a note and a small sack. Kealin picked up both, opening the note.

BROTHERS, *I knew you could and you have. I am done with her wail; I know it is time. Do well with these gifts, for I did not.*

HE OPENED up the sack and found several tiny shells of differing colors. "We have them," said Kealin.

"And it seems the faceless man has what he wished," said Taslun.

"Let us hurry back to Alri," Calak told them.

They exited the hovel as the body of the figure began to burn and the hovel itself caught fire. Within the glow of the burning structure, they stood, looking out at the bay and the tornado of ice. The funnel began to falter and then vanish into the clouds, a deep gust blowing upon them now.

Taslun looked to them and began forward, Kealin and Calak following.

WITHOUT THE TORNADO spinning a rain of ice upon them, the blustery winds of the night were not as bad as they had perceived before. They made their way with haste but not as quickly as the isle before where the imminent threat of attack was on their backs.

Ahead, Kealin could see the torches of the *Aela*

Sunrise. He looked up and noticed the constellations and that it was early morning now. The passage of time was quick within the lair of the demon.

He thought of the happenings before, his ability to speak to the demon and his sense of her attempting to look within his mind. He did not know how, but his ability to sense and decipher the unknown was growing. Where before it was a second of foresight allowing him to parry a blade or sidestep a thrust from his opponent on the arena floor, it had become more, and a power that both Vankou and his demon servant perhaps feared.

Drawing closer to the place where they had left the ship, they started smelling a salty burning smell. It was not the torches of the *Aela Sunrise.* A golden glow was in the air, shrouded in fog rolling over the shore. Taslun was thinking what Kealin feared; the *Aela Sunrise's* enchanted shield was up. At least it would provide safety in the event of an attack, but as they came closer, they saw no one on the deck.

"Where are they?" Calak asked.

Kealin and Taslun were silent. Looking at each other, they then went to opposite ends of the ship, searching at the water and then back up at the ship.

"Vals! Alri!" Kealin shouted. But there was no answer.

Charred and broken pieces of wood rolled in with the tide.

6

LOST

"They must've been attacked," said Taslun. "Check for tracks leading away from the ship. Perhaps he and Alri fled."

Kealin ran along the edge of the shore, away from the wreckage. He scanned the ground, looking for displaced snow or the imprint, at least, of something out of place. The ground was untouched. Not a single rock had been turned, nor ice broken in random pools that he was careful to not slip on. He stopped, scanning the dark horizon of the open expanse of the isle.

Alri. Where are you?

He turned to the water, and he saw what they had not before. A ship was beyond the *Aela Sunrise*, and a smaller boat was in the water, approaching his brothers. Upon the deck, stout men were busy loading into another boat. It was dwarves. Some of the same from the tavern back where they had run into Rugag and his crew. His brothers were not looking toward where the dwarves were coming from. The wind was howling over the water and they were likely hiding their faces from the icy cold.

He moved along the edge of the water himself. "Taslun! Calak!" he shouted. But the wind was not in his favor, and his voice did not carry to them.

The dwarves were upon them, and though Taslun drew his blade, he lowered it as Calak was taken to the ground at spear point. His elder brother dropped his blade and lifted his hands in surrender. Calak was pulled up and forced toward his brother as the other group of dwarves landed closer to Kealin and began to spread out in a half-circle.

He couldn't hear what was being said but needed to get closer. He looked behind him. An old pathway carved out by a long frozen-over river ran further down and would provide him some form of cover in the darkness. But taking this approach, he would still be seen. He felt he had no choice. It was then he heard the water break to his right. He glanced over.

It was a narwhal.

Hello, friend.

The narwhal seemed to turn to him. He heard melody and an echo in his mind. A word appeared, and he spoke it as he heard it in his mind.

Tulasiro?

"Is that your name?"

The narwhal blew air from its blow hole.

He smiled. There seemed to be a careful friendship developing between them. "Do you know where Alri and Vals are?"

The narwhal moved in the water, swimming outward to the open sea and then back to the shore.

"If they are gone, we cannot go that way yet. We must get the ship, and my brothers are in danger."

The narwhal turned to him, rolling his horn along the shore and blowing air.

"Will you help me?"

Kealin heard sounds in his mind as before, and felt calmness upon himself.

It was then a voice shouted across the winds. "Come on! A beast is on the shore."

They had spotted the narwhal, known now to Kealin as Tulasiro.

The dwarves closest to them, and most of those who had come in the second boat and not right by his brothers, were now coming his way. He lay down in the snow. Drawing his blade, he held it close. In the bleak darkness, he would look like little more than a dark patch.

The dwarves went to the water's edge, but Tulasiro had already left.

"Look around here. You know it will come back up. Stupid creature," the one growled to the others.

There were five in total. They each looked to the waters and not to where their own actual danger lay in waiting, at least, to Kealin's plan.

The one on the furthest edge would be the easiest to slay, but was not his first target. He would take the one in the front with a single stab in the open spot in his rusty armor that he had failed to maintain. Strange for a crafter of metals as were dwarves, but he had never seen dwarves like these. The second strike would come to whichever dwarf turned next to him, and then the next would be whoever was still standing. The last, who would have likely frozen in some form of shock, he would take as a tool for bargaining.

The dwarves looked at one another.

"Likely not even a whale. Why would one come into shore like this? Stupid creatures. Perhaps if the group of them wouldn't have run into that harbor, we would've never even have found them."

"You know how Rugag is, though, always thinking of that Vals. This ship was taken with ease beyond what we could've guessed. All of this time and we take it so simply! We got him and that little elven woman. I can't wait to get off this rock and to her."

The dwarf began a bellowing laugh as he thrust his hips.

"Patience, Luraa," the one on the edge said. "We need to find that other elf. Two are not enough. There is a third. We know it, and so do those two elves. I had thought them Urlas Blades, but they gave up without a fight. Weak Blades are more how I see them!"

The one speaking did not draw another breath as Kealin's blade slashed his neck and squirted a warm rush of fluids, casting a fog in the air.

The half-elf cracked the dwarf closest to him in the head, knocking him into the water, as he slashed the remaining dwarves across their chests in one arching spin. One of the two fell, and the other backed away in shock. His plan was working. He knew these bastards were weak. The winds worked to his advantage, for as another dwarf cried out, his sounds were muted by the gusts and his head was taken off.

Looking around, the last dwarf trembled, holding the spot with his open hand that Kealin had slashed. He backed up to the edge of the water and dropped his weapon.

Kealin grabbed him by the throat. He was heavy, but Kealin lifted him up, staring at him. He had a desire to kill him if he did not wish to use him as he did. His pulse thudded in his hands; he could feel his heart pounding in his chest. But that was not the way of an Urlas Blade, and it was not what he needed to do at this time.

He lowered him to the ground and kept him in grasp by gripping his armor. He squirmed as Kealin walked with him, approaching the group surrounding Taslun and Calak.

The other dwarves did not notice Kealin right away, but as he emerged from the darkness, they saw him, cursing and running forward before the half-elf lifted his quarry for the rest to see.

One of the dwarves slapped Taslun and then turned toward Kealin.

"Well, elf, it seems you are here. Your friend here had told me you were dead." He motioned to Taslun.

Kealin smiled. "Perhaps he meant you, if you do not answer my questions."

The dwarf laughed. "You threaten us? We outnumber you."

"So you do. But his friends did not seem to be able to do much against me." Kealin placed his blade against the neck of his prisoner.

The dwarf looked around with widened eyes. "He killed the others in cold blood, sir."

Kealin's grip turned tighter.

"You mean to tell me that an Urlas Blade murdered my men? Do you not have a code, Blade? Your enemy cannot have their back turned when you face them. A fair duel, you call it."

Kealin pressed his blade against the edge of the dwarf's neck. He screamed as it pierced the first layer of his skin, blood running down the blade.

Taslun looked on and looked to Calak. He was looking down at his blade that the dwarves had removed and tossed only a few feet from them.

"The Blades of the Urlas Woodlands do have such a code. I do not, for I am not a Blade," Kealin shouted. "Where is the elf taken from the *Aela Sunrise*? And tell me of Vals. Where are they?"

There was silence in the group of dwarves, and two of them slowly inched to his far left, almost out of sight. The other two, closest to his brothers, had walked toward his right. He looked to Taslun, who made eye motions to his sword lying in the snow.

"You will not murder him, elf. You are too pure for such an act as a dwarf might do."

Kealin tightened the grip on his blade. "You force my hand, dwarf, for I will learn what I want, in any way I must."

He pulled the blade through his quarry's neck, slicing his vessels and cutting through his tissues. The dwarf gargled and fell to the ground.

"What have you done?" the dwarf shouted.

The others around him began to back up as Kealin stretched out his blade. The dwarves, who before had been stalwart and confident, looked to their boat. Taslun and Calak went for their blades, and they were not hindered.

The dwarves turned and ran for their boat, the lead dwarf pushing one of his companions into Kealin's path as the remaining ones fled.

From the waters near where the boat floated, the narwhal Tulasiro came from the depths, shattering the vessel and throwing debris onto the shore.

The dwarves turned again, and their leader pushed them toward the elves. Calak and Taslun struck at their aggressors, as Kealin moved into the last one. He pointed his blade at his neck as Tulasiro came from behind, resting its horn against the dwarf's back.

"I . . . I . . . don't know what you want."

"Name where they have been taken!" Kealin yelled, his blade against the dwarf's neck.

"Rugag took them. He went south. I can take you!"

"Can you take us?" asked Calak.

"Yes! Yes! I will gladly take you. They head back to town, an isle like before. They will not be too far from here."

The dwarf smiled, but Kealin did not return it. Taslun placed his hand on his shoulder. "It is not the way of our people, Kealin. Do not kill him."

Kealin had no plan to.

He stepped back from the dwarf, lowering his blade, but before the dwarf could move a step, he buried the blade into his leg. The dwarf screamed and gripped his knee.

"Kealin!" Taslun said.

"They took our sister, and he was a part of it. Tell me you would not do the same. Do you wish to take him with us? I do not."

Kealin walked away toward the *Aela Sunrise* as Calak and Taslun looked at one another, speechless.

The shield around the *Aela Sunrise* was set and could not be passed by Kealin's knowledge. He tapped his sword on it and found it was not a riddle they could easily solve. He turned; Tulasiro had disappeared into the depths. He looked to the others. The dwarf was still wailing in pain.

"We have a ship, but it is that wretched dwarven one," he told them. "I know not the magic the *Aela Sunrise* is protected by."

"Nor do I," Taslun said. "We can use their ship. The other rowboat is over there."

The dwarf had become silent, and with their backs turned, they did not see his wobbling approach. In a last attempt of fight, the dwarf drew a knife, bleeding profusely from his leg as he did, running toward Kealin. Calak turned, seeing his approach, and slashed the dwarf down before driving the blade into the man's chest.

Kealin jerked around and looked to Calak with a nod. He then glanced up at Taslun. "Dwarves. At least in the Glacial Seas, they cannot be trusted," Calak said.

Taslun seemed thankful the threat had been dealt with, but the beliefs of the Blades still stuck in his mind.

Calak and Kealin went to the rowboat and steadied it. They boarded and rowed toward the ship. None of them really knew how to sail, and as they came closer, they noticed the battle scars left on it by the *Aela Sunrise*. Its sails had been burned to mere cinders. It seemed otherwise intact, though there was a lot of wood floating in the water. Kealin wondered how many ships Vals had taken down before he was captured.

Taslun pointed out, "A courageous man, Vals. He fought well to hold this ground, it seems."

The dwarven ship was easily boarded, being lower to the water and with the surf not as torrential as before. They made their way onto it and began to look around.

"Check what stores you can find. We must hope there are sails somewhere," Taslun said.

"Do you know how to sail, Brother?" Kealin questioned.

"I have not thought of how yet."

They each took turns looking through a large collection of nets and spears, more than a few bottles of wine, and dry goods. The dwarves were well stocked, but they could not find any sails.

Kealin walked along the rails, looking into the waters. Two massive ropes went out from the decks and followed around two large cogs. He guessed the anchors were below. Tulasiro broke the water, and as he stared into the waves, other narwhals appeared, their horns gleaming in the starlight.

What is it?

The narwhals all threw themselves forward, diving

down into the depths. Taslun and Calak came beside Kealin.

"What do the narwhals want with us?" Calak asked.

"Tulasiro," said Kealin.

"Who?"

"One of the narwhals. Its name is Tulasiro. It was the one who destroyed the boat, trapping the dwarves. I do not know what it and its brethren do, but—"

The ship began to lurch with the waves, and a moment later, the narwhals had appeared just below the surface. The ship began to move forward into the sea. The ropes hanging off the sides slipped forward, splintering the rails, and the elves steadied their feet as the ship dropped downward and then leveled out, a burst of frigid water coming over the rails of the vessel. Kealin went to the front of the ship.

The two lines that had been tied to the anchors now were straight out, and the flippers of the narwhals flapped as the ship was pulled forward.

"They must know," said Kealin. "Tulasiro spoke to me before; I believe they know where Vals and Alri are."

"As strange as your words are, we must hope that they do," Taslun stated.

It was some time they traveled before Taslun came to Kealin. Calak was eating a strange fruit he had found in storage, and Taslun had brought Kealin bread to share with him.

"You must keep your strength up, little brother."

Kealin glanced down at him and then back to the sea ahead, his eyes scanning the horizon for signs of Alri and Vals. "I do not need that," he told him.

Taslun stood, eating his own bread, but it was more than a snack he wanted with Kealin. "That dwarf, back on the shore, I wanted to talk to you about your actions."

Kealin glared at him. "Our sister has been taken. I will not let some scheming dwarf dishonor us in such a way by withholding what he knows."

"I know you do not have the respect for our people as I think you should, but you must embrace good conscience."

"My conscience is well, Brother. I know why I do what I do. I will strike someone from behind if it means saving any of you. Besides, he got what he deserved from Calak."

Taslun sighed. "Our brother is on the fence, and he could be as his people or resist like his brother."

"Then I hope you keep him near you, Taslun, for I would hate for him to also feel your judgment."

He went silent, but Kealin continued. "I may have resisted the ways of the Blades, but I listened to the Blade Master, learned what I could, and have increased my skills so that you may see that, if nothing else is true, I am worthy to stand beside you. I am not of pure elven blood; our people made sure to tell me that from a young age. I was not given pardon as you were."

"Brother, I only pray we use wisdom in all of our decisions."

"I do," he replied. "The wisdom imparted to me by our teacher."

The polar lights were above them, a greenish ribbon across the sky, turning red and purple as swift winds blew the clouds, showing the moon once again. The speed of the narwhals was magnificent, and Kealin was sure they were moving faster than they had aboard the *Aela Sunrise*, except, of course, when they had floated for a time above the sea itself.

In the distance, they could see blots on the horizon. At first, it looked to be more glaciers. A bit ago, they passed four large ones that had caused Kealin's attention to perk and then fall.

This was different. Four small glints of light were visible, and it seemed, at least from afar, they were the ships that they were looking for.

Kealin looked down into the water as one of the narwhals broke off from those towing and made eye contact with him.

He nodded after hearing its message, and looked to his brothers.

"The ships are ahead. Dey will lead us in. We are expecting other creatures to help. Vals is liked among those of the sea."

Kealin noticed his speech had changed for a moment, but thought nothing further of it. His blade was ready.

For the sake of those bastard sea-dwelling burrowers, Alri better be untouched.

Taslun and Calak stood beside him as the broken dwarven vessel gained upon the ships. The fact that it was a dwarven vessel worked to their advantage, for the large catapults on the four ships remained unlit and undrawn even as they ran along the stern of the ship on the far east side of the column.

As they looked along the enemy ship, they ducked

down, hiding behind the wreckage of the railings as other dwarves began to look on. Two ships over, there appeared to be a ship of grander design. It had bright green railings. It was the flagship of Rugag. The lost vessel of their fleet arriving, even with burned sails, was a very peculiar occurrence.

"We go together. Clear the decks one by one," said Taslun.

"Agreed," Kealin said. "If you spot Alri or Vals, stay with them. If we see Rugag, kill him. We move ship to ship all the way to the flagship."

Taslun looked at Kealin but said nothing of killing Rugag. "Together, Brothers."

The ships were next to each other, and it was clear the narwhals had left the ropes. Those aboard the dwarven vessel shouted to one another, talking of the burned sails and the lack of a crew. The elven brothers knelt with their blades. As dwarves began to board the ship, Kealin led the attack, jumping from one ship to the next.

He landed with little more than a thud. His eyes scanned the deck, and he squinted, looking for either his sister or Vals. His brothers landed next to him, and it was then the dwarves of the ship noticed they had been boarded.

Calak and Taslun went right, sliding into a stance with swords behind them. The dwarves charged them; one had a net, while another two had spears, and the remainder, coming from a galley at the aft of the ship, came with what weapons they could find. They were cut down one after another.

Kealin worked the opposite way, cutting down two dwarves near the deck-mounted crossbow. Shouts filled the air from the other ships as dwarves laid down planks to cross from one ship to the next. Kealin leaped onto the nearest one, slashing each dwarf who came between him and wherever it was Alri and Vals were. One by one, taking down the dwarves and spraying blood across the ice-encrusted deck, he began to feel frustrated. This ship, too, was lacking whom he searched for.

Calak and Taslun turned the wheel of the furthest ship, and it crushed into the one next to it, starting a chain reaction of colliding and splintered wood. They joined Kealin on the second vessel they had taken.

"Wake, Rugag!" someone shouted.

Kealin looked, spotting a trio of men running from the third ship, which he guessed was, in fact, the flag ship, into a locked room adorned with the jaws of sharks.

The dwarf at the helm turned the third ship away from the second ship as the fourth ship on the outside moved to protect it; its crossbow was readied and aimed at the second ship that the brothers had now managed to clear of breathing dwarves.

The crossbow fired. Its bolt tore across the deck. Its tail slapped just over Kealin, close enough for him to hear the buzz of its chain across his ears.

The fourth ship was moving along front of the second ship, now even further from the green-railed flag-ship of the dwarves that tried to move away from them.

From the depths of the sea, an explosion of ice and water came as Tulasiro broke the surface with its brethren, the pod of narwhals smashing into the side of the crossbow-firing ship. Tulasiro crushed the mechanisms of the crossbow, rolling off the side and back into the depths.

All across the ship, more narwhals struck the dwarves. The wooden deck splintered with their weight, and the dwarves fought back, sticking more than just one of the large white whales with spears and hacking at them with axes. The fourth dwarven vessel was destroyed.

The flagship of Rugag now moved alongside of them. Without their other ships, they would have to fight. The dwarves were much more prepared and now they were garbed in armor.

Taslun went to the crossbow and fired into the center mast of the ship. With a crack, the bolt slapped across the deck and took down many of the dwarves. Rugag appeared and shouted, climbing to the helm of his ship and twisting a crystal of similar design as the one on the *Aela Sunrise.*

The air began to sizzle, and a stream of fire shot across the bow of the ship from the flagship, catching the other two vessels on fire.

The dwarves boarded the ship, and the slicing and clanging of metals filled the air as the dwarves proved better opponents now that the surprise of the attack had worn off.

Kealin twisted his blade before arching back down on two dwarves who had pointed at him and proudly charged. Their mistake.

The ship under attack by narwhals had been reduced to a sinking mess, its occupants, both drowning in the frigid waters and being skewered by the horns of the narwhals, wailed into the night sky. Other creatures had come now, too, and enacted a long-awaited revenge on their hunters. The ocean was angry, and the waters were very much alive.

The dwarves were losing their hold on the elves, and Rugag knew it. He disappeared into a hidden recess under the helm with two of his dwarves, and returned dragging Alri and Vals.

Kealin shouted to alert his brothers. "Alri!"

Taslun and Calak looked, suddenly feeling a renewed vigor for battle.

Like some type of sudden blessing for Rugag, more dwarves swarmed the deck of the flagship and crossed over to attack the elves.

Each elf had at least four assailants at any moment, and as one would fall from the glowing red blade of an elf, another would take its place. The deck of the ship had become a slippery mess of bloody ice and sea foam.

Calak had broken through his attackers and leaped to the flagship; Rugag pushed the two dwarves near him, and he was engaged. The younger brother worked to slice his way to his sister. Alri was awake and could see what was happening. She looked to Rugag, and though she had been beaten more than once, she could see through her swollen eye enough to make out his knee. She kicked him, and a crack followed, the dwarf grasping at his leg.

She scurried up, weak but on her feet. Taslun and Kealin defeated the last of their attackers and made it to the ship. Calak cut down the remaining two dwarves and approached Rugag.

Taslun and Kealin went to Alri.

"You came. You didn't leave me."

"We would never, Alri," Taslun said. "Are you well?"

"She is not who you should worry of now," Rugag announced.

Rugag forced Vals to his knees. A circular collar of some design was now on his neck, and the dwarf held his finger on a trigger of sort, trembling. Kealin looked it up and down and did not know what device he held. His eyes met Vals', and the man wept.

"There," Rugag said. "Quietness. I am under no belief that I will survive this. I wished to have the *Aela Sunrise,* but it is out of reach due to this man's devices. I, at least, had him, and a nice elf for a bonus, but I did not know the sea would react as such. These beasts, good for oil and bones, not to mention the narwhals and their lovely horns, a good profit, but that is no more. My ships are sinking, and even now, what I had built is burning."

The fires of broken oil lanterns had engulfed the dwarven vessels. Flames had begun to catch even the flagship and were beyond extinguishing.

"But he will die first."

"Take care of them!" Vals shouted out. "They wait for—"

The dwarf pressed the trigger, and a blade severed the captain of the *Aela Sunrise's* neck. Blood squirted up and covered Rugag.

Rugag laughed, "Not soon enough. I have defeated

him after so many years. I have broken him and it is too bad I didn't get the rest of them."

The dwarf looked out at the sea, seeing the many narwhals around them. Kealin stepped forward and Rugag dropped Val's body.

"And now I die," Rugag said, "but not before I say this: your world, my world, will end. Darkness approaches the Glacial Seas. All you four do is for nothing but to prolong suffering in your own hearts. Even your path now takes you closer. This was all meant to happen like this. Vals was just a step. I am happy to know your ends come. May you sickening elves go the same way as Vals, but much slower and more horrendously."

Kealin stepped forward and slashed the dwarf, severing his head beside that of Vals. It was the most satisfying but yet most empty kill he had felt. Vals was dead, and there was nothing that could be done for him.

Taslun looked at him, but he had no protest to this killing.

"What did he mean?" asked Calak. "What darkness? How does he know of our intents or fate?"

"Put it from mind, Brother," Kealin said, "as you told me before. As it stands, we still go to serve Dimn."

"Hurry, Brothers. We are still not safe," Taslun said.

The ship was sinking around them, and there was not a nearby boat seaworthy enough to hold them.

Kealin looked to the waters where Tulasiro had been. As the sea rippled with the ships burning and cracking into the icy water, the elves ran to the highest point of the ship not engulfed by flames.

"What do we do?" asked Calak.

The narwhal pod came around the edge of the sinking ship and slowed. Kealin saw that Tulasiro was closest.

Do you wish me upon you, Tulasiro?

He heard the sound of the narwhal's song, and he smiled, leaping from the wrecked ship to the body of the narwhal. He caught hold around the form of its head. Its skin felt strange against his, and though he was not in the water completely, he was very cold. The others followed suit, jumping onto the narwhals as the ship began to disappear into the void of the ocean.

"My staff," Alri said.

Taslun looked back at the ship. "We will find you another one, Sister. Be happy we were able to save you."

Kealin looked back to see each of his siblings. He felt a strange hate for what had transpired, but at the same time, he was thankful. A stirring was within him. Vals had wished him to take care of the narwhals. For once, he felt purposed to do something beyond himself, but he did not know what to make of it. Vals was a good man, and in that, he found respect, a feeling he did not have for many. He thought of Rugag's words, as well, unsure of what to believe of them.

The pod of narwhals made their way away from the wreckage with a careful pace. It was difficult for them to keep the elves above the surface of the water while also propelling themselves forward.

Kealin did not know where they were being taken, only that his hands were aching from the cold water. He did not know how long he himself could hang on, much less Alri, who was not in great health to begin with.

He looked up at the sky. He could just see the constellation of a sea snail, but he had not been watching the time as of late. Tiredness filled his body, or was it the numbness in his fingertips spreading to his arm and causing it to be painful to take any amount of breath into his chest?

Vision clouding, he made out the polar lights bright above him. The water seemed to be moving faster, pushing them along. A strange current.

Meredaas. Master, Tulasiro said to him.

Your master, I thank him. We all do.

Tulasiro moved more quickly and broke through ice. Kealin pulled his arms up as much as he could muster to prevent the ice from scratching him. He turned to glance behind, and it seemed that Alri had fallen asleep. At least, he hoped it was that. Her condition of the wights was a mystery to him, and her true health was unknown.

He looked up to see the shore ahead. It was a cliff-faced island, and the beach itself was inside a rocky grotto lit with glowing flowers. It reminded him of some of the groves near Eldmer Lake back in the Urlas Woodlands, but it had been some time since he was able to look upon them himself.

The yellow, orange, and red flowers sparkling upward were dotted with fairies fluttering from bloom to bloom.

He felt himself rolled onto the shore, and then the thuds as his siblings were placed the same way by the narwhals. As the pod of narwhals left, the fairies floated over them, and he felt himself growing more tired and falling to sleep.

He looked around, seeing still the polar lights but then rocks and a blackness to their left. It was a cave. Within the dark, he saw two blue eyes looking back at him. He wished to sit up but could not. He fell asleep, unable to stay awake any longer, but very much not alone.

7

ICE DRAKE

Kealin opened his eyes. The sky was unchanged to his just wakening self. The winds were calm, and though he was very cold, his body felt restored. Aches from the past few days had been healed.

He sat up, seeing that Calak was up and walking around their stony surroundings. Taslun was some distance away, walking near the edge of the water, standing ankle-deep on a pebble beach. Alri, too, had just awoken. Taslun noticed her first and went to her.

"Alri, how do you feel?"

She smiled. "Better. Though I still feel the sickness within me, I feel as if I have been healed to some degree."

The fairies from before flew high above them. Kealin could see better now that they were in a large cave. He looked to his left and the darkness. He remembered the eyes from before but looked around, finding no sight of them.

"Kealin!" said Calak. "We are in some cavern, but we cannot find a way out. It seems we must wait for the narwhals. That is, if they come back. Did they say anything to you?"

Taslun turned to look at him also. It seemed the general belief was that he might know something, given his gift.

"I do not know. I just barely remember being placed here."

"Well, we took the time to search, and there is no way we can find. We had thought to climb out near the entrance and make our way up, but the stones are too slippery and we have nothing that will give us grip."

Kealin stood and walked toward the darkness of the back of the cave.

"We checked as far as we could. It is no good," Taslun told him.

What his brother had said was true. The edge of the cave dropped into a blackness with no discernible end that he could make out. For a time, they appeared trapped.

Kealin went back to Alri, who was still sitting on the ground.

He came behind her and embraced her, holding her tightly in his arms.

"I was worried, for a moment, that you had been lost."

"I, too, had worried of that. I had never been as happy to have heard a shouting clamor as I did as you three attacked the distant ship. Even from my cell, I knew it was you. I knew you would come for us, though Vals—he tried so hard to defend. They overwhelmed us at the *Aela Sunrise*."

Taslun and Calak, looking up and down the edge of a tidal pool in the cave, looked up as she began to speak.

"What did actually happen?" Kealin asked.

"It was sometime after you three left. I had awoken and questioned what transpired. He cared for me, preparing tea, and then he saw them. He pulled me into the storage area as bolts began to fly in, crashing on the deck. He moved along the bow, twisting crystals as he did. Flames leaped from the masts, striking what I would soon learn were the approaching dwarven ships. He attempted to raise the enchantments, but they were upon us before he could. They bound both of us, but as we were being pulled from the ship, he managed to hit a switch, and a dome surrounded the vessel. We were still pulled from it, but when Rugag attempted to return to the ship to capture it, he could not. Vals would not help him. He was struck many times because of it, too."

Kealin looked over to his brothers. Though they were listening, whatever they had seen in the tidal pool had led them further. It was clear they had found something. Taslun drew his sword and attempted to chip off pieces of the wall.

"I was beaten a few times," Alri continued, "but once they learned of my health being as it was, I was to be more of a trophy. Vals, though, I know you did not see it, but they had burned his back with hot iron. Rugag was angry. Angry for no reason I could understand.

"Vals told me he could not let the ship fall to one of them and he would die before he gave it up. He said the ship was sacred. He said he feared death. I heard what he said before, how if he feared death, he would die. That he was told this was how he would die but that by helping us, somehow, he had served a greater purpose... They screamed at him. They lashed him. They called him 'Stormborn' and claimed he was hiding something. But he would not tell them what they wanted. I guess it doesn't matter now. I feel bad. I fell asleep many times, so he was alone to suffer," she wept. "I don't know anything else. It is not good that in all this, my staff was lost. I am powerless."

Kealin kissed her forehead. "Do not worry of it, Sister."

"I think I have found something," Calak said.

Kealin looked over, standing up as his brother pointed.

"This is no cave. I do not know what it was for sure, but these writings are like those in the cave Vals had showed us. There is brickwork beneath the rock here."

"I wish that it helped us in some way," Taslun said. "This cave may be no more than the one before. If it is a ruin, the rocks are no help to us in finding our way out."

They spent a considerable amount of time exploring the cave or ruin, depending on which brother was asked and at which particular point of debate they came to. Alri too helped. Though thankful to the narwhals to have been brought here, they believed they were abandoned.

There were no supplies, no sources of food except

for the sea, which was almost pointless given there were no tools for fishing. Kealin at last resolved to stare into the blackness of the cave. He had seen something there the night they arrived. In time, he sat down, convinced that what he saw would return. The narwhals had picked this place for a reason.

It was many hours later when his siblings had gone to sleep, cold and hungry. He stared into the blackness. There was something more. He had heard a scratching sound below him, and now it was only a matter of waiting.

Kealin drew his blade and looked down further into the depths. The red glow of his sword permeated the shadows. It was then the cave quaked and he heard sliding in the ice. From below, what appeared to be two burning sapphires shined toward him.

"Elves of Urlas Woodlands, I had heard you were upon the Glacial Seas. The narwhals are holy beasts, and they brought you to my domain. Why?"

Kealin looked back to his siblings and noticed no one had awoken. "Come up to me," he said downward. "Let me know to whom I, Kealin, speak."

There was silence for a moment that was split by sudden scratching and a rush of cold air blew over Kealin. The others behind were stirred awake. Kealin looked on as, from the depths, a massive face appeared. Its eyes were as sapphires but were greater, their light shining down a scaly snout, and an icy breath blew over Kealin as a mouth full of teeth opened.

"Seen enough of me, elf? They do not have dragons in your woods, I suppose, which is not a surprise to me. This is my home you have intruded."

Now surrounded by his siblings, Kealin sheathed his sword. "We seek to go to Dimn, but the dwarf known as Rugag caused us to be taken well off course. We had been upon the *Aela Sunrise* with Valrin, but his ship is of no use to us now, and he has fallen."

"I do see, but why would the narwhals bring you here? I suppose my fairies healed your wounds?"

"Yes," said Alri. "We are thankful."

"A thankful elf, that is something hard to find. One of you speaks from within."

"What?"

"One of you can speak from the mind. I sense it. Who is it?"

Kealin closed his eyes. *Me.*

"I had thought it you. I watched you four this day; you seemed to have uncovered a secret within this old harbor, but you could not find the way out."

"There is just stone. There is no way that could be found. Or I assure you," Taslun said, pushing past Kealin, "we would have found it."

The dragon moved his head in close to them and snapped his teeth toward Taslun. "Your brother is whom I respect. You are an elf, pure as can be, by your assurance of what you do not know. Do you not know that we dragons have less than the lowest amount of respect for you elves? Do not speak with me as an inferior or even an equal. I speak to him, for I care much for him and the division he has begun in these seas.

"The one seeking death has been given it by Vankou. The Lord of Death is gaining power again, and yet you tell me you go to Dimn when it is clear you are in service to Vankou?"

"We are in no such service," said Kealin.

"But yet you defeated the demon on the lonely isle?"

"We did that for the shells of Meredaas."

The dragon turned his eye to them and blinked.

"Go toward the corner of the cave. I shall reveal to you what you missed, but do not feel bad. It is by my will alone you can leave. Otherwise, you would've become my snack."

The dragon dropped into the darkness, and a gust of wind and a splash followed.

Taslun turned to Kealin when the water further out at sea exploded, the dragon emerging some distance off and taking to the sky.

They ran toward the edge of the cave and looked up as the massive creature landed some place above them. There were scratches and rumblings above, and then, in a distant corner, the sky became visible as the quaking dropped rocks rolling all around them.

"Come on," said Taslun.

The four of them proceeded toward the opening and emerged on a large icy platform. The ice drake was on all fours, looming above them. Taller than many masts of the ships they had been on and capable of eating each of them at once with less than a single bite from its jaws, it lowered itself down on the ground, looking over each of them.

The rest of the island was built around a large

central mountain. Though icy and dark, the mountain smoked and a red glow pierced the night sky like a lone beacon on the sea.

Nestled in its shadow were what appeared build-ings, but rock covered most parts of them. Even the plat-form they were standing on had markings and signs of craftsmanship. Kealin noticed large harbors overrun with rubble of rocks that had come down from the mountain and went into the water.

"You four elves are the first in some time to be upon this ground. A seafaring race was destroyed many millennia ago here. Their legacy is now covered in stone. I have been here for some time, protecting it from eyes needing to see it. There is much to be found here to the right person, but that may not be why you are here? You seek Dimn. Why are you drawn to him?"

"He is in danger," Taslun said. "A darkness approaches his holy place."

"And you have seen this?" the dragon said. "Be wary of vision, for it can be clouded with simple words spoken beneath the breath."

"Not us," said Kealin. "Our shaman within the Urlas Woodlands. There was darkness already upon the gods of the North. Our parents went to assist them, but we, too, sought the shaman, learning of this darkness upon Dimn."

"If your parents needed your assistance, why did they not take you?"

"We are too young," said Calak.

"Young? Do you speak to a dragon like myself of age? Age does not matter in the way the world spins.

Perhaps you are not ready for such a task, but then, you have traveled far and became sick." The dragon looked to Alri. "The wights of Vankou's isle have infected you."

"They had," Alri stated, "but I feel better after the sleep I had here."

"A temporary healing. Though, I know a way to relieve your symptoms. It must be why the narwhals brought you here, as opposed to an inhabited isle. It is all making sense to this old dragon.

"But I still do not see why I should help those such as yourselves. Dimn is not one to waste time with rumors, but I will say I have spoken to him of late, and he is worried much of his brothers further south and rumors of dealings in those lands. Perhaps he, in his wisdom, has become careless. The Heart of the Winds may be at risk, and if that is so, we have greater worry than Dimn himself."

Taslun stepped forward. "That is why we are here. We are to assist Dimn and protect our people."

"But you know not what approaches. How will you help when you do not know how?"

"It doesn't matter," said Kealin. "We go to his assistance, no matter what he faces."

"And you, Kealin, you are most susceptible to lies. Your mind has power beyond simplicity of sword. You hold not your own creed as a Blade, yet you seek a holy one to protect. Guard your own mind, for you have released the one to death that was forbidden it. There is something else at work beyond what you know. But of that, I will watch for myself. Yes, Dimn is in danger. I am master of the skies of the Glacial Seas, and those of the Itsu do approach Dimn.

"Know, that I cannot harm them. Their ethereal bodies are not affected by dragon ice, and I do not care of the affairs of gods, only that of the world itself. Your blades are elven; your bodies carry the lifeblood of the earth. Be happy by my words that you can harm them."

"Is Dimn not a god?" asked Calak. "Can he not destroy them?"

"That is blasphemy in the eyes of a god, dear elf, but yes, he can. Only, he will not be able to stop them all. There is more. A being is within these Itsu. I cannot see it beyond a growing dark magic, but you four may be able to learn more. I do not know."

"We need a way to the place of the maelstroms," said Taslun. "We thank you for your assistance, but we must get to Dimn."

"I can provide a way, and I will do so. But it is your sister who needs assistance first. Go into the place beneath the mountain. Retrieve an amulet kept upon the altar in the center chamber. It is large, but you will be able to carry it with ease. Bring it to me, and I will heal this ailment. Think of it as payment for deeds beyond these today."

Taslun nodded. "It will be done."

The dragon growled and then took to the sky, its wings blowing snow and ice from the platform they stood upon.

"You agreed quickly," Kealin said.

"I didn't feel we had much a choice in the decision,"

Taslun said. "Why ask questions that we do not want an answer to?"

"Oh, you mean something like 'what is in this place we go to?'" Calak said. "At least it is not wights like before."

Alri shook her head. "I hope not, and I hope nothing of ill is here at all. I have no staff to assist you three."

From the platform, they followed a literally frozen road. Walking along areas not sheer with ice and made up of more rock, their way was precarious. Aside from falling, sharp rocks and tiny crevices large enough to break an ankle but not actually swallow you up ravaged their way. Passing to a lower portion of the path, they looked to either side of them. Kealin noticed wrecked ships preserved beneath the icy waters. Even with the many years under the surface, they had held up well. Their design reminded him of the *Aela Sunrise.*

He wondered of them. Between the caves where Vals had hidden them and now this place watched over by an ice drake, he knew not of what race these people were. The annals of his people had said nothing of a Glacial-Sea-dwelling culture, but perhaps it was not knowledge the elves embraced or agreed with.

Their path began upward. Three grand stairwells reached up toward the volcanic mountain, but instead of steady footing, they found their path even more difficult, as broken stairwells mauled with the sheer stone and ice forced them into a sluggish ascent.

Kealin drew his blade and smashed ice from a foothold. He leaped up and, in the same motion, drove his blade into the stone. He reached down for Alri.

"Come, I will push you up."

Alri followed, and he tossed her upward. She slid but found her footing as the others did, as Kealin did, working slowly to go upward. They were only another few paces from the top, but it was here where the damage dealt was the most severe.

As they made their way up, it was in deep scratches in the earth they found footing, but this was new damage in terms of the ruins. Kealin was the first up, and after helping the others, he looked around.

The rocks near a center door had been smashed. The door itself was recessed in and was ajar but frozen. Its blue paint was emblazoned with golden tridents and the effigy of a whale. Large scratches were made into the rocks going up the volcano, and cracks ran up toward the summit.

"Do you think it the dragon's doing?" asked Calak.

"Well, he would not fit in the door. Perhaps that is why he sent us," Alri replied to him. "We can fit. But I do wonder if we should."

"We don't have a choice," said Kealin. "Aside from the continuation of our quest, he can heal you."

Taslun lifted his blade and looked around the edge of the door. Kealin did the same as he stepped on the opposite side. Alri looked down at the ground. Kealin looked at her. She was scared.

Do not worry, Sister.

She looked up at him and smiled, but with a raised eyebrow, unsure of what she heard. He had gained more knowledge of his skill, and still he did not understand how. Since his time with Vankou, somehow he used it more. He smiled back. It was good he did not need to speak; he knew his tongue would change as it had before.

"Keep a keen eye, Brothers," Taslun commanded. "Alri, if there is trouble, stay near me."

Kealin entered first, with Taslun just behind. The world within the mountain was crystalline. The entire interior had been frozen. Beneath them, the lava of the mountain flowed but did not melt the ice. They walked in a cavern of corpses. Though it was difficult to make out, it was clear the race of seafarers that the dragon spoke of were not all destroyed by a cataclysmic eruption but had suffered a freezing from within. From the shapes of the ice, it seemed it had come from the door inward. Considering the fire beneath them, it was not any normal ice.

"I do not know where it is we should search," said Taslun. "The dragon had said it was in a center chamber."

"It is large, too, but able to be carried with ease," Calak quoted with a hint of sarcasm in his tone. "Let's just continue further in until we cannot go any further."

It was a good plan to Kealin. There was a stillness in the air that brought a colder chill to his skin. His blade glowed red as always, but he found himself wishing it gave off heat.

Alri shuddered. "It is very cold," she said.

"Do you feel well enough?" Kealin asked, stopping with her as Calak and Taslun went ahead.

"I feel more than a chill. I am dizzy. But I will manage." She forced a smile.

He took off his cloak and placed it around her.

"Alri, Kealin, come quick!" said Calak.

The two of them caught up with their brothers, finding they had made it into a large room more cavernous than the previous ones. There were more iced figures here. In their hands were what seemed like staves, pointed upward.

Kealin stared up. It appeared the stone covering was not like that of the rest of the mountain.

"I believe this room was open to the sky at some time," said Taslun. "Perhaps these were casters, providing a shield from an attack."

"So they were frozen as ice came upon them?" asked Calak. "That does not make much sense."

"It does when there is an ice drake outside wishing for us to retrieve something for him."

"That which I believe we have found," Kealin said, pointing.

In the center of the room was a large chest covered in stone. It was cracked down the center. A large white bone of some kind was stuck in it; the end of the bone sticking up into the air had been hacked away, or so it appeared.

They began removing stones, and as pieces were placed aside, a silver chain could be made out. Kealin looked to the strange bone in the one stone. He questioned what it was but could not explain it. He went back to work.

It took some time and many breaks, but at last they came to a final stone on the far end. It was a capstone, heavy, and even with many hands, unable to be removed.

They began to use their blades to chip away at it. One by one, the elven brothers worked their way, and the stone began to crumble into itself. Cracks formed with each strike, and with a shout, Calak delivered a strong blow, and the stone shattered. A black stone, the amulet, had now been unearthed once again.

"I look at this massive chain and do not believe our dragon acquaintance has told us the truth. How can it not weigh a ton?" Calak said.

He was right, or so Kealin thought. The chain itself was nearly as long as the *Aela Sunrise*. The amulet was easily the size of a boulder.

"I cannot guess what we have been lied to about, but he would have not sent us had he not assumed we could do it," Taslun said. "Let's lift it up and take it out. This cold is wretched, and I much prefer the winds outside."

They each took position at places along the chain. Kealin wrapped his hands around it and braced his back by tightening his stomach. He took a deep breath.

"On a count of two," Taslun said. "One, two."

Kealin lifted but found not at all the weight he was expecting. The amulet indeed was light and came upward without much muscle at all. Had he lifted it any harder, it likely would have flown upward out of his hands.

"Seems the dragon was right," said Calak.

They exited the room as they had come in. Though now holding a massive chain, they wormed their way between statues and walked with haste toward the still-cold but warmer world outside.

It was only a few paces from the doors when a gust came upon them from behind. At first they each ignored it; instead, their assumptions and excuses convinced them to not worry. But upon a second gust, Kealin looked behind, and a deep haze came upon them. A great light began to shine, and they dropped the amulet.

A voice came upon the air. "Do not take what we took to hinder them. We cannot assist again. You will awaken more than the one of music can as of now. Do not, we beg you. We will not harm you if you leave it, but flee this place now or face damnation."

The haze was upon them, almost as if choking them. It smelled horrid, and Kealin coughed.

"Go!" shouted Taslun.

Their view was obstructed, but they knew the gateway was just ahead. Kealin began to sprint, though it was not until they passed the void and returned to the outside that they could all see again. They knew not to stop. The gusts came upon them again, and the ground trembled. Kealin glanced behind them as he did; the others did too, and it seemed the haze had followed them.

They looked up, searching for the dragon, but could not see it. It hadn't returned as of now. They continued running toward the platform above the cave. There was no other path.

The ground rumbled more, and there was a shrill sound behind them.

A crack formed in their path, and they stumbled,

sliding to a stop as they looked behind. The fogs were converging together. From the top of the volcano, a dark smoke rose and a fiery blast rocketed into the air, arching downward and striking the fog. Lava spewed onto the ground around them and further split the earth they stood upon.

The fog began to glow red and black. Stones from the ruins flew toward the combining mass, and two white eyes stared at them.

Kealin scanned for another path. He saw one, but he was not sure if his brother had the same idea.

Taslun had already let go of the chain and drew his blade. He turned to them. "Go, do what you must to get the amulet to the platform. Continue on to Dimn. I will stop this beast."

"Yes, Brother!" Calak shouted. He, too, had seen the path Kealin saw, and began toward it, the amulet dragging behind them as Kealin and Alri now fell to the back part of the chain. They ascended upward and further up the frozen ground to the platform.

Kealin looked back to Taslun. His blade shimmered a bright red as he took a dueling stance with the creature, now brandishing a golden trident emblazoned with flames. In a few paces, Taslun walked to the side before charging in true Urlas Blade form.

His brother faced a being at least four times his size in height, but it made no difference, for in a great leap, he struck high, and the creature was pushed back. It stumbled before stabbing toward the flying elf. Taslun evaded, twisting and parrying the blade as he used the momentum to toss him back toward the ground.

Kealin stumbled, not watching his footing, as they began a last ascent up toward the platform. His legs ached, as did his throat. The cold now bothered him, after the frigid air of the cavern and then the burning fumes as they left. Reaching the platform, he dropped the chain. He drew his sword and then pointed to Calak. "Stay with Alri."

Looking up to the sky, he saw no dragon, and his brother was sacrificing himself for the act the dragon had commanded. It was not like the dragon was waiting outside to help them. They were alone, and Kealin had to act.

Taslun was locked in parry, blade versus the spikes of the creature's trident. It roared, the ravenous sound cutting through the cold as Taslun gripped his hilt tighter, his arms being forced out of his protective form as the creature began to glow brighter. A white opening appeared just below its eyes, and it spoke.

"You had a chance to leave it. I will stop you and return what we took from the one of songs."

The white opening closed, and the creature began to shrill again. Taslun began to falter. But it was then he perceived another approaching. He looked beyond the creature and spotted Kealin mid-jump, his blade angled downward, landing atop the creature with a rock-cracking downward thrust.

The creature recoiled, swiping Taslun away and throwing Kealin off of itself. Kealin rolled across the ground and stopped just short of the sea water in one of the harbors.

He shook himself; he had hit his ribs quite hard and

coughed as he went back toward the beast. His brother was again engaged with it, and his swipes were becoming sloppy, doing little more than deterring the trident.

Kealin ran forward again. The creature turned this time and slashed the prongs toward him. He ducked and rolled, making it inside the creature's attack range and slashing upward. His sword couldn't break its skin. The creature stomped at him, and vibrations sent him wheeling backward again.

It turned to Taslun now, raising the trident before smashing its boulder-like feet again, knocking the elder brother to the ground. It held its trident back, rearing for a final strike, when the air around it turned frosty and a blast of ice struck from above.

The dragon roared upon the ruins, and its form struck the creature, sending it into the opposite harbor in a roll of ice and flames, its stony form fragmenting and falling downward.

"Go to the others!" the dragon commanded.

Kealin went for Taslun and pulled him to his feet.

"Good work, Brother!"

They both began a careful flight to the others atop the platform. They went as quick as their feet would carry them, careful to not slip as the ground thundered behind them. Within a short time, they were with Alri and Calak. They turned to see the battling titans.

The creature had come again from the sea, its trident in hand. The very volcano seemed to be quaking beyond control as it struck at the dragon who took to the air, clawing the creature as it did. The dragon would then circle high, out of the reach of the fiery trident, before opening its mouth and casting a sheet of ice upon the creature.

Multiple attacks engulfed the creature, and each time, it recoiled, breaking from the purposed icy prison. It eventually ended up before the door of the volcano. The mountain quaked again, and lava flowed from the top; the flow of melted stones came upon the creature, and it began to grow in size.

The dragon flew over them, and they ducked. An icy fog fell upon them as the dragon arched up high before diving toward the creature. Magics swirled from the mountain and around the center of the creature's head. A single beam of light burst forward from a glowing crystal that emerged from the head of the creature. The beam itself nearly hitting the dragon in the neck.. But any hope it had to defeat the dragon fled as a blast of white and blue struck it, causing its form to be pushed against the stone. The dragon pummeled the mountain, and there was a final shrill sound. The dragon was upon the mountain for a moment and then flapped backward, landing near the ruins of the harbors.

The creature did not move, even as lava still poured upon its form. What life source or enrichment it was to be given from the fires was no more. The dragon had defeated it.

It took to the air again and landed upon the platform. Looking down on them and the amulet, it stuck its head through the chain and cocked its body; the chain rolled over the dragon's head and came to rest down its neck.

"I thank you four for your deeds. I see now why your journey brought you here, but merely not for my own terms to be met. I must do something for you." The dragon went back toward the harbor and dove down into the sea. In a few moments, it returned clutching several long objects that looked almost like strange logs. It dropped them into the harbor.

The elves made their way back to the water, and the dragon waited for them by the waterside. Kealin watched in the ruined harbor as the waters stirred. The narwhals had returned. One horn broke the water first, and Kealin knew at once that it was Tulasiro.

In the water, too, were four boats. They looked like they were made of black stone.

"These are boats of the race who built this place upon the rocks. They will do well to traverse the maelstroms, and know that the narwhals will be of great aid to you. They know the way to Dimn and will take you there."

"And our sister's healing?"

The dragon looked down upon them and then turned its head.

"That is of Dimn's healing power. I did have the way, as I said. This is my part of our agreement. Get to Dimn and do not wait."

Kealin did not care for the dragon's deceit. It knew well they expected immediate healing. "Why do you lie to us, dragon?"

"I did not lie in full. You will get your healing. Tell me who else was to direct you to Dimn without fail? There is not a soul. You will learn these icy realms are more than they seem. They are a desolate place of many imprisoned and tortured souls. You have assisted a greatness here, elves of Urlas Woodlands. Your part may soon be over, but at least know the narwhals will take you the rest of the way."

The dragon looked up to the sky and stretched out its wings. With a few flaps, it took to the air. Kealin stared at its feet, learning now what the bone had been inside the mountain. The dragon had a large claw from its right foot missing; a cruel stub remained. He did not know what they had done today, but indeed, more than they were told. The dragon needed them to retrieve the necklace, but Kealin sensed there was more to this plot. Like before, they had been used for another's purpose.

As the dragon disappeared into the night sky, the flow of the volcano had lessened, as what power had driven it to quake had dissipated, and it returned to the way it was when they first saw it. The lava flow had cooled and was hardening as the Glacial Sea winds began to blow hard upon the island.

"Look," Alri said.

Three fairies were floating over her, twisting up and down her arms and legs before encompassing her entire body.

They heal her one last time, but we must get you to Dimn. Evil is coming; we must go quickly, Tulasiro said to Kealin.

"We must go with de narwhals. Dey will take us to the true healing you needs."

Taslun nodded. "I will not understand your new gift, Brother, but I think I am happy you have it."

8

THE MAELSTROM

With the rumbles of the volcanic island beneath his feet, Kealin worked with the others to pull the ships to the shore. The vessels felt as if made of stone, but floated with ease. He climbed in and, after a short search, was not able to find paddles.

"How are we supposed to use these?" asked Calak.

Kealin look into the boat but found it mostly bare. He noticed a single latch built into the side. It was a crystal of design, like those of the *Aela Sunrise*. He pulled it, and from the front end of the boat, he heard a splash. A moment later, Tulasiro came to it, and he saw the horn of the narwhal make a dive below the boat. He steadied himself into a seat.

Friend, am I to ride as you pull?

The boat lurched forward, and he laughed. "Dis way. Move the crystals inside the boat!"

The others got in their boats and did the same, and each had a narwhal come to them. Kealin smiled, water lapping over the edge as Tulasiro pulled him faster away from the island. They circled and awaited the others to join them. The remaining narwhals seemed to come to each of the ones guiding the boats, and then departed. The four narwhals pulling them circled once and then headed east. The polar lights were above, shining down upon them and reaching to the far south in twisting waves.

Calak laughed. "Perhaps Wura also guides us to the realm of his brother Dimn?"

Kealin looked up, the sky rushing above them as they raced across the open sea pulled by the narwhals. He took a deep breath of the air and felt a warmness within himself. He was at peace upon the seas.

The narwhals began to swim faster, and the winds coming over them became beyond strong. He tucked down into the lowest portion of the boat. He now could only see the sky, but it seemed the best way to ride as they sped on. His siblings did the same.

He felt for the shells in his pocket. How they would play into their exact finding of Dimn or reaching Dimn, he did not know. He could feel the rush of water against the bow of the boat and felt the rhythmic flapping of the narwhal's fin beneath. With peace setting in and his body beckoning further rest, he closed his eyes.

HE AWOKE to a cold splash of water. He blinked,

clearing his vision, but then gripped the sides of the boat as he stared down, his feet against the opposite end of the boat. The sea was in front of him, not the sky like before. He was pulled upward as his belly sunk in.

Tulasiro!

But the narwhal did not respond; its form became visible for a moment as it jerked out of the towering water, slapping the boat the opposite direction before surging on, pulling him up the crest of a wave. The sea had turned turbulent. He pulled himself up as the boat prepared to dive again. He looked behind and noticed the other three boats trailed behind with his siblings in similarly precarious positions.

Alri was clinging to the back end, and Taslun hung from the front, his feet dangling back. Calak was somewhere in between, sliding one side to the other as his boat became airborne before crashing back into the sea.

Lightning flashed above in repeated dazzling white. There was no rain, only waves and rocks, many rocks. At times, it seemed either the ground had appeared below, the sea swallowed up in the waves around it, or there were indeed that many crags from below poking up. Slurries of ice splashed into the ship like tiny boulders on his legs.

Bracing himself, his fingers ached. The icy splinters attacking his joints and numbing his fingertips made every bit of movement difficult. He felt weightless again, and he prepared for the slam on the water as before. Kealin had no doubts as to why many had not dared go this way before.

The winds became horrendous, howling over the water as the towering waves of the sea became calm and stilled.

Kealin sat up and felt himself barely able to look over the edge of the boat. He was still shaking from his harsh awakening.

A towering column of fog shot up from the sea, interlacing a large rocky island with crafted stonework and sea-weathered stones. He looked up as far as he could, but the night sky was blotted out further by dark clouds. He could not see very much.

The winds shifted again, and a horn called out, or so it seemed. The mountain moaned, and a twisting blast of ice and winds tore out of the fog toward the edge of the horizon.

Is this it? Is this the mouth of the winds?

The wind died down as before, and the waves began again. The narwhals began pulling them faster; they were gaining speed as they went toward the island.

"Are we here at last?" shouted Calak.

"This looks like an old place, that I can see," replied Taslun.

"We have been to many old places. How do we know?" asked Alri.

Kealin turned and looked forward. He then shouted, "There is swirling ahead, and it is maelstroms we have sought beneath the palace of the wind god. Brothers, Sister: we have arrived, but I do not know how good this happening is."

He looked forward, and the winds cut over him

again, sliding the boat across the edge of the water. Tulasiro twisted its path, and it was clear what was happening to them. The horizon began to fade from view as they cut down into the sea, drawn into the twisting slope of a turbulent whirlpool.

Kealin braced himself against the boat. He did not know what it was they were supposed to do, for deep in the darkness there was no light, no guide, no arcane sign, just blackness and the icy reminder that the intent of this maelstrom was destruction.

He held shells in his pocket, but he still wondered at their purpose. He reached in, fumbling them between his fingers. It was then Tulasiro dove down into the wall of the maelstrom. He held his breath, feeling himself tugged under the water. Kealin opened his eyes for a moment. Through the darkness of the water, he was able to see the body of the great whirlpool. Tulasiro ripped them to the right, and he closed his eyes. He was out of the water suddenly, and he looked to see the narwhal had pulled them over the center of the maelstrom.

He looked down into the mouth of the beast of the sea. Beneath him were the skeletons of ships long lost seeking this place of holiness. There were many bolts of lightning, and in a flash, he spotted his siblings spinning around, their narwhals still holding to the edge.

Tulasiro had brought them to the other side and swung its tail to increase their speed again.

Shell.

The narwhal spoke to him, but he did not know what it meant. He felt the shells. There were many colors: orange, pink, blue, among others. He remembered the hooded man and his letter but couldn't remember the exact colors and their meanings. He took a blue one. The narwhal again dove and then ripped them across the mouth of the maelstrom. He tossed it into the swirling waves. In a few moments, a radiant light shined from beneath. The cyclones dropped from above them and became water spouts.

Not that one.

He braced as they slammed against the opposite side. He looked again. The orange one was in his hand. They returned to their path; he was pulled again into the water for a moment and then across the chasm they went. The shell was caught in the waves, and an orange flash shot flames into the air, nearly striking Kealin himself. The sky above them shined with a bright flame as the clouds became as flames above them.

Wrong.

He looked to his siblings. They were farther down the maelstrom. So far down that he had difficulty seeing them, and if not for the light above from the last shell, he would not know if they still were with him. The maelstrom churned, and Tulasiro struggled to keep a good path. The waters above had begun to be sucked into the center; the maelstrom was about to close upon them. He placed his fingers on another shell. Thinking to himself, he went to his mind. He imagined the maelstrom as he felt the shell. He saw the maelstrom collapse. He moved his finger to the next, the maelstrom swarmed with glaciers. He then grabbed another.

This one was different. He saw light shooting toward

the sky. The maelstrom faded, and there was bright light. He pulled the shell out. It was pink.

Tulasiro pulled them from the maelstrom, swam hard, and burst through the watery grip again. Kealin looked over the edge and tossed the shell. Wind caught him, and he was dumped from the boat. He struck the water and was beyond the reach of the narwhal. The shell struck the surf, and a blinding light followed. He felt himself go weightless, and then an icy feeling struck him that was more frigid than the water he found himself in. His eyes went dark, and then he opened his eyes to see glowing blue rocks above his head as his body was pulled down a waterway of some kind. It was only a moment later, and he felt his feet fly downward, and his face headed toward a pool. He pushed his hands out to break the impact, and he was underwater.

He looked up, kicking as he did and pulling himself to the surface. He glanced around. He was alone. There was a lone shore ahead. He swam to it and went to his feet as quickly as he could manage.

Kealin looked around. It was an underground cavern. He was alone, and where his siblings were now, he did not know. His eyes scanned the rocks around him. The unnatural blue glow was something he had not seen in the Urlas Woodlands. Runic etchings ran along the walls and were in an obscure dialect of elvish that he did not know.

The shoreline was sandy and had no vegetation. He began along it, searching for nothing more than a way out. Walking along a bare wall, there was no loose stone or hidden door that he could find.

This was no accidental cave, but he could find no
way out, and the way he had come in was not only out of
reach but flowed with water beyond anything he could
fight to climb back out of. He wondered if he was at the
bottom of the maelstrom or some other kind of trickery.
In all of his wonderings, he did not know what "out" was
or where he had ended up.

Making his way to the opposite side of the room, he
found a monolithic stone with runic inscriptions like the
wall, but now glowing as he approached.

It was then the entire room became bathed in light
as the runes covering the walls were now glowing. The
stone burst into red flames. The pool he had landed in
bubbled, and from the surface emerged a figure.

Kealin drew his sword, but it became heavy. His grip
was forced open, and his sword dropped to the ground.
He knelt to pick it up, but could not lift it.

The figure had turned to that of a woman made of
water. Her hair was a darker hue of black, but her
form was a constant renewal from the pool she
stood in.

"Kealin Half-Elf of the Urlas Woodlands, you have
come far to end up within my cave."

He pulled at his blade again.

She shook her head. "You do not need that here, but
soon you may wish you had your second blade."

He stood and pointed.

"How do you know of me?"

"I am of the sea, dear Kealin, the maelstrom beneath
the palace of Dimn. I know much of those who draw
near me."

"If you knew it was me, you knew the purpose of my siblings and me. Where are they? What have you done?"

"They are where they are supposed to be. I am but a maelstrom of the Glacial Seas and am tied to protecting the way to our lord, Dimn. You appeased me as needed, though."

She reached behind her head and revealed, in a strain of her watery hair, the pink shell.

"Then why, if I appeased you as you wished, was I brought here?"

"Kealin Half-Elf, I brought you to this place so that I may look upon you. There is much within these waters that has transpired, but the Glacial Seas have been of relative peace for some time. Your events, your gift of the mind, and the deaths of those you love is that which was foretold."

"Deaths of those I love? Where are my siblings?" Kealin shook his fist at her. "If you harmed them . . ."

"They are where they should be. The maelstrom does not lie, but there is fear in your steps. Death is awakened and released. Its demon was destroyed, its beast released. Those of the seafaring race who you've seen whispers of and visited the ruins of their city worked with great difficulty to do what you have undone.

"In truth, without your presence with them, your siblings would already be dead. You have kept them safe, but it was your sole quest to come here. I am afraid that fate has determined your path, and though it is here with the holy Dimn, I fear you do not realize what has been done."

"Stop speaking in your riddles. What has been done? I did no such awakening of death. How can you awaken a state of existence? I want to go to my siblings."

The woman spun about the pool, the tides increasing within the room. She paused as the watery chasm that he had come from before began to flow faster.

"I have warned you, and it is not as a maelstrom of death but as a force of the sea. The narwhals will not listen or help just anyone, and so, with you also having the shells of Meredaas, I knew there was more to you. But I am just a maelstrom, and you a half-elf. Perhaps I say too much out of turn. I never quite know when to stop turning, you see?"

Kealin was more confused, but the words he heard drove him to a near-madness. A maelstrom, of all forces of nature, had personified itself as a woman of water to speak with him.

"Kealin, doom is upon your heart. Guard yourself well, for there is life beyond the breaths you take here, and the sea will be your only comfort in those times. This place was made some time ago; I was happy to speak with a soul after so long. It is tiring dragging so many to death within my mouth."

The figure smiled and began to flow from its form into the room. The water was now at Kealin's knees. He picked up his sword and ran around the room, looking for a way out again. The waters were flowing in faster than ever.

In a few moments, he was floating, the water rising more. He shook his head, unsure of what to do next but still swimming, and then, the water pushed his head against the ceiling of the room. He gasped, breathing heavily and pushing himself against the rocks. The water crept up his face, covering his eyes, his nose, and then coldness consumed him.

He felt a tug to his feet and was powerless. His body was dragged with force, twisting and turning away from the room. There was a great current in the water, and then he felt himself leave the sea. His eyes saw only light and then a blinding flash. He felt himself fall to a hard surface, and he could breathe.

Kealin felt numbness all over. He was no longer cold. His skin was warmed from above, but still he could not see.

"Kealin."

He heard the voice but found it difficult to respond. He thought the words in his mind but could not lift his head.

"Alri, help me!" he heard.

He felt hands grip him, and he was rolled over. He blinked his eyes, but they were blinded by the light above.

"He is alive! Kealin, can you hear me?"

He nodded and blinked; his vision was getting better. He looked ahead, seeing Taslun and Calak. Alri supported him from behind.

"When you were lost to the water, we thought you were done, dear brother. I am relieved to see you well."

Kealin looked around. The ground was gray and like fog on the sea. It was daylight here. The sun shone brightly above them. Around him, it seemed the ground went out as far as he could see.

"What is this place?"

"We made it, Brother. We made it to Dimn."

"Well, we made it to his palace grounds. We have not been here more than a few moments before you arrived," Calak told him. "I noticed you tossing the shells and how they changed the maelstrom. I guess you picked the right one?"

"Yes."

Taslun gripped him under his arm. "Can you stand?"

Kealin nodded and stood, though his knees were shaky. He steadied himself and then felt for his sword.

"What happened?" asked Alri.

"I do not know. I fell into the maelstrom and ended up in a cave."

"A cave?"

He then realized what the woman of the maelstrom had told him. The dread upon the air suddenly felt heavy upon him. He looked at each of his siblings, and they stared back.

"What is it?" asked Taslun.

Kealin thought to tell them in full what had transpired, but they were words he wished to validate by speaking again. "A woman was there. She claimed to be the maelstrom itself. She was curious of one who wielded the shells of Meredaas."

"Why you get to speak to all of the females of these seas, I will never understand," said Calak.

Taslun laughed. "You forget about the truth that

while one was a mermaid, the other two were creatures of another type: a demon and a force of nature. Not exactly material for one to love."

"You cannot say that, older brother," Alri said. "Do you remember the elf who fell in love with a tree and spent the greater part of a thousand years waiting for it to speak to him?"

"Yes, but he died from starvation."

Alri winked. "Yes, that is what happened. But that proves love knows no boundary."

"Aye, food!" said Calak. "We have not eaten in some time."

Taslun shook his head. "Good brother, you never stop eating."

Kealin smiled at his siblings. The sun made them all livelier than they had been the entire journey.

"Let's go this way," he said to them.

A stone path was visible, still shrouded with the fog, but walkable. To their right, there was green grass, but it was still and there was a constant shroud of fog. This was a bizarre place. Up ahead, they could see a structure.

They began up the path that rose higher off the landing with each step they took. Coming closer, Kealin could see columns that surrounded a square stone building. Atop each of the columns, there appeared to be miniature tornadoes twisting upon their set platforms.

There was a set of four steps that went toward an entryway with open doors. Kealin paused on the first step and turned, waiting for his siblings to join him. The land around them was clouds. At the level he awoke, it was not obvious, but now above it all, he could tell.

As Taslun at last reached the stairwell, Kealin noticed he took a knee. He turned back to see a robed man looking at them. He bowed in turn.

"Elves of the Urlas Woodlands, you have traversed much to come here. I am Dimn, Northern God of the Winds."

Dimn was not what they expected. Not that they knew for sure what to expect, but he was a man not much different from them. Kealin heard his brother stand and looked over at him.

"Taslun, I am called. This here is Kealin, Calak, and Alri. We have traveled with news of greatest importance."

Dimn nodded. "I will hear your news, but I invite you into my home first. I have prepared food for you. We will speak of this news then."

Kealin stood with the others and followed Dimn inside.

The interior of the palace was a series of columns sparkling with what appeared to be actual stars within each of them. The floors were polished and sheer and reflected the glimmers from the pillars.

Dimn took them around a large pool of water and to a corridor to the right.

"The eastern corridor is this way. I have a place here for you four. I have made it to be comfortable for you. It has been some time since pilgrims have come to my place."

"Maelstroms do not help," said Calak.

Taslun glared at him.

"Do not judge your brother so harshly," said Dimn. "Calak tries much to appease you, Taslun."

Taslun looked away and up to Dimn. Kealin turned to Taslun and raised his eyebrow.

"My knowledge should not surprise any of you. The winds carry much through my temple. I hear names, whispers hushed but caught in passing. I feel the blow of northern snow and the burn of the far south sands. With all of that come words and stories of many times more than even a god cares to hear.

"But of the elves of the Urlas Woodlands, I keep an ear out of special regard. Your people are within a protected realm. It is that which surprised even the gods. I doubt you could have news beyond what I know already. Had I not heard you were approaching, I would've departed for my own business in the south, but for now, I take time for you."

The room they were taken into was made of glass. As Kealin walked in, he jumped at first, looking down, for he saw the open sky both above and below as he passed the entryway. Dimn walked well ahead of them and walked around a large table that appeared as if it was a massive bird's wing made of silver. Beneath it, and connecting it to the floor of the room, were tiny tornadoes spinning in place just as the ones outside the temple did.

On the table was every form of fruit and vegetable known. In the center was a large portion of meat.

"I do not eat," said Dimn. "I know of your love for nature, so I assumed what you might like. A sea kraken was of olden age, and it came time for his death. I knew of this and spoke with Meredaas; the creature was well to be sacrificed for your consumption."

Calak did not seem to mind. He sat down ahead of the rest and began to fill a bowl with many items, including the sea kraken meat. Though Alri and Taslun joined him, they were not nearly as enthusiastic.

Kealin sat beside them but did not touch the sea kraken. In truth, he was not hungry. Vals had only just been murdered in his mind, and the words of the maelstrom haunted him.

Dimn remained in the room with them, and as they each finished, he served them drinks in silver chalices.

Dimn was strange. Kealin had expected a much different entity, not a man. But there was no doubting the power he held. After pouring the drinks, they needed a stir. He pointed toward the liquids and swirled his fingers. Winds filled the room and stirred the drinks before he handed them out.

"Wine of the clouds and the headwinds of the west. Berries like these are hard to come by but do grow within the grove to the west of my palace."

Kealin sipped the wine; at least it was sweet and like that of a blueberry, but lighter. He set the cup down as Taslun began to speak.

"Dimn, the shaman of the Urlas Woodlands told us of darkness approaching this place. The Itsu approach."

Kealin expected a look of surprise from Dimn, something beyond the stare he gave to Taslun. He turned from them and looked out over the skies. "My brother Kel is dealing with the Itsu in the South. I am headed there to deal with what is at hand in those lands. The time would come when those of the Urlas Woodlands would come to me; I knew of it as long as I knew of the Prophecy of the Glacial Seas. There are workings now in motion.

"I had heard the Blades and archons made their way south to assist in the war, but then I learned of you four, and then I found the stench of death upon the air, and power had been reawakened. Old and foul energies flow outward. The song of Vankou is playing on the winds. The ice drake returns to its master."

"So it is true?" asked Kealin. "There was something to our journey beyond what we sought here with you. Our steps to reach you were not what we thought."

"If you mean that you inadvertently opened up a way for an evil long held in these lands to terrorize these seas, then, yes. You could not have known, but the way of an easy path to the shells of Meredaas should've been a clue to you. Though Vankou knew of other sources for these shells, he sent you to his demon instead. One of you speaks with the ethereal knowledge. Who is it?"

Kealin nodded.

"Then you are who was sensed by the Lord of Death. I knew not many of you were left. The steps you took were for Vankou, but you are here. I take your warning but do not feel it valid."

"Are you talking about his power that he developed?" Alri questioned. "It is like our shaman in our village. Their voices sound the same when he is using the power. We have all been confused but thankful for it."

"To do what you have done, Kealin, takes a mind of extreme power. I am surprised you still use the blade at your hip if you have access to such knowledge," said Dimn. "Who is this shaman?"

"An old man, not elven. He goes by the name Iouir and is older than most elves we know. He has lived within our realm for as long as I know," said Taslun.

Dimn opened his eyes wider. "A Dwemhar, then, one of the last, no doubt. Is it he who sent those of your people south to assist Kel and the elves there?"

"Yes."

Dimn turned away from them. "I may have misjudged you, then, my friends. I know much of your shaman, and he is a wise man and a devout follower of myself. He would have not sent you this way without knowing of the danger you, Kealin, possess."

"What I possess?" Kealin asked. "I did not ask for any gift. I am of elf and human blood, none else."

"A false statement," Dimn corrected. "You are of elf and Dwemhar blood. As are all of you, only that your brothers are more attuned to the elven attributes and you to the Dwemhar. Your sister is like you; however, her training may have tuned her energies away from the Dwemhar powers. I cannot know for sure."

"You are saying our mother is of this Dwemhar race?" asked Taslun. "How can we not know this?"

"Indeed, but do not let it surprise you that you do not know. Such descendants are very rare and become rarer. There are some who live to the south, but even they do not speak of it. The Dwemhar were greater than the other races in many ways, but of most importance was the power of their minds. The ability to manipulate the world around them, not like casting magic, but literal control over others' thoughts and actions, was a power that did not make others comfortable.

"Even Shaman Iouir is not full-blooded, though. The Dwemhar resided in many places of the ocean, including these very seas around you, but they left the realms many ages ago. Those who were not killed, at least. Your shaman must have seen it worth the risk, even with what has happened because of you four journeying here. He sent you four, too, a particular number to us gods.

"There is much happening in the world, but if the Itsu are coming to this place, they must seek something, and I think I know what it is. The Heart of the Winds must not be halted, or the world would become a nightmare of uncontrollable seasons, the balance of life would alter, and all would die. At least, those not of the gods. But still, I question the coming of Itsu. I had thought they were banned to their realm." He paused for a moment. "Come with me, all of you."

The wind god beckoned them to follow him back into the main chamber, walking them deeper into the temple. In a center portion, beyond a crystal column, was a large swirling vortex they could look within.

"This here is the source of the winds of the world, the clouds, fog, rains. Long have I guarded this place. If this place is defiled by the Itsu, I do not know what may come."

"How can we help you, Dimn?" asked Taslun.

"How can the elves of the Urlas Woodlands serve Dimn?"

"First, you can be helped by me, more than you can help me." Dimn looked to Alri. "You are unwell. Your soul has been bitten by a wight of Vankou; I feel though you seem well now, that its blackness is upon you."

"The ice drake said you could heal her," said Kealin.

"I do know the way, and I offer the advice to you freely, but one task remains. Alri can heal herself from within with a renewal spell. I know the words, but it is a staff you need, for it must be cast by the one who is afflicted. I can direct you to a staff, seeing as you do not have one."

"I did," said Alri, "but it was lost amid unfortunate events in the last few days."

"Many unfortunate events have happened as of late." Dimn began to walk away. "Follow me, elves."

He took them away from the Heart of the Winds, passing a large chamber opening up from the left.

Kealin noticed a crystal-walled case off the main path. It was between two large torch basins and, as was the theme of the temple, had tornadoes circling atop pillars beside it. Within the case was silver armor; it was sectioned and had from the arms what appeared to be wings hanging from it.

"What is that?" he asked.

Dimn stopped and turned. "It is wind armor of particular power to myself in the defense of this place, though it is not of just a god's use. I guard this place in the form that you see so that I may use it, if needed. My normal form is well, large, but the portal into this place is better defended with that armor. It allows me to go between the realm gates of the clouds and the maelstrom at will. But its use is not worth going beyond this place, for its power is tied to the mountain. My other form suffices when I leave."

Kealin noticed a large sword, as well as a curved spear, was crossed behind the suit.

"How would any assail this place?" asked Calak.

Dimn smiled. "The Itsu are crafty and places not as secure; at least, not with the way the world has come to. Others such as foolish dwarves, or men, or in some times long ago, elves, tried, but they drowned in my maelstrom's fury." He smiled. "This way."

They followed him as he wished, turning down a long corridor that made it appear they were soaring through the sky like birds. To either side, an open walkway was blown by clouds and torrential winds, but from within the hall, they could neither feel nor hear the sounds, only see the wisps of gray clouds twisting around the chamber. At the far end of the hall, a stairwell circled downward.

"Go down," he told them. "You will find the old worship places for pilgrims. It is beyond there, behind two sealed doors, that you will find the staff you seek. You receive a great object, Alri. Long ago, you would've needed much more in whim and power to claim one of my staves." He handed her a rolled parchment from his robes.

"Within are the words you will need to heal yourself. A scarce spell, also not typically given so easily."

Alri bowed to Dimn. "Thank you for helping me."

"The gods of the North are not of malevolent intent, but hurry back up and we will talk further of what troubles are imminent. If you four have come to help, you will assist me with the Itsu, if that is what approaches."

Alri began down first, followed by Taslun, who rushed ahead of her.

"You still have no weapon, little sister, and we do not know what evil may lie ahead."

9

DEMONS AT THE GATE

T hey proceeded down the curved stairwell for what seemed a longer time than was necessary. It was very dark, but after several steps, the passage straightened out. They could now see the way ahead. Their path was lit every few feet by faint red glowing stones, not much light at all, but it was just enough to see the steps.

Ahead, they could hear a whistling wind, but it was not clear where it came from. They came to an area where two green torches provided plenty of light. A doorway was there, with a veil hanging down. On the veil, a silver inlay of the four points of direction and a maelstrom. Alri put her hand out and walked first, disappearing beyond the veil. The others quickly followed.

Kealin found himself in a moonlit walkway. He looked to his left and could see the sea rippling in the distance and the dark skies of night. He looked behind him and noticed that where the veil had been was now solid stone. He pushed on it with no budge from the surface.

"Where are we?" asked Calak.

Alri walked ahead of them, and Kealin ran up beside her. The stone hallway ended abruptly at a wall and turned left. Kealin touched her shoulder and then drew his blade, moving up ahead of her.

It was a temple of some kind, with rows of pews in a square room with a high arching ceiling. Windows surrounded them, and snow and ice had built up on the outside. He moved through the center of the pews; a large doorway was at the end, and he went to it, attempting to open it. He pushed. Nothing.

Taslun stayed with Alri, who walked to another hallway around a center altar that mirrored the hallway they had come from.

With Calak's help, they both pushed on the doorway. It cracked and then creaked open with a gust of wind and snow. There was a landing just outside, and as the doors were forced open, Kealin and Calak walked outside. A ruined stairwell that led downward was broken apart halfway from a stone dock, but it was a great distance to that point. The sea tore upward at them. They were on the base of the mountain in the temple, and it was clear why few had come to visit Dimn, at least, in their normal realm.

"The veil must have been like the maelstrom, a split in the realms," said Kealin.

"Well, it is cold," said Calak. "And I do much prefer the realm of Dimn." Calak smiled. "Come on, Kealin."

Kealin took hold of the doors but found they had

already begun to freeze in the snow. He managed to free one, but even with his brother's help, they couldn't get the second.

Calak shook his head. "Leave it. It's not like someone will be coming up those steps anytime soon. But it is a bit draftier in here now."

They walked toward the other hallway where Alri and Taslun had gone, and found that they had progressed through a large door and were now at a second door. This one was stone with a silver runic inscription. Alri was reading it to herself.

"Did you enjoy making it the temperature of the Glacial Sea in here, little brothers?"

"It is a view to see, at least." Calak laughed.

"What does this say, Alri?"

By this time, she had knelt down and was reading the last of the inscriptions. "It was a decree, by the Saints of Dimn. Most fell in battle against some beast seeking its way into the mountain to reach the god. The last few made an inscription, remembering their struggle. It reads, as best I can translate:

To those who remain in the days that follow, know that we did what our god would have us do. To join in revelry of death against the Ice Demon of the Glacial Seas, we do recount our fall to the last patrons of Dimn. The stairwell is no more, and we have shut the doors. While they are sealed, this place is protected from the beasts. We have no food, but it is in Dimn we are strong.

I will be the last of the Saints to draw breath in these

hallowed walls, the sanctuary once kept warm by the prayers of the patrons of Dimn. It is beyond this wall I will seal myself away, awaiting the end, for my brothers and sisters have all become ill. The magic protecting our doorway has been made no more. I will go beyond the wall, my last act of sacrifice to Dimn. He has betrayed us to this fate."

"It seems the Saint was stalwart and then despaired," Taslun said. "So this is the second door Dimn spoke of?"

"I assume. I will attempt to open it as before."

Alri placed her hand on the door, and it began to glow; she spoke a word to herself, and the door cracked. Stepping back, Taslun stepped in front of her with his sword out.

The room was dark. A single form could be seen against the far wall and, as torchlight from the hall would provide, it was clear the Saint was true to his runes.

Sitting upon a stone bench, a recessed room of prayer had become a grave. The robed figure still clutched a staff in its hand, and there was nothing else to be found.

"Then that is the staff," said Kealin.

Alri stepped forward; placing her hand on the staff, she pulled it from the decomposed grip of its last owner. The bones of the hand cracked as she pulled it free. At once, the staff became alive with a radiant light, and she smiled.

"It is good to have a staff again," she said. Alri

unrolled the parchment Dimn had given her and murmured the words to herself.

"Well, heal yourself, dear sister," said Calak.

She placed the staff over herself, and it glowed slightly before a mist fell over her head and down to her shoulders. Her face brightened to that which Kealin knew before.

"I am well now," she said. "The words worked."

The parchment she was holding turned to dust.

"Then we have done what we came to do," Kealin said.

Taslun knelt down to the corpse. He placed his hand above the skeleton. "In death, you are honored, last of the Saints of Dimn. May your stand be remembered."

"To die to protect a place is strange to me," said Calak. "To defend your people, yes, but a god and his temple?"

"We honor him regardless, Calak. To die in a stand against odds beyond yourself is a glory beyond understanding, unless your sword is next to the one who does it. Such is that of the Blades of the Urlas Woodlands."

A roar shook the room they stood in, and pebbles fell from the ceiling. Kealin looked to Taslun, and they both filed to the end of the hallway, glancing into the temple hall.

Another roar rumbled through, and a blast of white shattered the windows on one side of the hall.

"Back to the other hallway," Taslun commanded.

"That door is sealed," said Kealin.

"There is some way out," said Taslun, "and it is not

out the door to the seas! Alri, your staff. I am sure of it; it will open the way back to Dimn."

They both peeked around the doorway again. It looked clear for the moment. They looked at one another and ran. A blast of ice shot through the open door, spraying the back wall of the hall and turning it to ice. Another roar followed. Kealin and Taslun had made it to the second hallway.

They peeked around as Calak and Alri did the same.

The doors swung open, and a plume of snowy dust flew in. Eyes stared in. It was the ice dragon from before.

"Vankou wishes his will upon you, elves. I thank you for my freedom, and I am happy to realize you made it through the maelstrom. But now, you will freeze."

It opened its mouth, cracking the foundations of the hall, causing the front half to shatter and fall to the sea. With a blue blast summoning around its mouth, Alri rushed forward, her staff out; she summoned a blast of wind, knocking the dragon's mouth back. Calak ran behind her for the hallway, and as the dragon recoiled and spewed its icy breath, she summoned a shield of fire that turned the breath to water. The blast had been thwarted, and as the dragon took to the sky, she joined the others in the hall.

She placed her staff at the wall, and the way began to materialize before them.

There came a strange laughing growl. Kealin looked back to the double doors leading outside. A form appeared, hunched and made of bone. It was very small, perhaps only coming to his waist in height. Following it were many others just like it, tiny skeletons, at least to that of the elves' standards. They held spears and ran for them.

The brothers ran to meet them, slashing and cracking at their bony forms, turning them to no more than piles of bones. Kealin took a glance at the now-gaping opening in the hall. Alri had opened the path. He then looked out one of the windows to the sea. It seemed the dragon had made an icy bridge from the sea to the hall, and a steady flow of the skeletal warriors were upon them.

Backing into the hallway, they slashed and parried those they faced with ease, but their numbers inundated the hallway.

"This way, come on."

Alri had opened the doorway, and they fled one by one. Crossing the dark void again, they watched, but they were not followed. They had escaped the attack upon them.

Taslun checked each of them, but they had escaped without injury. "Good. Let us go to Dimn."

"Will they not follow?" asked Calak.

"They cannot pass into this realm," said Alri. "We are safe."

They made their way back up the stairwell and were happy for once, to be warm again.

Following the way Dimn had taken them, they returned to the Heart of the Winds to find Dimn reading a book.

"We found the staff, although it was a less than happy occasion for us. The ice dragon we dealt with before has attacked, as well as skeletal creatures."

"We are safe from them here. They cannot cross into this realm, but they are of Vankou and more of what you four have unintentionally awakened. Can I see the staff?"

Alri came forward, showing the staff to Dimn, who took it in his hand.

"My Saints fought well."

"This is from the last one. His body was in the chamber."

"I knew it so," said Dimn. "Their prayers did not fall upon closed ears, but there is much in the ways of gods that our patrons do not understand."

"Is that our fate?" asked Kealin. "Do you not fight yourself? Could you have gone to them or, if not, brought them here to protect them?"

"The sickness that your sister was affected with had already taken them. Vankou was there. If I would have gone, there was danger for myself and all the realms. As I said, I must protect the winds. That is my intent and purpose. That drake below is full of ice, but nothing else. He was bound to his master, though he did not wish it. He could not help but complete his task. His amulet has been returned to him. It took many lives to take it the first time. He was sent to watch that path, I am sure. But it is of our other path we must speak now. You four are here to aid me, and I shall use you. It is quite simple. Protect this place. Even if I am unable to stem the tide, you must not let them here."

"We understand," said Taslun.

"Can you be killed?" asked Alri.

"Not by any force of your world, no, but the Itsu are

of my world, and, yes, though it would take much, I could be.

"Your fate is your own, dear elves, but if you will stand with me, I accept it. I want to show you something that may come of need."

He turned to a pillar that stood just the height of the rail of the Heart of the Winds. Placing his hand over the flat surface, a crystal appeared.

"This is to be used as the final move. If I fall and if you cannot hold them back, twisting this will lock down this temple. You will not have escape, but they will not be able to get in."

"And what would happen if we hop into this place here? Seems like an escape worth using," said Calak, looking into the swirling winds.

"I do not recommend it," said Dimn. "You would be gambling with fate beyond what I think you should."

Kealin looked over the edge and to Calak. "Keep your blade up, if it comes to that. We will not need that option." Calak smiled, as did Taslun. Blades had an unwritten rule of death before retreat, and it was well followed.

Dimn walked toward the doors of the temple and, leading them to the steps, stood looking up. The sun was nearly down, and the expanse of skies continued up above them. In the clouds below them, the edges of the polar lights stretched out like snakes in the grasses of clouds.

"This place has been my domain for as long as the skies were above the world below. It was in that time that the Heart of the Winds was first threatened, in the age when elves were but infants crying within the trees beside the lakes. It has remained almost unchanged since then. I added the way into the mountain for my followers, but that was a long time ago. The Saints of Dimn were once plentiful in the Glacial Seas."

"What is it that this Vankou wants?"

"To leave his island. Indeed, call it foolish for a god to not know, but his purpose is now lost to me. He has power beyond most, that of death itself. His music is the last a person hears prior to his demise. Kel banished him to that island."

"Is he a god?" asked Kealin.

"He is not in the form as I am a god. He is magic; he is an entity of the grave, dwelling within the realms. A dangerous place that can be both a prison and redemption."

"Can he cross into this realm?"

"He could, but only by way of the maelstrom, and he may try, but I do not fear him. It is the Itsu, the gods of the South, who grow in power. Kel has used much of my wind, accenting his own powers in the battle against them."

"Our parents are there," said Alri. "They went to assist Kel with haste."

Dimn looked to her. "I do wish I knew more of their purpose. While you four were below, I reached out to my brothers, and there was not a response. A shadow is upon the northern shore of the lands, as well as further south toward the deserts. Much evil is growing, and this is but one single front in what will become a larger war."

"What do the Itsu want with this place?" asked

Kealin. "What is there to rule over if the world is thrown into its own destruction?"

"It is not rule over the people they want; it is to destroy us gods. I cannot hope to tell you of a simple answer to the war between us gods, but know that besides destruction, the Itsu seek every weapon of war they can wield to defeat us. Kel's answer has been destruction of much, but I feel that, in time, will prove undoing. The strife of the south is poisoning the land."

"Other than your armor, do you have a weapon here they would seek?" asked Taslun.

Dimn nodded. "A weapon is any item that you use to harm others. A person's hands can comfort or choke. It is in the way you use them, correct? The power creating the gusts of the world is here. But if they do not seek to destroy this place, possibly, it is for but one other item."

He turned back into the temple and took them to the farthest reach of the hall. Past the Heart of the Winds and down a long open-air corridor, they came to a large black stone that towered above them.

Dimn rubbed his hands along the surface, and it split open; a crack of light shot upward as high as they could see.

A single white chest set on a shelf within a small chamber was now visible. Dimn turned a lock, and it opened. He lifted the lid and reached in. Pulling something out, he cupped it in his hands.

"Behold a power of the gods."

He opened his hands, which held a small orb. It was white and seemed to swirl in its center.

"Like enchantments that are placed upon staves of

magic, the Heart of the Winds must be watched and fed. The power within these orbs comes from the very life force of the skies. If used as intended, there is no harm, but if a staff was to be made with this, a person could have control over winds, fog, and the force that entails. This may be the point of such an approach by the Itsu, but we know nothing for sure."

Taslun approached, and Dimn offered him the orb. Taslun took it and then placed it back into the chest.

"They will not take them," he told him.

They each felt a rumble beneath their feet. Dimn looked out toward the entrance of the temple.

"The maelstrom is active. Someone is below."

They began a hasty walk toward the front of the temple. Though Kealin and the others were headed toward the gateway, Dimn turned and went to a wall. He moved his hands across it, and an image of the swirling seas appeared. The angry maelstrom was in full view. From the view they could see, Kealin could make out the arms twisting beneath the water, creating the whirlpool. Massive ships swirled in a circle.

"Why do they try?" asked Taslun. "Do they not know they will be destroyed?"

Another ship approached the maelstrom; this one fought to not go in. It turned hard; from its bow came flaming bolts, like streaks of red flying away, aimed at something veiled in clouds.

A blast of ice followed, and the flapping of the dragon's massive wings became visible.

"Vaugar," said Dimn.

"Vaugar?" asked Taslun.

"The ice drake's name is Vaugar. He is chasing ships into the maelstrom. He must have flown south, grabbed the vessels, and brought them here."

"Why?"

"I do not know."

The dragon swooped down. They could see the masts of the ship splinter, and the ship lurched backward. The maelstrom was filling with debris. The dragon hovered atop it and looked down within. A light blue surrounded its body. It let out a blast of white, and ice began to fill the mouth of the maelstrom. The arms of the maelstroms were caught in the ice. A shroud of blackness approached from the side. As the waters of the maelstrom slowed almost to a frozen halt, the blackness went into the maelstrom. A fire overtook the ice, first red, but then green, turning to a shade of gray, and then black.

"What does she do?" asked Kealin.

Dimn stared but did not speak.

The swirling fire began to reach upward in the image. Dimn walked toward the gateway and looked out.

"You can only get in with a shell, correct?" asked Calak.

"That is the way it is made."

"Was that black shroud the Itsu?"

"No," said Dimn, "but I will deal with it."

Dimn turned from them, moving with haste to the hallway where the wind armor was. They heard the sounds of metal clanking, and then Dimn emerged again. His armor was silver, and the wings were outstretched. His helmet had two large spikes, and down his back was a furling cape. In his hand was his spear, and down his back was his sword.

"I will return," he told them.

He ran outside and then leaped; his wings caught air, and he took to the sky before diving down into the clouds.

They ran back to where they could see the maelstrom, to see a golden light strike the heart of the maelstrom. Vaugar flew around helplessly, appearing to be trying to reach Dimn, who had passed beyond the ice drake's ability to harm him.

Watching the spinning black fire with no knowledge of what was going on within caused an uneasiness to befall the siblings.

Taslun paced between the gateway and the wall, while Alri and Calak just stared at the image. Kealin held his hand on his blade. He leaned against one wall of the temple and stared across the clouds below.

He had never thought he would be upon such a place as this in all his imaginings of his own life. A place such as this was not one that could be imagined. A literal temple within the clouds, high above the lands. Even to an elf, such a place was mystical.

The ground rumbled again, and Taslun went to the wall. "I cannot see anything. The image is gone."

Kealin drew his blade. "Prepare, Dimn may not have been able to stop this force." Calak and Alri both came beside him.

The clouds below the temple began to swirl, mixing with darker ones below and creating a funnel, sucking the winds from the temple inside. Small cracks began to fracture the ground.

Taslun drew his blade and stepped in front of Kealin. The force of the wind grew sharply, forcing them to lean back to keep their balance.

"We hold this ground. We do not falter, elves of Urlas."

A blast of ice came from beneath the clouds, spiraling upward into the sky, and the winds stilled.

"The dragon," said Alri.

"But it cannot come into this realm," said Calak.

"Little brother, not every belief is certain," said Taslun.

The head of Vaugar emerged from the clouds, the amulet they had retrieved glowing orange from the dragon's neck. It turned toward them, spewing a stream of ice.

Alri jumped to point at once. Her staff out, a fiery shield came up again, decimating the attack. The dragon flapped its wings, struggling to force itself up and out of the portal.

Kealin ran forward. He went to the edge of the path and just to where the clouds swirled. The dragon looked at him.

"What do you do, Kealin? Do you now know that Dimn's power fails?"

He ignored the dragon and attempted to step toward him. The dragon roared, and he stumbled back, nearly tripping backward and off the path itself. Taslun grabbed him just as he fell backward.

"We cannot leave the holy realm, Kealin."

The dragon snapped its jaws. "You were meant to assist us, Kealin. You can speak with my lord as none before. You must embrace your gift and see the error in your ways."

Kealin looked to the dragon, staring Vaugar in his eyes. He looked as deep as he could, trying to feel the dragon's persona, his emotions at the moment. He felt rage and pride; a coldness was in Vaugar's chest.

"Dis is not de time for fake words, dragon!"

The dragon cocked his head and laughed. His wings still flapped as his clawed legs slowly breached the cloud line of the sacred realm. Vaugar took in a deep breath, arching his neck.

"Come, Brother!" said Taslun.

Kealin ran with Taslun just as the icy breath struck the ground and traced behind them as they fled toward the temple.

Alri pointed her staff and closed her eyes, speaking to herself.

Her staff burned with white flames, and a blast of air struck the dragon, flipping its head back and causing the dragon to struggle to raise its head again.

"Into the temple," shouted Taslun. "We must wait for it to come closer. If we can get its head toward the doorway, we may have a chance."

Alri stood in the opening as Kealin and the others lined up along the wall surrounding the opening. The idea of facing a dragon that had defeated the seafaring people in a mountain set up just like this temple was not comforting to him.

Alri's staff let fly another blast, this one aimed not at

his head, but his body. Vaugar looked down and let out a shrill roar.

"That was not my strike that caused that wail," said Alri.

They peered around the corner to see the dragon sucked downward, its claws scraping and scratching to hold its place, as something dragged it back beneath the cloud layer.

Dimn emerged from the clouds, his form visible for a moment, before aiming his spear downward and plummeting back through the clouds.

They all filed outside. The clouds had stopped swirling but remained blackened. Kealin scanned the cloud line. He was tethered between the two thoughts. Either Dimn would come back up victorious, or he would be turned to a glacier by the ice drake and they would run back into the temple.

The clouds seemed to be shifting, and then, in a shining gleam, appeared Dimn. He landed on the road just below them, his wings flapping water from the feathers.

"I have thrown down the dragon, but I do not know if it will remain there," he said. "Come into the temple; time is short, and there is much that must be done."

He walked past them, and they followed.

Dimn moved with an annoyance, taking off his armor and placing it near the wall. He went to the Heart of the Winds and leaned over it. No one spoke, but instead they lined up, ready to serve him as needed. Kealin still had his sword out; unlike his brothers, he felt there was no reason to sheath it.

"Elves, it seems I may have been wrong about our situation. I do not blame you four, but you were betrayed to this fate. I am happy you have come, but it is in the path you took that Vankou gained an upper hand. He has said for ages he cared little of us gods, but the Itsu have made him care. I believe now that all gods of the North are in danger."

"Is Vankou now against you personally? Is he not held below the realm?" asked Calak.

"I cannot be sure. The dragon was able to breach the realm, but only while the maelstrom was silent. It seems the amulet it wields has power beyond what I knew, and Vankou does not seem to want it back, as of now."

"What is it that the amulet does?"

"It allows Vankou to go beyond the realms, but only in a way as to speak with us gods. It was given to him some time ago, but when those of the seafaring people went against him, they stole it in an attempt to further rob him of power. Then the gods bound him to the island, but there is too much confusion in the workings of the enemy.

"I do not know when Vaugar became his pet, but it seems Vankou wished to use the ice drake against you four and to pacify this temple."

"Does he seek the orbs?" asked Kealin.

"I do not think so. Vankou was attempting to slay the maelstrom itself, or at least, to quiet the storm. I dispelled him. But I sensed something else. The Itsu have grown in strength. Before I sent him away, Vankou mentioned their coming. They may have discovered a way to ascend to this realm from that of their own, using the normal realm as a bridge through Vankou's working.

"Perhaps Vankou had his own intent, too. I do believe he hoped to overwhelm the temple originally, but he fears the Dwemhar blood, so he sent his dragon. It failed, but now the maelstrom is weak. She will restore, but it will take time, time that I pray we have. The dragon has since returned to its task with the dead creatures and the holy place beneath us. It seems, for now, Vankou fears you, Kealin, so he will not attack himself."

"I am an elf; he is himself. Why does he fear me?"

"That, too, I do not know for sure. But the Dwemhar blood may play into that fear. That is not the point; if the Itsu come as Vankou stated would happen, he believes that my defenses will not hold. He hopes the Itsu can breach this place and kill you and the others."

"Can the gates be thwarted?" asked Taslun.

"No, not that I believe, for no power exists to my knowledge that can break the gates once they are sealed, save my own words. I alone have the key to open the gates. But I cannot doubt that the enemy may be more resourceful than I know."

"Is not the path underneath, from the Saints of Dimn's holy place, a danger? Can it be breached?"

"That path is veiled. Though it is not of the gates, it cannot be found unless known."

"The beasts knew," said Kealin. "They fought us up to its door. I can see no reason why they would not tell their master."

Dimn looked toward the hallway and then began a quick walk that way.

"I do not have time for this." He turned from them. "That pathway was sealed with a multi-layered veil magic, and in the times it was used, I had no fear of it being a route into this place. A folly of my own. They cannot get in easily, but eventually, they could get in if they have some degree of arcane knowledge."

They went down the hallway and to the stairwell. They were not even down the first few stairs when it became clear all was not well. The dark passage was cold, much colder than it had been. At the far end of the hallway, where the furling veil was, there was a deep orange glow beyond the doorway.

Dimn lifted his hand, and clouds began to flow in from above them, like rolling fog; they filled the hallway, before gathering together as a large gate between them and the doorway. He then went to the foggy mass and placed his hand. A wall solidified. "That will have to hold."

"Will it?" asked Taslun.

"I do not know."

Kealin was getting annoyed by the answers of the god. He followed behind the rest as they went back to the main hall.

"There is more," Dimn said to them. "The winds have spoken to me while I was within the other realms. The Itsu received a weapon from Vankou. I do not know if it is a weapon like the traditional type, or a bit of spell craft, but it is something that can kill a god, and in such, I must go south. I must warn my brothers, Kel and Wura. I believe the workings here were to keep me from intervening."

"What of the approaching Itsu, the shadow upon the northern shore?" asked Taslun.

"I will return, and I will bring Kel. Between the two of us, the Itsu stand no chance. I will hope to be gone no longer than I must. You will be well to stay in the temple. When I return, we will talk more of Vankou, and we will throw down the Itsu before we move to rid ourselves of that beast. Kealin, there is much to be discussed. I believe I know how we can halt Vankou, but as of now, I have no time. Walk with me, Kealin. I would like to speak to you privately."

As Dimn began out of the temple, Kealin followed.

"I tell you this away from your siblings but do not hold you to remain silent."

"Very well," he replied.

"You four survived the way to Vankou, but I tell you, no other living soul could have done that, and to only escape with one suffering a wight's bite—"

"It is good sword work."

"It is unheard of in the realms of elves and gods."

Kealin fell silent.

"I fear your place in all of this, Kealin. The power that your shaman has is an old one. To speak to the land of the ethereal is not common, nor even rare; it is beyond that. You four were pulled into this plot, and you will have to be the ones to end it. The gods have fought each other longer than worth speaking, but Vankou has never taken a side so directly.

"I will get back to this place to help you, but know that the Itsu may take me before I can."

"Why do you not tell Taslun? He is the eldest."

"He is not you, and not the one who can converse using the power of the Dwemhar. Your sister could, but she is naïve in power. Guard your mind and guard the winds. I will speak with you more on my return."

Dimn's form began to change from that of a man to wisps of clouds. In a white mass growing in size, he vanished beneath the cloud line.

SHATTERING OF THE SKIES

Kealin sheathed his sword and exhaled deeply. He wondered how he had become such a pivotal person in the events they had passed through. He had gone on this quest due to his siblings alone, and now, according to the maelstrom woman, they were going to die and he had made their situation worse.

The clouds before him were stilled and no longer shifted, although their black color increasingly darkened. The wind blew across the grounds of the temple, and he shivered. He no longer felt any comfort here; Dimn had taken that from him.

Kealin turned, joining his siblings in the entryway of the temple. Taslun looked up at him.

"So he will return?"

"Yes."

"Then I feel until then, we must prepare. I have already thought of our next steps. Alri can rest first. You can watch the cloud plains, I will watch the hallway, and Calak can bounce between the two of us. We can alternate resting, but assure we do keep watch."

Kealin looked down. "Brother, do you know we are beyond the help of any here?"

Alri looked to Kealin. "We knew we would be. Our parents have no help; we do not need help either."

"There is a difference," he said. "They have not only themselves but others, hundreds of Urlas elves, and even more from different regions. We four are the last line to this sacred place."

"You've never been bothered by thoughts such as this," said Calak.

"I do not feel good about it. Had I not been here, you three would likely not have found your way here."

"But," said Taslun, placing his hand on Kealin's shoulder, "that would mean we would be dead. You have helped us more than once with your ability. I do not understand it, and am thankful it hasn't gone to your head, but it is not by horrid deeds we have reached this place. We are here for a reason. I am confident in Dimn."

"So was the Saint in the chapel below; it served him well, I guess."

Kealin turned from them and heard his brother sigh but remain silent.

"Dimn told me we should all be dead," he told them. "That the wights of Vankou would have killed anyone else. I feel we are part of a plot, and one that is far beyond us."

"Have faith," Taslun said.

"I do not have faith in this god or any other."

"No, Brother, have faith in us. We will defeat any evil that assails us. I will stand beside you in battle, as will Alri and Calak. Do not despair, for that is what the Saint in the chapel below did. It is why he hid away. The last thing we will do is hide."

Kealin nodded as Taslun approached him. They embraced.

ALRI WENT TO LIE DOWN, still in the center hall just off to the side of the main hall. It became quiet throughout the temple. The footstep of Calak pacing between the gateway and the stairwell was the only sound other than a sudden gust of wind that periodically rushed through from the Mouth of Winds.

The sky was darkening, but Kealin had learned from before it never went completely dark. Sometime later, Calak and Alri switched spots, and now Taslun walked the path while Alri watched the doorway. Kealin remained where he was.

Taslun waited for Calak to be asleep and then went to Kealin.

"What do you know, Brother? You never despair as I saw a few hours ago. What else did Dimn tell you?"

Kealin stood. He had been slouched over his knees for a while, and his back cracked as he stretched.

"It does not matter," he told him. "Fate is not set; I do not believe that."

"So Dimn knows the future?"

"No."

"Then what troubles you? I may be older, and you may not agree with my ideals as a Blade, but we are brothers. I want to help and comfort you, if I can."

Kealin noticed that Taslun seemed genuinely concerned for him. He knew his brother cared, but glancing at his eyes, he saw a look their father gave them when he was concerned.

"I am a key to this. It was me, my power, that led us to this fate."

Taslun laughed. "So then, we might have a fight ahead of us. We will fight, together. As it should be, if you ask me! Have faith, little brother."

"I am trying." He smiled to him, and his brother embraced him.

"Don't worry; if I drop my blade, I know you will be quick to grab it and defeat one hundred enemies before I can arise again. Just please hold on to it. Don't throw it like that time in the arena. We may not get it back."

Kealin laughed. Had it not been for the pillar of the arena, the sword would have likely flown into the lake. Kealin remembered, too, that he had beaten his brother that day.

"That is a good memory, but I am tired," he told him.

"Calak has slept long enough. Go wake him."

Kealin stood and looked over to his brother. He was on his back, mouth agape, and jerking occasionally as he snored.

"Calak," Kealin shouted.

His hands jerked; he partially drew his sword as he glanced around. "To arms?"

"Not quite. It is your turn to keep watch. I'm going to sleep."

Kealin lay down, curling up on the floor. The thin blanket Calak had felt quite warm, and he went to sleep fast.

It was a rush of wind, but not like a gust of the Glacial Seas. There was the rapid clamor of someone running past. Kealin's eyes jerked open to see Alri. Her staff was alight, and a silver blast of air flew from the tip.

He had been sleeping well, too well. He focused his eyes as Calak ran past him, his sword drawn.

Kealin jumped to his feet, drawing his blade, and Alri looked to him.

"Go, Taslun needs you."

He ran past Alri. A flash passed over him as she released another spell into the chaos ahead. Reaching the steps, he paused for a moment.

The sky was red. Lightning shot up from the portal in the clouds, which was now colored the deepest black he had ever witnessed. The entire surface of the realm was churning. White beasts, running on all fours like dogs with red eyes and burning fire upon them, had breached the temple grounds.

He ran forward, his elvish blade up, before he slashed into the nearest one, turning its form to ash. Calak was to his right, but Taslun was much further in already. They fought their way nearly to the platform they had arrived on just hours before. Moving down the walkway in a loose formation with his brothers, he engaged the wave of creatures.

There was a horn call, and it seemed that more of the beasts clawed their way up from every place they could. There was no order to their assault, no sense to it, just a continued rage.

Kealin fought through them with ease. With a single strike, the creatures would shatter, dissipating to light and then passing as dust down into the portal. He reached Taslun just as he cleared the platform. They both looked down and could see all the way to the sea.

"Has the portal been broken?" asked Kealin.

"I do not know. But I can see the sea. The maelstrom is no more. There is no protection here. I do see something else below; it takes them time to reach this place, but they do come in waves."

Away from them a good distance was Calak, moving from beast to beast, hitting each in an elementary fashion compared to the sleek and confident style his older brothers had.

Kealin and Taslun joined him, fighting side by side; their sister came, too, and it was no time before the small creatures were gone.

"Itsu?" asked Alri.

"I assume as much," said Taslun. "They come up the portal. I think we can keep them down there longer, or at least hinder their advance."

"Could we close their way up?" suggested Calak. "Could we wake the maelstrom?"

"I do not see it possible," said Kealin.

"Alri, do you know a spell?"

"I do not know. I know much of wind magic, but that may be beyond it."

"It is too bad you are not an archon," said Calak.

"She is the closest we have," said Taslun. "And this magic is of the gods, not our realm. Very well, stay and watch for them. We know they are coming now. I will go check the doorway, and then, I will try something, something to keep them from this realm."

Kealin looked at him with a peculiar glare.

He smiled to him. "Trust me, little brother."

As Taslun went into the temple, Kealin went to Alri.

"Stay safe. If you must, fall back into the temple and seal it. If we fall—"

"Stop, Kealin. I am with you three. If one of us falls, we all will remain until the last. I will not retreat while you die."

"I know I cannot convince you. I know how you are when your mind is set upon the task. You are like our mother."

"I am glad you know that." She shook her head in confidence.

The lightning began to surge near the portal. It was clear that whatever spellcraft had been used to break into the realm, it was upon the creatures crossing into the realm when the lightning began.

Creatures began to appear on the outer edges, and Kealin and Calak went forward.

"Taslun, they have returned," Alri shouted. Her staff up, she gripped it, looking at her prey just beyond her two brothers. She felt the buzz in her hands, her staff glowing white, and then she released the spell, striking two at once.

As Kealin prepared to strike, he heard a sound above. He glanced up just to see Taslun indeed had a plan. He now wore the Wind Armor of Dimn, and it was of no difficulty in skill for the elder elf as he flew effortlessly down the portal.

He tore down into the clouds, his wings flapping, with the spear and the sword. Kealin rushed to the platform, the only space that he could easily look down and watch as the mass of white creatures engulfed his brother.

Calak joined him, but he noticed Alri had gone back into the temple.

"Alri?" he asked.

Calak looked over the edge, seeing the speck of Taslun going from one side to the next, slashing and turning the Itsu to flashes, a sign of their demise.

"That is hellish," he said.

"Where is Alri going?"

"Oh, she thought of something. Had to go into the temple. This is a nice way to battle," said Calak, with his attention obviously taken by the happenings below.

Kealin shook his head. "Only a start, I fear. Keep your blade ready, Brother."

Winds from the temple blew toward them, cutting through the black clouds. Taslun seemed to be floating upward, and it gusted more, pulling him as it shot below him and then back up. The Itsu attack seemed to have died down. He flapped just above them and then landed with a thump a few paces away.

His armor smoked, and he was breathing heavily. His spear and his sword were both reddened from the heat of the Itsu bodies, and he had glowing scratches covering his armor. He took a knee.

Kealin knelt down to him. "Brother, are you well?"

"There are many. I do not know how long I have gained us. They are gathering again. Larger ones approach, but it seems they are doing such with a group of the smaller ones—" Taslun was out of breath. He took several breaths and then continued. "I will go again, but be prepared up here."

"Let me take your armor. I can go, Taslun," Calak said, placing his hand on the spear.

"No, little brother, I will handle this. You and Kealin must protect Alri. She is the youngest of us and most prone. She was not well not too long ago."

Kealin knew that was a poor excuse, but ignored it.

Taslun stood and looked over the edge. "Keep well, Brother," he said to Kealin.

As a mass of white began an ascent up, he plummeted downward. Kealin watched as he tore into the flock of Itsu.

"Kealin, I will check on Alri," said Calak.

"Very well, hurry. Stay alert to fight if needed; we do not know what other tricks the enemy has."

Calak sprinted up the hill as Kealin paced the platform. He watched Taslun, a worry growing in his stomach, seeing his brother at odds such as this. The larger creatures were going for him now, as the smaller ones flew upward.

The creatures were gripping the edge of the plat-

form. Kealin swung his blade in repeated swipes downward, sending their ashes back to the sea.

A few moments later, and it was clear another
assault wave came upon the grounds of the temple. The
creatures swarmed again. Kealin was engaged with
multiple beasts on the platform. Calak emerged from the
temple with sword high, striking those nearest to him
that had gone for the temple doorway.

A large Itsu beast had made it past Taslun, and its
clawed hand struck the platform. Kealin looked down at
it, noticing it was nearly three times his size. He jabbed
his blade into its hand, and it recoiled, grabbing with the
other. Kealin went to stab this one, but the creature
pulled itself up. He stepped back, holding his sword in
front of him.

The Itsu creature was white like the other smaller
ones, but this one had armor of gray crystal. In its hand
was a sword, and it appeared less of a beast as it seemed
to sidestep slowly, studying Kealin. It had white eyes,
and a red raiment flew off its back.

It began to speak. "Half-elf, I call you. You are not
pure. You will not taste as good to my soul to kill."

"My apologies, I care little to be a decadence to your
soul."

Kealin stepped forward, feinting right before leaping
to the creature's left and swiping his sword into the creature's neck. The elven blade hesitated at first, caught in
the energy of the creature, jerking Kealin from the
smooth transition.

He swung himself into its back and kicked to pull his
sword free. The creature turned, white glowing fluid

pouring from his neck. It was the same as other enemies; it charged him, one hand on its gushing neck, the other haphazardly swinging his blade. Kealin dodged him and then swung through, cutting into its back and cracking its armor. The creature went to turn around again, and Kealin kicked it, throwing it from the platform.

Kealin checked his area and then looked to Calak; Alri was now with him, and they worked to push the creatures back. He looked over the edge of the platform; his brother came but had two of the larger creatures upon him. He flew high, missing the platform, flying toward the entrance to the temple. Landing with a rolling thud, he attempted to push himself up, but collapsed.

Kealin sprinted toward him. The two creatures were atop his brother, trying to rip at his arms and legs. Alri stabbed her staff into the ground. A blast of fire caught the first one, throwing it backward; it toppled and fell. The other rushed Calak, who parried the strike, but faltered, falling himself.

Kealin ran toward the one struck by Alri. It had begun to get up when, from behind, he grabbed its face, burning his hand as he did from its eye and the energies surging through its body. His blade severed its head, and it turned to ash. Alri smacked the one near Calak, and it turned its attack. Calak forced himself up and cut behind the knee of the creature; it was crippled. It fell to the ground and, by a well-placed blast of wind by Alri, broke its neck. Its ash flowed back down from the realm of Dimn.

Kealin ran to Taslun, who was struggling to stand.

He pulled the armor off, unclasping the main compo-
nents. From that, Taslun was pulled out. He pushed
Kealin off.

"I am fine, little brother. I just need to catch my
breath."

Taslun had a cut on his face and was trembling. Alri
held her staff over him, speaking a healing spell.

"He is weak, but I think I can get him a bit better, at
least. Kealin, I'm working on a spell to call forth the
maelstrom again. I saw its writing earlier, and I have
managed to learn part of the incantation."

"That is good," he replied.

He was listening to her, but his mind was on the
application of the wind god armor. He had it fastened
before Taslun noticed. He felt the armor as if it was his
own body, not bulky like the armor he had felt before,
freeing in a way. He thought of flying, and his wings
flapped with ease, and he was off the ground. He landed
and went to the spear and the sword, taking them in
hand.

"Kealin, no!" protested Taslun. "Little brother, it is
too much." He attempted to stand but could not.

"Let your body heal, Brother."

Calak nodded to him. "We will hold them here."

Kealin nodded back and flew toward the portal. He
looked down at the circling mass of white preparing to
come through. He closed his eyes and then dove down.

He felt himself falling. The wind rushing over his
face burned near his eyes and mouth. He tucked his lips
together, centering his sight on those below. He felt his

sword and his spear, feeling them brim with power, a slight buzz in the air.

It was not the same as fighting on the ground; he pointed himself toward his enemy and barreled into them, feeling their forms roll off of him as, with his sword, he cut into their passing bodies. He had reached the bottom of the portal itself. The rush of cold on his feet was more pronounced, and he looked to see the night sky. He looked back down as more of the creatures ascended. He flew with swiftness, his spear at his head. He slashed those he passed with the blade and stabbed those ahead of him, ascending in an arc back up the funnel before dropping down again, repeating the same.

As he reached the lower portion, six of the larger beasts were upon him, grabbing his spear and his sword. He used what force he could muster and spun, ripping the hands of those that held him, but was caught by the next. He let go of the spear and grasped his sword, pulling it free before flapping as fast as the wings would to ascend back up.

He had lost the spear.

Several of the smaller beasts had made it past him now, but he trusted Calak and Alri to deal with them.

"He is not of pure elven blood; how does he fight as this?" he heard in the air.

"Half-elf, but he has a stench of something else, too," another said.

The larger ones that had attacked him before were on him again, with a laugh in the air. He did not care. He swooped downward, slashing his blade and hewing three heads in a single pass.

He reached down to his hip and drew his elven blade. He held them in a cross toward the remaining three, landing upon the body of the one and forcing it down. He then pushed off, throwing himself into another, which he jabbed his dual blades into. He swung the beast off of him, and then, for the finale, he parried before a follow-through stab of his blade before it, too, fell to the "half-elf."

He looked out into the darkness of his world. There was a dark shroud over the seas with no end to it. The flow of Itsu had halted, and a single form came out of the shadows. It was large, larger than the rest of them, and it was veiled in a dark coat. In its hand was a staff, unadorned but silver.

A voice boomed over the sound of the winds. "Folly you have been found in, to face the Itsu as this. You are no god. Why do you wear his armor? You have killed many of my brethren with ease, yet I hear you are a half-elf."

Kealin felt his head aching; from beyond what his eyes could see, he saw a figure in the veil. He felt himself weakening to its glare. He tried to use his new powers to curve his mind away. The figure's image grew in his mind.

"Dat is enough!" he shouted.

"Your mind speaks well what your mouth does not. You wish to see my form. Well, dear half-elf, there isn't one in this realm. Soon you will see me as I am."

The veil of the creature was pulled back, and Kealin saw, at first, a bright flash. Then his ears went silent, his eyes tunneled. He looked up to the red skies of the realm of Dimn, and flew as fast as he could. He closed his eyes; in his mind, he tried to hide from the creature as he flew and noticed his wings flapping less as winds from the temple had caught him and drew him up.

He looked down to see his siblings at odds with some of the smaller Itsu. Taslun went to him as he landed. He was dizzy and worked to balance himself. His brother helped him.

"There is something else down there," Kealin told him.

"Fine," Taslun replied. "I will go after it. Out of the armor. Alri needs your help inside.

Alri ran up to them."

"Brother, there are words, written strangely, that speak as I try to read them. I feel you may understand them better than I. They are spoken like the shaman. "

He looked to the portal again and unlatched the armor.

"Are you sure you are well?" he asked Taslun.

"It will take more than some scratches to defeat me, little brother! Where is the spear?"

Kealin looked at him with a raised eyebrow. "I lost it."

"Ha! You just wanted two blades! I know it! Here, take mine as well, then! The time has passed for codes of our people. If we can survive if you wield two blades, so be it! I will take that back when this is over, though!"

He took the blade from his brother and tucked it into his belt. Taslun got back into the armor and flapped his wings. Calak was near the entrance to the temple, watching for their enemy. Kealin turned and ran in that direction. Alri had already gone inside.

"Watch yourself, Calak."

Calak nodded.

Kealin continued inside. He didn't see Alri yet, but he went to the doorway toward the temple, past where the wind armor had been kept. Alri was against a far wall. Runes floated in the air above her.

"This is it here," she told him.

"I do not hear anything."

"Walk into the runes and you will hear it."

Kealin stepped forward; the runes surrounded him, and his eyes saw the seas. A faint voice came upon him, and he heard it, just as if Alri was speaking to him.

Waters churning, thirst and yearning,
Like siren calling, dead birds falling.
Twisting, pulling, ocean calling,
Winds of Dimn contrived, conjoining.

"Dis is simple. It says dis." His speech then returned to normal, and he repeated it to her.

"Then that is the spell. The words were twisted when I heard it."

"Does this mean you can summon the maelstrom?"

"Yes, I believe I can. This wall has an image high above." She pointed.

It was a golden engraving of what looked like the

actual maelstrom.

"I thought I would take a look and, well, I saw signs like from my archon instruction back home." She smiled. "I wanted to really help you three."

He smiled back. "You have."

A scream pierced the air, shattering their moment of quietness. They both ran. Kealin drew both of his blades and leaped through the gateway.

He scanned, seeing no Itsu but Calak on his knees holding his brother. Taslun was down; his legs were bleeding, and his face was bloodied. Kealin ran to him, dropping his blades as Alri began trying to heal him again.

The bleeding wasn't stopping.

"Taslun!" shouted Kealin.

There was no response.

"Get the armor off of him. We need to stop the bleeding," Kealin said as he and Calak ripped at the fasteners, throwing the armor to the side.

A strike had landed beyond the armor and sliced his chest; a golden glow burned him, and his skin smoked. Kealin pulled his fingers through the wound. His fingertips burned, but the mark was cleared. Alri placed her staff on the wound, and it began to heal.

"I will return," Calak said.

Kealin looked up to find his young brother already in the armor of Dimn. At that moment, Taslun opened his eyes, gasping to breathe, and looked toward Calak.

"No!" he shouted.

Kealin jumped to stop him, but he was just out of reach.

"I will help you, Brothers. You've done your part."

With that, Calak flew straight up before twisting in the sky and shooting downward, his blade out before him.

"Kealin, that thing, that creature. It will kill him!"

Taslun worked to stand. His legs still bled, and Alri had begun to feel the effects of continued magic casting. Her skill was not fully developed. Her staff bounced, and her vision was blurring. Kealin pulled Taslun up.

"I will go to the platform. I can wait for him. I can see what happens and prepare."

"It is no good. There are too many. They've stopped coming at random. They have formed like a land army in formation. That creature with the staff, it is leading them. I know not what it is."

"Alri, can you cast the spell? Restart the maelstrom?" asked Kealin. Before Alri could answer, the portal erupted with lightning, and thunder shook the temple. A mass of the larger Itsu emerged. They formed a line on the edge of the portal, instead of their instantaneous attack before. Kealin grabbed his swords and pointed for Alri to go left.

From the portal came blasts of green magic that shot high into the sky before turning and diving toward them. Alri grabbed Kealin and pulled him to Taslun, dropping to her knees and pushing her staff upward. A shield of white expanded from it, and the ground shook as she struggled to hold up her staff against the weight of the blast.

The shield lowered, and Kealin was back on his feet. The pathway to the platform, and most of the road now, was no more. The blasts had destroyed them. The creatures began to emerge in the largest wave yet.

Taslun stood and pointed. "Get to the stairwell of the temple."

Alri was ahead of them already, managing to jump a small gap in the path, and from her staff, she sent a flurry of red flames that struck each of the Itsu creatures one after another.

Kealin brought his brother to the edge.

"I do not think I can jump," he said.

Kealin picked him up and jumped with both of them, reaching the ground near Alri, whose entire body had been engulfed in flames. She turned and looked at them. Her eyes gleamed red, and her hair furled from the arcane energies flowing off of her. She set her eyes on the Itsu and began to force multiple ones back.

Kealin ran forward, his blades out. He jumped upon one and used it to go to the next. He slashed that one and continued on, dragging a third and fourth down to the ground before burying his blades in each.

Alri had stopped her spellcraft as smaller Itsu were now approaching Taslun, who was unarmed, dragging him away from the gates. Overwhelmed, he punched the ones closest as Alri ran for him. Kealin saw that more of the larger Itsu emerged. Another line. Calak was still below them.

It was then one of the creatures grabbed him. He hacked at its arm, but he felt it fling him, tossing his body upon the steps of the temple. Alri was backing up as Taslun was shrouded and covered in the smaller Itsu. Kealin pulled himself up; his blades now lay a distance from him. The creatures were converging, and he saw Alri try to cast a spell but lower her head in weakness. Her last bout had taken all of her remaining energy. He grabbed her and pulled her up the steps, scanning a last time before dragging her into the temple.

Once inside a few paces, he released her. He looked back out. He paused. He prayed to see Calak but could see only more of the Itsu in the gateway. He turned and ran for the crystal at the Heart of the Winds. Smaller Itsu began to run toward him. He pulled the crystal, and a gust of wind struck the grounds, spreading out in all directions.

A slamming sound at the front of the temple followed, and a gate covered in lightning fell downward. The Itsu were sucked out, their forms annihilated by the gate as they were pulled into it. Kealin went to Alri. She nodded quickly and tried to catch her own breath.

Kealin went to the gate and looked out. The Itsu advance stopped, and the larger Itsu had formed a column, with packs of the smaller ones at their fore. It was then from the portal the veiled figure appeared.

Rising up, its hand grasped Calak's leg. It floated down to the steps of the gate and dropped him, the armor clanging on the steps. From the mass of Itsu, Taslun was dragged, still alive but moaning, beside Calak.

The veiled figure pointed the silver staff as it approached the gate. He was covered in white raiment.

Kealin stared at it.

It stopped at the gate and then spoke. "We need to speak together, Kealin Half-Elf."

11

TORMENTOR

Kealin looked out the gate at the figure.

"A hasty defense you threw up here against the many angels of the Itsu."

Its voice was like a strange cackle, higher in tone than Kealin heard before. It continued.

"You elves cost me many of my precious warriors. I would not have thought those who were like the others who came to face the Itsu with Kel would have put up such a fight. Why were you not with the others?"

Kealin said nothing.

"I do not care myself. I only wish to know to whom to tell that they were all killed." It snickered and then began to pace back and forth. It set its staff against the wall of the temple.

"I went through much to assure a simple taking of this temple. I spoke with the one you know as Vankou, convinced him of lies, his own grandeur, and then let him attack this place first. Dreadful show he put on, but still, through one working or another, it managed to convince Dimn to leave his holy house and head so hurriedly to the south. The dragon also did well to damage the maelstrom, allowing me an easier passage.

"I care little what the one of death and his pet lizard wish with Dimn. I was going to come here, do what I must to take care of a small deed, but then the noble elves of Urlas remained to defend the holy ground."

The figure turned from the gate and grabbed Taslun by the arm. Taslun looked up at him, bleeding from the mouth.

"Do you think he will open that gate?"

Taslun spit at him. "Curse you."

The figure stepped back. "You cannot curse me!" It shouted the words loud and deep before stomping Taslun's hand. His fingers were broken, and blood ran red from the splintered bones piercing his skin.

Kealin struck the gate. "Creature! Over here! You want to speak with me, do it. Do not hurt them."

The figure bobbed its head back and forth. "How wrong you are. Hurting them furthers the will of the Itsu!"

It went to Calak. "Wake up, elf!"

Calak opened his eyes, and his head bobbed. He then spotted the figure and tried to punch him. The figure laughed and then stuck a curved finger into his eye, ripping it out.

Calak let out a scream. The Itsu Priest threw it on the steps.

"Bastard!" shouted Kealin. "Get over to this gate! Speak with me!"

The figure rushed up to the gate and placed his ear toward Kealin. "What would you like to say? That you will open the gate?"

"It does not open," Kealin replied.

"Wrong again, half-elf. Is that why you are not full elf? You cannot comprehend basic truths? How about you, young one? Can you open it?"

Alri was still on the ground and weakened from before.

"Hmm, no response. Well, here is the deal I have for you. Dimn is gone, and if he was here, I would deal with him, but since you are here, I offer you this. Free passage home. You can take your brothers here and your sister there, and you may leave. I will simply take what I came for and be on my way."

"You want to destroy the winds; I cannot allow that."

The creature knelt down and stroked its head.

"When did anyone say that?" It stood back up. "I have need for an item within there. Nothing more. Your winds will be fine."

"What is your name, creature?"

The figure laughed. "My name is my own. You shall never know it! Call me creature, for now. I am a priest of the Itsu, and I come in their name."

"You command, though. You are not Itsu?"

"I am between realms, you might say. Like the one called Vankou. Although, I fancy the realm below. The people are more gullible than the deity types. Oh, how many ill happenings are caused by men corrupted to the lust of power. They are so easy to manipulate and betray."

Kealin stared at him, "So you admit you are untrustworthy. So why would I open the gates?"

"Because"—it spoke in a deep voice again—"you do not wish to see this."

It turned to Calak and crushed his hand just like Taslun. Blood now flowed from each of his brothers. Calak screamed.

"Stop it, creature!"

The figure placed its foot over Calak's broken hand and began to dig into it, smashing the bones and spreading them out over the stairs. Calak screamed and cried, slapping the foot with his other hand. The figure kicked him, knocking him out.

"I give you time. Time to think. Before I continue," the figure said.

Kealin jerked away from the gateway and walked toward Alri.

"What does it want?" she whimpered.

"For us to open the gate, but we cannot."

"It does not open, Kealin."

"I know. But our brothers, we must do something!"

Kealin picked her up, and she glanced over at the gateway; the figure stared in.

"This way," he said to her.

He took her past where the armor had been, and they stood near the stairwell.

"Do you know any spells, any single bit of magic that can help us?"

"No. I do not. My last spell took much from me, and the maelstrom cannot help us now."

"It says it can open the gate. It tortures Calak and Taslun before our eyes. Should we try?" Kealin turned from Alri, clutching his forehead. "Sister, I do not know what to do."

They began to hear the sounds of rocks being thrown near the stairwell leading to the old shrine. They looked downward and noticed orange glowing through the wall that had been erected by Dimn. The wall he had crafted was beginning to crack, and from tiny holes, claws could be seen picking at the wall.

"The dead creatures of Vankou, they are close to being within these walls," Alri said. Her voice choked. "I do not have enough magic to defeat them."

Kealin pulled his sister back up the stairwell, leading her near to where the armor was. He peered around the corner; the figure still stood waiting. He looked back to her.

"Could you move our brothers to the Heart of the Winds?"

"You mean into the Heart of the Winds?"

"Yes."

"I don't . . . don't . . . know. The gate would have to be down, but how long I could last to move them in . . . The Itsu would be upon us . . ."

"Do not mind them. I will deal with them. You could move them into the Winds and then escape yourself."

She shook her head. "Dimn said that was folly."

Kealin smiled. "He said it was 'gambling with fate.' I will take that chance."

"I will try. But I cannot promise I can."

"You can, Alri." He began to walk, but she grabbed him.

"What about you?"

He paused. "Once you have them and are gone yourself, I will join you."

She smirked and nodded. Kealin was glad. He didn't want to tell her the truth of his intentions.

As he walked toward the gates, Alri stood by the Heart of the Winds, her staff in hand.

"So have you thought of my offer, Kealin Half-Elf?"

"Yes, and I will open this gate. You will let us go free."

"Of course."

"Then tell me how."

The figure laughed. "When you faced me below, above the seas, I felt something within you. I believe you could even hear the words of the Itsu, a gift, and you would make a great asset to them. Tell me, will you join us?"

"I am to open this gate, nothing more."

It laughed again. "Pity, then. Well, the gate cannot be opened with one using powers such as yours, but between you and me, we can force the locks. It is not just a matter of how rare your gift is but also the blessings of the Itsu upon us. I can show you power beyond. Tell me, will you not join me?"

"I said I will open this gate, but I will not join you!"

The figure stared at him. "Use your mind and join with my own power; envision it, and it will be. There is indeed a power beyond the gods. Now, we must make this gate open."

Kealin closed his eyes and saw the gate and the figure's form. He began to try to open the gate, but it only shook.

"More!" the figure bellowed.

Kealin tried but could not muster the strength. Concentrating, he began to shake. The gate lifted a small fragment and then slammed shut.

"Need more inspiration, half-elf?"

Kealin opened his eyes, and the figure took hold of Taslun's other hand. He chopped off his thumb and threw it.

"Angry yet? Angry?"

"Stop!"

"You can make it stop. Open the gate."

He closed his eyes again, concentrating on the gate. He could see the magic holding the gate shut through his mind's sight. Ripples of power flowed from the temple to this center point.

"Do it, Kealin!"

He struggled and then heard Taslun scream again.

"He only has three more fingers! Open it!"

The gate began to lift again. The power of the temple seemed to work against him. He could hear the wailing of winds within, blowing toward him, but still he tried. Taslun screamed again.

"One more, half-elf! One more finger remains!"

He tightened his eyes and balled his fists. His head surged with pain, and he saw the gate lifting more and then slamming shut again. His eyes jerked open to

Taslun's wails. The figure cut off the final finger and then slashed his face prior to smashing his body with his foot over and over, blood splashed over the steps. Once the figure had finished, Taslun had stopped moving. He then went to Calak, who had just opened his eyes.

"You lost one brother! Open it, or I will kill the young one!"

Kealin closed his eyes. He made note of where his swords were between the Itsu Priest and the Itsu beyond. He knew he could force the gate. His heart thudded, and he sweated. Taslun, his elder brother, his friend since birth, was dead.

He would get to Calak.

The gate began to lift again, sliding quicker as a sharp southern wind struck him.

I am coming.

Kealin heard a voice in the wind. Dimn.

The gate began to slide down as he thought of Dimn's approach.

"Itsu, the god approaches. Do not let him near us! Open that gate!"

The figure drew a large curved blade from his robes and held it at Calak's neck. "Now, Kealin."

Kealin shook. He pushed the gate up but then felt the temple itself work against him. It began to fall again. He was failing. His mind could not keep up.

"Too late, half-elf! Open it. I will give you reason to open it."

The figure sliced into Calak's neck.

"Goodbye, Brot—" Calak's last words were gurgled in blood as the Itsu Priest cut through his throat.

"No!" shouted Alri.

Kealin cried out, and tears fell from his eyes. The gate shot up, fracturing the foundation of the temple. A blast of wind followed, and Kealin shouted, running for his blades, rolling on the ground as he took both his and his brother's swords in hand.

The Itsu angels ran toward him, and he cut into each of them. One, two, three, four, five. Their heads were sliced, turning them to ash. He turned to see the Itsu Priest running into the temple. Alri stood her ground. She held out her staff, but the Itsu Priest made a motion with his, and she flew against the Heart of the Winds, falling unconscious.

He ran into the temple. He went first to Alri. Grabbing her by an arm, he pulled her unconscious form up and held her above the Heart of the Winds. "Live on, my sister."

He dropped her in and watched her body disappear in the winds. From behind him, the Itsu angels were entering, the smaller ones first, sprinting toward him.

From the hallway, the dead creatures of Vankou had come wobbling in, pointing their blades at him. Against the distant wall, the Itsu Priest opened the vault containing the orbs. Kealin ran toward him. In a leap, he took to the air, flying toward the figure. It turned as he did and swung its staff.

The two fell into a duel, and Kealin spun, striking multiple times, the blades of the elves cutting his robes into tatters but not hurting the being beyond.

It struck Kealin with its staff, and he flew, rolling across the floor. He forced himself to his feet, still grasping his blades. Itsu and the dead creatures both came upon him. Within his mind, he heard the wails of Taslun and the last words his little brother had said cut short in a bloody gurgle.

He felt his heart surge, and his arms cut into all that faced him. He felt their blades burn his skin, slicing tissue, and his blood splattering their faces. His blades shimmered a brighter red, both from his bleeding arms and their natural elven glow. He broke through the thralls of enemies and again went toward the Itsu Priest.

"I will kill you."

It laughed and evaded Kealin's strike. He smacked the half-elf to the ground with his staff. Kealin landed facedown. The Itsu and the other beasts held their stance as the Itsu Priest walked around Kealin.

He tried to push himself up, but he couldn't. His arms trembled, and his face lay in a puddle of his own blood.

The Itsu Priest laughed. He picked him up by his arm and dragged him along the floor to the very center of the temple.

"You cannot harm me, foolish elf, and soon I will be untouchable by all within the realms. This was a mere test for me by my masters. Now, I will leave your body as a gift to Dimn."

He flipped Kealin over, and the half-elf stared upward. He coughed, and blood shot up. He still gripped his blades but lacked the strength to swing them. The Itsu Priest lifted his staff high into the air.

It was then a cyclone struck within the temple itself. The ceiling caved in, showering them in rubble. Kealin turned his head as rocks hit his face. A white mass flew in, blowing back all of the Itsu. The sounds were horrendous, and screeching winds tore into all. The priest cowered, and Kealin felt himself sucked into the air. His eyes scanned, and he saw the Heart of the Winds. His eyes went dark as he fell into it.

12

UPON THE SEAS

Kealin awoke to the sun shining upon him. He could not move. His head pounded still, and he was unable to do much but crack open his eyes. The sound of the sea with rolling waves was to his left. Something was over his eyes that made the already blinding sun worse to attempt to see through.

He could not remember what had happened, and for now, it was good. He wondered why his brothers and sister had not come to get him.

He fell asleep. Night came upon him, as it had many times since his arrival at this place. The sun came up the next morning, and then set again, although to him, he simply slept. Fairies visited the half-elf and continued to heal his many wounds.

He opened his eyes again, seeing the sunrise and now able to turn his head to witness waves rolling onto a black rock beach. He looked around but saw no one. Though someone was searching for him.

The days passed on, and still Kealin was weak. A crab walked near him, pinching his cheek, causing him to open his eyes in pain, but it was not with ill intent, for the crab sensed his weakness and offered him a slice of fruit to eat.

It was sweet to taste, and the crab remained with him, bringing him fruit unceasingly until he shook his head no more. It then crawled away. The next he knew, the moon was up again.

His mind thought to the Urlas Woodlands and his siblings. He still did not remember the horror of the events, but he saw them all upon the *Aela Sunrise*, and he saw Vals at the helm, smiling. He watched them soaring above the storms and crashing back to the sea. Narwhals appeared, and it was then he awoke from his drifting dream and looked to his left.

Tulasiro had come, and with a strange black object in tow. He blinked and then turned back over. He felt cold, a dread sadness upon him and a tone of music playing. Vankou. He then saw the image of the wights and the mouth of the maelstrom. He still felt the surge over his body as he was sucked downward into its grasp, and then he saw Dimn, his siblings standing beside the wind god. The image faded.

He rolled to his side. Thick hair fell into his face, and he looked at Tulasiro. The narwhal had brought the boat he had used before. He had not seen it since the incident at the maelstrom. He was remembering now.

"Do you know if Alri was healed of her sickness, friend?"

The narwhal dove under the surface of the water

and splashed him with its horn. Tulasiro then swam out and back toward him, releasing the bite line and letting the boat run up on the beach.

I have seen not sister . . . I found you. Others like me lost with the freezing sea.

I am sorry.

In time, a trio of fairies appeared. They floated over him, and he felt himself slowly healing. The cuts on his arms vanished; the pain in his back and neck ceased. When, at last, they floated away, he felt much better but was not perfect. He had been near death before. He was fortunate for the fairies.

Kealin sat up on the beach. The ground was barren and rocky. He was in some type of cove where the waves beat upon tall rocks behind him, casting sea foam high into the air. He felt his head. He had been here a while; his hair was longer than he normally kept it.

The crab that had fed him before brought him another piece of fruit, dropping it on his leg. He took it between two fingers and then watched the crab scurry into the thick bushes it had come from.

He ate it and then stood, wobbly but managing to keep his gait stable. His head still ached. He went to take a step, and his feet kicked something on the ground. He looked down and saw both his and Taslun's swords.

He reached down, picking them up. Looking at the sword of his brother, he saw his face at the gateway of the temple, the blood from his body. He then teared as he remembered again Calak and his throat being cut by the Itsu Priest.

They cannot be dead. They cannot be lost.

He began to pace, holding the swords. He then lifted them, driving them into the sand. He dropped to his knees, breathing fast and crying. To his side, Tulasiro beached herself and made a sound to him. He looked up to the narwhal.

"It is us now," he said. "We need to find Alri."

He grasped the hilts of his blades and tucked them into his belt.

I need to kill that Priest. I will kill that Priest.

It was then that a strong wind blew from the north. A parchment floated over him, and he snatched it from the air. It was a note, written in silver letters.

KEALIN HALF-ELF, you have escaped death by all degrees and have awoken where the winds wished.

Tulasiro has surely come to you by now.

I cannot say where your sister was sent, but the winds tell me she, too, is alive. The Heart of the Winds is safe, and my temple is once again secure. Of your siblings, I cannot say. Their blood remained, but their bodies were taken.

There was much confusion as to what transpired within the Glacial Seas. I will deal with what a god can, but your work is not done. The Prophecy of the Glacial Seas will come to pass, and though it is not understood by you, it will be in time. May the peace of Dimn be upon you.

Know that I am sorry that I failed to protect that which you loved.

. . .

HE FOLDED the parchment and placed it into a pocket.
He climbed into the boat on the beach and sat down,
shaking his head. Had this been the point of their quest,
for him to find himself upon the sea with a narwhal,
alone?

He had released a Lord of Death upon the Glacial
Seas, watched his brothers be slain by a figure calling
itself a priest, and lost his sister.

Tulasiro took hold of the lines, and they began out of
the bay, turning into the open sea with no destination yet
known. The boat flew across the water, headed south.

Kealin was deep in thought, wondering in his memories of the tranquil waters of the Urlas Woodlands, the
moon high above as he stared out over the sheer surface.
As a young boy, he had watched a swan take to flight and
go to the heavens. He had wished to do the same so long
ago, but that was then. He was no longer a young boy,
but neither was he the Blade he was training to be,
before the events that had passed in the past few days in
his mind.

He was friend to Tulasiro, wielder of the blade of
both himself and Taslun of Urlas, and in his heart, was a
zeal for his siblings and a wish upon his soul for
retribution on his brothers' murderer. First, he would
find Alri, and then he would have his revenge on all that
had set him upon this path.

Half-Bloods Rising was my first jump into the back story of Kealin Half-Elf of Urlas, a character that originally appeared in my Rogues of Magic series. I had many questions about him... from his strange speech to his narwhal companion, it was a series of questions I answered in a simple form with this story. What I didn't know was how the story would develop into a much deeper and longer series.

As for backstory, this story didn't have a ton of it but the half-elves themselves were exploring the world so I wanted to show it from their point of view, a new, unexplored place that was both dangerous yet exciting. A living world that was harsh yet seemingly unexplored.

The Secret History of the Dwemhar

The Dwemhar are an ancient race of gifted psychics that had many advanced technologies using a fusion of science and magic. Valrin's ship, the *Aela Sunrise*, was a later development and in this story, has only shown a small amount of its once-greater capacity.*

The Dwemhar ruled as one of the four original races made up of the Dwemhar, the Rusis, Elves, and Dwarves. As masters of esoteric magics, they focused on inner development and a path to enlightenment that was marred with vast technological achievements which seemed to divert their spiritual path to ascension. Their lands were of the greater North, before the floods which created the now Glacial Seas. The ruins where Kealin and the others met the dragon is one such reminder of a once greater race that has long since fell away... but other partial Dwemhar exist and two rather prominent ones are in the next book.

*Check out my *Stormborn Saga* series for a ton more on Valrin, his crew, and the secrets of the Dwemhar race!

My Writing Playlist

For each of these books, I'm including a playlist of several songs that I listened to while writing the book. Some of these might make zero sense from an outside point of view but I'm including them anyway. :) Some you might have heard of while others might not be anything you've ever heard of! I tend to gravitate to Symphonic/Viking/Folk metal for a lot of these books.

Half-Bloods Rising Playlist

1. 10th Man Down -Nightwish
2. Everdream -Nightwish
3. Inis Mona - Eluveitie
4. Thousandfall -Eluveitie
5. Everything Remains (as it never was) -Eluveitie
6. Quote The Raven -Eluveitie
7. You Will Know My Name - Arch Enemy

SEER OF LOST SANDS

Revised 2nd Edition

FIVE YEARS

I t had been five years of searching unceasingly. Five years since he was awakened on the icy shore with only his narwhal friend beside him. From the far northern Glacial Seas, he went from shore to shore, searching for a sign, a whisper, a chance that she was alive. Alri, his sister, once sickened by the Wights of Vankou and placed into the Heart of the Winds, was somewhere within the world. He feared her dead, but he would not give up.

He had chased rumors, sought out clues, and killed more than a few deserving souls in an attempt to find her. At last he had caught whispers of a mysterious old man who could find those of blood kin rumored to live in the Far South. A sandy region where the deserts to the west met up with great mountains. That was his next destination.

His journey had taken him around the northern horn of the far edge of Taria, and entering the straits of the western passage, he directed Tulasiro along the dock of a fishing village.

Kealin stood, stretching and looking at the dark rock beach and gray clouds rolling high above. Tulasiro squeaked.

"I know, friend. But I dare not force you to warmer waters. You are accustomed to the North, and I go to waters I fear too warm for your blood."

He gathered his belongings and tightened the scabbards of his blades. He touched the hilt of his brother's sword. His mind flashed to the gates of the Temple of Winds. His one brother was dead, his other bleeding and under the foot of the Itsu Priest. The memory, though in his mind many times, was still painful.

He wrapped himself in his coverings and jumped from the boat. The pebble beach crunched under his feet. It felt weird to not be on the ocean's tossing surface. He had spent many weeks in journey to this place. The moment he had learned of the man in the South, he headed toward the passage, but the warming waters had forced Tulasiro to slow her pace.

"You should take it up with your kin Meredaas, and perhaps the sea-god will make it so you may follow. You know I will not stay from the sea if I can help it, but I cannot wait. I sense Alri still, but it is fading. When I have her, I will come back to these waters if we have not reunited by then."

Tulasiro squelched and dove underwater, taking the boat underneath. Kealin watched until the waters calmed, the soft surf caressing underneath his feet. His new journey began.

He trudged up the shore. Drying racks for fish dotted the upper hills sparsely covered with moss and green grasses. Smoke rose in the distance. The village would hopefully have way of passage further south. It was a journey still to the desert, but his map showed no lack of villages and an even larger city at the mouth of the western passage. His first step was to reach that place.

He came to a low-built stone fence that ran the length around a small village of stone huts. Some people were about, but it was still early in the day. Passing through a gateway, he scared a trio of chickens that ran off further down the path. A woman carrying firewood back into her house turned and saw him. She jumped in surprise but then approached him.

"Stranger. We do not see many strangers, particularly of elven kind. I advise you to continue down the road if business is what you seek. This is just a camp."

"A camp made of stone?"

"Aye. Since the storm last year wiped out most who lived here for some time, it has been slow to have people return to it, but the fishing is good and the halibut doesn't seem to come much further south."

Kealin smiled. "That I know. I have a friend who quite enjoys the fish."

"Would you like a cup of tea?" she asked.

"I really must keep on, but I have been away from comfortable places for a while."

The woman led him into the house. It was a quaint abode with a bed and table. A cooking stove was against the far wall, and the shelves were stocked with jars of preserved vegetables and fish.

"Do you frequently let strangers in without even knowing their name?"

She laughed. "Sometimes. But the normal fare of strangers is not those who can speak back. White bears rummage through the camp on occasion, but not much else. We do not have robbers up this way. There is nothing of value anyway, except fish. My name is Marr."

"Kealin," he said to her with a smile.

She set down a cup and poured a dark brewed tea. On the shelf was a jar of honey which she offered him, and he stirred in just a spoonful.

"So you are an elf in the North? Call it common wisdom, but do you not prefer trees and warmer weather?"

"It is true, my kind are not those of the South. But there are places with such comforts that can still be had further north."

"Hmm, well, I haven't seen many trees up this way."

The conversation became awkwardly quiet for a moment. Kealin was the first to speak again.

"Do you live up here with someone or are you alone?"

"Alone. My father lives in the South but is ill, and the medicine he needs is not easily obtained. Furthermore, fairies help but are rarer in these parts, so we are forced to work extra to keep a supply of fresh ones. I have a brother who serves in the southern waters as part of the Highland Navies. Crime is rare here but becomes more common the warmer the water. The gulf region has so many foul places within its shores; we try to stay where we are safe. There is much evil in the lands."

"I make my way south. To the desert. I hope to avoid foul places, but I can deal with what I must."

She glanced down at his swords and then looked to his hands.

"You have scars from battle and weapons of fine craft?"

"They are and yes."

"Watch yourself going south. Mercenaries are common, as are those seeking wealth in any form. The kingdoms are literally at each other with blades for simple misunderstandings."

She stood and went to the shelf. She picked up a parchment and brought it to the table.

"You have a map, no?"

"I do."

"Let me see it."

He pulled out the map and unrolled it on the table. She unrolled her parchment, which was a map as his but more detailed and older.

"I mark a path that will lead you safely south."

As she scribbled a southern road along the coast that passed through a few of the villages already marked, he looked up at her. She was young and fair. Though he had no doubt in her skill as a fisher, he wondered why she would not find work somewhere else. He sensed something of her that she sought to hide. Something did not make sense. She looked up at him.

"You do sense it, don't you?"

He nodded.

"It seems my dreams are still of need in the world. I had thought my power quieted for good." She sighed. "I am of a dying kind. If you can sense it, you must know how much I must hide. The Dwemhar are rare, and even rarer will we admit who we are. My dreams told me of a stranger coming this way at morning light, and I have not had a dream as such in some time. I do not know your business, but I fear there is a greater darkness upon the lands that is beyond you or me. Perhaps you are to deal with such?"

Kealin shook his head. "I seek a man to help me find one of my own blood. My sister."

"Then I tell you, watch your path, for I fear there is much changing in the world."

He rolled the map back up and stood. She took his hand in hers.

"I can sense your sadness, elf. I also sense you are more than you seem."

"Such words are true, but do not worry of it. Care for your father and remain in hiding. There are men who would kill you."

Marr closed her hands around his. "With your hands, you will do what you seek. The gods of the North will watch over you. I will remain safe here for a time."

She led him back outside. The sun was rising higher and warmed the air, burning what fog remained.

"Fair luck on your journey. I must get to the water and the fish that hide from me."

He smiled and nodded to her with a slight wonder if he would see her again. He knew he was one of the last of Dwemhar blood and with the chance meeting of another like him he hoped it was a sign he was on the right course.

Turning to continue down the path, he looked up as the still-thick clouds obscured the sun again. He looked down at the map and the road still ahead. He tucked it away and began walking.

The road remained barren of other travelers for some time. In the next village, he found a man heading south with a bunch of crops. For a few coins, he managed to secure a ride through the next two villages. He was fortunate to have obtained money enough for many men over the last few years, so coinage was not a problem. His ways of earning the money was not always honorable, but he had reason enough to do whatever was needed.

In the next village, he departed from the cart and took back to the road. There were many more people bustling around stacked pallets and buckets of fish. He checked his map to assure he stayed on the path as marked. A stable on the edge of the "camp," as he understood they called it regardless of how many buildings they had, had a man outside who looked him up and down as he walked past.

"I see not bag or cart, so a traveling man such as yourself might want a horse."

Kealin stopped. There was a white mare standing near the corner, looking his way.

"Fair offer," Kealin said. "How much for the white one?"

"Oh, dear sir, I am afraid she is too scared and wild. Some of the horses were run up this way after a fight

further south with a manner of pirates and our regional
navies. No man has been able to calm that white one, so
I keep him well but have not had time to deal with the
behaviors."

Kealin walked to the edge of the fence, reaching his
hand out to the mare.

Friend, I know not your past and you know not mine,
but perhaps we may work together?

The horse neighed and walked toward him. It
lowered its head, and Kealin stroked its hair.

"De horse is good. Hows much for de horse?" His
speech abruptly changed having used the power within
his mind.

"I cannot believe it has approached you with not
even a jump or force of hand. Though mind your drink,
the way you're talking you might fall off that horse."

Kealin turned and looked at him. It was then the
man noticed his blades.

"I mean no disrespect, dear elf. Blades like that are
rare. I had thought you a normal man of the bottle. Your
words seem strange. If not the poisoned bottle, are you in
need of a healer?"

"There is no need for worry, and I am not ill. I only
ask for a fair price."

"Two hundred would be a more than fair offer. The
others go for three hundred."

Kealin counted out the coinage, and the man nodded
to him. "I thank you and wish you well on your travels."

He led the horse out and mounted him without any
issue. The horse keeper offered him a saddle, which he
took to ease the ride. He had ridden horses before, but it

had been sometime since then. The swordsmen of the Urlas Woodlands rarely rode upon any steed, so there was no need for it before now.

Kealin rubbed the horse's head and gave a tug of the reins, and they began to trot down the road. The sun was setting, but he at least wanted to make it a bit further down the road before resting. The next spot on the map was supposedly a larger town and would likely have a place with a proper bed and meal.

The moon was high in the sky as he came to the crest of the hill and to the promised town. There was a brown sign with the word *Maklak*.

He rode into the open gates that were one of the first to actually have standing guards. They looked him up and down as he entered but did not hassle him. He dismounted and began to walk his steed. There was an inn ahead. A sign hung outside of it swinging in the brisk wind. The image on the wooden plaque was a coin purse and a half moon with the words *Sleepy Rags Inn*. A strange name but it would work for him. He tied his horse out front and flipped a coin to the guard watching over them. He was a large man, not of the garb of the city guards, so likely a hired hand.

"I trust my horse will be well."

The man smiled. "As long as you do not drink too much and cause a ruckus. Then yes."

Kealin went to the door and pushed it open. The smell of herbs took him back to a springtime walk in the Urlas Woodlands. He looked around the room with a careful glance. Many simply didn't notice he was there. Either they were too busy with their own dealings or otherwise preoccupied. He noticed one of the patrons at the far corner of the room that was muttering to himself. Kealin walked to the bar.

"I need a room."

The barkeep turned and looked him up and down.

"You look a bit elven. What are you doing in these parts? Hadn't you heard some in the world want your kind dead?"

Kealin shook his head. "I haven't heard that, and I don't really care. I have coin if you will give me a room."

"Hmm, well then. A room is all you need?"

"Yes. A bit of food would be nice but is not necessary. I wouldn't want you to be inconvenienced by my presence." He moved his hand down to his hilt.

The man nodded. "I'm not at all. Very well, thirty pieces for the room and board. You should know we of these regions don't care for trouble."

Kealin smiled and went to reach into his pack when a stranger brushed up aside him.

"I'll pay for him."

The man dropped the coins on the bar. Kealin looked at him. He had dark hair and a long face. The man didn't seem too young or old in the age of men, but his clean-shaven face was strange in an inn of many with beards. That being as it was, Kealin had no facial hair, but it was clear this man was no elf.

The barkeep slid Kealin a key and set a plate of bread before him.

"Upstairs, room three, and roasted fish stew is coming," he said.

Kealin gave a deep nod to the man who had paid for him. "Thank you."

"A friendly gesture to hopefully earn a conversation of interest to a man like you."

They both sat down at the bar, and the man smiled and nodded as he took a sip from his drink. The barkeep brought the stew and then hurried over to two patrons who had begun to argue.

"As I said, I have a proposition," the man from before continued.

Kealin began to dip the bread into the bowl of fish stew.

"I have my own issues, and I mustn't be from them."

"Do you head south?"

"I do. To the sea and boat to ferry me further."

"Well then"—the man laughed—"we may be able to help each other. My brother and I have a boat that could take you further south."

"Many have boats, I am sure."

"Aye, but we won't charge you nearly as much as those swindling sea rats."

"Man, of whom I do not know your name, you do know that I neither care nor need to know your plight. Your word is worth as much as these supposed sea rats. I have spent the greater time of five years dealing with men of all kinds. I see not how you can provide proof of such a claim of excellence in a sea of a sad existence of men in which I have found these many months.

The man shook his head in a quaint understanding way.

"I may have misjudged you. I thought you were an elf mercenary. A great warrior, perhaps."

"My ability to fight has not come up. Speak clearly of your intentions or you will find my mood further soured than it is now. I do not even know your name."

"Apologies, dear elf. The name is Orolo."

"Well, there is one thing."

"And well, we just need to talk with my brother. He is not too far away. Staying at the Mrin Swamp to the west. We have an agreement with the master of the region to wait out his time until I can find someone to travel south with."

"Wait out his time?"

"We have accommodations there. An agreement long held. We only need to show up and explain we are done with such agreements, and we can head south to whatever . . . thing . . . you need to do."

"And my ability to fight is just a bonus point you make to me?"

"Robbers, dear elf. The path is fraught with dangers. I am but a man of simple blade. Your blades are of high quality, fine steel, if I might guess? You take me to the swamp and speak with my brother; we will help you south in return."

Kealin stared at the man. He was weary. He thought of his mind powers, but he had difficulty using them since the time at Dimn's palace and the events that transpired there. He had been lucky earlier with the horse.

The man appeared to be innocent enough in his asking, but Kealin questioned the task itself.

"I will see you to your brother, but I will not help

beyond that. If I sense foul play in your or your brother's words or actions, I will think little of killing you both."

"Fair, then."

The barkeep brought Kealin a glass of water.

"Orolo, if you are indeed done pestering this elf for protection, I will have my room key back. It seems you've spent the lot of your money buying help."

"Right away, good Rumb. I have it here."

Orolo passed the key to Rumb, who took it and shook his head as he tucked it into his shirt pocket. Orolo then looked back to Kealin. "Do you think I could borrow the floor of your room for the night?"

Kealin looked away and finished his soup. After dunking the bread into the juices, he looked back to the man who had bought his services of supposed protection just to now beg him for a place to sleep.

"I suppose, dear man."

Kealin stood from the bar and followed a stairwell near a crackling fire where a man with a lute played a somber tune to the sound of patrons tapping on the tables.

"They sing of the folly of the winter winds and the rough seasons they have had of late."

"Be happy there are winds at all," Kealin told him.

Kealin reached the top of the stairs as Orolo pointed toward a line of doors. They went to the door with a blackened three marked on it. Kealin walked in after his new acquaintance opened the door. It was a simple room with a bed and a chair next to a very small desk. A candle sat unlit. Orolo went back into the hallway and found another candle and lit the wick. He then shut the door and sat down at the table. Kealin removed his boots before lying down; his swords remained on him due to his strange visitor who so needed his help.

"I take it you and your brother are not from here?"

"No. We come from the mountains to the east."

"So you find yourselves making these lands home for what reason?"

"We are adventurers, I guess you might say. The home life is not our thing, and we will do whatever we can to remain free."

"So you have no actual jobs or meaning for life beyond wandering aimlessly?"

Orolo leaned back in the chair with his hands behind his back and closed his eyes. "We have purpose, but like you, we choose to not tell all our secrets at once."

Kealin could respect that.

"Just know, dear man, I have little patience for lies, and you better have a way to take me south after we meet up with your brother. Is this place you need to go too far?"

"Not too far, especially if you have a horse we can both ride."

Kealin closed his eyes for sleep as the man laid his head on the table and began to snore. He wondered what strange shenanigans he had agreed to.

2

SWAMP HOUSE

Morning came, and Kealin woke up to Orolo shaking him. In a quick motion he drew his blade.

"Time to awaken, not fight," Orolo stuttered.

He released his grip on the man's shirt and lowered his sword.

Kealin sat up and began to prepare to leave the room. He said nothing to his new companion as he slid on his boots. Orolo followed him downstairs but trailed behind still slightly afraid considering the mishap a few moments ago.

The inn was quiet, and other than crackling embers that remained in the fire, they were met with silence. Kealin placed the key on the bar and walked outside. His horse awaited him.

Orolo watched as he mounted. "So I take it there is no horse for me?" Kealin glared at him.

"Okay, okay, I was only kidding. Hold on."

Orolo disappeared around the corner and came back with a pale black steed. "I may have little money, but I do at least have a horse." He mounted, and they rode out of the village.

Kealin looked down at his map and noticed the man led him in the same direction he was already heading until just past dawn. They then turned down a less than traveled road leading north. Leaving further from what seemed partly civilized, Kealin looked up into old trees strewn with vines and strange flowers of red and purple that he had never seen before.

The road curved up a large hill and then back down. They descended into a valley that was mostly a large lake overgrown with trees. The water was just visible, catching the midday sun now arching across the sky.

"Where is it we go?" Kealin asked.

"The Swamp Home."

"A swamp? I am from the North, but I know this word. It is too cold for a swamp. What place do we really go to?"

Orolo shook his head yes. "The Swamp Home, as I said it is. I understand your doubts, but soon you will understand."

In all his careful maneuvers and even a few misgivings in his travels, he had learned to trust few in the lands, save himself. Of the most nefarious of issues was the betrayal of the dwarven hunter ship when he was still in the Glacial Seas. He was told of a young woman, a stranger to an island, who was of profound beauty. The entire ruse was a trap and one that Tulasiro had noticed first having found more than one body in the bay when

Kealin searched the remains of a village. When the dwarves attacked, as had become normal for Kealin's expectation of them, he killed them.

Then there were the elf traders from the South. He thought his own kin could prove true in assistance, but they simply attempted to swindle his money from him. Their extortion failed, and he collected a good deal of his coin from their coin purses. He headed south now out of desperation more than pure belief in this "man of knowledge," but at this point, he had no compass to direct his path. Alri was his sister. The last of his family he believed alive. He had heard nothing of his mother or father but only bloodshed between the races of magic.

This man led him to something, and he was not entirely sure it was a good thing. In the end, it would likely be his blades that sorted the lies from the truth. That was how it always ended anyway.

The road had turned to water. Not that it was raining or a sudden stream had overgrown its banks, the road literally led into the lake. It continued on ahead with a series of bridges and stone paths that were just visible beneath the surface.

"This way," Orolo said, leading them into the water.

"This Swamp House," Kealin began, "what sort of place is it?"

"Well, you should be fine. The last few I brought were not the greatest in the way of heart and sword, but I sense you will do well."

Kealin stopped, pulling his one blade from his scabbard. Orolo turned to him. "I wouldn't do that here."

"You are unarmed and I will not be told what to do."

Orolo turned. He held his hands up as if surrendering. His eyes shifted upward and around.

"Yes, but they are."

Kealin looked around him. At the edge of the trees and in the boughs above, men looked down on them. They looked as if they were part of the trees, dark and covered in leaves. Most held bows, but some had spears. He drew his second blade, and his horse became unsteady.

"Whoa," he said to her.

A whisper came from above. "Drop your blades and feel not the wrath of Gudru."

Kealin laughed. "Drop yours and you will not feel my own wrath, shadow speaker."

He felt his head suddenly become heavy. In his arm was a barbed point. He looked up. The figures appeared to be closer. He felt another prick in his back, and then another barbed point struck his other arm. The strange petals of the flowers he had noticed before were wrapped along the shaft of the small device. He was dizzy, and blackness overtook him.

KEALIN FELT HIMSELF LYING DOWN. There was commotion nearby, but he could not see yet. His body ached. He began to be able to move his hands and feet, and he set up. There was faint light across the room. He felt for his swords but found neither upon him. He was in simple garbs now and didn't even have his boots. Mud surrounded him and made a half circle where he noticed some type of metal formed bars. He walked up to them and took hold. He gave a firm pull, but they did not budge. He heard the commotion again. He looked through his bars and saw other bars. About that time, the door opened and men with torches entered.

"They're awake. Good."

The one who spoke walked forward, going at first to the cell next to Kealin's.

"No, no. Do not attempt escape again. As it is now, Gudru says you owe him five hundred pieces of gold just for your theft and escape last time. You will find yourself unable to dig out of this cell. We've learned we cannot keep you so humanly, thus, you and your friend come here."

Kealin could hear Orolo talk from the other cell.

"At least my friend did not kill anyone."

"Another thing we have learned with you and your brother. We silence all visitors the same now. It is unfortunate for true merchants, but you and your brother are no merchants. Nor were the others you sent to try to break him out. You should know by now that none can escape the Swamp House with such ease.

At this point, Kealin had mostly been ignored. That changed as the man came to the cell just out of Kealin's reach.

"And for you, pointed-ear fairy, what say your purpose at the Swamp House?"

Kealin glanced over to where Orolo was and then back to the man.

"I was seeking passage south by boat and this man asked me for help with his brother."

"Oh, well, did he bother to tell you that the great Gudru holds his brother as ransom for failure to deliver the mountain rock of the swamplands? A promised price forsaken when the lovely Srvivnann brothers attempted to steal from our treasury a mere trinket in comparison and pass it off as the mountain rock?"

"I know nothing of it," Kealin said, "and I hold no quarrel with you or your master."

"That is for our master to decide. I am Uev, warden of the Swamp House, the humble abode of the regal Gudru. You have been calm and thus I will treat you well, but remember the lovely swamp flowers have produced a valuable poison for our use. The first introduction of it causes paralysis, the second will kill you. That poison is always ready if needed, and know that all blades I and my people have is tainted as such."

Kealin shrugged off his sudden thought of fighting his way out, for the moment.

"I wish to talk with your master, then. I am sure arrangements can be made to return my belongings and see me on the road from this place."

Uev laughed. "Perhaps, but likely not so easy. Come."

The gate opened, and Kealin walked through. Orolo was released too but was placed in chains. Kealin remained unchained, which surprised him. They ascended a stairwell and to a wood platform. There was a waterfall in the distance, and mud walls made a dome over their heads that kept out most light. A river passed in front of them, with small vessels carrying loads of weapons and supplies. One of many boats came to stop near the edge.

"Still preparing for your war?" Orolo asked.

"Do not ask questions. You do not need knowledge of our business. Get on the boat!"

Kealin stepped forward with the others, joining them on the boat, and then gave an angered look at Orolo, who ignored him. They began down the river. The passage ahead was a cavern, and as they entered, Kealin looked up, seeing sunlight above him. They floated into another chamber, and instead of more mud walls, they found large walls made of tree trunks running along either side. A wood dock was to the left, and men with large spears lined a stone path leading up to a gateway.

The men here were strangely adorned. Large leaves made hats that stood well off of their heads. They had tree bark for armor, and their spears had purple etchings on the blades.

"The Swamp House," said Uev.

They disembarked and began up the path, coming to a covered area. A large doorway to their immediate right opened with the sounds of tensioning vines above them. They passed through, and Kealin noticed a large stone structure, not like dwarven design of sharp curves and angles or like that of elven with smooth nature-like architecture. This was different and not like the rest of the Swamp House.

Torch basins lined the walkway that went deep into the stone structure. More of the guards, like from before outside the gate, lined this path too. As they went into the structure, glowing stones took the job of the torch basins, and down a lit hallway, they came to another room, this one much larger and adorned with glowing crystals that ran up the wall.

Drums played with accompanied pipes as many slender women danced in two lines. The women were garbed in only leaves, their curves meant to distract all but the most centered minds. As Orolo began to look at them and slow his walk, Kealin looked up into the alcoves, counting the number of guards looking down. The lower portion of the room had at least thirty, and at least twenty looked down from the terraces above.

Ahead of them sitting in a large chair of wood with attendants to either side was a gluttonous creature. It may have been a man at some time, but his skin was scaly and he looked part lizard. His mouth was wide, and his teeth were like that of a creature of the deep sea. It belched as they approached. Kealin noticed his blades sitting on a table to the side of the creature. His first thought was to break from the group and take back what was his.

"Great Gudru, I bring you the rats from upon the trail. One you know as the lost brother Orolo. The other is an elf, a stranger to these parts."

"Why does Orolo return?" Gudru bellowed. "I told him that no more will I hear his pleas for his brother. The younger Srvivnann is mine, and I will keep him as so."

Gudru moved a switch next to his seat, and a cage dropped from the ceiling. Within it was a pale man with scraggly hair.

"Brethor!" Orolo shouted.

The man Kealin knew only as Brethor looked up and began to shake his head, pointing toward them.

"Foolish bastard, why did you come back again?"

"Ha!" said Uev. "Even your brother thinks you are crazy."

"I wish to go with my friend here," said Orolo, motioning to Kealin. "We will go into the temple and retrieve the stone you seek, Master Gudru."

"You had your chance to do what was needed," Gudru said.

"But the trials were too much for us mere men. I found the elf warrior; I know he can do it."

Kealin remained silent.

"What do you say, elf?" Gudru asked.

"I was asked to come get his brother in return for a ship to lead me south. I did not know he was in debt to you or that his brother was your prisoner."

Gudru nodded and motioned for a servant to bring him a platter of food. He took a handful of fruit and shoved it into his mouth. He began to chew, smacking as he did.

"What more do you seek?"

"Nothing of here."

"I question your reason for going south."

"I wish to keep such secrets as they are. I want to leave this place and get back to my own tasks."

"But you are a warrior of renown?

"I am a warrior, but I seek no further quarrel."

"Will he do, great Gudru?" questioned Orolo.

"He will, but he is not willing and the stench of elf is

strong. I do not wish to keep him, and he has not insulted me like you two. You wish to go, elf?"

"Yes."

"Then as it is, you may leave. I do not care for elves, but I will take your blades as payment of having to deal with you. Be gone from me."

A firm strike from a hand pushed Kealin away from the group. He looked at Gudru and then to his blades.

"I will have my blades first; I have no issue with you, but they are dear to me as are the rest of my belongings. I will have them back."

Uev motioned toward Kealin. "What is this? The great master releases you and you demand something of the great master?"

Kealin pushed himself back into the group and pushed Uev aside, walking before Gudru.

"I will have my blades back and my belongings."

Gudru stood. His obese form towered above the others. His clawed feet scratched into the ground in front of him.

"You dare approach me after I give you freedom? Do you not know who I am?"

"No. I care not and I fear not your threats or your poisons."

Gudru sat back down. "Orolo, perhaps you are right. Seeing as I have been disrespected, I will see to it you have your chance with the man here."

The Swamp House master then hit a switch on his throne. Kealin felt a crack under his feet and looked down as the floor gave way. Kealin dropped into a wet hole, sliding and twisting as he descended. He flipped and rolled as the passage widened, and then landed in a pool of water. He kicked himself up to the surface and then grabbed on to a stone platform nearby. He pulled himself out of the water just as he noticed Orolo and Brethor followed the same path he had taken into the pool.

Orolo made it to the platform first, and Kealin grabbed him by the arm, dragging him up.

"Oh, thank you. I had thought you'd be—"

Kealin punched him in the face and forced him against the ground. "You lied to me!"

A firm hand took hold of Kealin's shoulder, and a swift punch followed, throwing him across the platform.

"Do not touch my brother." Brethor shouted.

Orolo reached up for a hand from Brethor. Brethor shook his head and kicked him in the stomach. Orolo collapsed down wincing from the kick.

"You are stupid," Brethor said to him.

3

OLD TEMPLE

Kealin watched from afar as Brethor smacked Orolo again.

"We tried and we failed and your bastard self went on to drag someone else into it."

Orolo put his hand up to his brother. "I am no bastard and you know it!"

This seemed to only anger Brethor more. He kicked him again.

"Why do you joke no matter the circumstance?"

He kicked him again and exhaled in frustration. Brethor turned to Kealin and bowed to him.

"I am sorry you have been dragged into our issue. I am Brethor Srvivnann, and this is my brother, my brother who does not know when a task is failed and I am doomed to remain a prisoner. It seems you are stuck with us here for the time being."

"What is this place?"

"It is a sanctuary of the Dwemhar race. You are an

elf, so I know you may know something of them, but it is not riddle or higher knowledge that confuses us and hampers our path but the fact that a beast guards the treasure we promised to obtain for the frog of the swamp that sits on the thrown above us."

"You agreed to get this for him?"

"We did. In turn, our debts owed to others would be paid in full. It would also eliminate the debt we owed the Gudru himself. He gave us considerable coin to search the southern seas for rare items. Some we gave to him as instructed. Others we, well, lost . . . and in turn made more in profit from the treasure selling it to the highest bidder. He eventually sent bounty hunters and, well, here we are now. We must obtain this item to be free, but it is near impossible."

Orolo pushed himself up, wiping blood from his mouth and rubbing it on his shirt. "That is why I found him, a great warrior."

"A warrior without my blades," Kealin said. "If we must obtain this item, lead me to it. I will have my blades and freedom and be gone from you."

"Fair," said Brethor. "Though I daresay it will not be so simple."

Brethor walked to the edge of the platform and jumped to another platform near a wall. Vines ran up to the top and an opening.

"This way," he said.

Kealin made his way to the second platform and began to climb up. The vine had more than one thorn as he climbed up. Reaching the top, Brethor pulled him over the edge and then helped Orolo. Kealin looked around. The stones of the temple were dark, and crystalline lights lit their path going deeper into the temple.

Brethor sighed as he looked up with Kealin. "The item he seeks is one of great worth, a gem, red in color and capable of controlling the very air around us. It is what gives warmth to the regions around the lake and causes such growth and life as is. It was used to create this haven for the Dwemhar, a sanctuary for those who remained that was abandoned as the race slowly went more into the shadows." They began to walk again, "With it, he will likely sell it for profit and further his army of loyal followers. Many only serve him out of slavery or desire for wealth. Both essentially the same in my opinion."

Brethor turned down a hallway and then made an abrupt corner to a stairwell. "This place had numerous puzzles to solve. Be happy we figured those out on our own."

"You say there is a creature this way?" asked Kealin. "Do you have weapons of some sort?"

"We did. But most were used to navigate the traps. My dagger held a switch that opened the doorway we just went through. My brother's staff held a locking mechanism in another room that keeps the bolts in this very hallway from cutting us down. My sword was taken by the creature, and well, he lost his sword attempting to kill the creature. It threw it somewhere."

"Somewhere?"

"Wherever the pits beneath lead," commented Orolo.

"Yes, when we first encountered the creature, it was

in a chamber we thought led to the treasure, but we discovered it was only a mirage and a room of deep pits. The creature chased us, and we made it to the sanctuary of light."

"Aptly named," said Orolo. "There are large crystals in each corner that keep it very bright in said room."

Brethor led them into a large room with a single walkway that lead high above a labyrinth of other rooms below.

"We had spent the greater part of a week trying to navigate this place. When at last we faced the creature, I had the only weapon remaining, and now the creature itself has it."

They came to a sealed doorway. It seemed to have no lock or lever to actually open it.

"Believe me when I say, this was the easiest part of the temple to solve. We understand the workings of it ourselves but none but us could ever get this far. Go ahead, try it."

Kealin went to the door and attempted to push it. Nothing happened.

"See?"

Kealin pushed it again, and suddenly he felt a sensation in his head, like the feeling he had felt before when he was still with his siblings, and his speech changed. The door quaked and opened.

Brethor looked to Orolo and then back to Kealin.

"There is much we may need to speak of, but I am afraid we will need to get out of this situation first."

"I wish to only be free of this place," said Kealin. "I have only one desire in this life, and it is to the south."

Brethor walked ahead of them and hugged the wall. Bright lights shined from the chamber ahead. He instructed the others to do the same as him. They could hear heavy breathing ahead. Brethor stepped lightly down the path, and as they reached the far edge of the passage, he lay down and began to crawl. Kealin followed and crawled next to him as he overlooked the edge of the path.

Bright lights did shine down from the corners. Orolo was right, and the name of the chamber was appropriate. In the very center of the room was a red jewel.

"Is that it?" Kealin asked.

"It is. But I say to you, look into the darkness above."

Kealin looked up and noticed the webbed wings of a massive creature hanging down.

"Dragon?"

"No," said Brethor, "but it too likes caves. It has been here for some time from the looks of it."

Kealin was not sure if the creature smelled them or overheard their conversation, but it dropped from the ceiling, swooping down just near them, and let out a screech. It was a bat of horrific size. Its wings were made of bare bone, and its fur covering its body was missing in large patches. Brethor's sword was still in the creature's possession but not in the way he had thought. The blade was stuck in its head, yet the creature still lived.

"You did well to strike it, but clearly it wasn't enough," said Kealin.

"No. I should have sliced rather than stabbed."

The creature swooped back over them and went

back into the only darkness it could find, the cave above them.

"There are no weapons in this room, other than that sword?"

Brethor shook his head. "And we had almost got to the stone itself but it guards that spot. We must kill the creature."

Kealin looked down into the room, noticing a large, round metallic shield that set above the jewel. It was covered in symbols of a language he did not recognize, but it gave him an idea.

"Did the creature return frequently to that spot in the ceiling?"

"It did."

Kealin nodded. "Perhaps the light weakens it or at least bothers it."

He looked up to the crystals in the corners of the room.

"Those are the only light sources, but if we can direct the light up into the cave it hides, we may be able to weaken it enough to destroy it. That shield can deflect the light into its hiding space. It will not be able to recover, and between the three of us, we can retrieve your weapon and end this creature's existence."

"It is possible," said Brethor. "If we can break the crystal, it should give a blast of light before it dies. Catch it in that shield, and we may be able to stun the beast for a few moments."

Kealin stood up and looked down the stairwell that led to the ground floor. "Just find a way to produce the light. I will direct it where it needs to shine."

He went down the stairwell with careful footwork, and the creature above screeched. Orolo and Brethor began running down a side passage that led to another part of the same chamber. Their path led up the stepping stone walls of the room. Along the way, they picked up large stones and made their way toward the corner of the room and the crystal.

Kealin ran toward the shield as the winds shifted around him. The creature flapped closer, and he dove across the marbled floors as the creature nearly bit him. It missed but came close enough that the beat of its wings hurt his ears. It swooped back up and circled around. He took to his feet again, running past the jewel, which hummed as he approached. Kealin made it to where the large shield was. He took hold of it and lifted it from the pedestal. The shield itself held two large bronze spears hidden in its frame. Kealin stood but had a sudden fatigue and his mind began to feel heavy.

Descendant of blood, defeat the creature. Your mind has solved the puzzles of the temple. Now let it not stop you from your fears.

His strength returned. He did not know what voice spoke to him, but he freed one of the spears from the shield and prepared to face his opponent. Brethor and Orolo had made it to the crystal but not without gaining the attention of the creature. The bat screeched as it flew into the corner.

"Back, you damn beast!" Brethor shouted.

Kealin noticed that the crystal was cracked, but not enough. He gripped his spear and angled his toss. He released the shaft, and it flew true, striking the creature in the back. The spear stuck for a moment and then fell to the ground, making a clanging sound as it landed. The creature screeched again and flew toward him. As it swooped down to strike, the image of the bat's face, its yellow eyes and hairy body, turned to that of his own fear. The Itsu Priest was before him.

The voice had spoken of this, but he cowered down behind the shield as the bat bore down snapping and clawing the ground around him. The shield protected him for the moment. He took deep breaths and took the other spear in his hand. He knew the image his eyes saw was false. He stabbed from behind the shield, sticking the point into the bat's lower body.

Another screech. The bat took to the air again, rising up into its hiding spot. At that moment, a swarm of smaller bats swirled into the room. Brethor had failed to mention this part of why they could not get the jewel. Kealin used the shield to swat at the attackers as Brethor and Orolo did their part cracking the crystal. A burst of light shot across the room, and shielding his own eyes, Kealin directed the light up into the hiding spot of the beast. The light was brilliant, and the smaller bats fled. The larger bat no longer had a spot to hide.

It wailed, flapping and falling toward the ground. The spear Kealin had stuck into it fell to the ground, and as he ran to grab it, Brethor and Orolo hurried to his side.

Kealin took the spear and rushed upon the creature. It tried to snap at him with its jaws but as it did, Kealin swung the spear into its wing, breaking it, snapping the large bone. It flapped but could not take flight. The half-elf then ran up onto the creature's back. Taking hold of

Brethor's sword, he drew it out. The bat used his good wing and managed to flip, throwing Kealin off of it. He flew into Orolo and Brethor.

The bat screeched, and they each grasped their ears. Kealin felt for his spear and threw it at the face of the creature. The point embedded into its face, but still the creature lived. Brethor grabbed his sword and ran forward.

"You are dead!" he yelled out. In an arching swing, he hewed the head of the creature, and a gush of darkened blood covered him. The beast twitched, but as the flow of blood ceased, it became still. Kealin helped Orolo up, and they joined Brethor.

"We all did well," Brethor said.

Orolo went to the jewel and picked it up. "We have our freedom. Now let us return to Gudru and take leave of this place."

"How do we do that?" asked Kealin.

"Another thing of ease," said Brethor. "The temple itself provides a way." He led them back to the top of the room and the hallway they had come from. "We were fleeing the creature when we noticed this passage by chance."

Kealin too had not noticed the narrow passage, dark but quite visible from a different angle. He followed Brethor in.

Though it was a tight squeeze, the next room was large, with blue torches that lit up as they approached.

"Dwemhar blood has its advantages," Brethor said.

The floor began to glow as the three of them stood on an effigy in the ground. Brethor looked at his brother.

"That poor bat. What a weakness to be unable to be in the light."

Orolo laughed back, and Kealin watched as Brethor closed his eyes. Brethor had spoken of Dwemhar blood; Kealin was curious now of his companions. He felt his body lift up, and then came a flash of light.

4

WHAT IS NOT YOURS...

Kealin opened his eyes, and they found themselves back in the room before the great Gudru, master of the Swamp House. From the people standing in the room came gasps and sounds of surprise.

Gudru, seeing they had retrieved the stone, cleared the hall. The dancing women, the musicians, and all but the guards made their way out of the palace.

"Indeed you are a great elven warrior, though I know not your name."

"Gudru," said Brethor, "we have completed the task. We now demand our freedom."

Gudru nodded. "Yes, your freedom you have."

He stood from his chair and directed the guards to Brethor. One of them took hold of the stone, and a searing sound split the air. The guard dropped the stone, and his hands steamed with smoldering burns.

"What is this?" Gudru said.

"I do not know," Brethor commented. "I had no issue with holding it. Perhaps you need stronger men?"

The other guard approached with a piece of cloth and picked it up. At first it was fine. He walked toward Gudru quickly, but his hands too began to burn. He stammered forward and tripped. The stone flew toward his master and slid to a stop just to the left of his feet. Gudru placed his foot on it and quickly removed it.

"There is some trick on this device, but it is no matter. It is mine and I will do what I wish of it. Be gone, all three of you."

Brethor and Orolo turned but Kealin did not.

"You have some items of mine that I would like to have returned."

His belongings were on a small table to the right of Gudru. He motioned for his attendants, and they picked up the items and began down to Kealin. Piece by piece, he affixed his gauntlets and boots, his robes, and even his money bag. The last attendant held one of his blades, the blade that was originally his. The other, belonging to his eldest brother, was not there.

"I am missing a blade."

Gudru shook his flabby face. "No, that one I keep as my own."

"That will not do," Kealin stated. "I want my blade."

Brethor stepped to Kealin's side. "I will buy you a new blade myself if you come now. Angering Gudru is not the sanest of actions."

Kealin turned to him. "Go, Brethor. You have no further quarrel. I do."

Brethor took a few steps back and then looked at his

brother. Orolo motioned for them to leave. Brethor looked back to Kealin.

"Will you not come with us now? I can acquire you a blade of the highest quality, if you wish."

"I have a blade of high quality and significant meaning. I will have it back."

Gudru laughed. "I do not think so."

"Leave him, Brethor," his brother begged him.

The guards lining the walkway were cautious of the half-elf, but they should have been watching Brethor as well. He watched their hands and the poisoned staffs they held.

"I know not from where you come, elf, but I will give you but one last chance to go back to there and leave me. This blade is not worth your life."

Kealin moved his hand to his hilt. "That is right, Gudru, Swamp Master. It is worth more."

He drew his blade and slashed in a circular motion cutting into four different guards spraying blood across the path. Gudru looked towards him in horror. He reached down and took hold of one of the spears and tossed it at the creature. It struck but did not kill him. All around him, spear points flew from above, narrowly missing him as he began to run toward Gudru.

Orolo fell backward, but Brethor took advantage of the nearest guard's distraction on Kealin. He took hold of one of their spears and began striking down the guards. In a few moments, he had killed all in the immediate area of the lower doorway.

"Orolo, get the door."

"Always a scoundrel looking for a fight, aren't you?"

Orolo went to the doors, closing each in turn. Brethor let down a latch and locked it. The guards outside began to hammer the door, attempting to get in.

Kealin was upon the throne. He was mid-thrust into Gudru's flesh, when a spear point grazed his arm but didn't break skin. He jumped toward the wall, scaling up to the upper level. In slash after slash, he cleaved into the tree-like guards, moving to the next in a graceful attack and flash of elvish steel. When at last they were all dead, he leaped back down to where Gudru sat.

In all the exchange and loss of his guards, the master of the Swamp House had little choice. He brought out the blade he was hiding for himself and begged for mercy.

"I have angered you and was misplaced in such. You may have your blade back. Just leave us in peace."

Kealin took hold of his blade. Gudru was breathing heavily, and he stared him down. Kealin stepped into the remains of the Swamp Master's guards.

"Just go, please," Gudru begged.

Kealin reached down and picked up the stone they had retrieved from below.

Gudru shook his head. "No, you mustn't take that."

"I do not plan to. But this object is not yours."

"But there is a man who seeks it. A dangerous man. He must have it or I will be killed."

"I care little of your plight."

"You will. He is no normal man. He brings a darkness upon the lands. I could speak well of you to him, I could . . ." the creature stuttered.

The doorway was splintering as the many guards worked to come to the aid of their master.

Kealin turned. "Call off your guards."

As the guards swarmed in, Gudru stood up and shouted, "They have murdered your companions. They have moved against the great Gudru! Take back my precious stone."

Brethor and Orolo scrambled to take up weapons as Kealin tucked away the stone and charged forward with both blades. He slashed and tore at the guards, parrying their spears as he went. The Srvivnann brothers followed as quickly as they could. Kealin jumped down the steps and ran for the river. The raft they had taken before remained. Where he went, bloodshed followed. He quickly dispatched men on the raft, leaving it open for them. Brethor and Orolo jumped on, and they began down the waterway toward the cave.

Shouting filled the air, and other rafts made for the opening opposite the one they entered. A line of poisoned-spear-wielding men took stance. Kealin prepared to leap at them when Brethor took his spear, jabbing it into the earth of the cave and pushing the raft into another channel of the river.

Their pace increased.

"I did not know this path existed," said Kealin.

"Do not count us out of this yet. It leads through but one of the exits of this place, and I only know of it because I witnessed them disposing bodies down it before."

As they dropped to another level of the Swamp House, word spread of their escape. Spears bounced near them. The channel widened as the current carried them toward a massive gateway. Kealin scanned the opening and saw guards swarming their path of escape. The doors began to close. He noticed a path of rocky crags to their side, leading to the ramparts and wooden palisades of the gateway. He leaped from the boat and, with careful footing, jumped from rock to rock, slamming his blade into the body of one of the guards. He scaled up to the rampart and drove his blades into two of the guards twisting the mechanism that worked the gates. He ran to the top of the gate and looked down at the approaching raft with the brothers.

Sheathing his blades, he prepared to jump down when a pinch caused him to grab his side. One of the guards yet lived, and his tainted spear point had sliced his ribs. Dizziness struck him, and he fell forward. He felt hands grab him, and then his vision clouded. The poison had taken him.

He heard Brethor's voice. "Has he been struck before?"

"Yes, once before. He should already be dead."

"Not yet. He is elf, so he may have a chance. We must get him to the fountain of Eridea."

Kealin felt at complete peace and sleepy beyond what he had ever felt. It would be dark when he awoke again.

A TINGLING SENSATION overtook his face, and he opened his eyes. Just above him was a glowing orb. He could see a figure within it, but before he could focus, it flew away. Looking over to his side, he noticed a glimmering fountain with many other orbs gliding across the surface of the water. He heard crackling to his left. He turned to see both Brethor and Orolo. They had not noticed he had awoken, and both ate what appeared to be rabbit.

He could not guess how long he had been out, but more than a few hours was a good guess. It was the dead of night now. He felt his person and found that what injuries of scrapes and bruises he had acquired over the past few days were gone. Brethor looked over to him and then stood.

"We had thought you for dead after you did not wake up after the fairy's blessing."

He knelt down beside Kealin.

"Are you feeling better?"

Kealin sat up, looking around him at the dense woods he had awoke in.

"I guess so. Though I do not remember much past the gateway at the Swamp House."

Orolo offered him a hand to help him stand up. He took it and was surprised by how well he felt.

"You were struck by a poisoned tip, and any man of normal blood would have been dead. It seems your elven blood prolonged the effects of the curse upon your life force. We were able to get you to this fount in time."

"Fairies," said Brethor, "healers of many wounds and sorrows."

"So as I understand," Kealin said, "a young woman I

met some time ago told me that they could serve use to her ill father."

"And it takes the blood of an elf or that of a Srvivnann to do such a thing. Fairies do not help just anyone. We have rabbit if you are hungry."

Brethor led him back to the fire, and he took a leg of the brothers' quarry.

"You were out for over two days. We assured you continued to draw breath but could do little else save watch you."

"I thank you for your kindness and bringing me here."

"Do not mention it," Brethor said. "We helped each other in the Swamp House; we only wished to return the favor. Which leads me to another subject, that of my brother's promise to help."

"Speak nothing of it," Kealin told him. "Your brother sought a sword to rescue you. Make no excuse for what a brother will do for a brother. I know much of that."

Brethor nodded. "I know not of your plight but know you seek southern seas. I cannot provide a boat but I can help you to obtain a worthy captain in unsafe waters. Then I, too, can see you across the seas to whatever you may seek."

Kealin finished the leg and tossed it aside. "To what end do the Srvivnann brothers seek with me? Why help an elf at all? Do you not think as some men and that we are evil?"

"We know much of the struggles of the East. The Grand Protectorate is friend to few of magic kind, and seeing as the company we have in you, take heed that we are not simple men but those that have ancestry to the Dwemhar, the peoples of old."

"As to why the temple could be accessed by you," Kealin said.

"The same as you," Orolo pointed out.

"Then what I keep secret is brought out, but I would speak no more of it."

Brethor sighed. "That is why we must help one another. We can head south immediately and speed you to distant shores. What do you think?"

Kealin was in no place to refuse, and giving that he was with others who, like him, were half races, he did feel some comfort.

"Then let us begin to the coast." Kealin then felt about himself. The Dwemhar jewel he had taken was not there. "The jewel we found, did you take it?" he asked Brethor.

"No, there was no jewel on you. I knew you tucked it away, but it is likely lost to all. You fell from a great height into the boat. It would not be a surprise if it fell out. At least none of us will have it now. It is probably better that way."

Kealin nodded, agreeing.

After dousing the fire and bidding farewell to the fairies of the fountain, they began walking along a small path that led beside the water. In an abrupt turn, they then began into the woods. Kealin turned to look again at the fountain and saw nothing but woods. The location was veiled. He hurried to catch up with the brothers as they ran through the underbrush. He trailed behind, jumping stumps and limbs, and at last they made it to a more normal road, likely the same one he would have traveled had he never helped Orolo.

"We head to a port town called Frulak," Brethor explained, "and being so a port town, you can expect more than a small amount of activity. I guess we will get there by morning, but we must be careful. Between ships seeking privateers, you have pirates, slave traders, and all other manner of unkind types. The Highland Navy does have a presence, but it is fleeting at most. The best insurance you can have is something of value that you are willing to part with."

"Or provide," Orolo added. "Fighting skills are valuable."

THE ROAD TOOK them through open plains, rocky with windy stretches with a faint salty smell in the air. The moon was high above and a cold wind blew, a whistle upon the air.

"Storm must be gathering in the north. The clouds move swiftly above," said Brethor.

From afar they began to see lights both upon land and sea. To the east, sunrise was beginning. A spread of purples and deep reds glowed over the mountains. As they neared the port town of Frulak, Kealin noticed quite a bit of commotion. Fires burned upon some of the buildings, and from the sea came burning pots arching from ships up and into the city. Horn calls sounded.

"Frulak is under attack. What bastard pirate dare attack the port?" asked Orolo.

Instead of going toward the city, Brethor led them to

a hill rising on the outside of the city. They climbed up. Looking down gave them a much better view, as did the rising sun.

"I dare guess no pirate do such a foolish act, but perhaps we see something of worsening news. I see ships from the Far East, ships of the Grand Protectorate. We must get to the city, now!"

5

A DISMAL PORT

As they ran down the hill, two armed guards wearing red and black tunics stopped them. Kealin noticed their swords were already out.

"Speak that you are not of the Grand Protectorate and pass quickly to assist us."

"We are not of them," said Brethor. "We wish to help defend."

One of the two guards went inside the walls, motioning for them to follow. In a chest inside the gate, he pulled out two short swords and a knife.

"It is all we have to spare in such quick need. Do more travel with you?"

"No," Kealin said.

"Then let us lock the gate and hurry to the port. The bastards are burning it!"

Kealin ran to keep up with Brethor and Orolo. He glanced at the burning structures. It was soon obvious that fighting the fires would be more important than any man at the moment. A large building was aflame, and many worked to stop the fire. A contingent of men worked to fill buckets as others ran the buckets to the fire. Kealin joined in with Orolo, and Brethor ran to the edge of the dock.

After a few buckets of water, the fire died down and someone forced open the door.

"Port guards to the top!"

Kealin and Orolo watched as guards filed into the building and ascended a stairwell.

"Orolo and Kealin, let us find how we may help these people."

A ship was making ready for sail, and many men were piling on as it pushed off from shore.

"Three more!" said Brethor. The gangplank was raised, but they jumped on and into welcome arms.

At the helm was a tall man. He had metal brooches on his coat and wore a large black hat.

"Highland Navy," said Brethor.

The man began to speak. "I am Captain Eurna of the Highland Ship *Dismal Rain*. If you are not of the Highland Navy and are aboard, I simply ask one rule. Don't kill any of us in your fury. This enemy has come upon us but will flee as the cowards they are. Prepare yourselves."

Kealin looked back to the port. Atop the buildings, the port guard lit fires of their own, firing from ballistae toward the enemy ships. Looking back to the sea, he noticed ships of varied sizes sailing north for the Grand Protectorate ships.

"If ever will these ships fight together, it is against common enemy. The Grand Protectorate has large holdings on the distant coast and has been trying to expand west, but many forces have halted such advancement."

The ship glided across the water, taking formation just behind another ship.

"Ramming vessels of the Drean Navy. Another culture of people to the much farther south. These ships are likely pirated vessels, but their bows are strong."

The lead ships had collision courses for the Grand Protectorate ships. In moments, a thunderous crash halted the lead ships, and the *Dismal Rain* made way around the collision. Bolts flew past Kealin's head. Another Grand Protectorate ship smashed into their bow, and the ship was pushed against the sinking ship to their left.

Crew from the opposing vessel poured onto the deck. Those on the deck fought back. Kealin drew his blades, slashing and cutting down the men, eventually pushing them back onto their own ship. Another two vessels were on the opposite side and boarding. It seemed the pirates would have additional vessels. Another enemy ship was struck by a bolt from Frulak, bursting into flames. Horns began to sound from the enemy vessels, and the remaining ships turned from fight. A few ships continued in pursuit, but Captain Eurna made for port. His ship was not made for ramming, and the vessel that struck him had caused significant damage.

Men awaited to secure the ship as it arrived in the harbor. Crew members threw ropes to the dock, and others tied them off. One by one, they began to disembark. The captain followed after and stopped Kealin and the brothers just as they made it to the dock.

"I have seen many of the others who came to aid as regulars at the tavern, but," the Captain's gaze stopped on Kealin, "I have never seen you before."

"He is a traveler, heading south," said Brethor. "We had come to aid him in finding a ship to take him that way."

"A not so easy task of late. Come, let us go to my quarters at the Harbormaster Inn."

They followed him around the many wharfs and stone-lined bordered stalls of the port to a white stone building on its own inlet of the bay jutting out away from the port. Two firm knocks preceded an older woman opening the door.

"Is all the fighting done?"

"For now it is," Eurna said. "I would very well like some tea for my guests and me."

"Very good."

She opened the door, and Kealin walked in behind the rest.

The inn had a large sitting area for the size of the structure he had seen on the outside. The inside was well kept and was dimly lit where the sitting area was, but opposite the room he noticed large windows looking out to sea. Beyond the windows was a large deck and a few chairs. He joined the others sitting on a bench by a just-lit fire. The others had remained silent as well.

A few moments passed and the innkeeper came from a back room. Eurna took the cup of tea from the innkeeper and then motioned for the tray of cups she set down on a wooden table in front of them.

"I had just heated the water, so you are lucky," she told them.

The captain nodded. "Thank you, Silum!"

As the innkeeper left them, Eurna set down his cup.

"I know the battle seemed trivial, but if we do not respond in full force, they will become more daring. Already we have repelled land armies on some of the barrier islands. I understand that in the Far South, the once trivial colonies of the Protectorate have become havens for the bastards as well. If they do not bare the emblem, you can know they have their coin purses filled with Protectorate coin. Only lately have they attacked themselves. We are a simple people, but we value our independence. We see no point in an empire of men alone. I hope none of you desire the company of such men."

"I do not believe so," Brethor said.

"Do not believe so?" asked Eurna. "Before I give further help, I would hope to at least know the task you have in the South."

"I am seeking a man in the South," Kealin said, "A man of knowledge beyond that of normal men. He has wisdom that may lead me to my sister. She was taken from me some time ago."

"An honest endeavor. I too have a sister, in the North."

"Marr?"

The captain seemed surprised. "Yes. What were you doing near those villages?"

"I am a man of the Far North; the Glacial Seas is my home. I have searched the coastlines of my home and that of the northern lands and have only found bloodshed. The lands to the east have many of the same men who attacked you today. I have no plan to have happy dealings with them. I wish only to find my sister, and to do that, I must get to the southern desert."

"I understand," said Eurna. "You seek the Dashrin coast and possibly Sultan Amhe? He is a powerful ruler in the city of Eh-Rin. I know him by reputation only but have no ill will to his people. The issues you have are the colonies and the waters around them."

"A fast ship would serve us well," said Brethor.

"Us?" asked Kealin.

"You didn't think you would be rid of us so soon, did you?" asked Orolo. "We talked about it while you healed. We are going with you."

"It is true," said Brethor. "My brother and I have little more dealings on these shores, and we seek not our own. We will go with you."

Kealin was not expecting further company. Eurna took a drink of his tea and then cleared his throat.

"Take heed, man. You may not know of evils in these seas, but we all do. You would do well to have friends at your side if an event happened where you needed good blades."

"Thank you," Kealin said to both of them. He turned to Eurna. "But we still must have a ship."

"Indeed, you must. I have mind of a ship and a captain willing to take some passengers in need to go south. The man has dealings with both enemies and friends alike. Pay enough gold and see yourself well-traveled."

"Gold is no issue," Kealin stated.

"Then I will speak to him immediately and have him meet you here. He arrived before dawn with a shipment of supplies. I think some extra coin would pique his interest in returning to sea."

Eurna finished his tea and then stood. "I have issues to deal with regarding the morning attack. You are well to stay here and await the man I send to you."

The captain departed, leaving them to their tea and the warmth of the fire.

"A few steps in the right direction. Dare I say we are fortunate to of spoke with him first?" Orolo asked.

"Perhaps," Brethor added, "but we will see of this captain and just how much gold he requires if that is all he actually wants. How did your sister end up so far south? Do the slave ships come that far north?"

"No, and I have little desire to explain further due to the ears that could be about listening. We need no further evils chasing us."

"Are there evils we must worry about, then, on our journey?"

Kealin shook his head. "Not likely. I assure you, it is no slave ship that took my kin. Your land remains somewhat well, and it wouldn't have had I and my siblings failed."

"Dark tidings, but not something we are not familiar with. I tell you, I know of the lands south of the Iber way and the city of Finar in the north. There is the land of old gods, those called Itsu in our tongue."

Kealin made a fist, which Brethor noticed.

"You know of these?"

"In a way," he responded.

"They work with the Grand Protectorate. I cannot prove it, but most men are foolish and can be deceived into power. That is what folly strikes the North and what I fear will overtake this region soon. The gods have become silent at the holy spots in the mountains. My family has an estate that is safe from all such things, but I could never find myself stuck in such desolation."

"So you have a family of renown and wealth?" asked Kealin.

"More of honor and name with trusting friends with wealth and power," said Orolo. "Our family means well, and I've been sent to curve our brother's path back to truer purpose."

"Good so far." Kealin laughed.

Brethor sipped his tea. "I make plenty of trouble for myself."

They had finished their tea and neither had anyone come to meet them or the innkeeper come back to check on them. They went out to the back deck to look out to sea.

Kealin noticed the air of the South was much different than his home. The water was bluer it seemed, and the salt off the breeze seemed to stick to his arm. The air, too, was different. It was much warmer coming from the sandy lands they traveled towards. He didn't mind. In a way, he was happy to leave the cold behind.

"A great expanse filled with wonder and war," Brethor commented. "I dare to travel to the deserts. I made it south down this coastline but never across the sea. I have heard much of Sultan Amhe, and all of it has been good. If ever a friend to contest those we avoid, it is him."

"We just need to avoid the spread of culture from the East," said Orolo. "The Grand Protectorate would happily take new farmers or slave warriors or even legionnaires if they can get into your mind and convince you to join the legions."

"A difficult thing to do, convincing good people to join such ranks," Brethor said.

Kealin sighed. "I thank you both for going with me, though I cannot say what fate it holds. Skill with a blade will no doubt prove important."

"I have that," said Brethor, "and I might even have enough adventure to actually go back home for a time."

"Ha!" exclaimed Orolo. "I will believe that talk only when you say it after adventuring!"

They both laughed until they heard a door slam.

Kealin turned to find a man of shorter stature in a long dark cloak. He was hooded and walked over to the fire, removing his gloves before turning back toward them.

Brethor walked forward, entering the inn again. With an outstretched hand, he approached the man.

"Are you the one who sails south?"

The man let down his hood. He had dark red hair and a long beard. "I might be if the coin is right and I feel it worth the danger. I already dealt with the legion ships once, and I would rather not do it again."

Kealin walked around to the right of the man and

noticed the man scanned him up and down.

"You an elf?" the man asked.

"Something like that," said Orolo. "How much coin are you asking?"

The man looked to Orolo. "One thousand each, if the destination is as far south as you say. One thousand includes providing security for my ship if the need arises, as well as not asking questions that one would deem prying in any way."

"One thousand each is fair," said Kealin. "And in the event you need us, we will defend your vessel."

Kealin tossed a bag of coins to the man, who caught it in surprise. He tested the weight.

"Feels close. We set off at high noon. Be at the docks then."

Silum appeared with a wrapped bag and handed it to the captain. "Fresh biscuits for you."

"Thank you, ma'am."

She went back into the kitchen. He looked to the others. "I will see you all in a few hours." The man nodded and then headed back out, slamming the door as he left.

About then, the kitchen door opened again and Silum emerged with three trays of food. "Fresh from the bay and not even tainted by bastard Eastern blood that I'm sure our proud men poured into the water in victory."

They each took the trays of rock oysters and grilled fish. The woman then brought a tray of fresh tea.

"Thank you," Kealin said to her. "Your hospitality is welcome."

Brethor slurped an oyster and then stood from his chair. "Kealin, the simple matter of three thousand gold is quite steep. You do know that we cannot pay you back. At least, in not so simple of a transaction."

"I do and I did not ask it. Your company to the South is welcomed, as long as we can stay out of trouble."

"He keeps saying that, Brethor," Orolo said. "It is like he thinks we cause the trouble." Orolo gave a wink that his brother didn't return.

Brethor nodded, "We take a precarious journey and one fraught with old enemies and new ones. We must do what we can to avoid too many faces."

Kealin finished his food and stared at the brothers. Perhaps he was making a mistake traveling with them, but for the time, it would work. He had none save Tulasiro that he could call friend. The Srvivnann brothers were at least kind and did not ask too many questions. He hoped this trend would continue.

AT MIDDAY, they headed to the port and found the red-haired man they had spoken with before. The ship was smaller but of a narrow design meant to move fast over the water. The winds were picking up and would be perfect for sailing.

"All lines, check lines!" the man shouted out.

They were beginning to cast off as the three of them approached.

"Come on aboard, come on, come on."

Kealin remembered the last time he was on a vessel like this. He had become accustom to his small boat pulled by Tulasiro. He thought of Vals and the dwarf Rugag. It had been five years, but it was no less painful for him now. He looked to the two brothers and thought of his own fallen brothers. As he settled on a barrel near the edge of the ship, he wiped a single tear from his eye.

"Cast off all lines. Prepare to raise forward sails," the captain shouted.

Brethor went to the helm.

"Are you a sailing man?" the captain asked.

"No, but I do enjoy the ocean."

"The ocean has riches unlike any other, and I and my men work to find every last one. You can call me Kukra."

"Kukra. Good, then."

As the ship cast off from land and began into the open water, it quickly picked up speed as the sails were raised and the lines tied down. The air smelled much different than the Arctic regions. Kealin looked down at the water and then back up toward the open water.

The sky was a fair blue with little in the way of clouds. The sea was calm, and as they went over wave after wave, Kealin began to feel calmer. His time on land had been enough, and he was happy to be within Meredaas' regions. He wondered of Tulasiro and if she had managed to get to her god.

"So there are many ships in these waters?" Kealin asked Kukra.

"Helmsman, take the wheel," he said to one of his men. "Walk with me, elf. Let us share words."

As the Srvivnanns stood near the front of the ship, talking with other crew members, Kealin spoke with the captain.

"There are many ships of various flags across these waters. Many independents like myself who run cargo of varying kinds but also slave traders and occasionally Drean ships."

"Drean?"

"Yes, the Drean. They care little for most of us, but if a piece of old technology is found, they will send ships to determine if they wish to fight for it."

"You mean advanced weaponry of some kind?"

"In some cases, weapons, yes. But there is a device said to make desert ground fertile. Sultan Amhe has such a device. I think that is why the Grand Protectorate is coming this way now. With their unified armies, it is those like the sultan and the Drean who provide true contest to occupation, but already the islands of Cyr are under control from the East. It is there the many slaves work to extract Runite ore to make weapons of noble use, something beyond the purse of those in these regions. On each of the islands lay very old ruins, and it is from there that the occasional item is found that attracts unwanted attention to our seas."

"Why do you let the Protectorate in? Why not fight them out?"

"Because men like me prefer only our own bounty. You will find no closer family than that of your own ship, but with family comes tribulations no matter how calm the sea you sail across. I work to keep my family together and safe as much of the time as we can. If I let my guard down or do not listen to wise tongue, I am at fault."

Kealin nodded and looked out across the water.

"You are not like the others," Kukra said. "I am

unsure if the two brothers told you, but I do think they
are wanted in the lower seas. I cannot understand why
they would make this journey, but they have. You are
from the North?"

"The Glacial Seas."

"Seas upon which I will not find my ship if I can
help it. What do you hope to find in the deserts?"

"Answers to my questions."

Kealin intended for that answer to be sufficient, and
it was. Brethor walked toward them, and as he
approached, Kukra looked him up and down and walked
away.

"How friendly is our captain?" he asked Kealin.

"Friendly is a relative term. He is friendly for now,
but I have seen his type before. We are cargo, and extra
cargo at that. I should have made arrangements for half
payment of our fare."

Brethor looked up to where the captain stood.

"Do you think him dishonest?"

"No, but I think if forced into a choice, he would get
rid of us before risking his crew. As would I if in his
boots."

"I tell you, I already have sensed some disdain with
the crew. I fear of all the souls for you to find on your
journey, that my brother and I might not be the best."

"Well, when I met you, you were imprisoned by a
glob of a creature in a strange swamp."

"And that was due to a bad bargain and no breaking
of law. In many travels, we have made many friends and
enemies. I find our friends have dwindled as the wars in
the East have continued on. I fear more go toward the

side of men versus those of magic. The world is changing even as we speak.

"Years have gone by as I have scoured the lands, but the whispers of old evils in the South draw concern to finding items of magic to protect my family in the Far North."

"So that is why you do this? To protect your family?"

"Yes. It is why we go with you to the South. I hear there are powerful creatures in an oasis in the middle of sun-fired sand. Jinn, or something like that word. It is said they can grant wishes as if gods. It could be a useful for my family back home."

Kealin seemed unamused.

"In my experience with them, the gods are less than giving except for when death is upon their doorstep. But perhaps these Jinn are different."

"I hope. I am surprised to hear of your disdain to the gods given your race."

"My people honor the way of the sword and the elves of old. If it was not for the wars to the east, I might never have need come this way."

Brethor patted him on his shoulder. "Well, if it can be said, I am thankful you did. I would still be in that rat trap of a swamp otherwise. There is more to our workings than simple desires, that I am sure. To meet another with powers like my own is a rare thing. Our people were destroyed long ago, and many of the powerful races seek our devices for their own needs."

"So you know of the Cyr Islands?"

"Know? I've been there, but it is not a place for us to go for now."

Kealin noticed that the captain and his crew had huddled in a circle near the wheel of the ship. He stood and walked toward them. Upon seeing him, they began to file away. The captain smiled at him.

"A meeting of importance?"

"One more of necessity."

Kukra went to move the wheel, but it seemed to be caught on something. He jerked it a few times, but it would not turn as it should.

"The currents and tides can be unpredictable, so we will stop in the Cyr Islands to have it repaired."

Kealin looked back at Brethor, who immediately went toward Orolo.

"Are you sure we must stop to repair it?" asked Kealin.

He went to touch the wheel, but the captain stopped him. "I am sorry. You may not do that." The captain stared at him. "I will take care of the repairs. Your charge will remain unchanged. I bid you, go to your friends and remain with them."

The warm sea air had turned stale upon the ship.

"What did he say to you?" asked Brethor.

"The ship needs repairs."

"I have felt no strange movements or heard of any such thing," Orolo said.

"That is my fear," Kealin told him. "I am not too sure why we are stopping or if a repair is really needed."

The Srvivnann brothers looked at one another and then back to Kealin.

Brethor shook his head. "Our journey may soon become more perilous, and we are sorry in advance."

6

CYR ISLANDS

The Cyr Islands were up ahead. Though under a central name of Cyr, it was in fact multiple islands surrounding a larger island with ruins visible even from sea.

"A great lighthouse of Dwemhar rule," Brethor told him. "The ruins at Cyr are unlike many others. I believe Cyr was one of the last Dwemhar cities to fall."

"Who was their enemy?" Kealin questioned.

"The Rusis, to only have one city themselves, they were very daring in their attacks. Their people used power unlike that of other folks. What restraints the normal magic caster has, such as need of a wand or staff, is not an issue for the Rusis. The Dwemhar used the power of the mind, not that of elements, and where cohesion and unity should have bred came only strife."

As they drew closer to the islands, Kealin noticed the port was walled with large towers to protect from a sea attack. They took a narrow opening between two towers.

It was like a gateway. As they passed through, two ships of about equal size came alongside and directed them away from the harbor. Hooks clanked as the ships pulled themselves closer to their ship.

A man in an overlarge red jacket vest, with shorts and a large book, stood on the edge of his boat.

"State your name and business within port," he shouted.

"The name is Kukra," the captain answered. "Repair and supply."

The answer seemed sufficient enough.

"Welcome to Port Cyr, Kukra. Do you bring good offerings today?"

"Just a bit. I will see about my repairs first and then allow those seeking supplies to come to the docks. I'm seeking Rotfish. We will await you there."

The man gave an over-glamorous salute with his hand to his chest.

"Good tidings, then. I will see to it that proper buyers are acquired."

The chains and hooks were lifted off, and they were allowed to go.

The ship rocked forward as they shifted the sails and began toward a dock.

"Selling supplies as well?" Kealin asked.

"Just a few, and picking up some extra coin. I must make this landing a necessity without loss somehow. I thank you for our conversation earlier, Kealin."

The atmosphere aboard the ship had failed to improve after the notion that it went downhill. As they drew near the docks, Brethor and Orolo seemed nervous but didn't say anything. Captain Kukra motioned for them to join him in leaving the ship.

The water beneath the dock was clear and almost green in color. As they walked, Kealin noticed a school of small fish swimming away between the pylons.

"We will return, Kukra," Brethor said.

"Return? Where do you go?"

"It does not matter."

Kukra looked around them. "Hurry. I do not want to stay at port too long, and you leaving may lengthen our stay."

"We will."

The captain departed from them, and Orolo let out an audible sigh.

"What is it?" Kealin asked. "Why do you both act like we are lucky to be walking away from the ship right now?"

Orolo pulled a veil over his head as he pointed to a flier on the wall. Kealin went to it and pulled it free.

WANTED FOR THE COMMISSION OF VARIOUS INJUSTICES PERTAINING TO THEFT, DEFAMATION OF CHARACTER, AND MURDER. OROLO SRVIVNANN AND BRETHOR SRVIVNANN. CONSIDERED ARMED, UNRULY, AND DANGEROUS. UPON CAPTURE OR KILLING, AWARD OF TEN THOUSAND GOLD COINS.

"You are criminals?" asked Kealin. "And wanted for

a hefty sum."

"My brother got in an argument with a magistrate over ruins in the area. When the man demanded we leave, we refused. He then took my map and tried to throw both of us to the ground. When I pushed him back, he then attempted to stab me, and I threw him to the side where he inadvertently killed another man. We grabbed the map and ran for the harbor, stowing aboard a fishing trawler that we then convinced by way of blade to take us to the northern shores. It was a year ago, if not a bit longer, but it seems we are still wanted."

"Then it seems trouble does indeed follow you," said Kealin. "And this treasure is another artifact of the Dwemhar?"

"It is. Come this way."

Though the Srvivnanns were both covered with their cloaks, it seemed some within the market looked at them peculiarly, particularly the legionary guards standing on the terraces overlooking the port and market. They moved deeper into a city of white-stoned buildings that had fresh water running in troughs that were just above eye level. Plants grew near the troughs in hanging baskets that followed up the twisting, climbing road of the city.

As they made it to another large road, they descended and went directly next to a large stone edifice of a face long weathered down. Kealin looked to the sun. It was nearing the base of the horizon. They did not have too long. Looking back at Brethor now, he watched as he pushed on stones of different sizes. Brethor turned, looking behind them, and then gave a firm push. Nearby, a rock shifted, and they stood back. The face rose upward, revealing a small doorway.

"In," he said to them.

Kealin squeezed in first, followed by the others. It was a small room with a glowing stone above them. Brethor turned a stone, and the doorway sealed.

"This is a map room; it is small but will serve its purpose of showing what we wish to see."

In front of them, an opaque crystal became what looked like parchment but could be touched and moved around within the crystals.

"This device is one of many in the islands, but quite frankly, no one else knows how to operate them. It was the weathered face outside that helped lead us to the secret door of this place. You'd be amazed at what can hide in plain sight."

Kealin thought of the star map aboard the *Aela Sunrise*. This seemed very similar.

The image shifted and focused as Brethor made motions with his hands across it. At last, a single image of two objects appeared. A strange, runic phrase was just below the image.

"The word for sacred in Dwemhar," Brethor said. "This place is outside the city by the river. The rune still glows strong so the place has not been defiled by men. At least, not yet. We found the way into the ruins years ago but there were issues getting into the final room. I am sure we can now."

"Well, we will not have time today to find it. At least, we know it is untouched," Orolo commented.

"Perhaps after we find my sister," Kealin said.

Brethor nodded. "I like your thinking. As Orolo said, what we seek is untouched. If I'm right, it is a treasure unlike any other."

They exited the map room to the surprise of a young child skipping a rock down the road. As they emerged, he turned and jumped. Kealin reached down and passed the boy a coin.

"Surprises come when you least expect them."

The boy giggled.

The sun was quickly setting, and they hurried their pace to get back toward the ship.

Ahead on the deck of the ship, Kealin spotted the captain, who upon seeing their approach, did not look as welcoming as they expected. As they got to the edge of the dock, he pulled the ramp up.

"What is this?" asked Brethor.

"I must look after my family, and I fear that they speak against you and your brother. I have arranged your accommodations with the local magistrate, who was quite welcoming to your arrival."

Kealin felt the presence of many more around them. He turned, spotting a large number of the legionary guard at his fore. His hand went to one of his blades, but the captain spoke loudly to him.

"Kealin, I have no qualm with you, nor does my crew. You may come aboard, and I will forfeit the loss of coin to make right our arrangements. You need not tie yourself to these two."

About that time, a man approached with another host of men.

"Magistrate Lura," said Brethor. "Quite frankly, I

hoped to not ever see you again."

"Brethor Srvivnann and Orolo Srvivnann, I believe you. But fate has worked out for justice to be served."

Kealin stepped between the magistrate and the Srvivnann brothers.

"Another offering, Captain?"

"No," Kukra replied. "He is a traveling man seeking passage south. I had intended to take them all that way, but my men alerted me to who traveled with us. I brought them to port and arranged their transfer for the bounty offered."

"Yes, when I heard a bounty was cashed for them, I had to see for myself. You will find your bounty collectible upon their transfer. You do not commonly move prisoners or slaves, but I feel you have done well with this bounty."

Men moved in and bound Brethor and Orolo.

"Come aboard, Kealin. We will have you to the South in due time."

Kealin turned to Brethor, who looked down at the firm grip he had on his sword.

"No, go to your family. My family is here, and we will face our troubles alone. There are too many, even for an elf of considerable skill."

"Come, Kealin," Kukra said. "I ask only because I will be forced to sell you if you do not hurry."

"I am not yours to sell," Kealin said.

"Not for sale?" a man in the crowd said. "What is the point of the elf, then? They do good work in gardens."

"Move these prisoners out and you can do what you wish with the elf," said Lura.

As Brethor and Orolo were pushed down the dock, Kealin drew his blades. The gathering crowds moved backward, and a host of legionnaires filled the dock.

"I will have my friends back now and a transport vessel to take us away from this place."

"Dear Kealin," began Kukra, "I will gladly take you back aboard the ship for a fair price of—"

"No," a man shouted, "I will buy the elf. Twenty gold coins!"

More shouting began as offers were made on Kealin, who was beginning to lose sight of the Srvivnanns.

"Drop the blades," a legionnaire said.

Kealin smiled. "I cannot and I will not. Step aside, boy."

The guard went to seize Kealin's hand when the half-elf spun. Driving his blade down, he cut off the man's hand and then twirled his other blade, severing two other men's necks. In a rush of additional blades, they attacked Kealin, but he made short work of the men before jumping to the upper dock and running along the edge of the short wall.

The host with the Srvivnanns had stopped and forced them to the ground. A shield wall was ahead of him. He began to run when a shield caught one of his blades. He turned to smack his attacker and noticed an entire host was now upon the dock. Kealin pulled himself atop the shield and spun, slapping multiple strikes against his enemy. His blades turned red with continued bloodshed as person by person, he struck down his opponents. Two men approached, not bearing shield and sword but axes. He ran at the first one, parrying the swung ax with both blades before kneeing his attacker. The other man managed to jab him in the back with the point of the ax, but Kealin spun around, parrying the second stab before thrusting his blade into the man's stomach.

The first man ran at him, and Kealin locked blades above his head, preventing the ax from falling. As he pushed off the ground, he forced the man to stumble, before striking him three times in repeated fashion with both blades.

The man fell, dead.

Kealin went for the Srvivnanns. The two brothers took advantage of their captors funnel vision for the approaching half-elf, and began to kick and head-butt as he drew closer. Kealin cut into the guards, killing each one by one. They now had a chance.

"Thank you, Kealin. But now you have guilt worse than ours."

Kealin found the keys and unlocked both sets of bindings.

"Get a weapon. We must get off these docks and hide in the city," Kealin said. "We will escape after nightfall."

They ran up into the market and were met again by awaiting guards. Brethor and Orolo fought with acquired swords, and Kealin carved a deadly swathe as they worked their way through the men.

A horn sounded, and Kealin turned to find that guards marched in formation, surrounding them in a box.

"Do not let them close upon us!" Brethor shouted.

They ran forward, and Kealin leaped over the shield

wall, cutting into the formation. The formation shifted and opened up. He ran forward again but found his path blocked by a building. The guards had worked to corral him, forming multiple lines of shields going out from his position. Brethor and Orolo had already been captured again and forced to the ground. As Kealin took stance to continue fighting, he heard a sound.

Someone was clapping from within the legionnaires.

"It is rare to see such skill within the West. I am sure the magistrate will take a good deal of coin for you, and I can forgive such actions against my legion for exchange of a good show."

"Excuse me, but I care little for voices alone," Kealin said.

A line of shields some distance away parted and a man wearing silver armor walked through. He had dark hair, and in his right hand, he held a sword out toward Kealin.

"I am Admiral Urui, Tenth Expeditionary Legion of the Grand Protectorate and I am also one of their representatives within the Cyr Islands. I applaud you for such skill, but any further bloodshed is pointless."

"Pointless is to try to say that I will not go free."

"I will not say it, but I also will not say too much more. Your skill has kept you and your friends alive. Now, I will see it do more for more lucrative outcomes."

Kealin went to step forward, but he felt his body struck with an icy blow. His back felt frigid. He turned to see a man with an outstretched hand that glowed blue. He went to put his hand up when another blast of ice struck him. Unable to move, he collapsed.

7

SOLD

The fact was, Kealin awoke to a pounding headache and to blackness as before, only this time, he was more annoyed. He couldn't see, and his body shook with chills. He only remembered the icy blast from the man on the edge of the line of legionnaires. Somehow he also remembered laughing, but that had been the admiral. He couldn't remember for sure.

He sat up and looked around. He was in a stone room with bars on the far side. Candlelight from a nearby table gave some needed light, and fortunately he had awoken on a bed, not a floor like at the Swamp House. A woman walked into the room, holding a tray. She had her head down and moved quickly to his table before turning and walking back out.

"Excuse me?" he asked her, but she was gone already.

Kealin swung his feet over the side of the bed and put his head into his hands.

How did this happen again?

He was surprised he was not killed considering the failed escape attempt. He wondered too where Brethor and Orolo had ended up. Perhaps they were somewhere nearby or perhaps they were dead.

They had taken all of his clothing, and now he was garbed in a simple tunic. A pair of sandals sat next to the bed. He put them on and paced across the room, looking out of the bars and then back to his bed. He did not know where he was, but it was not as dark and dank as the prison he had found himself in before.

He went to the tray and found a decent serving of a cooked bread and lamb soup. He had eaten only a few bites when the woman from before came back to the gate. She twisted open the lock and opened the door. Kealin went for it and then noticed that the hallway to the right was lined in legionnaires. He stepped back away.

"Are you finished?" the woman asked.

"Yes, I am. But please tell me, where is it that I am? Are you master of this place?"

"I am not, sir, and I am a slave like you. Our master is Tubor, and you are to fight for him in honor of the Grand Protectorate."

She carried the tray out of the room, locking the door behind her.

He began to pace again when he heard a whistle. He went to the gate and looked out.

"Brethor! Orolo! Are you there?"

There was a stern cough from a cell across from his.

"I don't know who those people are, but it is best to not make many assumptions here."

A dwarf appeared at the door of the other cell. He was ragged and unkempt. As much as Kealin hated dwarves, this one was in as bad as a position as he was.

"They hold you here against your will, dwarf?"

"Aye, they do. The name is Bafnor. I am from the eastern mountains west of Taria in the North."

"What business does a dwarf of Taria have with the lands to the south?"

The dwarf laughed. "I could ask the same of an elf, but neither matters much."

"How long have you been here?"

"Me? Eight weeks. My companions have all died, but I held out the longest in the cave system beneath the city. We had nearly reached our way out when they found us. Thankfully, they did not find our escape but I doubt I could do it again."

"So you plan to attempt escape again?"

"I would like to, but I fear my death will come sooner than that. They will have blood games for the people of Cyr soon. In that, we will all die. It is the only guarantee and the only outcome of such games. Are you a well-trained gladiator?"

"I do not know that word."

"A warrior skilled in combat used for the profit of less-willing men."

"Then by the definition, no." Kealin laughed. "And I dare know anyone who would be willing to go by that."

"Well, take the name and embrace it," another voice said. This one was different and came from down the hallway.

"I shall not."

"You will," it said back.

Bafnor laughed to himself. "That is Riveaa. She is an elf from the South."

"Riveaa is indeed my name, but your stench of a mouth should not speak it."

"Perhaps we shouldn't seek to kill each other," suggested Kealin. "We are all stuck here. Plus, if we are to provide value to the master, I figured we would not all die."

"You and your hope and figuring," began Riveaa. "We are but the animals. The true gladiators have their place near the master's house. That admiral you met earlier has been searching for specimens for the gladiators to fight as an example of the might of men. You keep yourself well and perhaps you will live to be killed at another spectacle. Just ask the dwarf of his kinsmen."

"It is true," Bafnor confirmed. "We were set to die, but I survived and defeated all they threw at us. The people cheered and shouted my name, but in the end, it did nothing but anger the hierarchy of Cyr. I believe they seek to turn all against us."

"Who is the master?"

"A man of the Drean people, a foreigner, brought in because of his ideals of expansion and trade with the Grand Protectorate. He only works with them because they would take up arms against the sultan of the South, which the Drean have struggled against for years. It matters little."

The sound of shuffling feet came from down the hallway. A trio of men and a hooded figure approached the door of the cell.

"Step back from the door!"

Kealin walked backward as the door opened. Before he could say or do anything, the hooded person reached out, and his hands were forced behind his back.

"No talking. Do we just assume I know what is needed?"

"I take you to the master. He will speak with you."

Though Kealin did not know her name, he could tell by her voice that she was female. He followed the guards out and walked with the hooded woman behind him. They proceeded down the hallway and up the stairwell, coming to a barrier where two other hooded figures stood. Some type of veil was lowered into the ground. It was not cloth like in most places but a blue hued spell. As he stepped through he looked back and one of the hooded figures motioned with their hand, summoning the veil back up and sealing the way they had passed through.

Ahead, there was another gate. This one was flanked by two white stone towers. As they went into this one, he saw a courtyard of men fighting one another with wooden shields and swords. They paused for a moment.

"Your death awaits you at their blades," the hooded woman said.

She pushed him along as he ascended a stairwell and was now before a wooden door. He walked in and found himself standing on polished floors. Red linens hung down the length of the hallway, and the sound of a waterfall could be heard in the distance.

The guards escorted him down the hall and to a large room with an opening near one edge that let down the waters from a mountainous spring. The water rushed down the rocks and went down the length of the room before passing out of a grate on the far edge.

"Wait here," he was told.

Kealin stood watching as she walked around the edge of the pool, crossing a tiny bridge before entering a room on the opposite side. In a few moments, she returned with a man. He was very tall and had darker skin than any of the other people he had met yet. He wore a jewel on his head and had many bracelets and rings made of gold.

"Kealin, the elf," he said. He then turned to the hooded woman. "Thank you, Jesia. You are free to go for now. Guards, you too. I wish to speak with our guest."

Kealin was now alone with the Drean man he knew as Tubor.

The man approached him, waving a small golden rod over his magically bound hands. He felt his hands release.

"There is no need for that here. I trust your meal was good?"

"Surprisingly for a meal meant for a prisoner."

The man laughed. "You are being kept safe for a desired end. You are no prisoner."

"Then if I am no prisoner, release me from my cell."

"Demanding, aren't you? We must keep animals where they belong, Kealin, elf. Prisoners, or as I might say, slaves, are kept underneath the house of the master. You are kept where your kind belong, under the ground."

Kealin's eyes shifted around the room as his thoughts went to that of killing the man before him.

"The admiral and I have a special show planned, and I want you to be a part of it. In the market, you made a good large mess dealing with the legionnaires. Fighting of that skill level could be quite useful for entertainment at your death. I actually might find myself rooting for you! Although, you will have to understand I would do so silently. Good people do not like to see the beast actually win."

"Why am I here?" Kealin growled. "For you to insult and demean?"

"You are here for me to meet you. Your fellow kind, the elf, the dwarf, and a peculiar miniature stone giant we are keeping outside near my training grounds, are going to be in the Celebration of Cultures held at the arena in three days' time! Upon that day, you will be garbed in the very items you had on arrival, and then you will die well in front of a roaring crowd. A good death, I assure you."

"So that is it? You took me to let me die elsewhere?"

Tubor went to a small table and poured a glass of wine.

"You are all dead anyway, if not today or tomorrow, or in the arena. You will die soon. The world is changing, and there is little room for such kind as you. Your one hundred years' bickers with the dwarves, your eternal life unfairness. How do you feel of men? We have but one hundred years to live on average, and yet you kill us before we reach half that?"

"I only have killed as needed. I care little for these regions, and that includes the full-blooded elves of the East. What justification do you have for killing them?"

"Typical elf! Only care for yourself now? I am happy to send you to your death! The Celebration of Cultures will forever etch in the minds of the people the weakness of your own. Not to mention the financial gain will be substantial. I do not expect you to understand such things, but know tomorrow you will prepare. You will meet the men who will kill you. You will see the respected might that is what warriors we are capable of fielding."

"So you hate those of magic but you have the Rusis to do your bidding?"

"It is common and useful for those in power in these waters to have them. The Rusis are the rarest of magic peoples, and these serve the Drean. We have methods to keep them under control. They at least have the sense to side with a superior race of men, and in time they too will be killed, but not yet. Guards, I am done with him."

The guards from before came to either side of him. He walked back toward the cell area and, following the path down, he went back to his cell. As the door shut with a clang, Bafnor stood up. The guards departed.

"So you met the master?"

"He doesn't deserve the notation. He is a man, yes, but a poor excuse of one. What lies of that of elves and dwarves have been told to foster resentment to this level?"

"None. But in the East, we are quickly being centered as evil. The war is failing, and many have died. You say you are not of the East?"

"I am of the North. My parents went five years ago to

fight in the wars, but I have since lost contact with them."

"Riveaa fought before she was captured. Perhaps she knows of them?"

Riveaa laughed. "No, everyone I knew was killed in a bloody valley, left defenseless because the dwarves fell back at the last moment! Hammersong strong? Foolish dwarves! Their mighty Hammersong warriors fled! The lines broke as if wheat to the scythe! Your parents are dead, Kealin. Accept it."

"Elf, I daresay I have accepted quite a bit, and I suggest you watch your tone," Kealin said.

"I don't care, and I will not retract what I said. If it is not the bastard men, it's the black demon of the South. For the last year, this warrior has been attacking all upon the Eastern shores. There is rumor this warrior comes from the clan of Ur, and a dark foreboding that would be."

"Clan of Ur?"

"The demon god's followers, an alliance of the orc masters of old," Bafnor explained.

"Orcs were destroyed some time ago."

"Pray it stays such," Riveaa said. "The world is not what it was one hundred years ago. Have your hope, elf, but know I do not."

Bafnor shrugged.

Kealin walked away from the door and set down on the floor. He had not meditated in some time, but perhaps he could reawaken his mind, contact Brethor if such a thing was possible.

"Good, you rest," said Bafnor. "Dwarves need rest

too." The dwarf lay down, still visible to Kealin but asleep rather quickly given the amount of snoring.

Kealin concentrated his breathing. He took in air slow and held it. Then pressed it out. He felt himself become light and airy. His focus had been off for some time, relying more on physical strength than that of his mind. He felt the imbalance. His sword master back in the Urlas woodland frequently had sessions of centering and oneness with the woods. There were no woods here, but even so, Kealin soon felt himself above the cell. He could see the sea and a large yellowish moon arching across the sky.

Brethor. Brethor.

He called out in his mind hoping to hear something, someone.

Brethor. Brethor.

Still nothing. He then felt a rumbling in the air around him. A sensation, a feeling, as if something was near.

"Half-elf!" A shout came, rocking him from slumber.

He opened his eyes. He felt as if he had fallen asleep, but he was not sure.

It was the Rusis from before, but her veil was down. Her hair was a golden blonde, and her eyes were green. Behind confident eyes, she stared at him with a sadness.

"I am right, then?" she asked.

"Yes."

"I sensed it before, when I took you to Tubor."

Kealin stood up. "What of it?"

"You are not like the others I have met. Nothing like that bitch in the other cell."

"Maybe you would be the same if facing the same fate that we do?"

"That is true, but it is no secret between me and my kin that we do, just we do not know the hour."

Kealin began to pace. "Why is this important?"

"Why is a person like you cutting up an entire legion like it is nothing but quick blade work?"

"Have you never seen a good swordsman?"

"I have seen many. But none of your renown. The entire region whispers of you."

"Then the arena will be packed for my death. If you know so much, perhaps you can help me and tell me of my friends and their fate?"

"I do not know of them."

Kealin walked to the gate and looked through the bars.

"Brethor and Orolo Srvivnann."

"I will check on them."

The Rusis began to walk out when Kealin grabbed her by the shoulder. Her hand went up to his, and he felt a spark between them for a moment. Her eyes turned a deep blue and then back to green. He felt the ocean roll over him, and then took a breath.

"Are you just of the Rusis?"

"I am, but I am of the sea as well. Saved long ago by creatures from its waters."

"Then we have a common feeling toward things. I ask you, why do you offer help so freely?"

She smiled and then began to weep.

"We are all doomed to die by the hand of men. If we

are to escape, or even stand a chance of escape, I believe it be with you."

"Others think as you do?"

She smiled and then threw her veil over her head, walking quickly back down the hall.

Kealin stepped back from the gates and went back to his bed. He thought of his sister and his desire to be free of his bounds and now of the many others who, regardless if they said or not, looked to him for hope. He lay down on his bed and went to sleep.

THERE WERE NOT many windows in the jail cells, but still the smell of a morning near the sea crept in, and Kealin awoke as servants opened the doors and brought them trays. A Rusis, not Jesia but one of the other ones, watched over the servants. Kealin questioned why those as powerful as the Rusis had not broken themselves out. A question better waited until later to ask.

As soon as they had eaten, he and the others were brought out and bound by Rusis magic before being marched up and out to the main training courtyard. He turned to take a look at the elf. She glared at him with one eye, her other was cruelly taken evident by the still-healing scars over her face.

"Get a good look, elf. See what happens when you trust dwarves to hold a line."

Bafnor said nothing but seemed upset by the statement.

"Bafnor, how did you fair in battle? When were you caught?" Kealin asked.

"Probably running away," Riveaa said.

"Defending an elf village. I stayed to fight while they ran to safety. They had many little ones with them."

Riveaa seemed to ignore his words, and Kealin stood quiet between them. A host of men appeared from beneath the home of Tubor. They wore the simple dress of tunics and red leather vests.

Another man appeared from behind the rest. He was large and scarred beyond what any normal man of battle would be. His back showed evidence of whip marks layered to a degree that he had ripples of tissue showing. He wore a black tunic and came before them brandishing a metal chain.

"You are puke. You stand upon holy ground, bled upon by my men who stand beyond your pitiful races in all ways. The ceremony that will see your end will be one of necessity, not glory for my men. I am their master, their teacher, and their brother-in-arms. I have to assure that you rabble stay alive long enough to serve a glorious death as you are struck down by my masters of death."

He slapped the chain on the ground and then pointed at the men behind him.

"We train at all times, sleep little, and avoid the tainted drink except when we celebrate victory in the arena. You will train with us using wooden weapons, and you will abstain from dying until the arena. It is a mere two days away, so you should be able to make it. Also, you will learn that I am in control of you. Do not test me or I will beat your brains into the sand you stand in."

Kealin didn't care much for the theatrics, and at this point, he just wanted a sword, wooden or otherwise.

"You can call me as my men call me when they are new. Teacher. That is all you must know of it. Now, I will teach you to die well."

Two men brought out a wooden chest and flipped the lid open. They began to hand out a random assortment of wooden weapons. A sword, a hand ax, and a mace. They then went down the line, shoving a weapon to each of them. Kealin got the ax. It was lighter than he was used to and bore the marks of heavy practice.

"We almost forgot our prize catch," the man known as teacher said. "Bring him out of his cave!"

Kealin turned to see a large group of men, this one with actual armed legionary guards, pulling ropes and emerging from a dark cave. He expected to see some reluctant creature pulling back or attempting to fight. But as the tall, gray beast was dragged from the darkness, his elongated hands went to block out the sun and he whimpered as he was forced out.

"A stone giant for the deserts, a rare catch, but a vicious beast to be feared. He will use his hands as weapons."

Kealin could think of a word to describe this newest arrival, and it had nothing to do with vicious. Pitiful, or perhaps even sad, would be closer of a description.

"A depressing truth," began Riveaa. "That creature does not pose a danger to anyone. It is large, but that is it. It eats rocks and minds itself to a happy life of solitude."

Teacher noticed Riveaa's comment. "So you would like to try your hand at fighting one of my men first? Come, face those who will kill you soon."

Kealin observed Riveaa stepping out before the group of men. Her footing was balanced; she held her sword with confidence and form. One of the men approached from the far edge of the line. He was taller and at least twice the elf's size.

"Zibur is our reigning champion. A defeater of many of the greatest in the land. A warrior of descent from the gods themselves."

Zibur had a large sword of wood and a shield. He came within a few paces of Riveaa when she lunged at him. Her sword strikes fell hard, but Zibur parried each one. After a continued attack, he spun and dropped, striking her feet and knocking her to the ground.

"And that is it, the place all elves deserve to be. On the ground before the rightful masters of the lands. What difference would a bowstring make, nymph? Or is that more so what you might prefer, to act as a whore among men? We would have to check with the gods, perhaps a beast should not be with a man."

Riveaa's eyes squinted. She shouted and charged again. She parried his outstretched blade and leaped onto him, taking hold of his hair. He punched her twice, and her body fell limp. She rolled to the ground, and Zibur kicked her once. She moaned.

"What now," Teacher said. "Do you wish to give up? That was a poor excuse for fighting."

"I am a mage," Riveaa said. "I use magic."

"Well, not now. I would not allow magic's use so

freely, nor would our master. He controls magic within these walls. He keeps the Rusis in check, as those casters must be kept."

Kealin wondered of what was said. The Rusis had the power to use magic without aid of wand, staff, or device. Their elemental powers were beyond most magic, and it was strange they would be kept as slaves. He would try to ask Jesia about it later.

Teacher looked at him.

"You, elf. You are next."

As Riveaa was pulled from the sands, Kealin stepped forward. He would have preferred his blades, but he would have to do without them.

"Are you a mage too?" Zibur asked. "Are you going to whine as the whore did?"

Kealin remained silent. He set his footing and held his ax out. He did not move.

"You do not charge me as I would expect. Does fear overtake you?"

The other men on the training guard began to laugh.

"Do you wish to urinate on the ground before the might of Zibur?" he shouted.

The others began to cheer as Zibur reached up into the sky and turned in absorption of the cheering and shouts of his men. For a mere moment, he exposed his back to Kealin. The half-elf took that folly of pride to charge. Zibur's head turned just as Kealin smacked the ax into the back of his head. The giant of a man toppled forward and did not move.

8

BLOOD-LETTING

Silence overtook them all.

Kealin looked to Teacher, who seemed amazed and angry.

"You attack without honor? I will not have this."

He motioned his head, and three more men went for Kealin. He ran toward them, smacking and parrying as he had the many times upon the sands of the Urlas Woodlands. He dodged, parried, and took down the first man with an ax strike to his knee. The second one fell to a punch to the throat, followed by an elbow to the back of the head. By the time the third one came upon him, the man had begun to fear just as Kealin swung his ax head-up, striking the man in the jaw. Kealin grabbed hold of the man, forcing him to the ground. He struck the man repeatedly in the head, deforming his face more and more with each strike, splattering the ground and himself with blood.

"That is enough!" a voice shouted.

Kealin stopped, panting, and with a slight blood-stained smile, looked up. Master Tubor stood at the edge of the training grounds.

"Bring him to me."

Two Rusis appeared and forced Kealin's face into the sand then kicking the ax from his hand. He looked up at them with his cheek in the blood of the person he had just bludgeoned. Neither of the Rusis was Jesia. The pressure on his back released and he stood. Tubor motioned for him. He walked toward the man. Kealin glanced over to see Bafnor had a slight smile but hid it as they passed.

"You take training to mortal bloodshed?" Tubor asked.

Kealin smiled. "I know bloodshed. I have trained for longer than your lifetime and would not have myself made into a game before your men."

Tubor turned and motioned with his hand. "Come with me."

The magic hold on him was released, and Kealin followed the man back into the house. Tubor led him across the marbled-floor path back to the main room, where Kealin spotted his two blades lying on Tubor's table.

Tubor picked up one of the blades and held it out to him.

"Of elvish design, no doubt. A fair price they will earn me upon your death." He threw the blade onto the table. "I care little of your training. I know you can kill. It is why I want you to fight in our arena. I do have some respect for elves. You are resilient like the dwarves but have the accuracy of bow strike and blade work that competes with the greatest of men. You have seen many more sunsets than me, but it does not prevent foolishness on your part.

"I was a warrior once, but I learned then that given the chance, an elf will abandon a man to save their own kind."

"And that is why you take such joy in this coming fight? To see elves fall upon the field fighting against horrid odds by your standard?"

Tubor laughed. "You think me such a simple, cruel man? I have considerable coin invested in you. The others were cheap, but you, after what you did, were not. There is always a chance you will not die. Though this is not preferred, I have prepared such thoughts as to what I might do with you in the event."

"Well?" said Kealin.

Tubor began to pace. "You would become my new champion. A life of simple war as you live within these walls. You would have drink and food and women, be they of my or your own kind. You would fight and become renown across the lands as the great elf of Cyr, and there would be none to hold your name with disdain. They could see past the issue of what you are and see the warrior. I say that it would not be a foolish endeavor for you. Not to mention the wealth you could earn, even as a slave."

Kealin was not amused. "I care little for drink or what pleasures your coin can provide. I would still be a slave, and I will not be held here as such."

"Rusis!" Tubor said. He made an upward motion

with his hand, and Kealin was lifted into the air by a nearby Rusis. Tubor took one of Kealin's blades and held it up to him. With his other hand, he pulled a pendant from his shirt.

"This makes it so I have control over you. The Rusis were at once a powerful race of magic, but the few who remain have nowhere to call home. I keep these here to assure my own safety, and as long as I control them, I can control you."

Kealin was lowered down onto his blade's edge.

"All of your fancy blade work and quick movements mean nothing before the power of magic. A power I control."

Tubor lowered the blade, and Kealin was dropped onto the ground. He pushed himself up and slapped the sand off his tunic.

"Yet you still destroy the peoples of magic because of your hate?"

Tubor nodded with a cocky smile. "It is what has to be. It is an ironic truth I will not deny, but we shall see tomorrow how you fair. These women are my own property and kept safe and remain obedient." He tapped the amulet and gave another smile. "Take him to his cell, Rusis."

As Kealin was led away, Tubor spoke again.

"Be happy in that tomorrow you will be garbed in that which you had when captured. You will die with your blades of your kind—or not die and join me here."

As Tubor laughed, Kealin was pushed out of the house. The Rusis led him down to the cells, and he entered. As the Rusis began to walk away, he thought of Jesia.

"The one called Jesia, where is she?"

The Rusis seemed surprised by the question.

"She became ill and was taken into the city."

Kealin was surprised by the answer as the Rusis left. He wondered how he would ever get news of the Srvivnann brothers and what had befallen Jesia. He looked into the opposite cell and saw Bafnor lying on his back.

"Are you alive, dwarf?"

He heard a grunt. "Yes, the pain tells me so. I took a beating after you left. I think you nearly killing one of them set them in a sour mood."

"Apologies, then, for that."

"Ha, do not apologize. I quite enjoyed seeing his face smashed in after the treatment we have received."

"How did the giant creature fare?"

The dwarf sat up. "The troll creature wouldn't fight and was lashed for it. I fear he will be the first to fall tomorrow."

"Perhaps, but that might serve him well. The bastard king in the house has told me if I survive, I may join him as a slave within his warriors."

The dwarf laughed. "If we survive, he will have no warriors to speak of. We are to fight all of his men. This is not a common thing, this 'game,' as I heard it called. The Grand Protectorate has restarted this fighting long after we no longer did it. They are trying to make us elves and dwarves out as monsters and shower the opulent of Cyr with gifts and games, beyond the simple act of killing us."

"So those speculating tomorrow have already been primed with coin?"

"Yes, and our gear shall be sold as well. Most dwarves in this part of the world are gone. The mines in the eastern mountains have been quieted, and now legionnaires march down the roads my grandfather built. I would not be surprised if our very bodies are sold like specimens in the end. It is a sad day."

Kealin shook his head. "Perhaps we may live on? There is always a chance."

"The hope of elves seems to last as long as your lives. I only hope your chance plays out as you think. I must rest. Ponder my last breaths tomorrow."

Bafnor lay back down on the floor, obviously avoiding the bed he was provided. Kealin figured the dwarf preferred the stone.

Kealin's mind raced. He wished to try again to contact Brethor. What good was his Dwemhar blood if he could not?

He sat down on the floor and closed his eyes. He began to slow his breathing. He had tried many times to increase the power in his mind, to use it as he once did, but since, every time the images of his siblings clouded his thoughts.

Brethor.

Brethor.

He felt like he was sending words into an empty void. A realm where no one listened any longer. He wondered if Brethor was dead. The Srvivnanns were wanted for a considerable amount of coin. He turned his thoughts to tomorrow and those with him set to die. The troll was scared, but who would not be? The elf was without an eye or device to cast magic, and the dwarf was well in years. They were to die tomorrow. That was what was desired. But he could not.

Something jolted him out of his meditation. Tapping on metal. He opened his eyes and looked ahead, noticing but an outline of a figure.

"Kealin," the voice said.

He stood and walked toward the gate. It was a phantom of a person, just visible as a thin veil.

"The skills of the Rusis," Kealin commented. "Many forget your power to hide as such, Jesia."

"I have found your friends. They are alive, but after tomorrow, it will not be so."

"Are they to fight with me?"

She shook her head. "No, they are to be executed before then. The officiating powers will offer a sacrifice to their gods to bless their gladiators before facing you."

"I see little need for them to need blessing, by their own accord and pride."

"I had said your name had spread through Cyr. There is concern that you will not be killed by even the champions of this house."

"Tubor might have it so. He wishes to use me if I survive as his newest warrior."

"A good gladiator is profitable but hardly a life of anything but servitude. The people of this island did away with games when the last Western empire fell apart, but the people are roused to embrace these new games."

"So what is it we can do? Can you get me out?"

"I could, but it would serve little purpose. I have spoken with my fellow Rusis, but we cannot stand against the master yet. He has a device that we fear."

"I know something of it. I have seen it around his neck."

"If only it was removed, we could then be free to do as we wish. Otherwise, the device is capable of literally severing the mind of a Rusis."

"A powerful object."

"It is Dwemhar. I have spoken with the one named Brethor. He says he wishes to seek a treasure within the island."

"He had made mention of something before, but I am not too sure of its purpose."

"He says it may help us escape. I will return to the prison and I will make it so that they can be free. It will set the city into a bit of turmoil, but as long as the master thinks I am sick, I can move freely for a time. I will help your friends as long as I can."

Kealin smiled. "Keep yourself well."

Her face appeared for a moment, and her green eyes lit up. "I will." She smiled and then melded out of sight.

9

RELIC

"Orolo, I am telling you the chains cannot be busted no matter what leverage you put on them."

The Srvivnann brothers had spoken to the Rusis hours ago and frankly didn't expect her to return.

"Brethor, if you are fine to lay here and await our forthcoming death, that is all well for you, but I will not."

He continued to attempt to force his way out, and a passing guard looked in on them.

"Do you find your bed less than comfortable?" the guard asked, a laugh in his tone.

"Oh yes, wood and iron are my favorite items in bed," Brethor replied. "Particularly when it is your wife who is with me."

They had been bickering back and forth with this guard the last few hours, and it was amusing considering he did not have a key and could not open up the gate.

"You bastard thieves, if I could, I would destroy you where you are chained!"

"Odd, dear brother." Orolo laughed. "Did his wife not say that too?"

"Indeed she did, but I did not partake in that!"

They both laughed as the guard smacked the gate.

"You can laugh all you want, but I will be smiling in the arena as they separate your arms and legs and you scream in agony!"

On the far end of the corridor, the gate slammed the wall. It was the warden.

"Trouble on the outer walls. We sent men to investigate but keep the door here locked. How fair the prisoners?"

"Remarkably happy."

"Let me assure that this issue is dealt with and we will serve some lashings to them."

There was a pause, and the warden came into view. He looked at Brethor and Orolo and bobbed his head from side to side. "Here." The warden pushed the key to the guard. "Soften them up some before tomorrow."

There was a sudden sound, and a man screamed. The warden shook his head. "I will go see what is going on. I'm sure some guards are just getting too rowdy. Half of them aren't even sober and the other half just see this prison detail as a joke."

As the warden left, the guard locked the hall door and returned to them. He unlocked the cell gate and smiled.

"Your mouths have said much the past few hours. I will make you not so amicable to your situation."

The guard went to a far wall and unhooked a whip.

"Now, now, dear man. Let us not make things uncomfortable," Brethor said.

A moment later, the whip cracked, and he felt the sting from his neck to his lower back. Another crack and it struck again.

"Anymore words you would like to say of my wife?"

Orolo looked over at Brethor's face. He grimaced but had actually cracked a smile.

"Just one. I repeat what she said to me when I held the whip. 'Again.'"

The whip cracked again and struck his back, and then Brethor gasped as the man kicked him in the stomach.

"That will teach you to speak to those above you."

He then turned to Orolo and smacked him once. The whip tore clothing and flesh. Orolo grimaced from the sting.

"Neither of you seem to want to smile much now. Now it will be quiet as I walk by your cell. Good."

There came a clanging sound down the hallway. The guard dropped the whip and drew his sword. He hurried out of the cell and then looked down the hall. A moment later, the Srvivnanns closed their eyes as a bolt of lightning struck him, sending his body flying out of view.

Jesia appeared in the open cell doorway. Her hands were electrified, and small bolts wrapped around her fingers.

"I have come for you, but many come for me."

She went to each of them and opened the latches

holding them down. Brethor stood with difficulty, feeling the lash marks on his back crimp together with broken tissue.

"Thank you, Rusis."

"Please do not thank me until we get you from this place. Subterfuge is our only hope considering the amount of guards in this place."

Orolo went to the charred body of the guard and spit on him. He then bent down and took his dagger and his dropped sword that was a few paces back.

Brethor took the dagger, and the Rusis pointed.

"Let us go."

She led them out of the door and into a hallway. Neither Brethor nor Orolo had seen the way they were brought considering their faces were covered upon arrival at the prison. She led them past multiple charred guards and broken lamps to a splintered doorway. Brethor noticed the warden among the dead. She stepped through the doorway, and they followed into the night air. They were on a rampart leading away from the tower.

A large contingent of guards approached from the opposite way.

Brethor pointed. "This way. I see a stairwell to the ground."

They hurried toward the stairwell, passing by a door that sprung open just as they were happy it was closed. A trio of guards was now right upon them. They took the stairwell, and as they turned to snake down, one of the guards leaped for the Rusis. She rolled down the stairs with the guard wrapped up in her.

Brethor ran to assist when she blew the man away from her with a magic blast. Moments later, two more dropped down, and the contingent that pursued before were quickly catching up.

Orolo parried the thrusting blade of one man as Brethor dropped to knee, driving his dagger into another man's upper leg. Both fell to the ground. Jesia looked up the stairwell and reached out. An arching bolt struck the first group of guards, but then she stopped. She was out of breath.

"I tire. My powers have not been used as such in a long time."

Brethor grabbed her by the arm. "It is fine," he said. "Let us find a way out."

The structure itself was stone ramparts leading out from the tower in either direction with a wooden palisade wall running in a rectangular compound that provided housing and supply areas for the guards. There was a single gateway on the northern edge of the wall that led to a more rural region outside the main Cyr Island urban region.

"This way." Jesia pointed to the north. "The gateway out. There is a horse barn just near there."

They made their way through the rows of small shacks. Many patrols saw them and began to chase after. A bell tolled in the camp, and ahead the wooden gates sealed. A line of guards formed in front of the path.

"We will have to fight them," Orolo said.

As they ran toward the gateway, the Rusis lifted her hand. A thunderclap shook the ground and a bolt flew through the ones guarding the gate, splintering the closed gates. Orolo began to run through the open path when Brethor noticed the Rusis had collapsed. He ran toward her as guards closed in around her. He flung his dagger and reached for the spear of one of the fallen guards.

Orolo noticed his brother fell back but also that there were horses nearby. A small house, occupied by a stable hand, was dark except for a single torch near the door. The horses were kept in a fenced-in area next to the house. There were ropes hanging on a post by the gate. He grabbed them, making quick loops before tossing them over two horses and leading them into the road.

Brethor had struck down multiple guards, and now the main contingent was nearly on him. He scooped up the Rusis and pointed for Orolo to mount. He pushed Jesia on him.

"Ride! To the woods near the bend in the river path that leads to the sea!"

Brethor then mounted his own horse and rode into the stables, pushing the horses out and scattering them. He took a torch from the wall of the house and set fire to it, catching the thatch roof aflame. The guards fanned out as they approached, holding spears toward him. He threw the torch at them.

"This is what happens when you screw with the Srvivnanns!"

He kicked his horse and rode away. The fires from the house lit up the sky in smoke and light, and the other horses scattered, making pursuit nearly impossible.

. . .

Riding into the darkness, they went for the very area he had hoped to have time to go to. It was an old shrine by the river. Veiled in that of fallen trees and dense brush, it was a chance to find a lost object to aid them. He already knew of the fate Kealin faced in the morning. They had some time, and they would use it to complete their original purpose when they came to Cyr so long ago.

He found the river after just over half an hour and slowed his horse as he followed along its banks to a large rocky outcropping. Ahead, he noticed his brother's horse. Orolo had laid Jesia on the ground and placed a piece of river-water-soaked cloth on her head.

"How long will she be out?" Orolo asked.

"She must recover her powers, so I cannot say."

Orolo felt his back. "Lashes."

"I know. We have felt them before, and dare I say we will feel them again."

Beyond a large tree, there was a dark opening between two pillars. The image of a cyclone was set above the door.

"You seek that amulet again?" asked Orolo.

"Yes, we have killed three of those bastard guardians, after that bat. Surely that is enough."

"Kealin helped slay the last one."

"It must be enough, enough for him to give it to us."

"You act as if the god owes us."

"The Dwemhar respected the high ones unlike any of the other cultures. It is why many of them ascended in mind and became of the other realms. It is us who remain who must protect the world and in turn protect those fighting for it."

"Kealin fights for himself for his own goals," said Orolo. "He is not one for the world."

"Nevertheless, we will do what we can to save him. This amulet will help greatly. If he is just of his own goals, he would not have asked the Rusis to check on us. He would have found another way to get free himself."

Orolo was cautious but could see his brother's point.

"Did we make it?" Jesia said in a whisper.

"Yes, and thanks to you."

She gave a small smile and then slowly stood up. "I apologize. My powers weakened suddenly. I am not used to fighting anymore."

"A weakness of being able to cast without a tool, but your powers worked well to stop our enemy."

She sat up and looked around. "We are outside of the city?"

"We are."

"Then I must return to the city."

"Why?" asked Orolo.

"I am supposed to be ill. The master sends one of my fellow Rusis to check on me in the healers' quarters. Upon checking, they will find me missing. I am a known Rusis, and word of the incident at the prison tower will spread. If I am not where an ill person would be, I will have no alibi and my fellow kind will face the wrath of my master."

"Can you not just avoid him?"

"As I explained to Kealin, my master possesses a device that can kill me with a single press of an emblem.

If Kealin takes it from him and destroys it, I can be free. But until then, I must serve him."

Brethor brought a horse to her and helped her mount. She threw her hood over her head.

"Thank you, Rusis. I did not fully realize the danger you helping us put us in. If Kealin knows of how to free you and says he will, I believe he will."

"If he can. His death is to be tomorrow. I hope whatever you have in this place can indeed help him. He will be taken to the arena by midday and will fight at no more than an hour past that time. Good luck."

With that, Jesia rode away in a hurried thundering of her horse's hooves.

Orolo looked to Brethor. "Let us get in there."

They went to the entrance and stepped over a fallen log. The time before, they came with slaves, and an unfortunate amount fell to traps within the temple. As they descended into the main hall, they trudged through water and slick moss, eventually getting to the doorway, which was partially opened. They squeezed through the opening and continued walking down another stairwell that opened up to a large, open room.

Glass crystals, like in the temple at the Swamp House, came to life and lit their path. It had been some time since they were here, but the path was straight. Before, a series of chambers held pieces to the large bridge that spanned the monstrous chasm before them. Here, too, had been a gusty draft, only made still with an offering of Dwemhar blood. The path was bare and open to them. The massive doors of the chamber within were still sealed.

It was etched on these doors the notation of needed tasks that had taken the Srvivnann brothers on such a search for artifacts and temples, which led them to their capture at the Swamp House. Now those tasks had been complete.

The doorway came to life, opening slowly. They entered.

"Well, this trip was much easier than last time," said Orolo.

They went into the chamber, and a burning blue fire shot up like a whirlwind in the distance.

Brethor and Orolo knelt before the fire. A voice spoke from the flames. "What do you seek?"

"Your amulet, sacred god. We have completed the tasks of killing three guardians of Dwemhar treasure."

"Such an act I have noticed, but you come without all who helped you. I sense that another was within the temple to the north, a stranger to your company but not to myself."

"You speak of the half-elf Kealin. He is captured. We seek the amulet to help free him."

The fire surged to a bright white. "The elf of the Urlas Woodlands is a key to many puzzles, some that he has yet to contrive himself. He is who defended my home, for I am Dimn, Lord of Winds, but I am not as I was. You Srvivnanns abandon your abode in the mountains to seek profit, but finally you have a task worthy of Dwemhar blood. Know that the man you seek to help did more for the world than any know, but that also darkness is upon his blood."

A block before them slid to the side, and a golden box floated into the air. It opened, and a surge of wind spread out from it, causing the brothers to stagger.

"This amulet allows the wearer and those bound by hand with said wearer to traverse to places seen by the wearer's eyes. The bats of the wind will take you in their claws, and you will be able to travel great distances. I trust this to you, Brethor and Orolo Srvivnann."

"Thank you," Orolo said.

"We are honored, Dimn."

"Now go," Dimn spoke. "Prepare for the coming daylight and make preparations for your way away from this island."

The fire went dark.

"We will go to the arena and the port," said Brethor. "We will do as Dimn said so we may use his gift."

10

GLADIATORS

Kealin had slept most of the night without issue, but at early dawn, the entire cell block was awoken by the sounds of shouts and bangs on the cells. The legionary guard of the house had come with chains to bind each of them. Two Rusis were with them, but still he saw no sign of Jesia, and the worry crossed his mind of what had happened to her. He hoped she had not been killed in her attempt, but he hoped he would hear something of it soon.

Pushed into the hallway, he joined both Riveaa and Bafnor as they were marched into the courtyard from before. The sun was just rising, casting deep reds and purples into the sky.

The gladiators of the house of Tubor were assembled. A large cart with attached horses was just outside the far gate. As they walked in, the gladiators, in particular, Zibur, stared him down. He was surprised the oaf of a fool was able to stand up so soon after he had knocked him down. They halted near the gateway, and Master Tubor greeted them.

"A wonderful morning to be your last. I thank you for your time in my home and the sport you provided in your preparation for today. They questioned me when I said I wanted you here instead of the prison tower, but it seems an attack befell the prison and prisoners actually escaped. Now they cannot die as easily as you can. It is unfortunate that the one behind it had slipped from grasp, but"—he looked at Kealin—"we found her. She will have the attention one of her power deserves as will she have the end she has earned.

"My Rusis here will join you to the arena to assure you do not disobey. I have reminded them of their place once again." He held up a silver rod, pointing at their faces. "Isn't that right, Rusis?"

"Yes, sir," the one said.

He then pointed toward the other one. She coughed and spit blood.

"Yes, sir."

"You see?" he asked. "All is well within the house of Tubor. I will see all of you wonderful peoples of magic upon the sands."

They were pushed through the gates and into the open doors of the prison carriage. The two Rusis joined them inside and sat on the edge of the seats closest to the door. It was sealed and locked. A crate was then loaded on top of the carriage, and they began to travel down the road.

No one spoke, and the two Rusis stared, unmoving.

"Where is the troll?" Kealin questioned.

"Likely taken by a large horse-drawn cart. It is how they pulled him in," Bafnor replied.

"There are only two of you," Riveaa said to the Rusis. "Where is the other one?"

"Ask the other elf. He sent her to her doom," one of them replied.

Riveaa looked at Kealin. "What does she mean?"

"We are all to die. Jesia sought to free my friends and possibly help the other Rusis escape with us at the game."

"A foolish attempt," Riveaa said. "Foolish to lose her life for such strangers."

"We do not yet know if she is dead."

One of the Rusis let down her hood. "I know something of her fate. I am Muera, and my friend Krea does not feel we should be attempting to help you, but I knew of Jesia's work. However, when I went to check that she was at the house of healers, the legionary guard had already begun to take note of everyone there. It is indeed well known she is a Rusis, and the attack on the prison was obviously not a normal one. She was captured and taken before our master. He beat us, and when Krea spoke out against him, he struck her in the face. She is now blind in one eye."

"A fate shared," said Riveaa.

"We shall all share fate in the end," Kealin said. "That is why we must work together."

"But we Rusis are secure now. If our master senses betrayal, it will not be a rod but sudden death for me and my sisters of Rusis blood."

"I know what device controls you," said Kealin. "I

will attempt to destroy it upon proper chance, but I would beg you not act unless it is destroyed."

"We are with you three and the troll. There is no life beyond this attempt. I know after Jesia, he will not trust us as the same. Even though Krea fears our actions against Tubor, we could be a part of the next games in a month."

"Where is Jesia now?" Kealin asked.

"He has her." Muera said, "And all I can say for sure is that he is a cruel master."

From the bars on the rear of the carriage, Kealin could make out the sea. The orange sunrise was quickly lighting up the rest of the sky in a pale blue. They crossed a bridge and now entered the city through a large gateway. Even though it was early, many people were already moving about. With the games to begin at noon, more people would swell the city from surrounding areas and likely even further away, to view the recently reinstated games, as so the Grand Protectorate called them.

Moving through the city streets, it was obvious that those of magic were set in a negative light. Kealin made out sticks with figures of dwarves, elves, and small gnomes all with angry faces. Orators spoke of the end of magic kind and the profit in seeing them gone. There was even talk that troubles throughout the world were caused by "people different from the common man."

There was much hate in the air. Kealin figured if the people knew of who traveled in the carriage, they would have a riot. He questioned how the world could have changed to be so against them. He thought of five years ago and his mother and father leaving to fight in a war to protect all, but somehow now his kind were evil. Confusion did not describe what he felt.

They descended. He could not tell where they were, but he could feel them shift as the carriage went into darkness. After some time, the road leveled out and he could see the flicker of faint torchlight.

"Whoa," the driver said.

Legionary guards appeared at the back of the carriage, and Krea and Muera exited.

"You Rusis are to go to the upper levels. Your master has ordered you to the primary viewing box to join the others who have arrived. Your master will arrive soon, we hear."

As Kealin and the others exited, they were pushed around the cart and down a long, winding hallway that smelled of mold and rotting meat. The path was dry, but in the open cell doors to either side, there was a lot of debris, and many cells were covered in webs.

They continued walking until they came to a circular room. It was here they entered through a guarded and locked gate to another room that had a large ramp on the opposite side leading upward. A few torches along the walls provided light. Kealin looked behind them. The men carried a chest into the chamber and tossed it onto the ground.

"You have some time before you're needed. When the horns call three times, you will have only a few more moments to assure you are prepared before your sentence is to commence."

Bafnor raised his bound hand. "A sentence would

imply that a crime has been committed. What crime are we guilty of without trial?"

The guard chuckled. "Of being born as you are. Now line the far wall!"

They followed the command.

"Release their bounds."

As one of the men did this, the other guards filed out the door to wait for him to finish. Riveaa was first, followed by Kealin. As his hands were freed, he glanced down at the sheathed sword of his enemy. But then Bafnor was released, taking action as Kealin only thought of. In a quick motion, he drew the sword out, catching the guard by surprise. The dwarf toppled the man and drove the blade into his neck.

Another man entered the room, but Kealin ran forward. He kicked the man in the knee and then drove his fist into his neck twice. He looked up to see the gate shutting and the men nervously attempting to lock it. The man who was speaking before could barely keep his composure.

"You will pay for that! You will not continually harm us, you—you beasts!" The guards backed away, staring at them. Kealin looked back to Bafnor, who looked down, shaking his head.

"I had to try to secure escape."

"I know," said Kealin, "but plans may still be in the works. We have to survive against Tubor's men first. He has already stated that survivors will be given a chance to stay with him as warriors for his own coin. It is at least a forestall of death."

"Is that your plan, then?" Riveaa asked.

"That is when I will strike. I will be no slave, but I offer that you can follow me away from this place."

"Given the alternative, how can we not agree?" Bafnor said.

"Agreed," said Riveaa.

The box they had brought still remained unopened. Kealin went to the latch and opened it. He spotted his blades, tunic, and other belongings. There were other weapons and armor as well. A staff with a blue crystal as well as a large hammer and armor of like design. There were a set of robes as well.

"They return our weapons?" asked Riveaa.

"It seems they do," Kealin replied. He lifted his and his brother's blades and quickly affixed them to him. He found a few small trinkets but was most surprised to find his map.

"A map for treasure?" the dwarf asked.

"Hopefully, but not of the kinds of gold or jewels. I seek my sister." He looked up at Riveaa. "She seeks to be an elf archon."

The elf shook her head. "Tell her to become good with a bow or sword. Magic has many limits."

Both Riveaa and Bafnor collected their belongings and then began to pace around the room. The elf now wore dark blue robes and the dwarf wore the full armor of his people. Kealin looked at his own attire. They were each so very different but had all been put together for such a sullen reason.

"Fighting until death mentioned simply as 'games,'" said Bafnor. "And they call us the animals."

Riveaa sighed. "It does not surprise me in some ways.

There are many who dislike elves and dwarves for the vast wars we have had with common men. The battles became so fierce that blood would not flee the land for some time, poisoning the rivers, and only after a season would plants grow in such places. That was years ago. Though the hate is there, it seemed that we were in a temporary peace."

"My parents fought in those wars," said Kealin. "From the Urlas Woodlands, they went south."

"You are of an Urlas family?" she asked, a peculiar tone in her voice.

"I am."

"Then that explains your swordsmanship and why your parents came to help us of the South. I apologize for my quick judgment of you."

"It isn't necessary, and you are likely right. I do not know their fates, but I expect they fell."

"Many did, but still, many lived as well. I had spoken out of turn before. I feel it is important to rectify that now, at the end."

Some time passed, and a guard brought them food. He knelt down and began to shake, looking up. He looked into the cell with terror.

"Your food," he stuttered before scampering away.

"Why are they scared?" teased Bafnor.

"I do not know. They were confident before," Kealin said. "Perhaps because we have our weapons. Which is surprising now that I give it thought. Do you think you can use your staff against the gate?"

"No, though it surprises me they would know this. My staff must be exposed to either the sun or moon in order to recharge. It would not take long, but as it is right now, it would not work."

"Men read, particularly books of sacrilege as would be any of our people's texts. The master likely studies other arcane arts as well. It does make some sense. To understand your enemy is the best way to defeat them."

They took their food and ate. It was a simple porridge and a poor last meal considering that was the meaning of it. They knew the day was waning from morning to near noon, but without the sun, they could not tell the hour. But a deafening sound had begun to fill the air above them. The crowds had arrived. It would be soon.

"I believe this is worse than battle," Bafnor said. "To await the end so powerlessly. I am driven mad by it."

"It is the point," began Riveaa. "They care little other than our blood to run upon the sand and their support to rise in the region."

"I guess we will see it rise for them," Bafnor moaned.

"So you spoke of your siblings, Kealin," said Riveaa. "Where are they now?"

Kealin cracked his fingers and then rubbed his face. "My brothers are dead. My sister, well, she is lost. I have sought her for many years and will continue to do so. I am without other family, so I see my time best served looking for her."

"No friends in this world?" asked Bafnor.

"One. A whale of the North called a narwhal. A companion for a long time, since the mutual loss of our siblings. Many of her kind fell as well in the dark of the Glacial Seas. As of others like me or you, I have the occasional friendly acquaintance, but all things are temporary."

A horn sounded above them, loud and long, reverberating through the walls. Two more blasts followed in the same fashion. They scampered to their feet. Up the walkway, the door began to open, letting in light from the upper level.

"Now is the time," Kealin said. "Let us fight well together and defeat the gladiators. We must rally our troll friend as well; he may have some chance with us. We must encourage him."

They began up the steep path. Kealin gripped his swords and drew both out as he neared the edge of the passageway. He stepped onto the sands to the crowd's roar which turned to a booing sound as each of them emerged. Rocks flew from above, striking them as insults began.

"Tree sprites and a fat walking rock, as dumb as the gray beast from before!"

"At least one of the bastards is dead."

Kealin wondered for only a moment of what they spoke of. The stands around them formed a large circle. A single large pillar sat in the center of the arena. Chained to the pillar was the troll they had seen back at Tubor's house. The beast had been cut up. His head was disfigured with large sticks. His legs were torn from his torso. But even with these injuries, it still made an intermittent breathing sound. It was unconscious and dying but not yet dead.

A large box sat off from the arena just above the sands but far enough to be safe from striking distance.

Kealin walked with the others to a spot just in front of the arena. Admiral Urui, the man that had captured Kealin before, lifted his hands. The audience's shouting and roaring gradually quieted, and he began to speak.

"People of Cyr, welcome to the Celebration of Cultures!"

There was a slight laugh among those around him. He quieted them with his other hand.

"The Celebration of Cultures is but a taste of events to come. We started with the slaying of a beast by the grand gladiator warriors of the house of Tubor. Whilst his warriors prepare for the grand celebration we present you with, first, the competitors to the gladiators, the sickened races of elf and dwarf, those who have slaughtered hundreds in the wake of sunrise across our vast lands.

"We must unite as one race against the evils and travesty that you see. It is the Grand Protectorate that will unify you, men and women of the lands, against the evils within. The vast legions march in battle against their kind, and we will show you the weakness that is the common elf and dwarf. With your continued support of coin and bodies to fight within the legions, you will see these cursed beasts destroyed!"

A cheer erupted, and Kealin looked at both Bafnor and Riveaa. "Steady yourselves."

"But first," the man speaking before said, "a small word from the master of the gladiators you will soon see again and of the terrible events that struck our prisons last night."

Kealin noticed that Tubor stood to the left side. He

pointed, and a small gateway opened. Legionary guards drug something from the darkness.

"People of Cyr, last night a tragedy befell our men guarding the vile of the regions," Tubor shouted, "A rogue person, another of the cursed races, attacked the prison, causing havoc unlike seen before. The bitch of a creature then tried to act as if she was ill to cover up her deeds, but I daresay I knew her as one of my own, a Rusis by the name of Jesia!"

Kealin's hands gripped his swords tighter as the men dragged Jesia in front of them by just a few paces. She looked over to him with open eyes. They cut her bindings, and she sat up. Kealin went to her and pulled her toward them.

"Are you okay?" he asked.

"I am tired and bruised but well."

"I had thought to end her life," said Tubor. "I control her as a simple dog as the bitch is, but instead I will add to those here, seeing as one must be taken away."

Kealin looked to his side as men came behind Riveaa, ripping her staff from her and dragging her from the line.

"What are you doing?" she screamed.

"This one is part blind," noted Tubor, "an unwilling sacrifice to you, good people of Cyr. Just as the beast before was slain, we shall slay her as unfit to fight."

The men dragged her kicking and shouting toward the same chains where the troll was slayed.

While three men held her, others took chains and ran them around the pillar, locking them to cuffs that were slammed on to her arms. They pulled her body tight against the corpse of the creature, and a man took an ax out.

"Now wait," said Tubor. "I believe your dear lord wishes a special act here."

"The lord of Cyr indeed does."

A man wearing red robes stood up. "People of Cyr, I am gaining age, but my son is fresh in years. At twelve, he has seen much, but he will be the ruling hand for many more years. I would have him finish off the elf."

From the gateway they had dragged Jesia from came a larger contingent of legionary guards mixed in with what Kealin guessed were royal guards by their tall silver helms and differing armor. At their fore came a boy, large for his age with a prideful smile and likely no real skill with a blade. He was obviously pampered beyond reason, and weak, at least as Kealin saw him.

A cheer began again, but it was not for the boy but the arrival of Tubor's gladiators emerging from a passage opposite from the one they had ascended from.

"And who better to witness this but the gladiators of Tubor!" the lord of Cyr shouted. "One of the many houses of fine men to fight in our new games. Know that these are the finest, but we will soon host games against these wretched peoples of magic every month for the glory of the Grand Protectorate."

The gladiators approached, at least thirty-five of them in a large line standing just near the pillar.

Riveaa wept as the boy approached her.

"You are young of years," she said to him. "Do you not know what you do? Are you senseless to this?"

The boy laughed. "The elf calls out in fear, Father. Watch as I give her answer."

He rose the ax, chopping down on her knee in repeated strikes. He then took hold of her leg even as her other one kicked at him. He pulled at it, twisting and tearing her tendons. He jerked but could not free it. He hacked again, and she screamed.

Bafnor was restless. Kealin placed his hand on his shoulder.

The boy at last removed the leg and then, with a shout, lifted it up into the air to the reaction of cheering crowds. He took the ax and slammed it into her upper leg that had not been cut. She wailed and pouted.

"A dagger, Captain," he said to one of the guards.

He took hold of her hair, pulling up as a guard handed him a dagger. Kealin looked at her face, worn from battle, and her own eye sacrificed for those of magic. Her face ran red as the boy began to scalp her, cutting away at her forehead and pulling on her hair until the skin of her head was held up, as was her leg.

The elf was now slouched to one side and not moving. The boy picked up his ax again and, in several swings, hewed her head before tossing it toward Kealin's feet. It rolled after hitting his boot and came to rest against Bafnor's foot. The dwarf shook and boiled with anger.

The boy laughed and began to walk back toward his seat of privilege above the arena. The crowds roared with cheer as if he had just won a great battle, returning in triumph.

Bafnor reached down and picked up the head drip-

ping with warm blood. "They defile us like this," he said
to himself, looking down at the severed head. "No, elf.
You may have been called enemy by me before, but we
die as friends and you will take back what was stolen
from you. One way, or with my ax if necessary if this
fails, he will die."

Bafnor reared back with the skull of the elf and
threw it, just as he would an ax against an enemy,
sending it spiraling toward the boy as he passed. The
skull struck the youth with such a force, his own head
cracked, splattering blood as he collapsed, quivering.

The cheering stopped. Those around the boy
dropped to him and shouted for bandages and a cot. The
royal guards and legionary forces turned and stared at
the three of them. Kealin took a deep breath. He knew
what was coming.

"What are you waiting for?" shouted the lord of Cyr.
"Kill those animals, now! Gladiators, secure your glory in
taking down this evil. For the glory of the Grand Protectorate and all men!"

A roar of cheering reinvigorated the crowd. The
closest men to them began to charge when bolts of electricity struck them, sending them flying backward. Jesia
ran beside Kealin and Bafnor as the warriors slammed
into the royal guards and legionnaires. Bafnor arched a
swing into one man before spinning and cracking
through the legs of multiple others.

Kealin took two guards at once, driving his blade into
their stomachs. A man charged him with an outstretched
sword that Kealin parried before driving his knee into
the man's ribs. He then looked over the men he was

fighting to notice the gladiators had not charged in to fight. They waited a good distance away.

With a blast of more lightning and a few more well-placed thrusts, those of the guards were done. The three of them were winded but all unscathed.

Tubor stood up. "My men are well trained and would not charge in to some blood bath. You will face off as intended and die with glorious defeat. The injury to the lord's son has been fought, and the guards of the city failed. Now, reclaim the honor of the fallen boy and kill these magic wretches."

Kealin looked over the lines of faces. They were helmeted, wearing metal plate armor on their chests, with leather tunics ribbed in metal. Most of them had swords and shields, but a few had spiked clubs, maces, or an ax. He looked over all of them until his eyes locked with Zibur.

He spotted the man, and behind the half-covering metal mask, he saw the man smile, his teeth showing.

"Begin!" Tubor shouted.

Jesia fired a single bolt that flew into the far side, throwing back two guards as Bafnor charged in with outstretched ax. Kealin ran to the right. Using the body of the troll creature, he ascended before jumping down with swinging blades, cutting down four of the men. He was closer to Zibur but not to him yet. Kealin took stance and parried multiple jabs aimed for his stomach and then ducked as a blade flew near his neck. He thrust behind him and to his side, catching two more of the men. He pulled his blades out with a spray of blood.

Zibur came upon him swinging massive blades,

wielding two, just as Kealin did. Kealin sidestepped to avoid, and the blades shocked upon the ground, sending up a plume of dust. Kealin sprinted back his way, leaping up and slapping the open spot of his shoulder with the edge of his blade. It was a less than preferred strike, but the man had turned to the dwarf that was nearly on him.

Jesia had moved to using a broken spear with one hand and the occasional shocking touch, considering the conductive armor the men used. At least fifteen of the gladiators had fallen. Kealin had reengaged with Zibur. The brute of a man rushed him with an impressive rapid thrust of his blades, forcing the elf into a repeated parry exchange, leaving little room for attack.

From the far side, a blast of lightning exploded to the man's side and a spear cut into him a moment later. The Rusis had landed a strike. Jesia shouted, pointing to Kealin, but then a blade cut across her back, sending blood into the air.

Kealin turned to see two men with spears about to stab him. He parried both, catching the one on the left with a kick to the knee. The man fell to the ground before both the elvish blades cut into his neck. The other man yelled and stabbed at him just for his spear to deflect over Kealin's right blade and his ribcage to take the length of the left blade. He too was dead now.

Jesia was on the ground, covered in blood. Kealin looked up to the balcony where the slave master and other vile men sat. In the background, he noticed Krea and Muera. Even at a distance, he could see their distraught.

"Taste the ax of the dwarves!" Bafnor jeered. The dwarf struck two more men when an ax blow cut through his armor and tore a chunk out of his arm. He turned. In a fury, he swung his ax, driving it into the man who struck him, just to take a spear to the knee.

Kealin ran to his aid, but Zibur went for him again. The man laughed "Soon, you will taste that of sand and blood."

A cry rang out, and Bafnor wailed from repeated strikes to his neck. A moment later, his head was held into the air with a roar of applause and cheering from the crowd. Kealin remained alone.

He gave no time for any further words from Zibur. He focused his mind. The lifetime of men-in-training within the Urlas Woodlands had prepared him for such a task, but these men were not of sand like who he trained against. Their flesh ran red, and the smell of their death was thick in the air. He ran forward, leaping into the air. The beast of a man he attacked lifted his blades up to parry, but he was not going to strike. The half-elf brought one blade up to lock up Zibur's crossed blades while he dropped to his knees, driving his other blade into the abdomen of the defender. In a swift kick, he knocked Zibur to the ground. He then turned, moving from man to man who had lost the mental drive seeing their champion bleed upon the ground. When at last he had made it to the last one, he turned to find none remained. The crowd cheered. Zibur had made it to his knees but struggled to stand. Kealin looked up at those observing, the opulent rulers of Cyr.

11

EH-RIN

"Who now comes against me?"

The crowds roared. This was not the intent of those present, but thinking of what Tubor had said, this was a possibility to be expected. Tubor wanted Kealin as his own.

Tubor was standing and clapping but not to the approval of the lord of Tyr, the man whose son had been mortally injured only minutes before. The lord stood and made a signal to a guard standing near the gates. Kealin noticed the guard went through the main gates and disappeared.

From the metal gateway used by all coming from the podium emerged Tubor, as well as the two remaining Rusis girls and an accompaniment of guards. Kealin walked away from them, going to Jesia, who was covered in blood but breathing.

"Kealin! Proud warrior! You would fight well for the glory of the Grand Protectorate!" Tubor began to look around, attempting to quiet the crowd. "He has fought well. How would you like such a man to fight for the glory of you and the island of Cyr? A reborn elf of old, a man against that which he came."

"I did not agree to anything of this nature."

"You want to live," Tubor replied plainly. "Life equals servitude as a gladiator of my house, to train many others to be like you and to fight for my glory."

The guard from before that was sent away by the lord of Cyr returned with a host of royal guards who swarmed the arena grounds in a large swathe. Around the edge of the stands, archers appeared with bows drawn.

"This man does not deserve life but death, as was the intent," the lord of Cyr announced. "He must die."

"He is a proud warrior of the elven race," the Admiral boasted, "Perhaps he can understand reason and sanity when faced with death."

"Thank you, Admiral. Great lord of Cyr, have pause. He would fight for us. He did not kill your son. That was done by the dwarf who now has no head. Let him give us his answer and we will decide."

Kealin looked down. This was not an attempt for any except to draw his target closer. Tubor wore the necklace that held his Rusis hostage. Kealin would not go as a slave to a man into a life of pointless killing. The Rusis were powerful, and at this point, he was thinking in moments only a step ahead. If he was to fall to these circumstances, it would be in forward motion toward his enemy. The gateway from which they had come was built up, making it possible for one to climb if of considerable skill. He could make it up and out of the arena, hopefully taking the Rusis with him. But he could not simply leave Jesia. He was confused by his own decisions; he did not need to let any person distract him from his task.

But so far, his plan was working. His target had fallen to a simple show of emotion, false emotion.

Tubor placed his hand on Kealin's shoulder. "I know your hurt and the bloodshed before you, but know that it is only the beginning of blood spilled. You will forget this and all that troubles you, in the glow of your glory."

Kealin smiled. "You are right about but one thing."

Tubor smiled at him and patted his shoulder. "So you agree?"

"Bloodshed."

The half-elf brought his blades up, cutting through the lower portion of his robes, lacerating his stomach, and cutting up into the side of his neck, cutting the necklace off from around his neck. As warm blood squirted over him, Tubor fell to the ground. Kealin stabbed a blade into the device that could kill the Rusis and looked up to a shroud of blackness descending downward toward him.

Krea and Muera moved to his side, conjuring large walls of ice with their powers as arrows flew toward them. He took hold of Jesia and turned to see the massive Zibur billowing toward them. Jesia, though weakened, raised her hand, and a bolt of electricity struck him in the head. He stumbled backward.

Bats surrounded them, and then both Brethor and

Orolo appeared. Around Brethor's neck was an amulet glowing brightly.

"Grab one another," Brethor shouted.

The Rusis and Kealin took hold of Orolo and Brethor. As the guards came nearly to striking range, Brethor closed his eyes and the swarm of bats gripped them and they flew into the sky, rising high above the arena and the city. Kealin felt the tiny bats grip him tighter as he looked over, relieved to see the sea again. They flew over the edge of the island, heading south and leaving the horror behind. He noticed a lone ship on the waters. They floated downward to the deck, and the bats released them.

Kealin landed on his feet but then fell to his knees in exhaustion. He had survived the arena of Cyr.

HE COULD SMELL THE SEA, and not a better smell had it been to him ever before. He still worked to catch his breath, and the blood thick on his arms was not making him feel any better.

"Kealin, we came as soon as we were able," Brethor said. "We were lucky to have found a crew to take us, but it is amazing what mentioning of a severe disdain for the Grand Protectorate can do when you know you are looking at people from the Dashrin coast."

Kealin forced himself to sit up. "And what does a man of the Dashrin coast look like?"

He looked around the ship, noticing many men wearing bright white robes and strange wrappings around their heads. The men had skin that was dark just like Tubor. A man standing near the helm of the ship took notice of him and walked toward. He had a large jewel affixed to the front of his head and a curved silver sword at his belt. It too had jewels and as he walked closer, Kealin saw that his hands had rings of gold.

"You are well, then, half-elf of the North?" he asked.

"Beaten well but not dead."

The man looked over to a cot where Kealin noticed Muera and Krea stood above Jesia. One of the ship's men tended to her injury.

"You did better than her, but we have some of the best physicians in the lands. She will be well taken care of. Your friends here did more than pay us but also spoke of the gods, whom we revere beyond that of the heathen Grand Protectorate. They too mention of old races and their knowledge of such. A fine conversation that my sultan, Amhe, will have interest in."

"So you are friendly to those of magic, as we are deemed by those within Cyr?"

"We have few allies in these lands, but we need not friends other than those of your kind. We remember the old ways, and well, the sands tell us of other evils that we fear as of late, but of now we will not speak of such. I am captain of this vessel, but within the Eh-Rin Navy, I am an admiral. My name is Dala."

"Dala, I thank you for your kindness," Kealin told him, "but why does an admiral go on an obvious trading ship?"

"A great many enjoy an herb we grow in our region. It fetches great gold in the markets at Cyr, but it is not financial gain we seek but spying upon our enemy. That being as it is, the Drean have encroached on our coasts and are a separate issue altogether, particularly with their alliance with the Grand Protectorate. We have many enemies."

"Captain, first sun stone off the deck. Signal light forward."

"Aye, signal light. Let them know we are coming."

Brethor helped Kealin to his feet, as from the front of the ship, a crystal spun wildly on a pedestal, sending sparks toward a stone sitting in the water. The stone began to glow and shot a burst of light from the top of it to another stone further away. It appeared this continued on, but it was difficult to see.

"Signal stones that advise our approach to the port. We are still well out, but in the event it was our enemy, no said light would be sent and the stones would vibrate with a tone that we have the ability to hear from our port. It is an early warning system of a technical nature but a relic to the Dwemhar culture of the past. We have kept much alive from them, and you may be surprised, but at night we have light without the use of torch."

"Magic?" Kealin asked.

"Not at all." Dala bowed to him. "I must return to my duties for now. I leave you to your friend. We will make port in time."

Orolo had been below deck and emerged eating a bowl of berries.

"Good, Kealin, I am happy to see you."

"Was prison good, considering you and your brother here cannot stay out of such places?"

"Ha," Brethor replied. "We did quite well. A few lashings, but your friend Jesia worked well to get us out. We only wish she would had not suffered as she did. I did not count the bodies, but it seemed for you, an elf, a dwarf, and a troll, you killed quite a few."

"More so important if you realized they killed the troll and the elf without a fight before the match began. Jesia was put in the arena to fight with us and made a strike on the champion of the gladiators before she was cut down. I killed a few but frankly did not expect to escape."

Brethor pulled his necklace up. "This was the treasure we sought in the city and the reason for our travels to other temples. You helped in slaying one of the Dwemhar guardians, creatures meant to assure none of the sacred items fell to those undeserving and of lesser blood. This is an amulet of the god Dimn." Brethor paused. "A god who has a liking of you and knowledge of your deeds before now."

"It is clear we both have secrets." Kealin laughed.

"True, but ours was treasure seeking and guardian killing. The gods do not know our name like you."

"My siblings are who should be remembered by the gods, not myself. But I do know Dimn, the wind god of the Glacial Seas. My family's blood stains his temple that we defended against an old evil. It is how I lost those dear to me."

Brethor could tell Kealin was greatly saddened.

"I did not mean to pry, but I am honored to stand beside you. My brother and I wish to help you if we can."

"Yes," Orolo added. "We have spent too much time doing our own thing, for lack of a good word to say. I would like much to have purpose. Perhaps then I can convince my brother to return to our family."

Kealin nodded. "I am not sure you should follow me. The evil I deal with is beyond this world."

"Coastline!" one of the men shouted.

The three of them looked across the water to see a golden shine reaching as far as they could see. The Dashrin coasts were barren dune lands as far as could be seen, with the only mountains visible to the far south and away from where they were to make port.

Dala walked back toward them. "We are crossing into protected waters. I do not want you to worry as of now."

He pointed to a series of large stones that seemed to line up along the edge of the coast. Atop them were strange black stones that rose with four sides into the sky, coming to a point capped in gold.

"The obelisks take in the power of the sun, providing beacons of light at night, marking the coast as well as keeping those without the crystal on the front of the ship from passing. If it senses a ship of any other kind, it can burn it from the waters."

"Amazing," Brethor said "I have seen something of similar work in the Far North, but it is of Dwarven design. I can see how even without any friends you can do so well alone."

"None can compare to us with our sciences and astrology. The Drean come close with their ships, but they are still sub-par. We are the closest to a society of happiness as you can reach."

Their sailing continued through the day and into early evening. As the sun began to set, turning the sky to a hue of orange and red, Kealin noticed a faint light upon the dunes ahead as well as a large light in the darkening sky to the east. The obelisks turned toward the coast, and a large wall with torches atop it was ahead. They spotted a massive port gate that was opening to their vessel's arrival. To the left of the gateway was a large island of rock with a tower atop it, and as they came closer to the port, it was obvious that the glowing light in the sky was a massive lighthouse. Square at the base, it was circular going upward to the top, which was crowned with a massive glowing blue crystal. Off the edge of the lighthouse seemed to be another structure, like the keep of a fortress but with a large dome top.

"The depository of ancient knowledge guarded by the Sanguine monks, a source of much information but only accessible by those trusted by the sultan and the grandmaster of the monk order."

"I will have to apply for admittance," joked Brethor. "I would like to see such a place."

"Good luck with that endeavor. I am a trusted admiral and spy, and I have not even set eyes upon its interior."

They passed through the gateway and into a massive port. The masts of ships had to equal over fifty, and that was just what they could make out. There was a large dock that the ship came alongside. Deckhands and dock workers moved quickly to secure the ship. They extended a walkway and disembarked.

"You will go with me to the palace to meet the sultan. He will wish to know why you are here, of course, but he is a good ruler and will be kind."

"Thank you," said Kealin. "We have not been shown kindness such as this before now. I must ask, though, what of the injured Rusis? Where shall she be taken?"

"She will be taken to the sages of healing, and it is no problem, friend. We of Eh-Rin value knowledge and unity with those of like heart. You will have good allies here if you are not a friend of our enemies. You being elf, and well, you three being of higher descendants, you are who we call friend."

A cart was awaiting them as they made it to the edge of the docks. The city walls were massive and veiled the buildings of the city beyond. They boarded the cart and were taken through a gateway down a stone brick road. The city was made up of square buildings of stone smoothed by the desert sands and dust storms that frequented the region. They took a large road to an even grander roadway that would have fit at least eight carts side by side without issue. In the center of the road were more obelisks, each glowing like soft torch fire near the top.

"I presume those can be lethal as well?" asked Brethor.

"Indeed," Dala replied.

They began up the hill to a large structure with towers that had large domes near the top that glowed a soft blue, much like that of the lighthouse. It was the palace of Eh-Rin.

"Such is the home of the sultan and it's a grand place. The palace itself is built upon the foundations of a sacred mountain of old. Know that there are many inns within the city for travelers, but not often do we get those as yourselves. I believe you will call the palace home for the night, but I am not the sultan, so I will not say for sure."

They eventually came to another gateway. This one was made of blue stone decorated with the relief of a sun and its many rays shining down upon what looked as a copy of the palace. Upon the guards checking the cart, they were allowed passage and proceeded in.

Going down a now smooth road unlike the bumpy one before, they passed through a grand garden. A literal oasis in the desert with gazebos and flowing rivers that fed the many flowers and bushes along the road and across the green grasses just visible in the pale light of night. More of the obelisk lined this way, but they were also more ornate with gold lining their bases.

They came to a circular path that went around a white polished stone fountain that showed the image of an elephant with its trunk reaching to the sky. A large stairwell was before them.

"This way," said Dala.

They ascended many steps, coming to flat open levels that had guards on either side. The guards were garbed in white with black sashes and held long spiked staffs. They ascended two more platforms identical to the first and then at last came to a flat level with columns going off in either direction. Two silver doors were before them and closed. As the admiral led them further, the guards opened them and they entered the palace.

Kealin had never seen such a place as this. The pillars from outside continued inside, but now they walked on a blue and gold patterned rug that ran from the doorway down lines of columns to a large open room. The image of a large hanging sun set above the throne to their left. They stopped before it as a servant came to the admiral. They shared words, and then the servant departed. In a few moments, he returned and bowed before them.

"Grand visitors to the exalted Sultan Amhe, you are invited to share in dinner with the sultan. But, you must surrender your weapons here. They will be cleaned and returned to you."

Brethor and Orolo immediately complied, but Kealin was less than happy with the arrangement.

"I would prefer that we do not end up in prison here," said Brethor. "Trust that we have been treated well so far, Kealin."

What Brethor did not understand was that Kealin did not do well with surrendering weapons, and he knew that outside his homeland, he should never be without a blade.

Brethor noticed that the admiral and the servant stared at Kealin. "Seriously, friend, they will care for them well."

"If you have an issue with this, the sultan will not be insulted if you do not comply, only understand it is our custom," said Dala.

Kealin nodded. "You have been good to us so I will trust you."

He took his two swords and laid them with the others.

"It is well you have faith. Now," said Dala, "let us join the sultan."

They passed through a doorway that led to a grand table with many chairs. At the far end sat a man with a hat much like that of the admiral but larger. It had two feathers of a dark red with yellow ends. The admiral led them before the Sultan and bowed. They followed suit.

"Sultan Amhe, I was approached in the port island of Cyr by these two brothers. Their names are Brethor and Orolo Srvivnann, Dwemhar descendants that hail from the Far North. They had fallen to uncertain circumstances, as did their friend Kealin the half-elf, also Dwemhar from the Glacial Seas of the North. It is he who sought these lands with the Srvivnann brothers.

"I offered to bring them here, and they have been thankful of the gracious offering. I bring them to you to meet, and I feel you will enjoy each other's company for a time."

Kealin still was in a bow, as was Brethor and Orolo.

The sultan stood from his food. He approached them, holding a large silver rod with a crystal at its far end. He lifted it over each of them, where it began to glow before dimming slightly. He passed it over Orolo and then Brethor until finally reaching Kealin. The crystal became noticeably brighter. The sultan stared at him for a moment and then closed his eyes before bowing slightly.

"Welcome to Eh-Rin," the sultan said at last. "I am Amhe, ruler of these coasts and seas, and I deem you are what you claim. We revere the Dwemhar as the path to transcendence, and to have you here is indeed an honor. Now, please sit with me and eat."

The strange exchange became a simple dinner of exquisite tastes. There were oysters, different stews of fish, and a large cut of a strange toothed creature with a dark body. Pomegranates, a new fruit for Kealin, as well as figs and nuts and a bottle of wine were also served.

"Tell me," Amhe began, "what condition were you in when Admiral Dala found you? What reason do you have for coming to this shore?"

Brethor answered, "We sought an ally to rescue our friend here, Kealin. He was sentenced to die in the arena on Cyr. I had already secured a way to get him from the arena to safety but had to assure that safety giving our circumstance."

Brethor showed the amulet of Dimn to Amhe.

Amhe gasped. "Is this indeed the amulet used to summon the swarm of bats to move from one place to another?"

"It is," Brethor said. "I found your man at the port in a debate with a seller over goods. There was mention of the seller saying he was wasting time and how he wished to see the magic people killed, and your man had a face of disgust. I figured he would be a man to speak to in order to find safe travel. Once we freed Kealin, we traveled with the amulet to the deck of his ship and now we are here. I will leave Kealin to tell you of his purpose."

Kealin looked to Amhe. "I search for a man. An old

man. One who holds the power to find those lost, to find those of blood relation. My sister was lost to me, and I seek her."

Amhe nodded and poured himself more wine.

"The man you seek is in the distant east. A hermit near the mountains who has no known relatives or family. There have been some to question if the man is a man at all, others claim he is a sorcerer of old, but that is not for me to discuss. However, traveling there at the moment is not possible. There is a great storm to the east, and it has been as such for many days."

"Storms will pass," Kealin said.

"Indeed, in time. But this storm has been one of uncertain origin. It has not moved, and there is talk of strange dark creatures on the edge of the storm."

"Creatures of what kind?"

"None we have seen before, except in books. They have been called elf demons, lovers of mud and grime, the opposite of what we have here within the city and an unwelcome entity if its purpose is what we feel."

"You mean an orc," Kealin suggested. "Do you really think it an orc?"

"The term you use is harsher than a Dwemhar might say."

"I am elven too, and there is no better word for such a defeated race."

"There has been a growing darkness in the mountains to the far east, a rumored witch and the man of shadow with her. A great warrior, they say. We had begun to wonder of why such was happening, but with your arrival, we have hope. If you look around, we have done much to honor the Dwemhar. It can only be fate that you come here now."

"Not fate," Kealin said, "necessity for a purpose of my own. I know little of Dwemhar other than the name and a bit of history. I am an elf to my own dealings."

"Such may be true, but the gods work with whispers and shadows. What purpose you desire and the one you are to work can be different. But enough of this for the night. It is early, but I bid you three rest. With the rising sun, I will see you tended to further and we may discuss plans."

A trio of servants appeared.

"See these three to baths and beds of comfort."

Kealin stood with Brethor and Orolo. The meal was good, but his mind had begun to race. As they walked past the sultan, he bowed.

"May we unite ourselves with the will of the Dwemhar."

Kealin was not sure what to make of the report of the arrival of orcs. It had been at least two thousand years since the orc wars. A product of magic as wizards of the Far South unified with the death summoners of necromancy. They were elves, darkened with the malice of death reborn, under the life of their masters, with the stench of a corpse and the tribal mindset of mere but deadly war mongering.

They had some intelligence and were not as wraiths or those of walking corpses, but were an enemy relentless on the spread of destruction. It had taken many ages of fighting to at least turn the waves back into the earth. It was a grand day when all of the orcs were destroyed along with their masters. If the orcs had been reborn, it was a powerful witch to have summoned them again.

They were taken down grand halls with ceilings that rose many times over their heads. At a junction, they were each taken to slightly different rooms, obviously split for privacy, as separate pools of water steamed from warming sources far below.

Kealin noticed the room was scented with burning incense and had the ambiance of flickering lamps. Obviously added for that purpose due to the crystal lighting everywhere else. His attendant stood near the entrance.

"Was there something else?" Kealin asked.

"I am ready to tend to any need that may arise."

Kealin looked at her. "You can go."

She bowed and departed.

He disrobed and entered the warm waters. He had never been in such a bath except for the natural springs of his own homeland. There were many times after a vigorous training session with his brothers they would wander off and find one of the springs. He thought of home and how long he had been from the Urlas Woodlands. But returning now would only serve to worsen the pain of memories he barely kept down as it was.

He had felt increasingly worse about the ordeal as time went on. As every man, woman, or creature he fought fell dead, he felt more alienated from who he was. The mind powers he had before had become almost like a treasure beyond a walled obstacle. He could feel their presence in his mind, but that was it.

Kealin lay in the waters for some time before standing up and ascending back to a towel folded on a nearby bench. He wrapped the towel around him and then noticed a robe. He left the bathroom garbed in a white robe, holding in his arms the armor and clothing that for the longest time was the only clothing he had.

His servant had waited for him at the end of his hall. He was taken to another room where Brethor stood with a mug of hot beverage. He handed Kealin one as he entered.

"A warm bath. I must say I feel quite well and have not felt as this in some time," Brethor said,

Kealin took a drink. It had a feeling of a heavy mouthful and tasted slightly bitter.

"Coffee," Brethor told him. "I am told it is a treat of these regions. Found when a troll would not stay out of a man's garden and kept eating the red cherries from which they get such a drink."

Kealin took another sip. "It is good. A different-tasting beverage."

"Of many different happenings," Orolo said. "Did you two get the massage as well?"

"No, dear brother, I did not."

"Nor did I," said Kealin.

Orolo took the remaining mug on a nearby table. "Well, then you missed out. Did your servant not offer any service?"

"Yes, but that does not mean you must take it," Brethor told him. "I find it strange we are welcomed as such."

"After I turn in my blades, you have such a finding?" Kealin asked.

"I still do not feel we are meant harm, but friends such as this do not exist."

"And cities like this do not exist elsewhere. Even our home is not such a place."

"You speak much of your home but not where it is," said Kealin.

Brethor finished his coffee and then went to a chair. There was a large fire burning on the side of the room directly next to a nook with shelves of books and other oddities. Orolo and Kealin joined him near the fire.

"Our home is in the Far North, not so far as your Glacial Seas," he said to Kealin, "but far enough that it is secretive within the mountains. It was originally just a home of snow dwarves, but there is whisper of an evil growing in the South, and men have become increasingly violent against elves and dwarves. Our family has taken charge of an estate and city that will serve as a refuge in the coming travesties. A place of safety for all of magic."

"Do you not feel their own homelands safe enough?" asked Kealin.

"For the time, yes, but the evil of the Itsu is unending. Some feel that the inner workings of the Grand Protectorate has begun to fall to such an influence. But my family has no place except for that which we guard. The city is called Elinathrond and is a welcome place for all like us. Even you could come with us. If the war drew closer to the city, you would be free to fight as you wish to protect the city."

Kealin shook his head. "My place is upon the sea, not

in a walled city, but I am happy you would invite me. I will find my sister and then we will return to our home."

"Home," said Orolo. "A novel idea of returning to."

"In time, dear brother. We will return, but for now it is not necessary. We will help Kealin."

"I wish you to not."

"We have already spoke of this. We will follow your footsteps wherever they go. We Dwemhar blooded must remain together."

Kealin nodded. "If you insist, I will not stop you, but I cannot be sure of the path once I speak with the man who holds the ability to find my sister."

"To the journey, then, and what comes!" Orolo said, lifting his mug.

Kealin lifted his mug as well. He felt fortunate to have such companions.

SECRETS OF SANDS

The night had passed with little event. Kealin was led to a room with an open balcony that looked out over the city. There was a chilled breeze upon the air, and his bed was made of plump linens and the scent of jasmine. With the morning sun painting the sky a red hue, he arose and went to the railings, looking out over Eh-Rin.

He could hear reveled, almost lyrical, shouting over the city that he could just barely make out. It spoke of Dimn and Etha. It was a prayer of some kind being that Dimn was known as the god of the wind, and Etha, the god of the elves. He had not heard them worshiped like this in any point in his travels. He listened until he heard a knock at the door.

Opening it, he was met by a servant with a cup of coffee and a note.

. . .

WHEN YOU ARE DRESSED and well, meet me down below near the throne room. You will hear music. Come speak to me.

Amhe

A PERSONALIZED MESSAGE from the sultan was not something he expected. He had little to gather or prepare, so with his cup in hand, he began back to the throne room.

He did not see Brethor or Orolo but saw many servants attending hanging plants and gardens, decorating the stretch of ground before the throne. Early morning light from above gave life to the plants, and oil lamps filled the halls with scents he could not describe. He could hear the sound of music and walked toward its source.

He walked through a large arched opening into a room filled with men and women meditating around a large platform covered in pillows. The sultan was playing a soft melody, walking around those meditating. In the corners of the room, men stood blowing into flutes but holding the same tone.

The sultan looked up.

"The resonance of the mind is one of melody and tone."

"You had asked me to join you," Kealin said.

"I did, for I sense there is more to you than is obvious. You have a sense about you and one that even one of much power in the city has felt, but before him, I wish to speak with you in private."

The sultan made a gesture toward a closed doorway. Kealin nodded. Amhe led him through the doors onto a balcony overlooking the vast dunes of the desert. The sun was rising still, and the sky was beginning to turn from a deep to light blue. There were two chairs sitting next to a table. A strange object set in the center. It appeared to have glass at the bottom filled with water and a cylindrical metal tube that rose above it. What looked like tubular ropes came off it near the top.

"Please sit," the sultan said.

Kealin sat down on the chair as the sultan did the same. Amhe picked up one of the tubes and put it to his lips. He was smoking but not in a way Kealin had seen before.

"I invite you to try."

Kealin picked up the pipe. It was metal and intricately carved. Small effigies of sea birds were set in gold with a red jewel to the center. He drew in the smoke. It was stronger than he expected but smooth. He felt the sapping tinge to the smoke and exhaled.

"Do you like it?"

Kealin nodded. "It is different than I am used to, but I do not smoke much. I find it distracts the mind."

Amhe drew again on the pipe and exhaled. "Yes, and that is what I wish to speak of. What do you think of our city and port?"

"It appears advanced and beyond that of the rest of the lands. I have traveled over many seas and been to many ports and have not seen many of this size. Your obelisks are something I have never seen."

"They were here before us but covered in rock. The

Dwemhar covered many items with stone, so you may see a mesa in the desert and dig to find it is actually a temple. Nothing is as it seems. The island Cyr was actually a newer construction compared to what is in the deserts. But that is not the true treasure. The knowledge troves we have found, the stone books and those of metals are repositories of knowledge, and then the sacraments, the holiest of objects, are the last of the ancient civilization. Your people."

"I am afraid you confuse my lineage. I am of elf and only part Dwemhar. These powers I have are of Dwemhar origin, but—"

"You are Dwemhar and of a not diluted quality as many but half elf and half Dwemhar, an odd combination but one of significance and purity that is rare. Tell me, how long have you been able to use your powers?"

"For a short time, and only near the gods of the North. My mind has been shrouded since . . . well, for a while now."

Amhe nodded. "You are troubled. I wish for you, if willing to do something. I feel you should meet with someone. Your friends are not worthy, but you are what we have waited for and the time has come."

"I am a simple elf," Kealin said. "A man of blade and desire for revenge and that which was taken from me."

"And you seek a man of the desert, a man who can bend thought to your own blood?"

"Yes."

"Then embrace what I wish to have you do, and it will be so. The storms have lessened, but we have word that our villages were attacked. I will be sending my forces that way as the clouds recede, but I ask you, talk with whom I wish and learn. You are the key to a greater puzzle."

Kealin had no understanding of what Amhe spoke, but he would flatter him. Amhe stood and beckoned Kealin to follow him to a far wall. The sultan touched a stone and pressed it in. A stone panel appeared with multiple symbols. Amhe pressed them in a certain order, and the stone wall vanished, leaving a passageway.

"Go down this path, and when you get to the doorway, press your hand against it."

Kealin nodded.

"I will tend to your friends and entertain with stories for lesser minds. Do not worry of them."

Kealin began to walk, and as he did, the path behind him began to vanish. Ahead, he could see light from open windows and, walking past, noticed he was suspended in the air beyond that of a simple bridge. The city and the port were far below him. He continued walking until he reached a blue door. Upon the door were the inscriptions similar to the panel before and the ruins in Cyr and in the Swamp House temple. He pressed his hand against the door as instructed, and it cracked open. He entered.

As he walked through, he found himself in a large atrium. There were books on shelves that reached high up a great distance farther than any man could reach. A large stairwell was a few feet from him, and a door opened on the far end of the hall.

From the dark room came a procession of hooded men wearing deep red full-body cloaks. They wore silver necklaces and walked with a slight chant to their voices. He could not make out the words, but they paid no mind to him as he passed. He went to the stairwell and began up when a voice spoke behind him.

"Kealin of Urlas, you have traveled a great distance."

He turned to see a man with a pale face. His hair was gray and hung down straight. He had a large pointy beard and in his right hand was a silver staff. A crystal on it glowed blue, and as the man walked toward him, Kealin noticed his eyes were a bright blue.

There was a hum in the air, noticeable more as the man approached him.

"I am Kealin," he said, "elf from Urlas seeking my sister lost to me."

"You fought the evil ones, defended the great shrine of wind?"

"How do you know of that?"

"We are the Sanguine, purveyor of pure thoughts, actions, and wisdoms of such to come. The blood of the lost cleanse our robes, and we are free of the burden of the world. I am one with old powers and have foreseen such acts. Come, let us speak in more comfortable settings."

The monk walked past him and began up the stairwell in silence. Kealin followed, and the wrapping path took them high above the many books. The way was open, and Kealin looked out, able to see over many walls to a large gathering of monks in a massive room surrounded by windows looking out to the ocean. They continued up until they came to an open room, circular, with a central pillar and a massive crystal. There was a large carpet with simple pillows surrounding it. The monk went to a pillow and sat. Kealin followed suit.

"I am the Grandmaster, and if you were sent to me so soon, it is true what I have felt."

"I do not know what you have felt, but I came upon bidding of the sultan. I have traveled far to seek out the location of my lost sister. I had no intent of further issues upon anyone."

"Your sister was cast into the winds and lost five years ago. You moved with a creature of Meredaas, searching for clues of her to no avail until you caught a hint of a man to the south and hurried here, and that is why you have come?"

"Yes."

"So seeking one of blood upon the ocean's current, you moved from lands of ice to burning desert and seek the man of spoken mysteries finding Eh-Rin, the jewel of the Dashrin coasts. A war-blade that stood against the evils of the Itsu. Kealin, you are a man of prophecy. A coming darkness will see your blades thirsting and your mind unlocked, a Dwemhar warrior of renown but half-elf feared by all."

"I hear your words but know not how they help me. I heard such whispers of prophecy in the North but have put it from mind. I do not know how I can be a part of any prophecy. First it was the Glacial Seas, and now this?"

"You are of the Dwemhar," he began. "It is what your people did. They foretold and were foretold upon. Some came to pass for good and others for darkness. It is the true disadvantage of foresight and knowledge; you know and yet you can do everything as well as nothing to prevent a forsaken future."

"I do not understand," Kealin said to him. He walked toward the Grandmaster. "I cannot see any future prophecy or foretell anything."

"It is a good fact that you are of the elves too, Kealin."

The Grandmaster lifted his hand to signal Kealin to stop. The half-elf shook his head.

"I don't care of elves, Dwemhar prophecies, or any other task but saving the last of my family, Alri, my sister. Everything else is nothing but whispers of distraction."

"It is in the whispers, Kealin, that you must listen the most carefully. Now close your eyes."

"What good is that? If you wish me to meditate, you must—"

The room darkened, and the monk began to glow a deep blue. "You do not know all!" the monk bellowed. "Some secrets were made so not to be awakened, but you have opened up an old power! Calm now and do as I ask!"

Kealin closed his eyes and felt the room still and a slight hum return to the air.

"All in balance," the monk said, returning to his calmer demeanor.

The monk began to hum, and from his closed eyes, Kealin began to feel a tinge atop his skin, the voice of the monk moving over him. He felt sadness and anger but then happiness and elation; his mind felt as if it was being pulled in many directions. He then felt himself floating, and he opened his eyes but saw only the sea.

"From the creation of the world, there has been that of the soul, an ever-giving life force bound to the bodies of the earthly by the mind and is lost to so many. The Dwemhar ascended from the plane of life, through that of the ethereal gods, to that of one above all. A power tapped by some that are trained and by others by the blood pumping through their veins. The power to create and destroy. To see before happenings.

"Such says the prophecy:

When comes the one from the Far North with eye on love and strength of an eternal race, said darkness rising shall gain foothold in the world, and by the hand of such a spirit shall come both the end and the beginning of the world.

"Such completeness is the prophecy in you. With your sadness will come pain and from pain will come sadness. You will not know peace without war and your spirit will remain strong as your connection to that you love. But I fear with the enemies you have made and the infliction upon you, that your spirit already wanes. Your blades will act the will of the gods and in time will serve great purpose, beyond that of comprehension."

Kealin found himself not above the sea anymore but seeing only blackness. There was then a single light ahead of him, blue and glowing. It began to grow brighter and then flashed. He covered his eyes but felt himself pushed back and held against the ground. He saw a starry sky and then the two blue eyes of the Grandmaster, "Awaken, Kealin, Dwemhar, elf. Awaken."

He opened his eyes and saw many faces around him. Other monks sat on the pillows surrounding him, and somehow he had moved to the center of the massive rug. He sat up and then looked around. A hand appeared in front of him. It was the Grandmaster.

"The hint of power you had before has been awakened fully, but take care, you are not pure in blood and as such your speech will change to that of a strange slur like that of too much drink. You may have experienced this to some degree before, but as you release old pains, your power of mind will increase."

"A wise man of my woodlands, a shaman, he too had such a voice. I had it happen before when I faced the ones called Itsu."

"It is a power of the mind, Kealin. Awakened by the power gathered here. The great crystal is called the Realm of the Sea. You entered it and your mind was made anew. But beware the words I spoke before. A darkness is upon you, a darkness beyond that of mere suffering, and reason for you to be wary of your thoughts."

Kealin stood and looked at those around him. "To be honest, monks, I do not know what all of your prophecies and poetic words mean, but I understand the essence of the Dwemhar as a people of spirit. You honor me with this notion of my mind anew, but the pain I feel is still real."

"You will go," the Grandmaster said, "and find one of your blood by the wisdom of the man of the sands. Beware the shifting dunes and that of the spirit realm that dwell within crooked peaks of shadows."

Kealin looked around as the monks began to recede, floating along the floor. There was a snapping sound, and he was back on the bridge way above the city and island. He could see a red door. He approached it and placed his hand, and as with the other door, it opened. He was back on the balcony that he had sat with the sultan early in the morning.

He made his way back to the throne room and saw the sultan sitting with Orolo and Brethor. Brethor stood as he approached.

"You have been gone a while. Tending to the needs of an elf?"

"Fresh air is nice," he said.

"It is, and I plan to have more. The storms to the east are still great, and the good sultan's men left to check if the way is clear. They shall return at night, and if given the clear to depart, the sultan will provide camels and supplies."

"It is true," Amhe said. "I have received message that your friend, the Rusis, is doing better and has sought your presence."

A servant came up as Amhe spoke this.

"My servant Emers will take you to her."

Kealin looked to the Srvivnanns.

"She asked for you. We will speak with her soon enough."

Kealin nodded and went with the servant.

"Good sir, I will take you the way to the healers."

Kealin followed to his side as they exited the palace and began down the steps. Reaching the main gate just past the gardens and the small river, he made a motion with his hand, and the gates opened.

"How long have you been in service for Sultan Amhe?"

"Since I was twelve. My parents died, and he made me a member of the court. The term servant is but a title, for all within the court are trained in languages, arts, mathematics, and that of meditation and the centering of energies."

"A well-learned person is valuable to many."

"It is one's self who must be learned to find value in who they are. Such are the proverbs of the old ones."

The servant led him down the main road for a good many blocks before turning down a winding side road lined with streams of fresh water.

"This water flows from a city oasis near the palace of the sultan. It serves us with constant fresh water. It is by the blessing of the gods that this place is allowed to exist in the harsh climate."

They took another road east and came to a large building surrounded by trees that reached up the walls. A tiny monkey looked down at him from an overhanging branch as it ate a piece of fruit. They passed through an open doorway and came to a line of beds. A cat jumped from an upper level and began to walk near them. Kealin stroked its back as he passed.

"Welcome to the Healing Gardens of Eh-Rin."

Kealin watched as the cat jumped back up into an alcove.

"You keep cats here too?"

"The cats ward off the demons of sickness, a helpful

act when the injured come. This place has studied the
works of the body for some time, and even in death, you
can be useful."

"Your people study the dead body?"

"The inside vessels and spirits. You can learn much
this way."

He continued leading him down another hall and to
a large open room. It was an oasis of sorts with a large
pool and many green plants growing in rich soil that
lined the pool. There was a lone female figure standing
in the water with her back to him. She was nude, and as
he approached, two attendants garbed her and she began
to get out of the water. It was Jesia.

Upon seeing him, she bound her robe and then ran
toward him.

"You indeed are well!" he said.

She embraced him and he returned it. "I am, thanks
to you and the Srvivnanns. Though we barely escaped
the arena. I only remember the look of the man about to
strike you and then I felt a tearing pain upon my back.
Everything else flees from memory. But seeing my fellow
Rusis well too made me elated. They have told me
where we are, but I still do not understand. The wound
on my back is healed completely."

"The city is called Eh-Rin," Kealin said to her as they
walked from the pool. "An enemy of the Grand Protectorate and the Drean. Sultan Amhe seems to be one with
the old ways. Have they said how much longer must you
remain here?"

"The healers said I may leave now if I wish. I had
taken the time to relax a bit more, but I wish to go wher-

ever you are. My friends are at a nearby inn. We can stop and get them."

"If you wish, I believe the sultan would be happy to meet you. My trip east has been delayed, so we have time."

He led her back out of the Healing Gardens and back onto the road. After receiving directions to the appropriate inn, they made their way to it.

"So you still go east?"

"For now. The next step in my journey lies there, and from where I go then, I do not know."

"I have no path myself."

Kealin could tell she was leading to go with him, to wherever it was he was going. The Srvivnanns already felt the same. He only expected more death to come from his actions.

"I am sure you will find one. This city is no friend to those who would cause us harm."

They made it to the inn just to find the other two Rusis walking out. They ran toward Jesia and embraced her with tears rolling down their faces.

"Sisters, we are free of that wretched man! No more master and servant, no more rules against when to talk or whom to talk to." Jesia was wrapped in the embrace of Krea and Muera.

"You must see this city, Jesia," Muera began. "It is like the stories of old. Crystal lights, energy you can feel vibrating through the street."

"Yes!" Krea continued. "Our powers have surged since we've been here. This is a true oasis in every meaning of it!"

Kealin smiled at their happiness and then turned to see a rising dust and a clamor of shouting coming up the road. He stepped out of the way as a line of camels and a large cart made their way closer. Warriors with pointed metal helmets and long spears cleared the roadway further. As they passed the inn, Kealin noticed there were injured men, cut up, bloodied, and many missing arms or legs. It was then he was stricken with horror. They were not injured men of Eh-Rin, but men of the Grand Protectorate's legions.

THE SWORD THAT FLIES TOWARD COMMON FOE

Kealin followed after the cart, leaving the Rusis behind. From the paths it took, he figured the cart was going toward the healers.

When the cart reached the Healing Gardens, many of them came out and began looking over the injured, pointing to whom they wanted first.

"You man, standing there."

Kealin looked toward one of the men dismounting from his camel.

"Yes?"

"We need extra hands. Help carry them in."

The man pushed back Kealin and began to lift up a man. Kealin took hold of the man's legs. This man wore heavier armor than the rest. He had a medallion on his chest of an eagle grasping a sword. His armor was upturned and torn outward near his stomach. Kealin noticed parts of his bowels were showing.

"Quickly, take this one to the main table," a healer said.

Down a walkway to the right, he carried the man to a large stone surface. Other healers surrounded a man standing at the stone platform, sharpening different knives before rubbing a yellow fruit on the blade and then dipping it into water.

Kealin lifted the man onto the platform and stepped back. The healer with the knife removed the clothes of the legionnaire and surveyed his body. The man was not conscious, but he was breathing. The healer took a mixture of herbs and covered them with warm water. Then he began working it with wooden spoons and directed an assistant to add in a white powder.

Kealin was not sure what to make of what he saw. The man he had helped carry in this soldier stood at his side.

"You are not from Eh-Rin?" the man asked.

"I am not."

"Then as you see, our medicine works well. They will take the mixture they make, a blend of healing herbs and pain-reducing leaves, and pack it into the wound. We work to be careful of spreading further sickness with our blades so we clean them with the juice of the lemon and another herb that acts as something to numb if cutting is needed."

The man's bowels were placed back into his stomach and the salve applied. The healer then moved a large wooden stick over the wound, and a bright light poured from the tip. The man's stomach began to stretch down, covering the wound completely.

"He will recover in time, and good he does. His information will be vital to the sultan."

"What information?"

"That information is for the sultan," the man replied plainly. He then left Kealin staring at the healers still working with the injured man.

Kealin took his leave of the healers.

He was anxious to head east, and he felt that waiting within the city was pointless. It was a wondrous place, but he was uncomfortable by the stark contrast it was to the rest of the world. He felt safe but like he was being watched at every moment, and now the enemy had been brought into the city. He was curious of such information and its value to the sultan.

Kealin made his way back to the palace, finding Brethor kicking his feet, sitting on the edge of the platform that overlooked the stairwell.

"How does she fair?"

"Well, she is up and has been rejoined with the others. I am eager to leave for the East. I have seen our enemy taken in and cared for as allies."

"Hmm, we should not judge too quickly. A group of men hurried into the palace not too long ago, and we were asked to step out while they and the sultan conversed. I do not know the meaning but have no doubt we shall know soon."

"Yes, yes, soon enough," Orolo mocked. He walked from around the corner of a nearby pillar he had been attempting to translate for some time.

"Any luck, Brother?"

He shook his head. "No, I made out some of the

words as 'Pillars of One Society Laws to Govern,' but that is it."

"So the title, then?"

"Yes, and a word or two below it, but it's in an obscure version of Dwemhar."

"Likely a blend of their native tongue with that they wish to emulate. They do seem a different society than one would expect to find."

"A target," Orolo commented. "They do things which make them out to be different. They feel secure with their vast technological advancements versus other cultures, but they have no allies. I wonder how they feel they can remain safe."

"Are we no different?" Brethor asked. "We of magic trying to survive. You know of our home and its intended purpose as a refuge. Do you think we will not feel we can resist the ever changing tide of society and war?"

Orolo shook his head in indifference. "It is strange here."

Kealin nodded his head in agreement. "I am ready to go. I have peace here, but my mind feels restless. We must seek out the one I came to find."

At that moment, the door opened and a servant shouted to them.

"Visitors from afar, the great sultan seeks audience with you."

Brethor stood, and Kealin followed him and Orolo inside. They proceeded to the throne room to find multiple tables out with many of the high-ranking commanders of the army looking over maps and talking between themselves. There was a woman sitting before the throne, marking numbers on a parchment. The sultan smiled as he saw them.

"My apologies for asking you two to leave, but I see you found Kealin and you are all well."

"We did and it is," Brethor said. "It appears, considering the company within this room, you plan for battle."

"Indeed I do." He nodded. "Seer, what luck and fortune have the numbers provided?"

"Fogs upon the future. As veiled as a cloudy night are the moves from this point on. But I hear the one of prophecy is near. Perhaps he will have advice?"

Kealin went from looking at her to Sultan Amhe, who stared at him. Brethor slightly turned toward him and then looked back to the sultan.

"I have not advice on what I do not know."

The seer looked toward the sultan.

The sultan stood and walked toward one of the maps on the table. "You three know I sent scouts east at first light as the storm moved away. What we found was complete destruction from something unlike these sands and sun have seen in some time. My forces pressed forward and entered the fleeing storm to the sounds of cackling and the clamor of metal.

"Though we did not face the enemy, we came upon those who did. The legionary forces of the Grand Protectorate. Our generals took action and pulled back our forces to a safe distance with the injured of the legion."

"I saw such," confirmed Kealin. "Helping your enemy?"

"An enemy who stood against like enemy and

needed help. You must help those who need it no matter the cost or risk to your own, and the gods will protect you."

"What of this enemy?" asked Brethor.

The sultan went to the throne and picked up something sitting on the arm. He brought it back to the table and tossed it down.

It was a black-hilted blade wrapped in red leather. The end of the sword was notched in three places and was jagged.

"I have not seen a blade like this used by anyone of these lands," said Kealin.

"Because none that have been present upon these lands for many ages use such a blade. It is a southern-forged blade, a remnant of the old gods, the Itsu. In particular, it was used by the Drear orcs, creatures of elven blood and that of beasts. Savage and without souls of the gods."

"Such beasts were defeated," Kealin said.

Kealin remembered vague tales, spoken of as almost rumor since the time had passed so long ago. It was near the time of one of the first wars of the gods of the greater North and those of the South. A time before men. Orcs were mortal enemies of elves and in so were imprisoned to the grave in caves across the lands.

"If orcs have returned, there must be one who summons them," Kealin told them.

"We know nothing but that we must meet them if they encroach upon our sands. We are augmenting our forces marching east and sending part of our armada to watch the coast."

A door slammed open and shouting began.

"Take me to your sultan!"

A rush of guards made their way to the door, and the sultan walked quickly that direction. They followed.

The man who had previously been split open and Kealin had watched be healed knelt, restrained by the palace guards.

"Did he have any weapon?" Amhe asked.

"No, but he would not comply with our orders to stop."

The man was breathing heavily and looked at everyone with a fear and anxiousness in his eyes.

"I ... need ... to talk ... with the ... sultan," he said.

"Then talk to me. Tell me your name and rank and whatever you wish to speak. Let him up and give him a seat before the throne."

The man was walked but yet still somewhat corralled by guards to the throne room. Maps were covered as the man walked between the tables, and Sultan Amhe sat upon his throne.

"I am Iruis, general legatus of the 12th Western Legion of the Grand Protectorate. I call the mountain city of Vueric home. My men and I entered the desert in pursuit of a mad woman, a witch, and her captured kind."

"Captured kind?" Amhe questioned.

"The witch is an elf, a horrible being in itself, but the elves she took were not as many may say—evil."

"You speak ill of elves and then say that these were not evil? Explain your words."

"I mean no offense, but the wars of the North are

not the same as the ones here. I know the title I hold
and men's disdain toward magic, but these elves were
kind and treated us fairly. We have guarded the mountains for some time with little in the word of ill happenings. At first, an attack came in the night, stealing
horses, making a bloody mess of them near the stables,
but then they came after an elven woodland region. I
sent legionnaires, but then scouts reported the elven
homes were burning. I sent more troops to intercept
these reported stalking creatures, but then my centu-
rions reported a man of shadow, unmatched with a
sword, who cut down with ease all men who faced
him."

Kealin questioned the man's words, curious of this
blade-wielding man. He had fought some before who
claimed much pride and skill with a blade, but none of
them were validated by another actual warrior. It was
always cheap bar talk and words spewed when they had
drunk too much beer.

The general continued. "They take the prisoners and
then they murder them. An entire hillside is littered
with corpses of the dead. We searched for some time
against the orders of my own upper commanders, and a
few days ago, we found a mountain peak that had
become bathed in lightning from a large storm. We
pressed attack and were met by ranks of the creatures
flowing out of the caves like ants upon a piece of meat.
They were horrid and spoke only in growls. We pushed
our way into the mountain, and the woman fled from us
before we could capture her. She went into the desert,
kicking up a sandstorm to veil her path. I took some of

my best men in an attempt to find her, but the next I knew, I awoke here."

"My men found you upon checking of the storm you spoke of," Amhe clarified. "No witch or woman or elf was found."

"She was there. She has returned to the mountain, I am sure. But I must get my men back to Vueric."

"You will be allowed to return to your home. You are not a prisoner. Take rest for now."

The man smiled. "Thank you, Sultan. You would not believe the rumors I have heard of Eh-Rin and you, Sultan, but you have proved them wrong just in what little time I have been here."

"I do believe them and their harshness. I am happy to meet a man of the Grand Protectorate who is not trying to convince me of my own wrongs. Servants," he shouted out, "bring this man food and see to his other men that they have good dwellings and have needs met."

Kealin went to the sultan. "I must seek my belongings and depart for the east."

Amhe glanced at him. "I would hope with recent news you might hold off on traveling east. The storm is gone, yes, but it seems a new storm is brewing. My troops are rallying and will work to secure the path."

"I do not head to the mountains but to the old man."

"I get your argument and thus can point you toward him, but my concern remains of the path. Servant!" he said, before one of his men came to him. "Get this man's gear and that of his companions."

Brethor and Orolo approached.

"Kealin," began Amhe, "I fear of what is to come, and

if you understand the peace we within Eh-Rin so fever-
ishly seek, you understand why this is alarming. The
return of the orcs requires the blood of elves, and there is
much we do not know about in the eastern desert and
the mountains."

"It is a risk, but I must find my sister, Amhe. She is
my blood."

The servant returned with their gear and black
robes. They took their belongings.

"Very well. Follow me, all of you."

The sultan led them through the door where Kealin
had found him earlier in the morning. They went to the
back wall, and the sultan pressed on a block, opening up
another passage. He led them down a stairwell that was
only dimly lit with the faint blue light of crystal. They
walked to a landing and to a large room with many rolled
parchments. On the top shelf of one of the many rows of
books was an unadorned box. Amhe reached up and
pulled it off before setting it on a nearby table.

"Treasure in plain sight," he told them. He opened
the chest and pulled out a map with a large hole in the
center.

"Dwemhar ruins are one thing. But the mirage of the
old man is another. I have been to him once and can tell
you that with naked eye you will find only sand, but
looking through the center of this parchment, you will
see the stone archway that leads to his realm.

"Prepare yourself upon entering," he warned. "It is
not an experience taken with easy heart, and his region
has long been known as the Lost Sands."

"What does the parchment say?" asked Orolo.

"It is of the visions of a mad man, a soul lost to the Jinn, the devils of the sand. Beware them, for simple shelter can quickly turn to that of a nightmare. Do not trust a word they say if you happen upon them."

"We have blades," said Brethor. "We worry little of anything."

"Jinn cannot be defeated with such. Watch your minds and center your thoughts away from desire of the flesh. They will tempt you. Just be careful of the unexpected in the dunes and take heed the old man's words you seek out, Kealin. Many a man has found his way to death seeking out desires of the heart, no matter how innocent they were.

"Head east from the city along the rising sun road. You will come to an old caravan shack before your path turns to the dunes. Head south and then begin scanning the horizon with the map."

The Srvivnanns and Kealin changed into their original clothes, adding the black robes to help with the heat of the journey. Kealin felt the edges of his swords and noticed they were expertly sharpened.

"Close to the elven smiths?" Amhe asked.

"Close, and perhaps greater. Your skill with metal and the cleaning of my blades is well worth the time they have not been on my sides."

Kealin went to the sultan and bowed; the sultan returned the bow.

"I wish that you would not go and that you would embrace that which we have built here."

"I must go."

"Know that I send a large force to contend this new

evil. They are your friends, and the commanders know of you and your friends. If you find yourself in trouble, seek us and our fleet, if your journey takes you to sea."

"Thank you, Sultan Amhe."

"At the far gate, give the camel master the word 'Sandwalker,' and he will set you up with animals for your journey."

"I will."

Kealin was happy to have his items back and began to walk out, following the stairwell. Brethor and Orolo stopped and spoke to Amhe.

"I am happy to know of your work in the far northern mountains. Know that this, too, is a safe place for all of magic."

"Thank you," Orolo said.

"We will return when we can, Amhe."

"I welcome it."

They shared a bow and then hurried to catch up with Kealin.

14

MIRAGES

Leaving the palace behind, he took the main road, knowing all well that the Srvivnanns followed behind but that he wished they didn't. He walked toward the inn that the Rusis were at to tell them goodbye, especially Jesia, whom he cared for but could not bear to see follow him to whatever end he was to have. He already had to deal with Brethor and Orolo.

Reaching the door, he entered, finding the three Rusis sitting on a bench reading a book. Jesia turned and smiled.

"Kealin, it is good you came back. I was hoping to get to explore the city with you."

She set down the book and went to him.

"Thank you again for your actions at the arena. I would be dead had you not grabbed me."

"And I dead," he replied, "had you not told me of that large man."

They both smiled.

"Jesia, I am departing for the East, and I do not want you to come."

"You will come back and I will wait for you until you do."

Kealin looked down. "So far most I have deemed dear to me have been lost. I would not have you wait for me in any way, but I will return."

The other two Rusis stood and placed their hands on her shoulders. She kissed Kealin on the cheek.

"Take care of yourself, and your two friends."

He nodded without returning the kiss or saying anything. He took a few steps back and then turned, leaving the Rusis and stepping back outside into a sandy wind. Kealin had no intent on returning, but he would not steal that happiness from her.

Looking back up the path, he did not see the Srvivnanns, but then looking down, he saw they walked together, appearing to look around for him. He jogged a few paces to them and touched them on the shoulder. They startled and turned.

"We had thought you had actually hid from us to keep us from going," Orolo joked.

"No, but I will recommend again that you not follow."

"It is happening," Brethor told him. "We will go with you and you will see that your unhappy ending will not be so. You can't kill us that easily."

"I, maybe not, but who knows what is out there that can," Kealin said.

They made it to the eastern gate in all of its grand

spectacle. The gateway was massively tall with a large torch basin burning atop it.

Just before the gateway, a camel herder looked at them.

Kealin went to him and gave him the password. He immediately went and prepared three camels.

"You go to do the sultan's work?" he asked.

"Yes," Brethor replied.

"Good tidings, then."

"What? Would there be no good tidings if it wasn't?" Orolo asked.

The man laughed. "No, it would just mean you had overheard the words and were extorting me, and that would end badly for you." He laughed again and passed the ropes to them. "I wish a good journey to you."

Kealin nodded and led his camel outside.

Just outside the gates, they tried their hand at making the camels sit with tongue clicks, and eventually a passerby offered proper help.

"They are good animals," he assured. "Better than horses and strong."

Kealin felt somewhat comfortable on his mount, but he had never even seen a camel. It was definitely an odd animal. The creatures' fur was stiffer than that of a horse, and the smell was different. As the sand blew upon them from a strong coastal gust, they covered their mouths with their robes and began the arduous walk east.

The sun was setting behind them, and with that came less heat and a blast of cool air, even though it was

still somewhat humid. The road did not actually go due
east but turned slightly south, leading them through
valleys of massive dunes that left Kealin questioning if
some Dwemhar ruin lay waiting just beneath the surface.

As sunset turned to night and a vast array of bright
stars covered the sky, Orolo began into a verse, a bit
unexpected but relaxing still.

Stars alight in darkening void
I see familiar faces white,
Though southern path far from home,
Looking up I feel it's right.

Many days we've walked our own,
And long I've waited to go home,
One more journey to sandy South,
Then at last the end to waking roam.

"Now come, dear brother. Do you really hate our
adventuring so much?"

Orolo chuckled. "Not at all. Hate is not the correct
word. Dislike, maybe. But we've been going for so long, it
would be nice to be with our family."

Brethor sighed. "Yes, I do agree. You should come
with us, Kealin."

Kealin turned and looked at them before looking

back to the path ahead. "I could not. But perhaps if that is what Alri wants."

"Alri?" Brethor asked.

"Alri is my sister, the one I search for. The one of my blood. If I can find her and maybe even something of my mother and father, perhaps then I can truly rest."

Brethor did not say something for some time, and neither did Orolo. Their path went past ruins of what they each assumed was the trading post Sultan Amhe had mentioned. They turned south. After a good while more of silence, Brethor rode a bit closer to Kealin. "Your sister, I know you will not stop until she is found. That is why we are by your side. You've watched out for us, and us you, but it is more than mere companionship. Our blood binds us, and we will help you find Alri."

Kealin gave Brethor a smile but then looked away again. He feared what he led the Srvivnann brothers to. He took out the parchment and peered through the hole as Amhe had said. Nothing but dunes.

The moon had well risen and trekked halfway across the sky when they found an outcropping of a few boulders and a single tree in a small valley. They dismounted their camels and, using the few fire-making supplies available to them, got a small fire going. It was enough to barely keep warm. The camels were sitting not too far from them as Kealin looked over the dunes at the stars. They reminded him of the waves of the sea. The way the sand wisped off the top, carried away like sea foam. Once again he felt he had been too far from the water, and he wondered of Tulasiro. Had she managed to reach her god? Perhaps he would not know until he made it back North. Hopefully with Alri at his side.

The morning sun came quicker than expected, but Kealin awakened before it fully rose. He woke the others and then stood. He had missed it in the night, but looking ahead, he saw two crooked peaks that looked like fangs rising out of the sands. His mind shifted to the Sanguine monks, and he felt fear come upon him.

"We need to get moving," he told the others.

Orolo stood up and began tending to his camel when Kealin saw his attention set on something in the distance.

"Look, a trading caravan, and aside from what looks like some good fruit, they have a few women I might like too."

Brethor looked but did not see. "Brother, perhaps you need more water. There is nothing there."

It was then Brethor appeared to turn his own attention to something. "Why is there a child alone out on the hill?"

Kealin looked but did not see anything. Orolo had already begun to walk away from them, and now Brethor was about to do the same.

Kealin smacked Brethor in the back. "Friend, it is not real."

A voice whispered across the winds. "Kealin?"

He jumped. It was Alri's.

"Kealin?" it said again.

He climbed onto the rocks, looking for the source, but he didn't see anything.

"Alri!" he yelled out.

He thought to himself. *This is fake, Kealin. She is not in the desert wandering like a ghost. This is not HER!*

But again he heard it. "Kealin. Kealin, hurry!"

He had centered where the voice was coming from. He began to run to it. The shadowy crags were before him, and though he had warning in his mind of where he ran toward, he did so continually, unable to resist. He had to find his sister.

"Kealin," he heard again.

He now stood before the crags. Staring upward, an image of his sister appeared as clear as the night sky above.

"Kealin."

"I am here."

"Kealin!" The voice paused. "Slayer of Itsu." The tone changed from that of his sister to that of a raspy high voice. "Slayer of many since. The gods speak of you in both curse and praise."

"Who are you?" he cried out, drawing his blades.

"So simple of a person," the voice said again.

The image of Alri faded. A black and blue fire burst from between the crags. A face of light appeared and then swooped toward him before everything went dark.

He awoke, standing in a room. His blades were still in his hands.

"Where am I?" he yelled.

There was no response. A moment later, someone appeared at the edge of the room.

"Orolo?" The voice sounded like Brethor.

"No, Kealin."

Another figure appeared.

"Please tell me that the two I can barely make out is Kealin and Brethor," Orolo said.

"It is, dear brother," Brethor said.

"Well, it looks like we are—"

"Trapped again," Kealin finished.

"Since when do mirages do that?"

"It wasn't a mirage," Kealin said. "We were warned. It is these things called Jinn."

A cackle filled the cave, echoing off the walls as if it was all around them. They each backed into one another, looking around. A smokeless fire floated around them out of the darkness and spun faster and faster.

"We do not fear you, Jinn!"

The cackle grew louder, and then the fire stopped high upon a rock that towered above the room. A figure appeared, black with the thin outline of a wispy blue fire. It had white eyes and wore similar garb to that of those at Eh-Rin.

"Kealin, half-elf of the Urlas Woodlands. How I know you do not fear. It is how I know of you at all. The two with you are like baggage to a grand soul. One who would stand up to the Itsu while serving the ones of the North, but what creed holds you now? A whisper of a hope that your dear sister lives?"

"Shut up, fireball," Orolo said. "We need not your evil here."

The entity laughed. "How do you know I am evil? I have said nothing to indicate such. My name is Asa-

Twu, Jinn of the eternal sands. I hold no stance to either those deemed good or evil by your own accord but also hold neither of them in favorable light."

"So why are we here?" Kealin asked. "I have no time to deal with someone who takes us for sport."

"Well, you were no doubt warned of falling for desires of the heart? I do not like being alone. I hear much of what the gods say and find your story, Kealin, to be interesting. There have been whispers of prophecy of the fall of gods, of your own fall. In time, that is."

"I care little for prophecies," Kealin said.

"I listen to the voices of gods, traversing over mountains, rivers, and the heavens and seas. I know hidden truths and blatant lies. I know if your sister lives and care little if you do not."

"Then why are we here?"

"Because you wished it. You sought information and wished it. I heard your wish and did so in giving you what you wanted."

"We made no such wish," said Brethor. "So much for my original thoughts on the Jinn and granting a wish or two."

"Your wishes, no. But the conversation is nice," the Jinn laughed. "Look at your skin, dear fellows, and see what the sun does to it."

Kealin looked down at his skin and noticed it was extremely dry and cracked.

"What did you do to us?" Orolo asked.

"I did nothing but distract. The sun has done that. I am not the only one deemed evil in the stories. You must beware all within the sands."

Kealin closed his eyes and began to see that around him. The walls of the cave wobbled and warped before him.

"What are you doing, half-elf?" he heard.

He could see their camels in the distance, and he turned, seeing the archway crags where the image of Alri had been. Just below that, he saw himself, Brethor, and Orolo lying on the ground. They were in a mirage; the Jinn had distracted their minds.

He centered his thoughts on the pillars and spoke aloud. "De path is not what we think. Dis is not real."

You are Dwemhar. The rumor is true.

Kealin turned his thoughts back to the cave. "Free us."

"No," Asa-Twu replied.

"Maybe we can escape with my pendant," Brethor suggested.

"There is no escape needed. Close your eyes, friend. Center your thoughts on me and that of our awaiting camels."

"Dwemhar blood," Asa-Twu said. "Powerful and beyond that of many. You will see its use soon in a more complete action in the mountains that are filled with death."

Kealin had begun to glow. "De path away from the Jinn is visible to me. Dis way."

The three of them began to rise, and the Jinn cackled.

"It was wonderful to meet the one who has caused such turmoil within the very realms of the gods."

Kealin heard the voice and then opened his eyes.

They stood before the crags, and the Srvivnanns looked at him in shock.

"What happened?" Brethor asked.

"I do not know, but I learned at Eh-Rin of power within stronger than most. My Dwemhar blood is purer than others."

"Your speech," said Orolo. "It was strange."

"A side effect of the blending of bloods, but the powers helped free us from the grasp of the Jinn."

The sun was again setting. They had been laying in the sun an entire day in what seemed only moments before the Jinn. It was clear that was how many died seeking mirages. Any of their skin that exposed was now burned. The Jinn took pleasure in the suffering and death of wary travelers.

They went toward the camels.

"The Jinn seemed a fan of yours," said Brethor, "but what did he mean by Dwemhar blood and what you will see soon in the mountains?"

"I do not know," Kealin said, mounting.

They began out of the valley and back along the dunes in a southerly direction. In time, a large white moon rose above them and the cool winds blew over.

Kealin's skin ached, and he enjoyed that the cooler air seemed to reduce the pain.

"I see now why the robes are so valuable here," Orolo said.

"It does make sense," Brethor said, "and they are valuable, but my arms still hurt. I cannot imagine having to remain garbed over completely just to live somewhere. I actually like the feel of the sun warming my arms."

"It definitely warmed it, Brother."

They came to a rocky region dotted with monolithic stones that went out as far as they could see in either direction. There was enough space to walk between them, but then there was another line of stones that curved inward to an oasis of bright green trees. The sun had begun to rise in the east.

"Water," Orolo gasped.

"It is not even that hot," Brethor said to him.

"But it will be," Kealin said. He took out the parchment and looked through the hole. He could see the towering rocks, but beyond he saw just sands. There was no oasis. He looked to his right and left and saw nothing but what his normal eyes saw. He then looked back through the rocks and made out a path not visible to the others.

"We need to go this way," he told them.

"Ah! The oasis it is," Orolo jeered.

"No," Kealin corrected him, "the oasis is a mirage, and we have learned already to avoid those. There is a path visible through the parchment. We will follow that."

KEALIN DIRECTED his camel through the tight space between the rocks and jumped when the sky turned to a dark purple. The feeling in the air changed, and what coolness he had felt before became a plain temperature neither warm nor cold. He turned to see Brethor and Orolo both noticing the change as well. Orolo went to back his camel up but found the rocky monoliths that were there before now were part of a massive wall too high to even climb.

"Another Jinn trick?" Brethor questioned.

"I don't know. I don't feel the same presence that I did with the Jinn."

He looked back through the parchment and could see the road plainly. He looked around and up to the sky. The image through the parchment did not look as strange as the one he saw with his own eyes.

"The path appears unchanged when I see it through the parchment, but looking around, I do not understand what I am seeing."

They began to walk, and the ground changed from desert sands to that of grass. The sky clouded with fast-moving clouds, and winds swept leaves scattering along the path.

Kealin would check the parchment every so often to assure they stayed on the path, but otherwise he tried to figure out the many images he saw.

Fish floated above them, as if they were under the sea. Orolo reached out to touch one, but Brethor pulled his hand down.

"I don't know what this place is, but I can assume we shouldn't touch anything."

Sometime after they had walked a good distance, they came to a large lake. The water did not move. The surface was pristine, and along the bank, there was not even a ripple. A man fished in the distance, but it was way off the road.

In the field to the right, a caravan of men walked. They had a large empty cart, and their eyes were filled with fire. The caravan cut across the road in front of them but then continued on. Kealin noticed that they did not seem to even see him or the Srvivnanns.

"Good sir," Orolo shouted out.

Neither those of the caravan nor the man fishing seemed to hear him.

"Let's keep walking," Kealin suggested.

The path visible in the parchment began to show mountains ahead of them, but Kealin saw only trees when he looked ahead. The only part of that which made sense was the path visible leading into the mountains could actually be seen in this alternate world as a roadway through the woods.

They entered the forest, and Kealin recognized the sounds of an owl hooting as they did.

"Sounds like a white mountain owl," Brethor said. "An omen of good luck."

"A nice change if so," Kealin said. "The path appears to darken, according to the parchment, but just looking, it seems the road goes on."

They continued on, but did so carefully. The woods were empty of life save the sound of the owl when they first entered. In all directions before them, they could see only dense trees and nothing else. As the parchment became useless, darkening completely, Kealin kept much more alert than he had been when simply following the veiled path. There was a rumble in the ground, and Kealin looked around as the trees faded, and instead of woods, he saw rocks and torches. They were in a chamber, similar to that of the Jinn, except that it was furnished and brightly lit.

On an elevated platform, sitting on a large rug with a steaming pot of tea and a large smoking device like Amhe used, there was a man with long gray hair. His eyes were closed, and as he exhaled a plume of smoke, Kealin inhaled it, feeling relaxed. He turned to look behind him and saw the path leading back out of the cave and the mountains and, in the far distance, the moonlit sky and the sand dunes.

"You have traveled through much toil to meet with me," the man said.

"Are you the one whom can tell me of my blood? Can you help me find my sister?"

The man opened his eyes, and Kealin noticed a slight flicker of ember in his eyes. "I am the Seer of Lost Sands, and I can see much from my cave here, but I reside in that path which you and your friends took. Of the three of you, I will speak but to two, for there is dishonesty in the heart of one."

Kealin looked around, noticing that neither Brethor nor Orolo were there.

"Where are my friends?"

"Within the woods of my realm and safe, for you came with the parchment of old and they walked with you. I have also seen your burns healed. The Jinn stops most all who come unerringly to the abyss of the sands. Anyone who comes this far into the nothingness knows of my existence or of the rumor of riches, but few have ever had need or been of mindful purpose to do so and succeed as you have.

"The mirages do well to distract. As you can tell, within my realm, some have become lost. Those who make it past the barrier without good intent for the world will remain in my lands, forever trapped. You saw the caravan wandering? They sought palpable fortune, that which I do not have. They now feel a hunger never satisfied. The man fishing is hungry and will be so now without the ability to catch the many fish his eyes see. He had sought a way to murder without true cause a man innocent by all regard. I keep them here as I do many others.

"I know your intent, Kealin of Urlas, but you tell me, why do you feel so strongly to get one of your blood?"

"My family means the most to me. I have lost much, and Alri is but the last. My brothers fell five years ago in the Glacial Seas, and my parents fell fighting in the wars of the North. I must find her."

The man took a sip of tea. "So you say you do so because she is the last. Would you not seek her otherwise?"

"I would not seek her alone otherwise. But I would still go after her regardless."

"So you would put others at risk to find her? You would have their blood on your hands for her?"

Kealin wondered of the questioning the seer was doing. This man of wisdom knew such answers but was forcing him to answer other questions. He was not sure what to make of him but continued to answer.

"I would bloody my own hands to rescue her. If my siblings or my parents were alive, they would do the same."

The man took another drag of his pipe and exhaled

over Kealin. The cave became dark, and he saw figures of smoke and fire.

"Urlas blades will falter soon. Death will take those deemed dead. An old death will be made alive once again and vessels of the blood of love will spill upon unhallowed ground. That which you seek, one of your own blood, is within the mountains to the North. Be wary that your footsteps lead you to more of that which you seek to forget.

"You are not to find peace, Kealin. Death follows you. Death will haunt you. There is but work undone that you have abandoned. There is more than one prophecy that your feet tread within."

Kealin's eyes could now see the old man again.

"That which has been spoken is to be. Your hand can do little to stop the coming evils, Kealin, half-elf. But you have the power to curb such tidings to good. Good journey to you."

Then the Seer and the cave in which Kealin stood disappeared. He turned around to see Brethor and Orolo staring at him. The camels were behind them, and the mountains rose to either side in the narrow valley they stood in. Kealin's arms suddenly felt strange and then all of his burns healed.

"What happened to the woods?" asked Orolo.

"Mirages," said Kealin.

"I take it you met with whom you were seeking. What did the man of the mountain say to you?" asked Brethor.

"The mountains to the north, where the witch is that

the legatus spoke of. We must go there. But how did you know of the Seer?"

"I spoke to him too."

"What are you two talking about?" Orolo asked. "We were all three in the woods."

"You did not see the old man smoking and drinking tea?" Brethor asked his brother.

"No, we were in the woods. That was it. I felt my arms and face tingle and the burns heal, but nothing else."

"What did he say to you, Brethor?" Kealin asked.

"I saw a burning sun, blood, and wolves. I saw shadows upon the woods and polar lights burning brightly above the seas. I was told in time I would understand, but I don't know. It seemed strange. What did he say to you?"

Kealin shook his head. "That death follows me and will haunt me."

He turned away from them and got onto his camel. The others did the same.

"It sounds like I was favored by not speaking to the man," Orolo worriedly teased.

Kealin thought about Orolo's words and remembered that the Seer of Lost Sands was only to talk to two of them. The two of them with honest hearts. He thought of Orolo and what that could mean, but put it out of mind. He had to get north.

15

THUNDER AND LIGHTNING

The path back out of the mountain valley and into another night sky had thrown off Kealin's sense of time. It seemed that after each experience they had on this journey, first with the Jinn and then with the Seer of Lost Sands, more time was lost.

"We will go with you," Brethor said. "You go to a place of danger, and I will not have you go alone."

"Did you not hear what I said before? Death is following me, and I have already lost many I cared for."

"Then don't care for us." Brethor laughed. "But we are coming."

Orolo nodded. "You will have us. Or we will simply follow. An extra blade or two on your side will even the odds ever so slightly."

Kealin shook his head. "I thank you both. When this is done, perhaps we can go with Alri to your home for a time before we head back north."

"You see?" said Brethor to his brother. "Finally, a path

that leads home for me, just like what you've said was needed."

"Except just in the last two weeks, it has taken two imprisonments, nearly dying more than a few times, a Jinn, and the strangest of journeys I have ever seen, to convince you to do it!"

The three of them laughed.

Taking a straight path from the mountain valley and back out of the rings of monolithic stones, Kealin turned around to see only dunes. The mirage made him wonder if he had even been where he knew he just was. He knew where Alri was, and now it was a matter of reaching her. They continued along the road they had come to until they reached the ruins of the trading post. It was once again nearing morning.

"I feel like sunrise is bad luck for us. Something keeps happening every time I see just a glimpse of the sun," Orolo said.

"That could be true," said Brethor, "but I say we take actual rest for once. These ruins may not be much, but they will shield us from the sun for a time."

Kealin entered the shell of the stone hut and looked around. He could use some rest as well. As much as he was ready to reach Alri, he would need his strength up as well. Besides, if the Srvivnanns were coming with him, they needed rest. They did not have the endurance that he did.

Kealin laid down as Orolo did the same, and Brethor kicked open a wooden chest.

"Yes, yes," he said.

Brethor pulled out a bottle of wine. The etchings on

the side were worn, but it didn't stop him from popping the cork and taking a sniff.

"Strange berry smell, seems dry."

"Much like the desert we lay in," Orolo said.

Brethor took a swig and spat it out.

"You would think someone would be able to get a proper winemaker in a place like this!"

"An arid desert?" Orolo asked. "That's like saying we could get one in the icy mountains of the Far North. There's no point, and it won't happen. Once we find his sister, we can get a good drink. I'm sure we could all use one. This mountain and all the wondrous happiness that I heard the legatus say of it has me just knowing we will need one!"

Kealin closed his eyes. He rethought of the images shown to him by the seer. Then he thought of his words, wondering of what truth they held. Was the man a soothsayer of prophecy that could happen or were his words turning to truth no matter what?

The man had questioned him over and over, almost like he was forcing him to speak words into existence. He said death haunted him, and he thought of the one of the Glacial Seas. Vankou. The mysterious entity of death. It was his hand that helped overwhelm the defenses of Dimn's palace. He had played into the Itsu's hands then and given his place among the gods. He would know that Kealin had not died.

But as it was, he had seen no Wights of the Bleaklands and had not heard the organ. But he remembered the sounds, that drear he felt standing there with his siblings. Thinking of death, he remembered Calak and

Taslun's last moments and began to cry. He turned over and thought of Alri. He had to save her, and he would do so or die trying.

When Kealin awoke, the sun was just past midday. He sat up and joined Brethor and Orolo, who had lit a fire and were roasting a small animal.

"Some kind of rat," Orolo said. "There isn't much else to find out here, and the supplies on the camels were not the tastiest."

"Picky," Brethor teased.

"I like good food!"

"Do you both feel rested?" Kealin asked.

"Good as we can be," Brethor said. "I have thought of our path. Rummaging through some old parchment, I found an old map. If we head east from here, we can follow an old trading road north to the mountains. I also took note of the mountains. There seems to be a storm hovering above the southernmost peaks. You can see it from here."

Kealin stood, walking around the edge of the ruins. To the north, he could make out the dark clouds Brethor spoke of. A periodic bolt of lightning flashed against the blackness. He turned back to them.

"Are you sure you two wish to come with me?"

"I will get the camels ready," Orolo said with a wink.

Kealin had his answer.

This was the first day the sun really beat down on them. Their water supply was holding, but they would need to refill within the next day or two. The road that turned north was still traveled often, and they passed more than one caravan making their way south.

"Traders headed to the Iber peninsula," said Brethor. "There is a pass to the far, far south that is an easier trek than crossing the mountains."

"Not to mention less thieves," Orolo added.

With nightfall, they came to a small trading village at yet another crossroad. There were few people, but there was a well and fresh water. They tied up the camels and then each got a cold drink from the well. A man saw them and approached.

"Where do you head?"

"To the north," Kealin said.

"You know about those beasts?"

"We have heard."

The man looked nervously over them. "We are headed west, all of us. Enjoy the water and use our homes if you need rest, but the creatures came last night, and if it hadn't been for the paid guards, we would be dead. Sultan Amhe has made a place for us near Eh-Rin, a place for refugees. I would say you should come with us and not risk the northern road."

"Thank you," Brethor told him, "but we have some in danger to the north. We will send any others we find your way in hope they will be cared for."

"They will. Good luck to you brave souls. The terror of the mountains is no small fright. I will pray to the gods for you three."

The man then went to a door and knocked. Another man met him with a bag in hand.

"Do they come with us?" he asked him.

"No, they go to their deaths. Let us get back to our families and pray this storm is quelled."

The men's conversation was morbid, but the three of them didn't care.

Gusts began to blow into the village as the men mounted camels and sped off toward the west. Kealin began to refill his water pouch, and Orolo sat with his back against the well.

"They offer prayers to the gods and then doom us to death?"

"No fate is set, Orolo," Kealin said to him, "but prayers to the gods may see fate to our side. I have seen the power of the gods bring salvation once, but then again, there was much death leading to it."

They made their way back to their camels and covered their faces the best they could. The winds were violent and unceasing as they continued north. The mountain loomed closer.

To the east of them, tornadoes kicked up the sand and howled. Though they were wary of them, it did not stop their journey and there was little they could do but watch them. It seemed at every turn, he was reminded of the Glacial Seas. A reminder of the extreme danger he felt he was leading the Srvivnanns toward.

It seemed that in times before what had befallen the mountain, the rivers from the peaks had watered the regions they now traveled through. Though the grass was torn up and browned, the burned trees that grew were massive. Looking up the growing rock face, it seemed the scorch marks had scarred the mountain.

"I see no orcs," Brethor said.

"It is too bright for them," Kealin told them. "They need either the cover of the storm or darkness. They do not care for the light. We should look to find a way into the mountains. I'm sure there is a cave system of some kind. If orcs are moving through here frequently, we should see some sign of it. They are not the cleanest of creatures."

They walked along the sheer cliffs, eventually finding a lone goat standing on a cliff above them.

"He didn't fly up there," Orolo pointed out.

Brethor ran ahead of them and turned, looking back along the cliffs. "Yes, I agree, and I see a small path barely visible. Enough room for our feet, but it gets us in. Orcs are climbers, so what path they take may not be of use for us to find, but this will work."

They began up a very narrow path. Kealin worked to keep his footing flat along the jutting rock that went out no further than the width of his foot. They made it to the level of the goat and caught whiff of the smell of rotting flesh. The lone goat standing nearby was the survivor of a massacre of other goats. All over the rocks were multiple mangled bodies of goats and deer.

"Feeding grounds," Brethor said.

Kealin drew one of his blades. "I agree. They may be near."

The storm clouds swirled above them, and the lightning which had lessened in severity began to increase. Another round of storms blowing over the peaks caused the air to drop in temperature.

"We will need to find shelter," Brethor said. "Let's continue on."

They walked along a narrow path that turned into the mountains between two large fangs. The occasional rumble of falling rocks kept them all carefully looking up as they hurried under open sky for cover. Lightning struck above them.

Kealin felt a tingling in the air. That strike was close. He ran around a corner and found himself staring at a skull on a stake. The flesh was still rotting, and flies buzzed around it. He drew his other blade, and Brethor did the same. There was a cave ahead, but it was what was outside it that made them the most nervous. Small huts and several camp-size fires. Kealin moved along the fires, careful to keep quiet. Brethor was just at his side.

It was then Orolo began to shout. "I found a cave back here. Hurry this way."

Kealin heard a growl and a cackle in front of him. "Elf beasts come for supper! Bring me their heads!"

The order came from a distant cave and in a raspy, shrill voice.

From within the darkness came several hunched-over creatures just shorter than Kealin, flooding out of the opening. They were grotesque and held wooden clubs, not orcs but rock trolls. Much smaller than the troll from the arena, they happened upon travelers that drew too close to their homes and made too much noise. Kealin hastily slashed at the first one that was upon him but did little damage against their rocky scale hides. It jumped back for a moment and growled.

"This way, Kealin!" Brethor shouted.

They began to run, going toward Orolo, who pointed to a cave up the mountain a bit. They began to climb as the creatures came around the corner. Orolo drew his sword and held it out. Kealin had made it to the mouth of the cave and turned to helped Brethor up.

"Orolo! Come quickly!" Brethor shouted.

Orolo turned to run, and Brethor reached up to grab Kealin's hand. They heard Orolo's sword clang on the ground. They looked over the edge and saw Orolo standing with his arms out, holding a strange pendant. Lightning struck the mountain above them, and an avalanche of rocks began rolling down. Kealin and Brethor fell backward into the cave as the way leading back out was sealed.

16

THE LOST

Brethor ran toward the rocky seal, scraping at rocks but unable to move the larger boulders. Lightning flashing above gave what little light could be had every few moments.

"Damn it!" he yelled as tears fell from his eyes.

Kealin looked at the other side of the cave and noticed a passage leading down.

"This way," he said. "We will try to find a way to your brother."

They moved quickly down the rather large cave passage. Cracks of light gave them just enough life. They were not going back out to Orolo, but perhaps they would be led to somewhere they could get to him.

In a strangeness, they happened upon a larger area lit by torches. They moved along the shadows, wary of the dark spots in the distance and the unseen dangers that possibly lay there. They came to a fork and took the path leading outside to a drenching rain.

"This weather is strange. The skies were darkened, but this is a large storm to come up in less than a few minutes," Brethor said.

They stood on a platform overlooking a valley underneath the storm. Kealin looked down to where the valley itself had begun to swell. In the water, he noticed bones and parts of broken armor and weapons. He had never seen one before, but the skull he saw floating beneath them looked as he had heard orcs described.

"This is a tomb," he told Brethor.

But Brethor did not say anything.

He turned to find Brethor now against the mountain. A dark-cloaked figure held a large blade at his neck.

"Drop your weapons."

Kealin lifted his swords up. "I will not."

The figure didn't move. He seemed to be staring at Kealin. The figure dropped his sword from Brethor's neck and pushed him away. He threw back his hood, and Kealin dropped his blades.

"Son, why have you came to this place?"

In a rush of emotion like a small child, Kealin ran to his father, embracing him. He gripped him and began to shake. He could not fathom what was happening.

"I had thought you dead. I had heard of the battles and wars. I even met an elf who said she knew most were dead."

Kealin's father laughed and cried at the same time. "No, but we should be."

"Where is Mother?" he asked.

His father sheathed his sword and motioned for them to follow.

"Let us get out of the rain."

After Kealin collected his blades, his father led them through a passage and up a narrow opening into a small cave fairly inaccessible unless one knew where to look. It seemed like he had been here for some time. There was bedding and a small pile of embers that his father added kindling to.

"I am sorry, sir," he said to Brethor. "I had left to scout again, and when I happened upon you, I could not take a chance. What is your name?"

"Brethor, and it's understandable," he said.

"Where are the others?" asked his father. "Your brothers and sister. Why have you four come here?"

"They have fallen."

"What? How?"

Taslun and Calak fell defending the palace of the wind god five years ago."

"Five years? Five years my children have been dead and I did not know?"

"I have searched for Alri, who is not dead, ever since. I journeyed to the South to seek out information and learned one of my blood was here. I am here to save her."

"You sought the old man of the mountain. The seer. I know of him but also know he leaves out some information. But first I will explain my and your mother's absence. We went south to fight against those of men. We won many battles but lost many too. Nothing in these wars are what they seem.

"Your mother and I were stuck with a strange curse from a follower of the southern gods. We had sought a cure, following many strange paths, but then it happened that your mother was pregnant. She bore another brother for you, and it was then we had the last piece to cure the curse, but we were betrayed. There is no cure. Not even the magic of Urlas can save us, but I have traveled great distance in pursuit of the one who betrayed us. She has your mother and your brother. They are held in a cavern below. I worry, though. I have not seen Alri.

"There is a witch, an elf witch, turned evil by the Itsu, who seeks to awaken the Drear orcs sealed here. Many have been brought to life, but it is the purity of an elf mother and her offspring she seeks. With their blood, her task will be complete.

"This is our fault, our fault for seeking a cure that led us to this witch who now stands on the brink of extreme power. But you are here now, Kealin. You may help me. You are still a boy to me, but one does not survive this world acting as an elf child."

"Elf and Dwemhar."

"Then you know the truth. Embrace it, son. Know that your mother's blood is even more powerful than what elf blood the witch seeks."

"My brother," interrupted Brethor, "Orolo. He was taken by the trolls."

"The trolls take everyone to the witch. We will go to get your brother. I scouted tonight again to be sure of my path. It is fate that brought you here, Kealin. We will free your mother and brother and then we will find your sister."

His father looked out of the cave. "She has stopped the rain for now. The device she uses must cycle through a seasonal shift even if the magic is not used. However, it is accelerated greatly. The rain will return."

"Device?" asked Kealin.

"A few days ago, before the storms began as they do now, the witch obtained a Dwemhar jewel, red in color. She added it to a device that can control the seasons."

"A red jewel?" asked Brethor.

"Yes."

"We helped pull one from a Dwemhar temple some time ago. Your son helped us. It is true; it can be used to manipulate the air, but that would've meant that Gudru would have found it and retrieved it from the waters of the river."

"The witch has a servant," Kealin's father said. "Two, in fact. One is like her and uses magic. A wizard of some sort. I believe he is her son.

"The other is much different. He leads the raids that I have witnessed when I first made it to the mountains. They are not just like her but are very skilled on their own. We do not know how deep the betrayal goes within the peoples of these lands, but the only consistent thought I have is that we must prevent the rise of the orc. There are at least five thousand of them here. We must do as Blades, Kealin. Seek out our targets and kill this witch, and in doing so, free your mother and the child while preventing the rise of the orcs. Brethor, we will find your brother as well."

"We will do what we must." Brethor nodded. "I am with you."

Kealin's father led them out of the cave and back to the twisting rocky path. They ran along a narrow precipice that stretched over a chasm of shifting waters and orc parts.

"They were turned to dust by elven archons, cast into chasms in the mountains. This witch returns water to their forms as part of her dark magic."

They made it to the other side and took a wooden bridge to the very edge of another chasm. There were mines and forges here. Most appeared newly constructed but were not alight with fire.

"When she has managed to awaken orcs for a short time with necromancy, she has used them to build many things. From the bridge we just took, to at least the finishing touches to these forges. She has used weaker elf blood to prolong the necromantic orcs before now, but it is that of the magnitude of the Dwemhar she seeks."

"So you have always known of her lineage?"

"Of course I knew, dear son, but there was no need to say of it. Dwemhar were reveled and feared. Their items are of power unimaginable in most arcane groups, and the unfortunate fact such protections on their devices can now be beaten with Itsu powers is more fearful than any of us can realize at this moment. Now it is her blood which will fully awaken the orcs because of her Dwemhar ancestry. Now, come."

His father led them to another cavern, and snaking down wooden palisades that went down to larger open floor, he stopped them near a large rock. There were trolls nearby.

"I believe they have your brother," he said to Brethor.

They peeked around the edge of the rock to see Orolo bound in rope.

Two men stood before the trio of trolls that had brought the prisoner.

The shorter of the two men stared down at them. He wore a hooded robe with red armor along his forearms. He pointed with a crudely shaped staff. "The Matriarch is about to unleash the blood offering, and you come here with this low-life scum talking of how he claims allegiance to Gudru and seeks asylum?"

"He was with others. An elf and another man."

"And again you trouble me with him when you should be guarding our home!"

The man's staff flashed, and a bolt of ice splintered the troll's skull, splashing blood against the rock behind him. The remaining trolls cowered, holding onto Orolo's bounds.

"Leave this trash and attend to the prisoners. Assure they get to the High Rock and then pray the Matriarch does not seek your heads for wasting time."

The trolls dropped Orolo and scurried off. Orolo looked up at the two figures.

"The Matriarch cannot be bothered with this as of now," the man with the staff said. "If we are to secure our place, we must assure everything is done as she wants to that very moment."

"Agreed," the other man said. His voice was deep, and his face was not visible behind a silver mask. He was well armored. Kealin assumed this was the man he had heard so many rumors about.

"You are Orolo, are you not?" the man with the staff asked.

"I am."

"You and your friends caused quite the mayhem at the Swamp House. We agreed to buy the artifact for a good price from you, but you couldn't even deliver it. We had to retrieve it from the bottom of the river, and not until that bumbling oaf of a monster finally admitted he had lost it."

"I am sorry."

"Why did you come here? Speak quickly."

Orolo was silent.

"I have no more time. You deal with this. I do not want to see him again."

The man with the staff stormed away, disappearing down a passage. The masked man stepped toward Orolo.

"Please, no. Please!" Orolo begged.

The man reached down, gripping Orolo by the neck. Brethor tightened his grip on his sword. As his brother was strangled before him, the Srvivnann appeared from behind the rock and charged to his aid. Blade in hand, he cut at the arm holding Orolo's neck. His blade deflected, and in a flash, the masked man drew his blade, running upon him. He parried once and then was thrown into a roll by the second attempted parry.

The masked man approached him but was struck by Kealin and his father from behind. In a flurry of blades, the three fought. Kealin moved with haste to distract the man from Brethor, but the masked swordsman was skilled beyond what he had faced in some time. Kealin brought both blades down toward the man's head but found he was too slow. The man was upon him, head butting him away. Kealin rolled across the floor.

Brethor made his way to Orolo. He was barely breathing. Kealin watched as his father moved effortlessly against the swordsman, his Urlas blade singing in the cave air with a quiet hum with each swipe, causing the other swordsman to recoil. He parried and punched the man, cracking his mask with a single strike. The man recoiled, stammering backward. He seemed weary, and Kealin's father was unforgiving. He gave no quarter. He charged the man and, with an arching swing, struck the man in the chest, casting him off the edge of the cliff. His father knelt and sheathed his sword.

Kealin stood up unsteadily as his father approached.

"You still have much to learn, and perhaps two swords are not better than one!"

Kealin smiled and then made his way to Brethor and Orolo.

"I am sorry," Orolo choked. "I betrayed you."

"I saw nothing of betrayal," Brethor told him. "You saved us back there."

Orolo smiled but then coughed more.

"Go, Brethor," Kealin said.

"I told you I would help you get your family."

"Take care of your own," Kealin said. He looked behind Brethor, seeing a passage and a large open doorway. "I see light far down this very hall. Perhaps it is a way out of the mountain, and again, fate has made it so. The trolls should be busy in here, and there is a chance this region could be swarmed with whatever else is guarding this place. You can use the necklace to get him to Eh-Rin. Perhaps it is not too late."

"Kealin, I wish to help you, friend."

"Then make sure no one else dies needlessly. I will see you when this is done."

Brethor nodded and lifted his brother up, beginning a struggling trudge toward the door.

Kealin's father joined him and patted him on the back. "Son, let us go save your mother and brother."

They followed in the direction the man with the staff went. This "Matriarch" was a key to the awakening of the orcs, and Kealin would go for her.

They came to a large open cavern. The sloshing of water far below filled with the stench of long rotting bodies preserved in the coldness of the caves was pungent to their noses. There was a large center pillar, high above the waters, and a land bridge accessible from a portion of ground on a slope from where they were.

"Bring the sacrifices forward!" a voice cackled.

Kealin fell against the wall as his father peeked out, looking up.

He then looked to the left and fell back to where Kealin hid.

"They come this way. They go toward that center stone. That is what they call the High Stone. It is there they will attempt the sacrifice."

He stared into his father's eyes. A Blade of Urlas. A warrior of many battles, but his stalwart mind was troubled and he saw fear as he looked at him.

"There is a way up to that one we heard before. It is a woman of some kind, but from what we heard earlier, she is a key to this. Kill her, Kealin. Now is not the time for anything but bloodshed."

"Father, I will do it."

His father smiled at him. "I will save your mother and your baby brother. I am proud to fight with you, Son. Even if you use two blades. You always did like the stories of Riakar."

They shared a smile and then both moved closer to the corner of the passage. He smiled again, thinking of Riakar, the dual-blade-wielding warrior from eons ago. His mother and father had both told him those stories. The last time he heard that name, he had been with his brothers and sister. He wept a single tear and then focused his mind. They crept near the edge of the passage.

He spotted his mother. She was frail now; her supple skin and fair hair was now cut, bruised, and ragged. She bled from her arms, and within them, she clung to a bundle of cloth. He spotted the dangling leg of his brother. He could not have been more than a year old.

Multiple trolls, including the two from before, marched them down the slope and to the pillar. The two leading were the smallest. The other trolls were massive and three times the size of a normal elf. Kealin looked up, seeing stones that led up to a wooden platform. His father nodded and pointed for him to go upward. Kealin began to climb. His hands slipped on the moist rocks, but he dug his fingers in and straddled the stone as he made his way up.

A reddish hue began to flow up into the air from the

platform above. He began to hear an enchantment over the sounds of the water far below.

"Long have they rested, demon spawns of elven kind. With waters from the heavens, called forth by the power of the ancient race, let sacrifice bring forth life to rancid shells and black blood flow once more.

"Let not another moon rise without the shriek of the orc! Let the rumbles of the mountain caves fill with the footfall of servants to the will of the Black Star of Ur, demon of the Far South. Let not another day pass without prophecy fulfilled. This I do as a high servant to growing powers."

Kealin had reached the top. He could see the woman who spoke. She was shorter, with scraggly blond hair and a face aged from unnatural powers. A horrid sight to see. Her son was nearby. He held aloft his staff, adding to the enchantment in a wave of red magic that swarmed above them.

Kealin heard a sudden cruel shout below. "Stop him!"

He ducked down to the ground, turning to see his father move with haste upon the trolls, spinning his silver blade and hewing the head of the first one he came upon.

In a leap from the ground, Kealin drew his blades as the Matriarch moved forward in anger. She was too caught up in seeing what the shouting was to have noticed him on the edge of the rocks. Her eyes grew large as his blades passed in a scissor motion toward her head, cutting tissue and severing arteries, spraying her nearby son in blood.

The woman's body burst into a black fire that leaped from her and consumed her son. Kealin looked at the man who dropped his staff. He was stunned for the moment, his eyes open and his mouth in a large grin. He ran forward with his blades and went to strike the man but was knocked back just as their metal went near him. He landed on his back, and the man began to laugh.

"I knew you were there before and now you have done what I was bound not to do! It was my time for power, and now that bitch is done. I shall command the armies of orcs upon the lands!"

Kealin found his feet again and noticed that though the man spoke, he was caught in some spell or transfer of power from the corpse of the Matriarch. Kealin turned to see his father. The man moved with haste, unceasingly striking down each troll, their bodies falling into the waters below until at last the original two they had seen remained. They held a knife to his mother, and his father stepped forward.

The trolls lost courage and turned, falling to their deaths instead of facing the Blade of Urlas. Kealin made his way back down and began to run to the land bridge. He saw his father grip his mother, his brother held between them.

Behind him, a bright flash splashed the cave in light. There was a thunderous sound, and he looked to see the masked man appear on the far edge of the cavern.

"Do it now, servant! Destroy them!" the man above Kealin shouted.

Kealin turned his run. His target was now the masked man, but before he could get close, a silver flash cut through the air. The masked man's blade flew in a spin, arching over to where his father and mother stood, piercing his father in his upper back and slamming into his mother, pinning them against the rock.

He slid to change his path, running now to his parents as the man above them cackled. He made it to the land bridge, seeing as his parents' blood flowed off the rock and dropped down into the water below. He reached them. His father was slumped dead, and his mother had a loosening grip on his brother. He heard the baby's cry and took him in his arms after sheathing one of his swords.

"Kealin," his mother whispered.

"Yes, Mother?" He began to cry.

"Take him and keep him well. And make them pay for this! I will give you what time I can."

His mother's eyes turned white, her archon powers enraged in a last moment that was a mix of a mother's fury and that of a side he had never seen. A sizzling white fireball flew upward and then split, striking both the masked man and the man above. As the last of her power dwindled, Kealin ran back across the land bridge.

The ground began to tremble, and hisses and shrieks began to sound all around him. He looked over the edge and noticed that the surface of the water was no more. The walls of the caves moved, and creatures were swarming. He ran for the passageway that his father and he had come through when on the opposite end. What seemed like hundreds of the creatures appeared. He turned, running back toward where the masked man was.

The white fire from his mother that had enveloped the two of his adversaries had faded, and he ran toward his foe with a single blade. He leaped, gripping his brother but did not seek to kill his enemy but use the parry to propel him past. The move worked, and he flipped up, landing paces away from the masked man where he continued to run, spotting another land bridge. He ran across it as a blast of air flew just near his head, striking a rock ahead, turning it to pebbles. The wizard followed, as did the masked man. He turned down a passage and was met by the cackles of orcs.

They were half his size but wielded weapons still dripping with water. They had pointed ears and long noses, and many had gray hair. Upon seeing him, they went into a frenzy, crawling the walls and leaping for him.

He cut into them in defense, showering himself in black blood. He jumped up, using their heads as steps as he ran over the top of them until eventually he was barreling again through them. They stabbed at him, cutting his arms and legs. He held his brother close, using his blade to deflect blows that would have struck the child. He made it through the passage and tripped, rolling over other orcs and landing in an underground river. He sat up and saw sunlight and what seemed like a waterfall leading out.

Orcs were upon him, and a glow from the passage he had come from told him the other two were coming. The surrounding orcs growled.

"Die!" he cried out. In multiple spins, he cut down the orcs, slicing through their flesh one after the other as more moved against him. He spun left and right, slashing them, slowly forming a mound of corpses. He side-stepped toward the falls when the masked man leaped from above, nearly striking him.

He stumbled back to avoid the blow and fell down the falls.

TORN REVELATIONS

He thought of his brother. As the torrential current pulled him down and then spit him out a rocky crevice, he gripped the child in his arms and curled around him as they landed in the pool below the falls. He kicked upward and broke the surface of the water, gasping and lifting the child up, who coughed and cried. A good sign. He swam to the edge of a large lake and waded out. He sheathed his sword and looked at the child. He appeared uninjured.

Kealin closed his eyes for a moment and exhaled before turning to look behind him. The sea sparkled with sunlight. He trudged toward it and in so went away from the source of aching pain in his heart. Not only had he not found Alri but he met up with his father and mother only long enough for them to die. He was too used to his own actions resulting in more death.

He cradled his brother, looking down at the innocent child's eyes. They had witnessed much death; the spirit of darkness had been upon him. Kealin began to walk along the shore of the lake. The shoreline was ahead of him. It was then he saw masts of a familiar type. Amhe's navy, the ships sent to scout out the rumors of orcs within the mountains, was moving just outside that of the beaches.

He heard growls behind him. Orcs had begun to slide down the falls and fill the basin beneath. As more of the vile creatures began to appear, others came from caves in the rocks, hurrying down toward him. Kealin ran, drawing his blade once again as the rocks above began to reveal caves like that of ants, opening up with fresh orcs jumping down to the ground near him. His blade sung, hewing a path forward as more of the beasts were upon him. One of five ships was closing in on the inlet. There was a narrow passage of deep waters, and as the ship pointed its bow toward the lake, an electrified stream of light shot out across the water with a sizzling sound. It struck behind Kealin, burning the orcs in a horrid flash.

As he neared the beach, another wave of orcs burst from a passageway near the edge of the mountain. He turned, taking stance as two jagged blades swung for him. He parried the first, stepping forward and striking the beast with an elbow before pushing his blade into a second parry. He sliced the neck of his attacker just as a renewed wave swarmed him. He fell back toward the water. A rush of electricity surged over him, striking the orcs as the Rusis trio jumped from the ship, casting balls of flame and ice. Multiple Eh-Rin guards followed.

"You must go!" Kealin shouted. "There come many

more orcs and a man of arcane powers beyond us. We must get the child to safety."

Jesia looked down to whom Kealin held.

"A baby?"

"My brother, entrusted to me by my parents, who fell dead within the caves not too long ago."

Dala appeared, drawing his blade as his men rushed upon the orcs, slicing into the ever-growing ranks.

"Brethor told us of what has happened that he witnessed. We saw him upon a distant shore not too far away. He was to head to Eh-Rin. We have confirmed that the orcs are here." He paused, looking at Kealin's brother. "A child? Come, we must get you and that child to safety. To the ship."

The other ships of the fleet were nearing position along the beaches. The crystals aboard their bows whirred to life, beginning a cascading flow of lightning upon the shores. The orcs were burned to cinders, a flow of black ash mixed with blood. At that moment, Kealin spotted the man of magic from before. He stood upon the mountain next to the falls. He lifted his staff up, white fire leaping from it into the air and clouds spinning the pale sky to a black whirlwind. The tornado shifted over the water, tearing into one of the ships, ripping its deck and men apart.

"We must go!" Dala shouted.

The Rusis were boarding ahead of Kealin, who looked back down to the beach. The men of Amhe fell back, and looking back up the rope ladder, he saw Jesia's hand.

A roar louder than the orcs' clamor filled the air.

Kealin turned back to see the swordsman from before suddenly upon the beach, cutting down the men of Eh-Rin. It was the masked one. In moments he could be upon the ship's deck.

He pushed his brother up to Jesia, who took him in his arms.

"Keep my blood well. Take him to Eh-Rin so he will be safe. I will come for him."

Kealin dropped back to the water. As one of the last of the men of Amhe fell, Kealin rushed forward, drawing both blades, catching the masked man as he went to jump for the ship. He sliced into the man's side, taking a blow to his own shoulder with the man's blade as they both fell into the surf. Kealin pushed himself up, noticing his blood flowing into the water.

Dala moved the ship away from the inlet as the wizard began to turn the tornado to that of ice, attempting to capture or destroy all who stood against the orcs. Kealin fell back away from the beaches, drawing the masked man away from the vicinity of the fleet. He stepped backward through the sludge of burned corpses. The ships of Eh-Rin were down to their last two, including the ship of Dala.

Watching as the tornado of ice spun closer to the flagship, a spinning light shot out around the ship, shielding it from the icy blast, but the water around the ship had frozen, trapping it. The Rusis aboard seemed to be casting fire, attempting to melt the ice from beneath the protection of the shield, but the tornado was relentless.

Kealin jumped up to the rocks and saw a path

toward the wizard. He had to distract him to allow the ship to escape. More orcs emerged, but Kealin ran quickly along the rocks. The masked man was following him but was slower. As Kealin reached the summit of the rocks, he took hold of a stone and threw it with great force toward the wizard. It struck him, and he recoiled, falling down for a moment. The tornado, empowered by his staff, faltered, and the ship had a chance to escape.

Kealin ran for the wizard and slashed both blades toward him. The wizard parried the attacks, his own staff whirring with undulating winds as he pushed against the half-elf.

"You are a great warrior, but you must know that magic is supreme," he jeered.

Wind began to surge toward them as Kealin felt his grip loosening on his own blades. He kicked the wizard in the knee and then felt himself flung off the rocks, cast down to the shore beside the lake.

The ground shook some distance from where he landed, as the masked man had jumped down to him. Kealin pushed himself up, glancing toward the ship. It had escaped. Its protective veil was still up, but it seemed that while the crystalline protection worked well, it took up the power of the crystal and they could not help him. The whirlwind came upon the lake, freezing its surface before dissipating. The orcs filled the lake behind him as the wizard descended to his level.

Kealin stood uneasily, his shoulder surging from the injury from before. Obvious blood ran down his body. The masked man held his blade out to him as the wizard approached.

"You killed my mother, a witch of power beyond you but frail in mind and body. Thank you, for you released her matriarchal powers to myself, thus securing my position as the arch wizard. I am of a sect, one not unlike others of magic that exist, but perhaps we can make an arrangement with you?"

Kealin was not hearing the man. His mind surged with that of his mother, father, and fallen brothers. Whatever lies or bargaining this man wanted, Kealin cared little. With a last lunge, he drove his blade forward, the tip aiming for the wizard's chest, but the masked swordsman parried it away. His blade sliced the shoulder of the wizard. Cloth, tissue, and squirting blood followed as he turned his attack and once again engaged the masked warrior.

The wizard fell back in half-amazement of Kealin's nerve and watched as the two of them fought. Kealin slid across the ice, bracing himself as the masked man slammed into him in a fury of strikes. The orcs stepped back, leaving a large circle around them to duel.

Kealin and the man locked blades.

"Who are you?" Kealin yelled. He recognized the fighting style, the blade work, the form.

"Death."

Kealin pushed off the man and into the air before driving the hilt of his blade down into his face. The mask he was wearing cracked further, and the man recoiled, falling back.

He ran forward, dodging the blade again and aiming for the man's head. As his blade cracked on the lower jaw of the mask, it shattered, throwing the man against the ice. Kealin had gained the upper hand. He ran forward and jumped toward his target with both blades.

The man held out his hand to Kealin, and as he scanned his face, he parted his blades, thrusting them into the ice at either side of his target's head.

"Taslun?"

"Kealin!"

Between his blades was his brother, his face scarred and filled with tears.

"You were dead," Kealin said.

"I have done horrible things, Brother."

The mask began to slowly fly back toward his face. Taslun screamed in agony as the pieces fused.

"What is this?" Kealin asked.

"Cannot . . . withstand . . . the powers . . ."

The pieces fused one by one until the mask was nearly complete again.

"Brother, go to Risdannia—" Taslun begged. "Save me."

"Taslun, this mask, get it off!"

Kealin pried at the edge of the mask as the last few pieces fused. The eye holes flashed white, and Taslun struck him center chest, throwing him off and sliding across the ice. He opened his eyes to see Taslun mid-flight, a furious white fire engulfing him as the power upon him surged.

In this moment, Kealin felt the ice shattering to his side, and in a rush of water and large pieces of ice, a massive horn struck Taslun in the side. The ice gave way and as Kealin fell in, he spotted his narwhal friend, Tulasiro, with his boat in tow.

Taslun was stunned, lying on the ice. Tulasiro now wore a headband of gold and slid upon the ice, cracking it as she turned in the water. Kealin's boat was in tow, and having been dragged onto the ice, it was free of water. He leaped into it as more of the ice gave way and began to crack, taking many orcs with it as the entire icy shelf began to shatter. Tulasiro began to pound her tail, and they took off across the icy surface.

Kealin turned to see the wizard grasping his brother's body and hovering over the water with him. He looked to the path ahead and the few orcs that remained. As they flew past them, reaching more slushy water, Kealin swung at their heads, taking them off in passing. They reached the sea, and Kealin noticed that though they went to what would be warmer waters, the bluish glow of the narwhal seemed to give off a radiant chill. Meredaas had indeed blessed his friend.

But the wizard still pursued. He was high in the air, supported by his spell craft. A blast of wind struck near them in the water, and Tulasiro turned the ship sharply.

"Friend, you cannot face this one. We must flee to the far south. The city of Eh-Rin," Kealin told her.

As they headed toward the wizard, he knelt down low in the boat. The wizard shot another blast of wind, and it struck Kealin, knocking him back into the boat. He felt suddenly dizzy and had difficulty seeing.

Tulasiro thundered forward. The golden crown on her head turned yellow, and a blast flew from the narwhal, striking the wizard, throwing him back into the rocky cliffs with a plume of rocks exploding into the air.

The narwhal turned and began to pull them out to

sea again. The narwhal was taking him to a place of purpose, but not Eh-Rin as he wanted. As the orcs now awakened sunk back into the caves, the narwhal and Kealin headed back north. He tried to sit up but could not. Blackness overtook him.

DARK TIDINGS

Brethor sat beside Orolo at the Healing Gardens of Eh-Rin. He awaited news of Kealin. Since alerting the fleet of Eh-Rin and reaching the healers, they had heard nothing.

It had been some time, perhaps a day or more, since those events, and he had been without sleep, awaiting news.

"Brethor," Orolo said at last.

"Brother! I was worried of your condition."

"Did they do it?"

"I do not know of Kealin and his father, but the orcs did arise. I await to hear news of our friend." Brethor paused, looking down at the emotionless stare of his brother. "What do you mean exactly by your question?"

"You have answered it. The orcs are now alive."

"Brother, the orcs are not friends of our kind."

"They are not friends of our enemies either, and more will come."

Brethor sat back away from his brother. "Your betrayal is known, but perhaps I do not understand how far."

Orolo sat up. The strain on his throat had been healed. He stood.

"Yes, I sought profit from the jewel, but I must not deny that the witch has good use of the orcs. She will use them to ravage the lands and, with it, those against us. They will help turn the tide against men."

"The orcs are vile. They will not stop with men. They will plunder all lands and kill all without regard."

"We are outnumbered. Half-bloods, Dwemhar descendants, elves, dwarves. We must do what is necessary."

Orolo's eyes traced behind Brethor, and he turned to see Jesia. Her face was red and tears ran down her cheeks. He looked in her arms, seeing Kealin's brother.

"What is this? Where is Kealin?" he paused, "Who is this child?"

"The brother of the half-elf. The last of his line. I... I believe Kealin is dead."

Seer of Lost Sands answered the question of what happened to Kealin's parents. While now, they are both dead, Kealin has learned that he not only still seeks Alri but also a way to save Taslun... and war is coming.

Orcs

A bastardized race, created in part by the powers of the Itsu gods, thrown down by the heroes and heroines of the Western elves. The world now trembles under the control of a madman that seeks to destroy the West. Right? That's what it might seem like. Friends become enemies and enemies could become friends but that is the danger in the coming war. Who is truly the allies to our friends?

The elves have a near zealous hate of the orc, spurred by years that they themselves had to deal with the orcs and still fresh from their war against the vampires and demon men, they will not stand idle to the threat that approaches.

But with orcs come trolls, goblins, and all manners of beasts. At their forefront, Taslun himself. Engorged with dark magic...

I wrote this partially as a narrative to racism in our own history. Racism goes back to many countries and regions where another culture was deemed lesser due to color, beliefs, religion, or some combination of these. Orcs as these that have been resurrected are not the orcs of old. They do not have the cohesion of the old orc hordes. They are unified, albeit, my magic, under a single power but tell that to the elves. I have many armies coming together, working through their differences to face a greater evil, but what is the greater evil? Orcs or the memory of what orcs were? You'll soon see.

Brethor and Orolo

The duo treasure hunters that I modeled after Indiana Jones and Rick O'Connell from The Mummy (The early 2000s version NOT the one with Tom Cruise) I wouldn't mind writing a story just with these two clowns moving across the lands looking for ancient Dwemhar treasure...

Gladiators and Cyr

The Island of Cyr is a place of the opulent of the Grand Protectorate, a place that has little to do with Kealin in this series and more to do with the historical significance of what the Grand Protectorate had built in the shadows of their own society. The arena serves to show the future that is to come for those of magic, where they are used as a slave race, to fight for the entertainment of others.

Where their lives hold little value and the race of men is made numb to their subsequent torture and execution.

Of course, it would be a question of why the elves of the West would allow such a travesty just across the water from them but the elves have been at war in their own lands and if evident by the map and the "desolation of demon men", it did not go well for them.

It should be noted that Kealin's actions in the arena did not go unseen and a figure to come witnessed the "Elf Warrior of Cyr".

Jinn, Amhe, and Eh-Rin.

The desert of Lost Sands and the Dashrin Coast are a bit of mystery of their own. While the far northern Glacial Seas were once land, this region was at one time a vast jungle. Furthermore, in the desert, they are careful to keep a direct path or risk being "lost" much like in The Legend of Zelda Ocarina of Time. (there will be more Zelda references, watch for them in the next book!)

As for Amhe, I wanted a calm and peaceful ruler, someone to offer a peaceful almost "father-like" character for Kealin, who has up to this point been enslaved twice and has had no moments of peace since leaving Urlas. Eh-Rin, is truly a jewel of a city. Akin to another city, Aieclo, from another time in the Dwemhar world, it is powered by massive crystals and even on the surface is much more of a technological marvel than anything else around it. Also, as a home to the Sanguine Monks, it is a place of focus for Kealin as he develops his power as a half-Dwemhar, something that will become significantly more important to him as the series progresses.

My Writing Playlist

This list is a bit shorter. Not any particular reason except that maybe TV soundtracks are longer and I generally write in twenty to thirty minute sprints.

Seer of Lost Sands Playlist

1. Deku Palace -Koji Kondo (The Legend of Zelda OOT)

2. ALL of the Starz Spartacus TV show songs through Season Three

3. Gladiator Soundtrack "The Battle" -Yvonne S. Moriaty

SHADOW OF THE ORC STAR

HALF-ELF CHRONICLES BOOK 3

Revised 2nd Edition

THE LOST WOODS

He gave up on convincing Tulasiro to change her path. For many hours, she had pulled them through a deep fog, and the only hint he had was they were headed north. The truth was, she was following what she was meant to follow. In the time his narwhal had left, went to Meredaas, and saved him from the wizard and his own brother, she had changed, and Kealin could do nothing to dissuade where he was being taken.

"We need to go south," Kealin said plainly.

But their course didn't change. It had been only a few days since his parents' deaths. The same day he pushed his baby brother onto an Eh-Rin ship into the care of a Rusis that seemed as confused as he was at that moment.

Worse, he now knew his brother was alive but trapped by a mask.

Risdannia. He would find that place. Wherever it was. He still questioned where he was.

At sunrise of the second day, they turned east and now traveled down a large river with leaf-covered banks on either side. The trees reached over them and darkened out the sunlight above. They were almost taller than the ones of Urlas. The woods were strangely devoid of life, be they beast, elf, dwarf, or others.

They came to a narrower region of the river, and Tulasiro stopped, releasing the rope from her mouth and swimming in a circle before diving back underwater.

"I see that the sea-god gave you the ability to leave the ocean and go into a river, but . . ." The narwhal began to swim away. "Tulasiro, where are you going?"

She ignored him and kept swimming, leaving him alone on the shoreline. Now he was stuck, and he had no clue where he actually was. A yellow bird flew down from a tree and landed on the edge of his boat.

"I don't guess you can actually tell me where I am?"

The bird flew away. That served as a summary of his exact situation.

Kealin felt his head. It was still swollen from the blow to his skull during the fighting. His arms still ached from the scratches, but they had at least scabbed over. He had no food and no narwhal.

Some friend.

Kealin stood up in the boat and stepped onshore. The woods were old. He could feel it in the earth. Deep vibrations in the soil, like it had been untouched by any foot for a long time. There was a whisper in the wind, but he struggled to make it out. He needed to figure out where he was, and ahead he could see a hill that might give him some idea of that.

He began to walk toward it, but he couldn't find an absolutely straight path. Large tree trunks forced him around and down into valleys of rock before he would work his way back up to find that he had gone too far north or west. He walked back the other way, attempting to snake his way down a path that would lead him to where he wanted, but then again realized that he went back past the hill and found ruins so weathered, he could only barely see the fact it was crafted stone.

Attempting to avert the overall issue of walking in any direction again, he began up into the trees. A large pine reached high into the boughs, and in a quick fashion, he climbed up the tree. He scanned his surroundings.

Not only could he not see any other hills or ruins, he saw only more trees. He had now lost the river as well, and soon he would lose any light and chance to get out of the woods.

He found a fork in a tree and laid back.

If I'm stuck here, I may as well keep a good view outward.

As the sun sank and a pale moon rose over the trees, he caught a glimmer of water in the far distance. It was a lake. He pulled out his map but noticed he only had the coastline of this new land. He made out where he might be in reference to time and what he saw, but if this was true, he was stuck between two mountain ranges.

He saw a spark of light beneath his feet. He sat up and looked down. It was a fairy, zipping and shooting around the branches, ascending to where he was sitting. It floated in front of him for a moment and seemed to laugh.

"What?"

The fairy shook and then struck him in the head before floating down to the branch below them.

He rubbed the spot the fairy had hit.

"Do you want me to come to that branch?"

The fairy dropped again, and Kealin checked his grip before dropping down branch by branch as the fairy took him to ground level. The sounds of bugs and singing crickets filled the air. An owl screeched in the distance, and he heard the flutter of its wings and saw a shadow as it flew off.

The fairy danced a path through the trees that Kealin followed. He was careful not to get left by the swift sprite. Up a fallen tree and across an offshoot of the river, they then went through an open archway of tree limbs and to rockier ground where large stones littered the landscape. Climbing up to the top of a boulder, he found that the fairy danced above a stone bridge that led to an open area of green grass bare of trees. He then saw a shadow to his right. His hands went to his hilts.

He glanced around, and a gust blew through the trees. A shadow again, this time to his right. He drew his blades, and the fairy that had led him darkened and fluttered away.

He closed his eyes and took a deep breath. For a moment, he felt again at the arena in Urlas, shifting shadows around him, his blade in hand as Master Rukes watched over him.

A nimble footfall was in the air. It moved with elegance, in silence, except for Kealin's attuned ear. It moved like an elf.

He opened his eyes to see the carved edge of a wooden staff swinging toward his head. He jerked his blade up to catch it and twisted his other blade in a thrust.

Smack. There was another attacker behind him. He did a defensive spin, knocking back a total of three attackers. A thrown knife spun toward him, and he deflected it to the side just as an arrow whistled in the air. He ducked and then rolled into one of the attackers. They stumbled. He made a low slash that was parried before he kicked the attacker. The wooden staff came diagonally down toward his head. He pushed off the staff with his blades and knelt down to the ground in preparation for another attack, scanning his sides, but now his attackers were still.

A man stood off to the side with a large owl on his shoulder. He clapped twice.

"Kealin of Urlas, half-elf of renown. Indeed, it is you. We seek your help."

2

SCIONS

He stood up slowly, and the other three cloaked warriors lowered their weapons. The man with the owl approached him.

"Please, we do not mean you harm, but we did have to test you. Perhaps you are as strong as they say?"

The man bowed to him.

"I am Ruak, of the Scions of Starfall, and I hope you will forgive our rash welcome."

Kealin sheathed his swords but did not return the bow. "It depends on the true manner of your welcome. You fight surprisingly well. I did not expect to find ones like you in these dank woods on the edge of nowhere. I have been lost for hours trying to find my way out."

"These are the Lost Woods of Resip. It is an enchanted region that spans both sides of the river and up into the elven lands of Fikmark. It is a safeguard against those who would do us harm. Come, let us take you to somewhere more comfortable."

Kealin followed the small group calling themselves Scions. They proceeded down a bleak stone path that crossed the grassy glade and continued on toward a stone road lit with torchlights that stood on stone pedestals at hip level.

"You have seen much death?" Ruak asked directly.

"I have, but it matters little. Whatever you feel you need from me, I am sure it does not mean as much as my own desires. I am a mere elf from the North."

"Indeed, we know of Urlas and of your father and mother."

Kealin looked at him. "Then you will be saddened to know they have died."

The traveling group paused.

Ruak stared back at him. "The Urlas Blade and the archon have fallen?"

"A sacrifice. To revive the orcs."

Two of the other elves chattered between themselves, but Kealin could not make out the words.

"I knew your father was looking for your brother and mother. Him and I spoke frequently of many things in the past few months. There were rumors they had been taken by the Ur. It seems the mad Matriarch finally got what she wanted."

They came to a large wooden wall built into trunks of several trees that veiled the forest path. From the trees above, a woman descended to the ground.

"You found the half-elf?"

The woman was slender and had blond hair that was long down her back.

"We did."

The woman nodded and made a hand signal into the trees. The wall vanished, and they walked through. Kealin turned around to see the wall solidify again. There was a circle of stone structures with high steeples and a great tree in the center of the elven buildings.

"Welcome to our humble abode," Ruak said.

"You live away from others?"

"Away, yes. From others, well, that is a bit more complicated. We work for the others, but we are considered fringe followers of the elven kingdoms."

"Scions of Starfall. You make reference to the Starfall Concordat, I am sure," Kealin said.

"Indeed, but the concordat was really just a ceasefire, not any real agreement of peace."

"Scions were true elves," the blonde said. "They did what was needed no matter the cost."

"This is Elaca, one of the best archers in all of the trees that stretch within elven lands."

Elaca bowed. "The rumors heard on the coast towns speak of an arena elf that killed more guards than I believe possible."

"Perhaps it is so," said Kealin. "Many things of late have seemed impossible. I do not understand why my narwhal friend led me right to you. What is this about?"

"The sea creature came to our druids as they sought the knowledge of the darkness to the south. The druids saw your zeal upon her mind and the belief that you were of Urlas."

They came to a circular table near the large tree. Kealin sat down with Elaca as Ruak motioned to the others to leave them alone. Kealin looked up into the trees, spotting the moon and a very clear night. The owl that Ruak had on his shoulder now sat on a perch to their right. Ruak took a torch and lit basins of red rocks surrounding them.

"This region is protected, Kealin. Do not worry about your enemy here."

"I don't frequently worry about them when they are standing next to me."

"Of course." He smiled. "An Urlas Blade does not have such lowly beliefs as fear."

"I am not a Blade."

Elaca shifted her eyes toward Ruak. He took a seat and bowed his head.

"So you are the one he spoke of? Your father mentioned his son who preferred two blades to one and does not embrace the Urlas ways."

"The Urlas ways did not embrace me. We lived on the fringe, away from other elves. If you didn't know, some feel that half-elves aren't up to living near the holy places."

"Elves of the southern lands can be stubborn but not quite that isolating. We do not have time for such ceremony or racist preference in recent years. But still, there are rules to society."

"So what are we doing? Are you questioning my place here in your world? Looking for what's wrong with me? I have somewhere to go, and I would like to find my friend Tulasiro."

"Tulasiro, this is the narwhal?"

He nodded.

"She will meet you down by the river. The druids are

down there gathering herbs, and we can see her soon if
you wish. We are your friend, Kealin. I said we need
your help, and in good faith, you can know that we, too,
are not so welcome among the elven councils. This is the
Varmark Elven Realm. Though we are elves, we are the
arm of elven power who doesn't always follow the council's wishes but stay more loyal to the heart of what it
means to be elves. We have gone south to face a new
enemy with the Rangers of the Riverlands. We have
dealt with the dwarves of the far eastern Tikens Mountains before they were destroyed by some random fire
that engulfed their mines. An accident, supposedly, but I
feel there is a deeper malice at work. Of stranger occurrence, I'm sure to you, we've more than once stolen and
taken life from our own people. Elves can be stubborn,
and coercing can be difficult.

"We are the last willing to do whatever is necessary
to secure our world. We called for the Urlas forces. The
elves fought to the north against a sect of demon men
brought about by another terrible race of creatures. That
fight has only recently lessened. Some have said that the
Grand Protectorate instilled the desire to worship such
false gods in the men, but others claim it not true. Men
themselves have claimed it evil elves who fought us."

Elaca snickered. "Those men fought like men.
Sloppy and unskilled but with numbers that increase
every day. The old fight with the young. You could say
that men are fortunate. It has been some time since seed
elves were born. There are no elven children in this
region. Ever since the cities to the east fell under the
protection of the Protectorate, that is. There is a curse

upon us. The city they took had many alchemists, and though they denounce it, they use magic, and I swear they are behind the tribulations that we deal with now."

Ruak went to a stove and stoked a fire before setting a kettle to warm water.

"You wonder why we brought you here, so I will get to it. The Grand Protectorate wages a war from afar, but they are not our issue. You know of the Matriarch and her son, obviously. The orcs now dwell to the south. It is the Order of Ur, the demon god of the Itsu, who we fear. They attempt to resurrect an old evil and take advantage of the chaos of elves, dwarves, and all of magic and men alike to take power from the good in the world. We need your help in stopping them."

The water on the stove had begun to boil. Ruak added some tea and then brought it to the table. Kealin stood as he did and started to pace.

"I killed the Matriarch."

Ruak glanced to him. "That is a good start, and the bastard son?"

"Stood to the side and let me kill her before absorbing his mother's power. He is a wizard, and one not afraid to use his skills. That was before a dark swordsman threw his sword, piercing my father and my mother against a sacrificial post. The orcs swarmed the caverns of the mountains, and with my baby brother, I fled. I took the child to a ship of Eh-Rin, and then while dueling the swordsman and the wizard, I discovered the identity of the dark blade I fought. My eldest brother is trapped in a mask that forces him to the will of that wizard and whatever worshipers of Ur you speak of. I

already search for my sister, Alri, lost from the realm of
the god Dimn, and now I search for a place known as
Risdannia."

Elaca and Ruak looked at one another.

"We know of the place," Elaca said.

"It is true," Ruak confirmed. "It is to the east, but it is
not so simple to just stroll in. Much like the Urlas realm,
it is protected, and not by mere magic as protects the
borders of these lands. You speak of Eh-Rin, so Amhe
knows of your toil?"

Kealin shook his head. "They all likely think I'm
dead. I worked with a Rusis and two men of Dwemhar
blood."

"You have powerful friends, then."

"I have the desire and need to save my family. What
is left of them."

Ruak stood holding a cup of tea. He walked to
Kealin and offered him the cup. He looked down at it.

"It isn't poison. If we wanted you dead, I believe we
might have been able to do it earlier." Ruak laughed.

He took the cup and took a sip. The tea was minty
and had a slight tinge near the back of his throat.

"Good?"

Kealin nodded.

Ruak went back to the table and picked up his own
cup. "The Scions have long stood by elves and men as
a force to do what is necessary. You will find no more
dedicated friends than us. I can direct you to Risdannia, but know that the Moon Elves who dwell there
are not easily waned to matters of the heart. We have
little time. The elven kings in these lands will not

commit forces to deal with the orcs until they have to, and we Scions will prevent that if we can. There is a device, the Orc Star of Ur. It is what unifies the orc tribes, makes them malleable and controllable. It has many names but they are all the same. Some call it the Star of Ur or Black Star. The wars against the orcs were thrown down by the elf kingdom of old. We Scions will honor that. Your father shared with me the secret of your lineage. You are Dwemhar, and your powers may help us find the Orc Star before it falls to the Ur."

"So you needed me for that. To find some star?"

"If you value the lives of your brothers and sister, you will help us find it. It was my father who destroyed the Great Black One, the Lord of Orc, almost five thousand years ago at the end of the orc invasions. I will not let his work be undone by some religious sect of men. You are a great warrior, and we need both the power of your mind and your blade. The Orc Star is of Dwemhar design, used to herd them, but dark magic tainted it. If we find it, we can prevent the second rise of the orcs. I will personally take you to Risdannia, but then you must go with us back to Vueric and the king who dwells there. If the orcs have begun to unify, our task will become more difficult."

Kealin drank his tea and then exhaled. "I wish to see Tulasiro."

Ruak seemed taken back by Kealin's statement. "Yes, but will you help us?"

"I wish to speak with my friend." Kealin had heard plenty of talk at this point. He was curious of Tulasiro and, frankly, needed time to think of what he had been told.

"Then I will take you to the narwhal," Ruak said.

As they walked from the great tree and into a wide green field, he could hear the water rushing against the shores of the grassy area. To the east, there was a massive lake with a yellow-hued splash of moonlight from above.

"Lake Traseen," Ruak told him. "Its shore reaches around near all the major elven kingdoms, and from the river, you can return to the sea or take a southern river toward the Great Isira and to Vueric. The second one will be our path after Risdannia."

Kealin spotted two elves with large branches coming off their shoulders. They had long nails on their hands and glowing bracelets. They each looked up at him with a respectful nod as they reached over the water and Tulasiro emerged.

He went into the river knee deep.

"You left me."

Tulasiro rocked her horn back in forth and then splashed as she swam around.

One of the druids pointed at her and laughed. "Your friend is magnificent. I had called out in my visions to one that could lead us in our path, and when I awoke, this lovely creature had come upon the shore. She is far south for a creature rumored to be in the Glacial Seas, but it seems that all is not as it seems."

"Meredaas," he said to her.

"It does seem the great one of the seas has blessed her. Know she is safe in these waters. As long as the elves are upon these shores, this place will be a safe haven for your creature."

"It is across the waters we will go soon," Ruak said. "But first, we should rest. At first light, we will take you to the far shore and the border of the Great Varmark Woods. Risdannia is deep within."

Kealin noticed that Tulasiro broke the surface of the water and then dove back down. It seemed like she was chasing prey as she had done many times before.

"Plenty of fish to keep her satisfied. Show me to this rest. I could use it."

3

HEIR OF THE DWEMHAR

She cradled the baby's head as he slept. The milk from the goats of the palace of Eh-Rin worked as the perfect food for him since she had gotten back. Jesia sat on the balcony of the sultan, looking over the dunes and at a pale moon. She thought of Kealin and his look toward her as he pushed the baby into her arms.

Amhe walked onto the terrace, but she could tell he had no news of the kind she wanted.

"Dala has returned. I believe Brethor took a fall into a crevice for some amount of time, and he thinks he saw orcs, but other than the bodies of my fallen soldiers, we could not find Kealin. I refuse to believe he is dead."

Jesia wiped a tear from her eye.

"You were close to him?" Amhe said. "I had not known he had feelings for anyone in particular."

"He was a good friend. Why do I say that? He still is a good friend! He isn't dead! You have to look harder!"

The baby began to cry, and Amhe took him. Jesia

protested at first, but then, as the sultan rocked the baby in his arms, making a whistling sound, the child began to sleep.

"I remember when my own son was this small. I was a proud father. I still remember when he first learned to ride a camel! I couldn't keep him off of it. He loved riding."

Jesia stood and solemnly stared at him.

"When his mother died, he was distraught, but he learned to center his energies and release them into the world." Amhe paused. "If only such abilities could have saved him from the blast of the Drean ship that ended his life."

Amhe sniffled and then turned to see Brethor in the doorway.

"I assume Orolo hasn't been an issue?" he said.

"He hasn't," Amhe confirmed. "But I still question locking him up."

"He is a traitor."

"Perhaps so, or perhaps not. He does not believe himself a traitor, and though he did betray you, his purpose was to save others."

Brethor shook his head. "My family would not agree, and I do not. Plus, my friend is now gone."

Amhe nodded and handed the baby back to Jesia. "Excuse me, dear Rusis."

Amhe led Brethor back into the throne room. Dala stood near the other commanders, sipping coffee as Brethor looked at the table map. Iruis, the legatus of the Grand Protectorate, was there as well.

"They tell me there were orcs," Iruis said.

"A few," confirmed Brethor.

"Perhaps you will wish to help against them? Help us to secure the lands of men. The kingdom of Vueric is a vulnerable place."

"And Vueric's King Firda is not easily moved to change," Amhe said. "War is coming to our shores. It is coming to all shores, trees, and mountains, and we as the light of the city of Eh-Rin must be ready to have the courage to charge into the coming darkness."

"Courage is useful, but you need more than courage," Brethor said.

"You are right. I am sending you, the Rusis girls, your brother, and the legatus and his men along with Dala to confer with the good king and form an alliance. Furthermore, you will secure alliances with the elves as we move to stop the scourge of orcs rising in the mountains."

"We are to leave?" Jesia said, entering from the balcony.

"You are."

Jesia pulled the child closer to her.

"The baby will remain here and be safe. He is an heir of the Dwemhar, and the servants of the house of Amhe will care to his every need until such a later time. There is no safer place for him, and you seek Kealin. Perhaps, in this journey, you will find him again."

"Your plan to defeat the orcs is an abrupt one," said Brethor.

Amhe turned back to the assembly of men. "It is, but it must be. Though some of us know of the Order of Ur already, not everyone may have knowledge of the more arcane matters. I will recall why we fear the orcs.

"In the primordial times, as the gods battled one another, and men, elves, dwarves, Dwemhar, and all manner of creatures still slumbered in creation, the demon Ur arose as a god of evil. Take in mind this is before the Itsu separated from the gods of the North. They would align with Ur in time and spirit, but not yet.

The gods created life, and in Ur's desire for creation, he inspired those who would be called wizards and those of necromantic power to rise and form the followers of Ur. The orcs were born wild. A twist on elves themselves. They were unteachable and were more beast than creature of knowledge. He created a device known as the Black Orc Star of Ur and, with the accursed ethereal tool, was able to bring order to his creation.

"But the other gods were angry, spurring their own creations to destroy the orcs. Thus the Great Orc Wars began. The orcs were eventually beaten down by the great races. The elves, in particular, killed thousands, knowing these creatures were bastardized versions of themselves. In the end, all of the followers of Ur were thrown down, and the demon god was sealed away."

"But the orcs have returned," Dala said. "The elves are much less in number now. Two of the old races are destroyed, and men, elves, and dwarves must stand together."

The legatus pointed toward the eastern lands.

"The Grand Protectorate has its issues with elves, but I feel given the circumstance, I can contact them and they will send legions to help us."

"I know little of King Firda, but I would assume the

king will take that as an approach against his power,"
Brethor said.

"Then we must be sure that all truly are united."
Amhe motioned to the legatus. "There is no room for
betrayal in these events. We do not know why the Drear
Orcs have returned, or much of the ones who have awakened them, but we must be united in our response."

Jesia was now joined by Krea and Muera.

"Good, the other Rusis are here," Amhe said. "We do
not know how to destroy the orcs, but we will hold our
ground. The Black Star of Ur is the key. There is a
rumor that a repository of Dwemhar knowledge is held
within the city of Vueric. Brethor, I want you to
convince the king that you need access, using any way
you can. It is there you must learn if there is any mention
of the Black Star. We must do this before it is too late."

"When do we leave?" Brethor asked.

"As soon as you are ready."

BRETHOR WENT down to the cell beneath the palace. It
had been a few days since he petitioned the sultan to
place Orolo there. His brother had betrayed him, and it
was by his own brother's hand the orcs were now a threat
to all.

"Good, Brother," Orolo said, seeing him. "You've
come to finally get me out."

"Open the gate," Brethor said to the lone guard
watching him.

The guard unhinged the lock, and Brethor
stepped in.

"Brethor, I am happy you came to your senses."

Brethor punched his face, sending blood splattering against the wall.

Orolo fell down, grabbing his nose as blood ran over his hands. "You're still mad."

Brethor kicked his foot. "We are leaving."

"To return to Elinathrond?"

"To fix what you did."

"Brother, I have explained my actions to Amhe. He sees my side of it."

"Amhe is a man of patience that which I am not. He can see what he wishes; I see only a traitor."

The guard behind Brethor suddenly shifted his stance. Brethor turned to see Sultan Amhe.

"Brothers at war shall cause more trials than peace."

Amhe went to Orolo and knelt before helping him up.

"Guard, remove this man's bindings." He looked to Brethor. "You are right in many ways, but the truth of all is that men have long moved against those of magic. I cannot see the future, and I will not proclaim I know what is to come, only that the orcs are a scourge. Your brother and you are no mere explorers. You have defeated Dwemhar temples. Embrace your brother in forgiveness, and journey to save all you fight for."

Orolo bowed to Amhe as the sultan went back into the palace.

Brethor was silent. As Orolo went to say something, he shook his head and left him in the cell.

. . .

Jesia stood on the docks, the moon lowering its course and her own eyes heavy with sleep. Muera and Krea were at her side as the legionnaires of the legatus walked up to them. The legatus followed and threw down a sack at their feet.

"I know we do not know each other, but I do believe we can all work together."

"Well, that's good," Krea said. "I would hate for you to develop an issue with us."

The legatus stared at them. "I know you may not trust me or my kind but—"

"We were slaves to a man in Cyr with pigs like you that he called his friend!" Krea shouted.

Jesia raised her hand. "We will do what we must in order to work together."

The legatus smiled, but Krea and even Muera were less than pleased to exchange any form of pleasantries.

A few moments later, Brethor joined them, along with Dala, with Orolo following far behind. A large contingent of Eh-Rin soldiers was traveling with them.

"Then we are all well, I see," said Dala.

"Good as can be. I have not set eyes on these shores for some time," said Brethor.

"Neither have I, but the seas are generally calm. We can be thankful for that."

Boarding the ship, they began out of the harbor in quick work, putting the city of Eh-Rin to failing sight as a massive moon loomed above them. The Srvivnanns and the Rusis went to sleep. It would be a bit of a journey to the coastline of Vueric.

4

IN THE ELVEN REALM

Kealin had a comfortable bed, but it barely reminded him of the one at Eh-Rin. He awoke at sunrise to a plate of berries and another cup of tea. He ate and drank before gathering his things. Walking outside, he noticed that Ruak, Elaca, and both of the elves from the night before waited for him. Ruak took a sip of tea as he approached and introduced them.

"I want you to meet Kealin Half-Elf from Urlas."

The man bowed to him, and Kealin immediately noticed his sword and the inlay of a dragon's head.

"You use a blade well," the man told him.

"I've had some practice."

"The name is Ivasel, swordsman of the Fikmark elves, originally."

The other elf approached. "That was before he joined our little gang of happy sprites, and I say sprites in a good way."

This man's staff hummed as he approached. Its tip began to glow white.

"A healer," Kealin said.

"You must know some of the archon arts?"

"My sister, Alri, she was studying as an archon. She tried to heal a cut once and ended up turning part of my hand into a stone."

The man laughed. "An unfortunate mistake, but young archons typically struggle to perform healing spells correctly. I am Teusk, archon from, well, the Greater Varmark. My home was destroyed around ten years ago. The ruins are to the far north, and the site of the battle is now considered a holy one."

Kealin nodded to the man's sadness and the obvious grief still upon him.

"But that aside now, you still need healing, even after the fairy helped you from before."

Teusk placed his staff over his head and made circular motions. A cloudy haze circled around him, and he felt a vibration on his skin before what aches and pains he had faded.

"Well, now that we are introduced," Ruak began, "we can begin the journey."

The Scions and Kealin walked across the field to the water where Kealin had seen Tulasiro the night before. He went to the shoreline and reached into his shirt. Reaching down, he tapped a small silver hammer on a rock. In a few moments, several long-necked creatures rose to the surface. They had bodies like small dragons, but instead of feet, they had flippers.

"Water horses of Traseen from a temple deep

beneath its surface. One of the patron spirits of these regions is Tras. He resides deep underwater in an old temple. When an elf is christened of age at two hundred years, they must dive down to retrieve a crystal from him. The crystal is seen as a sign of acceptance in his realm, and thus you may continue to dwell in the realms of the woodlands."

"Or what?" Kealin asked him.

"They say you will be banished, but the thought alone kept most from ever failing."

"And the ones who did?"

"A few were saved; a few more than that died."

His nonchalant attitude of the supposed sacred rite of his people amused Kealin, reminding him slightly of himself to some strange degree.

The water horses waddled up on the shore, and they mounted their backs. There was one for each of them, and as Kealin settled into the notch on the creature's neck, he kicked his feet, which were just above the water.

Ruak led them as they took off across the surface, moving at a speed almost as fast as Tulasiro in the open sea. He glanced around as the morning sun burned off the lake fog. The trees that stretched around them were massive and dark. The forest has been untouched, guarded for many thousand years by the elves of the region. He could tell the magic of the elves was strong. Mountains rose in the distance, and a large white spire split through the canopies.

"Fikmark, one of the chief kingdoms."

"It's not all that you might think it is," Ivasel stated.

"Ivasel here wasn't happy in his place of lowly luxury in Fikmark."

Ivasel coughed. "It wasn't what you would expect. My father is not the easiest of people to deal with."

"Your father doesn't miss you?" Kealin questioned, wondering more of Ivasel himself.

"Oh, he does, just not for the reasons of, say, a simple good father desiring his son's company."

"It is unfortunate when the heir runs off," said Ruak, "and joins the Scions who you can't deny exist but want to."

"You are a prince of the king, then?"

Ivasel shook his head. "I am Ivasel, and I care little of royal birthrights."

Kealin was beginning to like the group he had ended up with more with every new thing he learned.

REACHING THE OTHER SIDE, the water horses climbed to shore, and they got off. The woods teamed with life, birds fluttering from tree to tree and bees buzzing across the morning dew. Ruak began to walk toward the tree line and noticed a torch burning in a tree.

"The Fikmark still keep their torches lit at all hours. Even with the ban made by the lower kingdom on guide lights."

"Guide lights?" Kealin questioned.

"They are helpful, perhaps more decorative than needed, but you can follow the torches along the road to reach the city. Not a worry in the past, but there is the talk of if a dragon was used by our enemy to assail us or drop off intruders, well, I guess the lower kingdom must worry of such invasions first, anyway, but thankfully, there have been no dragons yet."

Kealin followed Ruak as he walked along the shore.

"The way we take doesn't go near the actual city. We head into the woods and down paths rarely taken as of late. Be happy we avoided attention as of now. You go to a place that for any other elf requires permission by the king of Fikmark. We, of course, are not obtaining that."

They turned from the green shores and began into the trees. The forest floor was clear and easily walkable, as if the path itself had been swept clean.

Kealin looked ahead and noticed tall creatures walking between the trees. "You have Druid Keepers here?"

"Yes, they typically stay in hiding during the day, but there have been reports of strange creatures coming from the east and invading the woods. Elves typically let creatures come and go, as the woods are not only ours but nature's as well. But something has been driving them in. They haven't hurt anyone, but the Druid Keepers were spooked by, I think it was large rabbits, a few weeks ago. Nothing moves through the woods without an elf knowing of it."

An arrowhead appeared suddenly in Kealin's face. He felt another behind his back, and in a sudden shifting of leaves, they were surrounded by other elves.

"Scions," a stoic voice said.

"Fikmarkian guardians," Ruak said. "You are really pushing the reach of your territory. We are barely on the outskirts of your realm."

The bows lowered, and Kealin's hands released his hilts.

The Fikmark elf captain had long brown hair, and his bow was made from stag horns. The others with him took a step back, and he embraced Ruak. "You have avoided these shores for many moons."

Ruak patted him on the shoulder. "It is true and unfortunately not something I desire to do so quickly again, but my work to the south requires it. It is good to see you, Hariv."

"You talk of the south. The king doesn't believe there is any problem to worry of," Hariv stated.

Ivasel sneered. "The king hasn't been running protection for the villages near Vueric."

He bowed. "Prince Ivasel, I have not seen you in some time, my lord."

"I do not need a title, only for the elves of Fikmark to do what is needed at every moment regardless of what border our kingdoms are tied to."

"The king is doing something, and of concern at the moment is the half-elf among you. You enter the Varmark Woods with a half-blood?"

"My name is Kealin, if you desire it."

"Kealin, you may be part elf, but your passage through these woods must be allowed by the order of the king of Fikmark. I am sure the Scions will want to keep good relations, and though Ruak and the others I count among my friends, I must do as my lord commands."

Kealin nodded. This Hariv seemed a decent enough elf.

"Then let us go speak to your king," Kealin said.

The Scions and the Fikmark elves began away from their northwest trek and took to the road leading toward Fikmark. As they walked, Ruak and Hariv continued to talk.

"There has been word of orcs to the south, but the king refuses to commit forces to aid. You know he, along with King Rasune, feel that the return of the orcs is a fallacy to distract from other issues," Hariv said.

"The only issue is ignoring this one. The demon men from the North have gone quiet, and though that loss is still heavy upon us, we must not turn a blind eye to the South. Besides, the orcs of Ur and the demon men may be of allegiance to one another."

"That is a possible fact. Of a great concern as well is a question many have wondered. Does not the king of Vueric work with the Grand Protectorate?"

"Not that I have seen. His Rangers still fight to keep their border secure, and without further reinforcements, they will fail to protect the threatened villages. Although, many might have already fallen."

"I know the Rangers are good men and women, but can you continue to trust men who would just as soon turn against us? The dwarves looked at men as allies. And now, after the tragedy of Michranok and their disappearance, we are supposed to assume their city just happened to have a catastrophic accident?"

Ruak shook his head. "The dwarves are fighters but made poor choices choosing trade partners in men. They both swindle each other to try to keep or make a profit. I will not talk of dwarves when so many of our own race are at risk right now."

Kealin noticed the path was widening. Ahead was a large white spire that reached straight up into the sky, circled by a wisp of clouds that crowned its summit.

"I see you admire the spire?" Hariv said.

"It is something I haven't seen before."

Hariv laughed. "It helps channel magic into the very world. We have some of the greatest Moon Cullers. Their sourcing of magic from the night sky feeds into all of the world. It is part of why these woodlands are so fiercely guarded. Do not let my words seem too harsh; we have not always kept all from beneath the boughs. Men walked here once, and many were fine souls who respected our ways and customs. But men *always change.*"

The elf seemed to suddenly anger with those last words, and stopped talking.

As they approached two large stone columns, Hariv waved his hand, and a guard just coming visible took to a knee and flipped a switch on the column. Torches lit up on both columns, and the path behind them was covered in the earth of the forest.

"So you veil the path now, during the day?" Ruak asked.

Hariv nodded. "You caught that? Well, yes. I must make a good impression for you."

Ruak smiled in amusement.

A gateway ahead, crowned in the image of a large tree, opened as they approached. Kealin looked around at how different this place was compared to Urlas. Though he hadn't lived near the actual city, Urlas had not walls or magical roads that led around. Entering the city, the elven guard, standing in green armor on either side of the doorway, shifted their eyes in a careful glance. Their armor was worn and scratched, not pristine as he expected.

"Keeping with the old traditions, Kealin, we keep the signs of our battles evident on our chests. When there is peace for all elves again, we will polish our armor, but unlike the other elves of Varmark, those of Fikmark proudly show the evidence of our deeds. As in all such orders, we do as the king commands."

Kealin noticed a few who looked at him with a peculiar glare. Entering a long stretch of cylindrical houses that had large trees growing atop them, he saw many elves busy with their day-to-day activities, but there was a sadness in the air. As they came to a large circular opening, they paused. A procession moved through, carrying what appeared as a grayed tree and of an odd shape.

Ruak lowered his head. "You still have some dying?" he asked.

Hariv nodded. "The loss of the few remaining children continues to be a heavy burden to us. Some elves have considered migrating to the east. It seems Narisond still has young, but I feel it is only a question of how long they will last."

The procession went past them and to a large river that ran through the city.

"She was an expectant mother. A product of elf magic and old lore, along with the blessings of Etha in abundance. But it was not enough."

Kealin felt a tug in his heart as the body of a fellow

elf went past. Elves did not die like this, and though he did not embrace the full culture of his people, he could not ignore the emotion emanating off everyone around. He thought of his own very young brother and wondered of his safety.

5

BURNING ASH

Crossing the Vindas Sea, they sailed for the greater part of two days, and as night befell upon them again, a lone beacon appeared in the far distance.

"That is the lighthouse of the king. We near our destination," Dala announced.

The legatus had been lying with his head against the railings of the ship with his eyes closed. Jesia watched him as he looked around and then stood with a nervous look toward the shoreline.

"Are there no actual ships of the Grand Protectorate near these shores?" Brethor asked.

"There was, but I do not see them now," Iruis said with a nervous voice. Jesia joined them, looking toward the shore as both Muera and Krea stood nearby.

The shoreline was very dark, and the sea was calm. There was a thick line of trees further up the coasts, but the bare shore barely had any sand at all, only rocks.

"We will bring the ship north of the Isira River and make landfall there. I assume we will have to prove our goodwill rather quickly."

"If there is anyone to meet us. The Tenth Legion had a camp on these shores when I was last here. I see no sign of anyone."

Jesia looked over to Iruis and for once saw the stalwart man fearful.

In the far distance, there was the city of Vueric itself. It was shadowy in the cloudy night, and there seemed to be a haze in the air. As the ship drifted up on a palely lit lighthouse, they finally spotted another person. A duo of guards walking by torchlight on the road up ahead.

"Men of the legion?" Brethor asked.

"No, likely Knights Guard from the city, or perhaps Rangers of the river," Iruis told them. There was another lighthouse that sat off the coast and before the great bridge that led over the Isira River.

The Rusis girls stood together now.

"I have never heard of Vueric," Muera said.

"Likely another Rusis-enslaving filth hole," Krea spat. "We should be on guard."

"You are right," Brethor commented. "You should be. As should we all."

Jesia smiled at the man's comment as Krea shook her head at it. They had known nothing but slavery before this, and now, at least in partial action, she couldn't deny feeling purpose. Something she hadn't felt since she broke out the Srvivnanns and rebelled against her master. The Rusis were once much stronger of a race, and they held it in their hands to be much more than they had ever been.

As she took a deep breath, watching the two guards on the coasts, she suddenly spotted something in the shadows. A moment later, the torches the two guards held went dark.

"Brethor, did you see that?"

"What?"

"The guards."

He scanned the coasts and then looked to Dala.

Dala took out a viewing scope and scanned the coastline. After a few passes, he shook his head. "I can see nothing in the darkness."

A bell began to toll, and torch basins near the lighthouse were stoked. An arrow shot out from the lighthouse, striking a large pyre, and flames shot up into the sky. The light revealed a true horror. Orcs in the hundreds approached the lighthouse.

The helmsman shouted out, and a horn blew across the deck of the ship. The crystal at the front of the ship spun and began to illuminate the air around it. The soldiers of Eh-Rin prepared for battle.

"What better way to prove loyalty," Brethor said, "than slaying orcs?"

Dala gave his orders. "Guide the ship along the coastline and angle the crystal just before the great pyre. Prepare to disembark!"

The sails of the ship shifted, and they came into the edge of a sandbar with an abrupt rumbling beneath the bow. They had done this before when they were helping Kealin. The ships could divert energy from the crystals topside to power the ship away. It was a unique advantage of Eh-Rin vessels.

The legatus and his men were the first into the water, followed by Dala's men, and then Brethor. As Jesia landed in knee-deep water, she cracked her knuckles and felt the sizzle of electricity hum through her body. She heard the sounds of rushing winds, and then a pink blast shot out from the ship, striking into the lines of orcs, sending a ripple of fire and energy from the border of the lighthouse defenses marked at the pyre all the way back to the beach they were heading toward.

The legionnaires formed a shield wall as they made it to the beach. The Eh-Rin soldiers filed along either side of them. Legatus Iruis pointed up the beach. The orcs were scurrying forward down the coast and took no notice of the ship that had just decimated some of their hordes.

"They don't care about us," a legionnaire said.

"Or they are so focused on their task, they didn't realize a ship was there," the legatus suggested. "They are quite dim-witted unless someone is literally leading them."

The legatus looked up the beach toward the lighthouse. Fiery arrows streaked from the palisade walls surrounding the structure as the orcs slammed rams into the walls.

"We wheel left. Keep the line tight as we push onto the road. Men of Eh-Rin, guard the flank as we move up the road. We will attempt to break the siege before it takes hold."

"So simple your task?" Muera asked.

"Rusis, do what you do," Brethor said. "We must get to the king for the sake of all of us, and we must gain the trust of these defenders."

Iruis took out a horn and blew it twice. The legion sound for a charge. The front rank of shields moved forward, slamming into the massed orcs.

Jesia pointed forward, moving beside Brethor, and from her palm, a bolt of lightning erupted forward, throwing back three orcs and pushing back others. The other Rusis cast their spells, and ice and flames tore into the lines. Brethor and Orolo pushed into the line of shields. Brethor forced his sword between a gap in the shields and withdrew, spilling black blood on the ground. The orcs moved in, closing the escape to the sea but staying far enough back to be outside sword reach. The men of Eh-Rin kept the sides clear of stragglers, and the Rusis kept the bulk of the horde from approaching them from behind.

Brethor looked up at the battlements as more of the orcs fell in their wake, and noticed a hooded man pointing and shouting. A horn call went out, and the doors of the wall parted open.

The host filed inside, and the gates were shut behind them. As Jesia turned around, an arrow was pointed at her, as well as at all of the others.

"State your business upon the King's Road," one of the men said.

"Ranger Vaden," Iruis said.

"Legatus Iruis. I thought you dead." He kept a straight face and his arrow to cheek.

"Near, but the forces of Amhe came to our aid."

"Too bad you couldn't tell your men. Most of the Tenth Legion tucked their swords in their asses and fled. A bunch of cowards. I reckon you will be doing the same?"

"No, we seek an audience with your king," Brethor said.

The gateway was suddenly shaken by one of the battering rams.

"Rangers, concentrate fire on the roadway. Prepare an orc shocker!"

Men up on a walkway, built up one side of the light-house, began to heave a large log into the air and onto a platform.

"I don't know you, and your females look a bit fresh to be the type of use."

Krea and Jesia both lifted their hands, producing a flame and an icy bolt respectively. Jesia tossed the bolt to the ground, causing a shockwave.

Vaden gave a smug smile. "Rusis. Rare and beautiful. Especially beautiful, if I might notice."

"We aren't here to give you something to look at. Let us help you," the legatus said.

"Fine. We need able soldiers as much as beautiful ladies." He pointed at an area of logs. "Reinforce the gateway and get archers to the upper battlements. We will push them back, but it takes a bit to get the shocker ready."

As Brethor began to help reinforce the gate, Jesia went up the battlements. The men defending were all Rangers of the Riverlands. They wore cloaks of dark gray and had bows of Wyte Oak, a sacred tree to some elves for just the purpose of bow making. As she leaned over the battlements, they fired another volley into the horde. There were still hundreds. They were like a nest of maggots, cringing and moving erratically. They were simple-minded, as Iruis had said. As she concentrated spells down into the mob, she looked as Krea and Muera both worked to secure the gateway. A section of the palisade gave way, and men jumped from the battlements onto the ground. One of them threw back their hood, and Jesia noticed that it was indeed a woman.

Vaden ran over to her and picked her up. "My love?"

"Get away, you sappy bastard. I'm fine!" She gave him a kiss and drew back her bow. The wall gave way further, and orcs began to pour into the opening. Jesia summoned a large icy blast and shoved it down toward the opening as the legionnaires moved forward. Krea and Muera released their own magics.

"What is your plan, Vaden?" Iruis said.

"Relax, dear legatus. It is ready."

The Ranger gave a thumbs-up, and the men on the walkways above lit pieces of a giant log on fire. They then pushed it down a rampart that led over the wall. The entire wooden structure swayed and creaked as the log with the enlarging flaming tips made its way over the edge of the wall and into the host of orcs. Jesia watched as it rolled down the road a good distance and then began sparking.

"Get down!" a Ranger yelled.

She hid behind the rampart, and a blinding flash filled the air, and what was like thunder shook her.

Shrill screams filled the air. She looked over the

edge, and the many orcs remaining began to fall away from the walls, grabbing at their faces and tripping over one another to retreat. Many fell to the ground, quivering before gagging and dying as blood ran from their noses and ears.

Jesia stood with the Rangers near her, who gave her nods of approval. She then ran down below.

"WHAT WAS THAT, GOOD RANGER?" Brethor asked.

"That was dwarf dust. Good for clearing rock. Even better for clearing orcs! It messes with their eyes, ears, heck, whatever gives them sense. If we had more, it would be great, but we do not. We seem to be running out of a lot of supplies."

"I cannot believe the legion fled," Iruis said. "I apologize."

"Do not. The king gave your master their answer. Our lord will remain independent and will not join any protectorate, be it grand or lesser. There is still power in men. We do not need to give it over to a bunch of fools in the east. We already trusted the elves, and even they have fallen back."

Vaden went to a keg and poured himself a glass of ale. He slurped it down and then beckoned them to follow him.

"I saw your ship, a very advanced weapon. A few of those ships would be useful to our cause."

"Amhe of Eh-Rin seeks an alliance with your king," Brethor said.

"Well, we need it. The Knights Guard is faltering in

numbers and is spread too thin. We have been attacked every night for the past few nights, and each attack grows stronger. We built a fort here just after the attack that took the legatus east. I don't know. These orcs are relentless, and sunlight buys us time, but I think the orcs are getting used to it."

He led them into a stable and set saddles on the horses. Brethor finished saddling them one by one for Jesia and the others. Orolo came up behind them and took the one given to Jesia.

"Brothers before your kind."

Brethor gave him a glare before passing the reins to another horse to her. "Ignore his ignorance," he said.

They rode out of a postern gate and began down a road that went right to a massive bridge and then followed the ocean toward the city.

The bridge itself was a white stone, with ornate stones forming a circular pattern every few paces that continued the entire length of the structure. The bridge was large enough to line up ten men abreast with ease. It was clear the lighthouse fortress was an important defense for the bridge. The pattern continued down the grand road that led to the city gates.

Offshore, the Eh-Rin ship had anchored up the road, and now three boats were rowing to shore. As they reached the other side of the bridge and began toward the beach, Vaden turned his horse to await their arrival.

"Who is this twat here?" Vaden said.

"Dala, an officer of the sultan's navy," Iruis told him.

"Very well, then."

As the boats made it to the beach, Dala got out and

bowed before them. For a few moments, there was silence. The sounds of the surf rolling onto the beach and strange stares were eventually broken by Dala.

"The battle is won, and now we may talk about what more we can do to help. I am Dala, of the . . ."

"Sultan Amhe, yes, I am aware. I'm the leader of the River Rangers and the front line defense against this scourge."

He bowed in return to a slightly shocked Dala.

"He is taking us to Vueric," Brethor said.

Dala nodded and smiled. "Very good, then."

"Very good, then!" Vaden laughed. "He has never met our good king. He doesn't take well to most outsiders." Vaden laughed again and then began to ride down the road.

"I have room," Brethor said, motioning to his horse. "We can carry some of you."

"We insist on walking, but thank you." Dala motioned for his men to follow.

It was a long road at a slow speed. The path was riddled with bodies of orcs and broken arms and armor. Dead horses became plentiful as they crossed over trampled gardens and muddied streams. The remnants of a large village were to their right.

"When the orcs first assaulted this region, many died before we could get them into the castle," Vaden explained. "It was more than the raids; they would've gone straight into the city if it wasn't for the patrols who held them at the bridge."

"We were coming from scouting upriver when we saw the fires in the fields. We fought our way to them but it was too late. The few legionnaires who remained held the ground with several dozens of the Knights Guard, but by morning light, they were all dead."

Iruis cleared his throat. "Well, it is good some remembered their vows."

"Indeed. Vows are nice. Money is better. More than half of our castle guards are sellswords from the northern villages. They probably welcome the reinforced walls of the castle only because the elves won't help us, but we have the coin if they have the blade. Heck, even without a blade, they can eventually be useful. I am thankful for the aid your people gave us. I might be headed to the Great Poet myself, otherwise."

"So you have religion here?" Jesia asked.

"Yes, something of it. You don't live near elves for so long and not hear something of the gods once and a while."

As they approached the gates, there were several horn calls before the massive wooden doors began to creak open. The walls were blackened with scorch marks, and the ground was thick with orc blood and littered with broken spears and arrows.

"Our happy home," Vaden said.

As they entered, Brethor immediately thought of his home in the far north, Elinathrond. Passing through the entryway, tall buildings lined the wide street with alleys filled with activity on either side. There were no snow-capped roofs here. In some cases, there were no roofs at all and only charred outlines of what were once buildings. But the people were strong. Those of Vueric were not a simple or easy people. The city itself had seen construction by a dwarven-human alliance, occupation by elves, and retaking by men in its long history as a city. There was even more within a city of such size. They dismounted their horses and followed the path upward into increasingly denser buildings before the path opened up to a large square that sat beneath the shadow of another wall. Brethor noticed a large statue built into the second line of curtain walls. As he stared, he could feel something from it, almost as if it watched ominously over them.

"I know of my history, but that statue is not of any normal relief I have seen before, at least, this openly."

Vaden shrugged. "It is Dwemhar, I believe. Some say the Dwemhar had a secret hidden here. I say it's just a nice statue. But I am just a Ranger of the river." He laughed again.

Brethor looked up at the statue as they passed, and bowed before it. He had seen images in books of such grandeur, but never had he seen one in person.

They came to another gate and the large wall that led to a larger area of stately homes that looked over the cliffs toward the lower city.

"The opulent of Vueric," Vaden told them. "I never cared for these types too much."

The next gateway was an iron portcullis and one of many that lifted up in a straight line.

"The path of teeth." Vaden laughed again. "When the jaws shut, may no enemy pass."

Looking to either side, there were multiple rope-drawn spiked traps of every cruel design imaginable. Smoke rose from upper walls where smelters were ready to further murder would-be attackers. It was a place very different from Elinathrond. Brethor's home was a refuge; this was a city not afraid of war where its people evidently were ready at a single horn call to join the battlements in defense of their home.

"It has been a long time since these traps were used. We Rangers guard the way into the city. We guard the river. May no enemy ever need to die within these walls as long as we guard the Riverlands!"

Passing through the final gate in the path of teeth, they came to a large courtyard and a massive keep built at the summit of the mountains. Looking out, they could see toward the valley to the south and the sea to the west. There were also several more statues lining the doorway of the keep and the image of a fiery mountain emblazoned into the stones above.

"A mark of Kel, the war-god of the North. They say his presence protects this place."

The statues were that of standing eagles with large blades in either hand. Their stone forms were blacker than the ash before the city. The doorway of the keep itself was colored a dark red and made of stone.

"This city would make Kel happy, I guess," Brethor said.

The Ranger laughed again. "Come, let me lead the happy company to our great king."

Approaching the doorway, two silver-armored men opened the giant red doors and allowed them in. As they entered, another man in full armor, save his helmet, approached them.

"Master Vaden, I heard of the events from the watch. I hope we can acquire more of the dwarf dust."

They embraced.

"Captain Tiris, indeed, I do as well. I have messengers from Eh-Rin for our good king. How is his mood?"

"It is as expected without adequate coffee. The shipments fell under pirates again, and well, he is not taking the tea as a replacement."

He looked over to Brethor, Dala, and the Rusis. "Welcome to the Palace of the King. Our lordship is this way."

They followed him into what they learned was an ancient building. Through a large atrium with the image of the moon built into the skylight above them, they walked through two large wooden doors and into what seemed like a cathedral with large statues of the gods of the North represented in the image of man. There was Wura of the Northern Lights, Etha of the Great Woods, Throka, the mountain god, and Dimn, the god of the winds.

Jesia looked at the image of the gods, represented not as she had heard their forms, but as men might imagine them. It was strange and alien to see statues of the gods.

At the far end of the room was a tall throne wrapped in gold snakes and crowned with axes formed in a circle curving over a man sunken into his chair. A nearby servant approached with a tray of fruit but was waved off as the man sat up as his guests arrived.

"My lord Firda, these messengers have come to seek an audience with the great king of Vueric," Captain Tiris stated.

King Firda stood, and Tiris bowed, as did the other servants entering the room from the left and those in the host before the throne. He went to Vaden and placed his hand on his shoulder.

"Your Rangers, are they well?"

"They are, King. We pushed them off, just as we have done at every attack."

"Good. I have had men searching for more dwarf powder but have not found it."

King Firda looked over, scanning the men from Eh-Rin, Brethor, Orolo, and the Rusis.

"What do you make of them?"

"They are warriors who helped me in battle."

"Really? I assume the ones who looked like they fight did. I'm talking about the men of Eh-Rin. What did they do?"

"A few came with the others. I believe most stayed on their ship."

The king looked up, smiling. "As I expect of the sultan."

Legatus Iruis knelt before the king. "I have returned to assist you. I bring what men remain."

"Oh, I imagine more remain. They just happen to reside to the far east now and not in the camp they had made. The camp you promised would remain next to the ships that would help guard our coast."

The king walked past the kneeling man and went to Dala. "You are from Eh-Rin?"

Dala bowed. "Yes, Your Excellency. I am Dala of Eh-Rin, sent in the name of Sultan Amhe, Lord of the Sands and the Dashrin Coast, to seek your alliance."

King Firda grabbed him by the shoulders, "An alliance, with me? Oh, let me bring out the royal chairs for you to rest your desert selves on. What kind of joke is this? Did you come all this way just to woo me with grand offerings? I can't even get a cup of coffee, and I can get an alliance with Amhe of the Sands, the great ruler."

Dala brandished his sword, which was followed by the hasty approach of palace guards but a stern smile by King Firda.

"Most men would be dead now, had I given the order. You, sir, prove me wrong. A dangerous sentiment on its own, but at least it seems the desert people are more than fancy builders. Put the blade away. You can draw it again to fight your true enemy soon enough. Truthfully, I just wonder if you have a ration of coffee."

Dala searched his persons and revealed a small bag. "It is yours."

"Servant!"

A man ran over and bowed to the king.

"Well, now you have no excuse. Coffee, if you do not mind." The servant departed, and King Firda turned back to Dala. "So what is next? Will Amhe take me on his carpet again?"

Dala seemed to not understand what the king was asking.

"You know, the big golden flying carpet thing."

Dala shook his head. "I know not of what you speak."

"Oh, yes. I forget. It doesn't exist. Okay, my apologies. Sometimes an old king loses his mind. Especially seeing that orcs invade my lands."

"Good king, I urge you to consider the alliance with

the Grand Protectorate still," Legatus Iruis began. "We have legions of men to assist—"

"Listen, you protectorate prick, the orcs swarm our lands, the elves disappear into the woods, and my Rangers and Knights Guard fight day and night just to keep the fields from burning. I can take any alliance I can, save one that takes my kingship. The Grand Protectorate can continue to try, dear legatus, but I am the king of these lands and will not become an official of some protectorate as long as I live. These lands will be ruled by my family as long as my bloodline continues. Lord Kiras, Lord Meask, and Lord Ridau are my sons and the future rulers of this land. Understand that and know we need no help from your people."

He looked to Dala. "I normally would not do something such as this, especially before some decent coffee," he shouted toward the direction the servant had gone, "but I will accept your offer of alliance seeing as I don't have a choice."

The servant appeared with the cup of coffee, and the king took it from him at the very moment he came within arm's reach.

After a long slurping taste, King Firda exhaled. "Good, now, on to the rest of the rabble here."

Brethor bowed before the king, and Orolo followed suit. Jesia, Muera, and Krea bowed as well.

"I am Brethor of Elinathrond, and this is Orolo, my brother. These three women with me are Rusis, freed from Cyr and faithful companions to our cause and the cause that is against the orcs."

"Well, welcome to the city of Vueric and the killing

that has become as common as a man in a whorehouse."
He clapped his hands, and servants came from the sides
of the room. "See that our guests are given rooms and a
place to rest. I must see to my wife coming from the
northern reach with hopefully more allies and my dear
sons. We shall have a feast tonight, as best as can be had."

He slurped his coffee again. "This has been quite a
morning."

6

HIGH KING

The arrival of the Scions spurred a particular curiosity within Fikmark. Though many elves looked at them, few said much and seemed to just watch them as they passed. The scent of mint was heavy in the air, and as the wind shifted, the mint would give way to that of a heavy pollen scent. There were many squirrels cutting across the path. Though, not uncommon in the forest, seeing them carry small packs of cloth and even smaller wagons of different nuts was very strange.

Upon reaching the palace gateway, they were left before its doors with simple instructions to stay put.

Kealin looked straight up at the spire and struggled to not lose his balance. It was massive. Every few moments, a spark of energy would ripple off of it in the form of a bouncing bolt of lightning and dissipate into the clouds.

He turned back to the doorway. It was wooden with a border of gold. The inlay of drawings conveyed the birth of the world and then the emergence of the first tree. Down toward the lower parts of the door, he could make out the image of orcs and a great battle. He smirked, noticing the image of what was obviously an Urlas Blade in the picture.

The doorway opened, and a small creature no larger than a raccoon opened the door. It was furry and red, with a high-pitched voice.

"The king is this way and is awaiting you."

Kealin followed behind the Scions and Hariv. They followed a bright corridor with ceilings reaching high above. Tree branches formed the actual roof, and tiny lights floated in the air as fairies raced from limb to the floor and back.

Ahead there was a large tree, a carved-out chair, and two stairwells that went along either side of it. The chair was high above the ground, and a man with pale skin sat on the throne. There were orc skulls along the base of his chair. Two elves in black chest armor stood at the very base of the throne. Holding long staves with blades of white fire, Kealin saw that these two were rough in appearance. One seemed to be missing an eye, and the other had a scar along his arm.

Hariv went before the throne and bowed. "Sire, the Scions of Starfall and the half-blood."

The figure on the statue stood before moving down the stairs in a rapid fashion. Hariv still was in bow as the king tapped his shoulder. Hariv stood and turned. The king walked along the Scions and looked at each. Ruak cocked his head at the king, and he laughed in response.

"Good Scions, it has been a long time since your faces graced the halls of Fikmark. Tell me, what stirs you to come this way? I'm sure it is not any type of royal duty."

He had a mocking tone and now stared at Ivasel.

"You are a son of my blood but not of mind. You dwell with these near criminals on the verge of fair lands."

His son smiled at him, staring back with the same tone of look that his father had. "The fair lands of the Resip are quite nice for elves who don't consider themselves above their fellow elf."

The king turned away from Ivasel and went to Ruak. "Why do you come here and disturb my peace? Was not the desolation of the northern woods enough? We fought for years to secure that ground, and at last we do, you run down south to cause more issues."

"Good King Suvasel, you are not protecting the elven villages that border near Vueric anymore. The Rangers called for aid, and we answered. There is a new evil about. The orcs return to the south."

King Suvasel stared for a moment and then let out a laugh. "Foolish! Did you not know whom you speak to? I killed those vile beasts myself. I stormed the southern lands, searching out every last one of them, sending their corpses into the crevices of mountains and gorges of hills. The archons of many elven families came together and sealed them away. The orcs and the Order of Ur, the demon piss god, is no more. Your own father saw to that, Ruak!"

"I know what my father did, but it is all folly. The lands to the south already swarm with orcs. Vueric will be under attack before we know it. You must see that all of the Varmark Woods are ready for war and to march for Vueric. The demon men were of considerable power, and now we deal with another evil, an older, and I daresay, darker power."

The king drew out a long blade kept at his waist. It teamed with purple lightning. The hilt of it had the imagery of an orc skull, and he passed it through the air, sending crackles out as he did.

"This sword is called *Vank-Rus*, the *Orc Biter*. I killed more than ten thousand orcs with this blade near the time of the Dawn of Knowledge. Back when both Dwemhar and Rusis ruled the lands in equal with us. Now, I and others of our kin have fought to protect our own, even as new enemies stand against us. I cannot believe orcs have returned. I will not. My elves are the most elite of the warriors of the woods. We care little for sheen metal and the looks of clean armor. Our blades are sharpened by the forges of the sun's fire and cannot be broken. We did not get this way chasing false claims."

Kealin stepped in front of Ruak and drew both of his blades. "Blades of Urlas, King Suvasel. The one on my right, my own. The other, the blade of my elder brother, Taslun. Made of ruinite, a fine ore only found in one sacred place. My parents fought in the North, called to the South from the Glacial Seas in a time of dire need to help elves like you. Now they are both dead, and I assure you now, the orcs have returned. These blades, too, have killed many, and only a few days ago that was!"

The king sheathed his sword. "You're the half-blood I sensed entering the woods, but yet I am confused." He began to pace. "You did not come with the others, but you come now, alone, and seeking entrance to my domain?"

"He seeks the Moon Elves of Risdannia," Ruak specified.

"Then I am intrigued, for none but our own know of that place anymore. How would a stranger come to know of it?"

"My brother. He was lost to me before the gates of Dimn and taken by the Itsu. He is now a twisted and masked servant to the clan of Ur. I faced him in battle, and in a small moment, he was himself. He spoke of Risdannia."

The king crossed his arms. "You speak of a god of the North, the Itsu, and of your own kin who now serves the enemy? Then I say to you, Ruak, why have you come to these shores? To allow the stranger passage to a most sacred place?"

"The Moon Elves will decide his worth. His name is Kealin. He is of Urlas, and his parents fought with us in the North. He seeks out a place of peace and wisdom."

Kealin sheathed his blades. "I seek only a way to what family I still have. I care nothing of small quarrels between father and son, or perceptions of my worth."

King Suvasel ascended back to his throne. "We will investigate the threat of these orcs, Ruak. But I dare not open my lands to incursion by any. I fear the men of the

East and their desire to control. I do not need to speak of our distrust of men. Vueric is an old alliance city, but I will not leave the woods unguarded unless I must."

Ruak bowed. "Good king, my elves and I will work to assure you do not need to. We will get him to where he wishes to go, and then we head south in haste."

"Then my blessing is given for passage into the Varmark Woods."

They all bowed to the king and turned for the doors.

"Kealin!" the king shouted out.

He turned.

"The Blades of Urlas reinforced our lines and saved many lives. The archons of Urlas helped hold ground for many days that would have fallen to the demonic forces of the North. I respect your kind beyond understanding. I hope one day, we may fight together if the need arises."

Kealin nodded. "If it is fate, King."

THEY PROCEEDED from the citadel back down the road. Elaca looked back behind them.

"I'm surprised we're not under arrest."

"He knows better," said Ruak, "and I think he likes Kealin."

Kealin shook his head. "He seems like other elves I know, stuck in his own mind. Wise beyond reason, and only because of self-claim to it."

"My father is a strong man," Ivasel said. "He may not respond as he should, but if I can say one good thing about him. If the war reaches the trees, it will not go past the bark of the first saplings."

The archon with them sent a spark to the ground with his staff. "It is not through the trees the orcs will traverse. They're great burrowers, and from the ground, they can come up like field moles, or so I read. The orcs were destroyed for a reason. I even fear their return."

Back down a second and third ring of gateways, they came again to the city center, and this time, they stopped near a large waterway that passed through the city. There were many merchants along the water, and the Scions took a moment to check their supplies.

"Kealin," Ruak said. "Do you have any food with you?"

"Nothing."

He tossed him four nuts that were red in appearance. "Do they have those in Urlas?"

"No, I haven't even seen anything like this."

"They are Varmark Pine nuts. Eating one will stave off hunger for some time and provide all of what you need anyway."

The other elves seemed to all have some as well. Teusk was busy shifting his staff between his arms as he checked other alchemical devices kept at his belt. Elaca had gone to the nearest merchant and returned with more of the nuts.

"So you plan to go south as soon as I am taken to Risdannia?"

"We do."

"And if I am not going south?"

"I keep faith that you will, for wherever your sister is, destroying the orcs will play into her safety at some point. Not to mention, it is likely where your brother will be too."

Kealin took one of the pine nuts and ate it. It crunched and had a strangely sweet taste. His body had a sudden chill, and he took a deep breath.

"I make no promise to you, Ruak, that I do not know if I can honor."

"Good enough, friend."

They looked up at Teusk, who suddenly stabbed his staff into the ground.

"All well, my archon friend?"

"Yes, the merchant had what little I needed. But did you see where Elaca went?"

The elven archer then appeared crossing back over the waterway, having gone to a distant merchant specializing in the type of wares only an archer would want. She fiddled with a string, putting it on her bow. It flashed blue for a moment.

"An enchanted one?" Ruak asked.

"Yes. If there are any beasts in the woods, I don't want to need to shoot twice."

Ivasel stood up from his crouching position. "That's why you take off their heads with a sword," he teased.

Kealin laughed as well and was surprised. Being with the Scions reminded him of his own siblings to a degree.

As they took to the path, with many a wary eye looking on them, and their strange ensemble leaving the final gateway, they passed by Hariv, who shook hands with Ruak.

"Blessed passage, friend. I spoke with the king; know

the elves of Greater Varmark will stand beside you even if the king seems unsure."

Ruak embraced him. "If you can get there in time and I haven't killed them all."

They laughed, and then Ruak followed the rest of them out. The gates of Fikmark shut, and the sun shined high above. They turned off the path and began deep into the woods. They would need to hurry to reach the spot, according to Ruak.

Teusk checked a parchment and then nodded.

They began to run in an attempt to make up time. They came to a path that, while slightly overgrown on its border, was clear ahead.

Ruak was in the lead and began to hasten the pace. "It is a good path. Let us hope it stays this way."

The woods stretched far into a slightly growing darkness devoid of light except for the canopy above. The woods were very old, and moss covered every tree except a strange pine of red color that grew sporadically.

"Blood Pine," Ruak said. "You will find that more of them will appear the further north we go. It is said that for every elf who dies before their time, another tree will bleed."

"There must be quite a few bleeding trees, then, seeing as death among elves has been more common," Kealin commented.

"A sad truth," Ivasel said.

Elaca ascended a small hill ahead of them and then drew back on her bow. The others fanned out to her sides. Kealin looked ahead and did not immediately see what had caused the alarm.

"In the clearing," she said.

Ruak went forward. "Spread around to the sides, everyone. Keep yourselves ready. Kealin, come with me."

As he followed the wary elf, he noticed a large white stag lying in a clearing. It had been torn apart, recognizable only because of its antlers that remained on its decapitated head.

"I know we have spoken of the demon men of the North, but I did not explain to you what they actually were."

Kealin remained silent, scanning through the woods ahead as the other Scions did the same.

"They are men in a form, but there are beasts to the north, blood-sucking creatures that take the form as you and I and even men, but behind the facade of normalcy, they thirst for the blood of their victims. We had peace with them for many hundreds of years. They remained hidden in a castle within our woods under a careful understanding, but their thirst is unending. Eventually, they got a taste for elven blood, and you can imagine the good King Suvasel and the elven kingdoms of the North did not care for such a gluttony as the bloodsuckers wished."

Ruak knelt and dusted a fine powder over the body of the stag. Insects swarmed its body, devouring its flesh and bone. In a few moments, the insects disappeared back into the woods and the bloody grass turned to a burning blaze, blackening before new plants grew in its place.

Teusk approached. "Ruak, there are none of the creatures in the vicinity. They must be gone."

"A troubling fact, but it means it wasn't the vampires themselves. It is their servants, the demon men."

"How did they get past the forest guardians?" Kealin asked.

"There are many secrets to the woods, and as many elves as we have, our numbers are not what they were nor our eyes as keen to the movements of the demon men. They lack the warmth of other creatures. They are cold, heartless, and move almost silently. I have burned the stag, for once bitten, you will turn to that of a beast, and if you are torn apart as this stag, you will infect others with a horrid sickness that will make you wish you were dead. It is troubling to me that we came upon such a thing in these once tranquil woods. We must keep moving forward and get you to the place we promised."

It was now turning dusk as they moved with a much more nervous watch to the darkening woods surrounding them. Faint lights moved through the woods. As the lights began to cross their path, Kealin noticed that they were indeed fairies.

"They sense the trouble in the woods," Teusk said. "Their powers are affected by the demon men, and they move away from the source of the dread."

Ivasel snickered. "If only the path could be tracked back to the bastards, we could do what the elven kingdoms won't—attack them."

"If you have the army, why not?" Kealin questioned.

"Because my father wishes us to hold our kingdom itself and not risk more falling to the bloodsuckers."

"Seems I understand why you called the Urlas Blades."

"And thanks to them," Ruak said, "many of the blood-suckers fell. At least, that is what I understand. If only that was the lone evil upon the lands."

7

MOONRISE

Darkness was upon them. They formed a smaller line, and Kealin noticed that the moon was rising but not high enough to light their actual path. Glowing stones dotting the pathway gave some guidance to their trek, but once again Elaca drew back on her bow. There was no stag this time, not that Kealin could see. The trees near them seemed to be drier. The leaves of bushes were shriveled, and the magic of the elven woods felt as he could only describe as depleted. Footfalls came from all directions, and a growling sound shrieked toward them. Kealin drew his blades, and out of the underbrush, it lunged at them.

Kealin jumped backward as Ruak swung his blade at the beast. It was a large wolf, drooling and snapping at them. Its eyes were glowing white, and its hair was missing in large patches. The wolf had already been injured, evident from its decaying flesh on its legs. Teusk lifted his staff, and the beast was splashed in an eye-blinding white light. Elaca released a bolt that found its target in the creature's upper neck before Ruak and Ivasel stabbed their swords into its head. The beast trembled and fell lifeless. Kealin was in awe at the creature's appearance. He went to turn to check their flank when a man appeared out of the shadows with a bony staff.

Kealin sidestepped, parrying the swung staff before severing the man's head with a scissoring strike. Elaca fired another arrow just to his left as from all sides, more men wearing bone armor appeared.

"Kealin, do not let them bite or scratch you!" Ruak yelled.

Teusk's staff became bright, and then from the tip, a ball of light shot into the sky. Shrieking sounds shot through the forest, and it seemed every bush moved with the strange beings.

Kealin moved into the bushes, striking the beasts and knocking down one after the next as Ruak and Ivasel moved to his side.

"Don't go too far away. We will not win this pushing forward. They are trying to draw us out," Ruak warned.

Teusk's staff glowed red, and he struck the ground with it. Red sparks shot out in all directions before the entire perimeter around them became as a wall of white fire. The creatures within the circle fell to the ground and were quickly killed. The creatures stood motionless outside the circle as Ruak walked toward them.

"Go, tell your masters of your failures. You cannot live within our sacred woods. Remain past the moment of this spell and know the woods themselves will punish you."

Kealin noticed the assembled demon men seemed to look into the trees and tremble with fear. One by one, they sunk away from the wall of magic and fled from sight.

"The woods will punish them? They listen to that?" Kealin asked.

Ruak smiled. "Sometimes. But they are as simple as can be in truth. They have pride in numbers and darkness, and taking away either will break them."

"The issue is that your ability to channel magic gives out with prolonged combat," Teusk said. "Even archons have limited powers, and in battles, we lose many of our archons before they can construct such a spell as I did."

Ruak nodded. "We Scions are happy to have such a veteran archon in our presence."

Teusk smiled at the words. Ivasel knelt down and picked a beetle off the ground.

"The presence of the bloodsuckers didn't spoil everyone. This friend can help us let those know who should know of the events here."

"Your father?" asked Ruak.

"He may concern himself more with the demon men than the orcs, but he must know how far they are coming. It seems the silence was just to increase their numbers. It seems the Fikmarkian guardians have been blinded."

Ivasel inscribed a note and affixed it to the beetle's body. "Take it to the king of the woods with much haste, friend."

The beetle seemed to acknowledge the words by a quick flap of its wings, and then scurried away.

"Well," Ruak said, "it appears our journey has been fraught with events so far. Let us move quickly to reach even more uncertain odds."

He smirked at Kealin with a double eyebrow raise. As they began walking again, Kealin walked beside him. "Do you feel this is pointless?"

"If I felt it was pointless, I would tell you. But Risdannia is not a commonly traveled to place. At least, not anymore. The fact that these woods along this path have become an ambush point by the demon men concerns me almost as much as the orcs to the south. Our enemies surround us, and I hope to have your blades when it comes time to fight."

The woods began to thin out, but it was not plains, but great rocks and fogged mountaintops that came into view.

The road became wider. Large stones every few paces marked strange statues that Kealin did not recognize.

"You walk a path of the gods, Kealin," Ruak said, "and I hope you understand that we elves have reasons for not coming this way as before."

Kealin noticed ahead that there was a large altar made of gray stone and covered in a sheen black stone. In the center of the stone was a single blade with the hilt of a raven's head. The blade was a sheen white, and the rising moon was now high enough for its light to glint out of the blade.

"I don't right like this part of it," Ivasel said.

Elaca walked around the altar and toward the open gateway just behind it. There was a stairwell that led up and around a sheer cliff. As she reached the gateway, it slammed shut. "I have never walked this path. So I may not continue. I have no need for the Moon Elves."

Kealin looked at her and then back to Ruak. "Scared, dear elf?"

He picked up the blade and offered it to Kealin. "To pass this gateway requires a sacrifice of blood. The pain is temporary, but what will happen to you in their presence is not. This practice is not as common as it once was. Elaca is under no guilt to choose not to take this journey."

Kealin grasped the hilt and noticed the eyes of the raven glowed blue. "Just a few drops?"

He pressed the blade against his finger and pierced the skin. The blood began to drop on the blade when Teusk grabbed his hand and the blade, pushing them together, causing a rush of blood from the serrated skin.

Kealin grimaced and offered the blade back to Ruak as he glared toward the archon.

"It takes more than a few drops of life to embrace the wisdom of time," Teusk said.

"Now go to the gate," Ruak said. "Place your hand on the plate in the center, and the gate will open again."

He went to the gate. It was unnaturally white and tall. Curved leaves of whatever material it was made of had almost crystalline qualities as he watched the path beyond the gate. He placed his cut hand on the plate in the center of the gateway, and the white turned to a fiery bright blue that was cold against his skin. The gateway opened.

Teusk, Ruak, and Ivasel went to follow him.

"Are you sure you do not want to come with us, Elaca?" Kealin asked.

"Doesn't want to hurt her draw hand," Teusk teased. "A good excuse for one who is afraid."

Ruak made an annoyed expression behind Teusk but also gave no objection to the assessment.

Kealin turned, and they began the trek up.

The path was strangely well kept. Small torches lit their path from carved basins that set in the face of the wall to their right. There were no spots that were overgrown or any broken stones, at least, that was originally carved to start with, and the ascent was not as difficult as Kealin expected.

As the moon continued upward, fogs veiled their view, and it became much more difficult to continue forward.

"Does anyone remember fog on your own journeys here?" Ivasel asked.

"No," Ruak said.

The archon remained silent.

Kealin looked toward him as he lifted his staff upward. A bright light began to glow, and the fogs receded in their direct path.

"It would take more than fog to make this journey arduous for the likes of me," he said.

"So why did you make the journeys?" Kealin asked.

"It is a rite once we each hit one hundred years. A strange task, but one to separate us from the children we once were to the men we were becoming. Though one hundred is not old, it became the new definition as leaving our childhood. The rite itself is about fear and blood. Fear drives you to do what you may not normally do. Blood reminds you of a sure path. To a child, this is much more than to us now, obviously. After the first pilgrimage to the top, few return unless on business to the Moon Elves. In the times long before now, the Moon Cullers would come to this place for their staves to be blessed by the goddess Etha, but in time, the Moon Elves banned the practice, claiming it took too much from their natural abode to have the Cullers present."

"Do they not create magic from moonlight?"

"They do, but the area directly below them loses magic for a short time."

"It can happen to archons too," Teusk said. "If too many of us are close together, our energies negate and we will lose our magic until we are apart. A way for the Great Poet to limit our powers."

"I have never heard the term 'Great Poet,'" Kealin told them.

"What do they teach in the North?" Ruak said. "The Great Poet is the creator, the one who wrote us into existence when the world was barren."

Kealin shrugged. "If this poet can assist me in getting my sister, I will believe in him."

"That is not how the Great Poet works," Ivasel said. "You must pray to the sleeping one and pray the Great Poet will dream in your fairness."

"I prefer blades and places I can use them."

Ruak laughed. "We shall have plenty of that in time."

They soon came to another gate just as before, but this one had a large circular disk affixed to the top where the crystalline leaves were on the first gate. As Kealin looked to Ruak for an explanation, the Scion knelt down before the gate and looked up.

"And it's perfect. Go ahead, Kealin."

He went to the gateway and pressed his bloody hand on the metal. It became engulfed in a green fire and then opened.

"It was the first moon lock," Ruak explained. "Depending on the trek of the moon will depend on how quickly you can ascend. This time, we were lucky and its placement was perfect. On up, we have a bit more way to go now."

In time, they reached the end of a stairwell, and Kealin found himself staring down a stone bridge across a narrow gorge. Coming to the edge, he looked over and noticed billowing fogs and no sign of an end to a sudden fall. Ruak suddenly drew his sword and stepped forward.

"In the name of the realm of Fikmark, throw down your weapon!"

Kealin jerked his gaze down the bridge, curious of what Ruak saw. Teusk ran ahead of them all, his staff glowing brighter and then fading as he came to a slow jog about midway across the bridge.

The rest of them came running up to find a single skeleton, charred beyond any form of knowing who this man was, at least in Kealin's opinion.

Ruak pushed around the charred remains to find a single button with what appeared to be a brooch of some kind. It was partially melted, but Kealin noticed the figure seemed to have large teeth.

"It is true," said Ivasel. "The dragons have been near our lands."

"It seems worse that they would come here, of all places."

Kealin gestured to hold the brooch. "Perhaps it is different in the South, but I have never known a dragon to have a brooch. Do you think this just because of the scorch mark on the bridge? It could've been a spell, right?"

"It is not the scorch that concerns me," Ruak began. "It is that this brooch has come to fall in our lands. There was once a guild of men, hunters of beasts. They did it for the mere thrill of a kill. Then they found the great dragons to be the quarry they sought, but in time, it became something else entirely. Instead of killing the creatures, they befriended, trained, or as some may say, enslaved. They are known as the Grey Scourge. They are of the South, and in such, not an issue to us elves, but there was talk they may come this way."

Kealin kicked the bones at his feet. "What happened to this one?"

"They are explorers as much as beast hunters and trainers," Ivasel said. "This one found the bridge and decided to defile it. The magic of this place cleansed him, and by Etha's light, he is free."

"What of the dragon?" Kealin asked.

"Moon Elves," Ruak said. "They love dragon meat. Come this way. Leave the bones for the beasts of the mountain."

. . .

Across the bridge, there was another platform and a stone stairwell. This one was glowing, unlike any he had yet seen. The soft blue hue of the stairs made it no issue to see the path, but difficult to see the view of rolling mountains. Kealin wondered of his sister, thinking of her as he moved around a more jagged jutting rock face and a narrow flat walkway to another platform. This one had two large braziers and a large white tree. He glanced off the mountain and noticed the end of the grand forest they had journeyed through. From high above, he could see a barren landscape that reached as far as he could see. As high as he was now, he could see the edge of the northern passage. A solemn feeling struck him.

"You look upon the northern lands of the elves and the barren place it is now. That is the place your brethren from Urlas, at least some of them, fell in battle."

"Foolish fighting," Kealin said. "I do not understand where such an evil would come from. My father said he did the will of the gods when he departed. He said the gods called to them."

"Indeed they did," Teusk said. "How are we to know the difference of the gods' works to that of elves? We are not, but we can say we were inspired by visions, goodness, and necessity. The last one is a stretch in meaning, but know that your father and mother's fate were not a waste."

"I know, especially when they served as sacrifices to bring back orcs."

Kealin forced the thought of his parents away. He stepped ahead of the rest, noticing at first the glowing crystals in the white tree before turning to see a large circular stone platform hovering above the rocks of the mountain itself. There was sheen silver writing across the entire surface. As he stepped up onto it, a large red swirling mass in the clouds appeared. He stared into it and watched as tiny lights seemed to slowly circulate out of it and wrap around the platform. At that moment, all went dark, and now Ruak and the others stood next to him.

"You saw a hint of what is to come," Ruak said to him.

Where the strange swirling mass had been was now a massive white gate with large stone statues of each phase of the moon lining the top of it. As he stared at it, he noticed the clouds parting to splash it with moonlight for a moment. The gate seemed to vibrate but remained sealed. He walked up to the center plate of the gate as he had done many times before. His hand was no longer bleeding, but he parted the skin with his fingers, and droplets began to flow. He pushed the gateway, but it didn't give.

"This gate is not like the others," Ruak said. "Now that we are here, it will be the will of those we wish to speak with that will open the way. But I'm sure the blood offering doesn't hurt."

He laughed at Kealin and motioned for him to come toward him. They had each taken a seat on standing stones upon the platform. He noticed the platform they were sitting on was slowly moving in a circular path. Different parts of the silver inscriptions began to light up as it twisted, but he did not understand the symbols.

"It is a form of elvish that not any of our realm still remembers. Frankly, I expected you to perhaps know something of it."

"I've never seen writing as this."

Ruak shrugged. "Well, now we wait. Teusk will continue to rotate his staff in his hands as he is doing now, and Ivasel will think of his home and act like he isn't."

Ivasel looked up from his blank stare toward the ground. "I worry of all elves."

"With the supposed coming battles, I am not surprised," Kealin began, "But after that last exchange with Hariv, I wonder how easy it will be to defeat the orcs. If I remember correctly, he laughed."

"We laugh, for if we do not, there will be despair," Ruak replied. "I cannot imagine the state of the lower coasts. The orcs will come in force, something beyond that of the lords of men and the king of the city by the sea. There are still elves there, but not many. It will take the forces of the elven woods to reinforce the city."

"You will need them to defeat one of the ones who lead them, and he will not give ground easily."

"Your brother is not fully lost, Kealin. Have faith that he did send you here for a reason. That mask is one of many that have been used through the ages. It is something to completely control one who would not be so simply used otherwise. Some say it was the Dwemhar who originally crafted them. Their way to control the ones who were more prone to mindless actions. Others claim it was the actual clan of Ur, the demon god himself. That was back before the great sinking of the lands of the South in times that, frankly, I rather not recall even though I was not even born yet."

"That was the time of the damn orcs," Teusk said. "It is when they first crawled out."

"And before we forced them back," stated Ivasel.

Ruak nodded. "Very true. But that is why we must find the Orc Star of Ur. I know with your help we can secure it before those of Ur. You already killed the Matriarch."

"Do not forget who now leads them. The half-elf was quite clear it was her son who controls the orcs."

"He is no son of hers. He held an adopted title due to his own elf lineage."

"The man was an elf?" Kealin asked.

"In form, at one time," Ruak said. "He became angry with the peaceful wisdom of the elves and began to fear that men were a greater threat to us. He sought power that was beyond his own grasp. Not all who seek to be archons are allowed. It takes balance in mind and spirit. He had both a mind and a strong spirit but failed to find balance. He has much knowledge in magical arts. The term wizard is a loose one, but one he claims. His original name is cursed to speak upon such a place as this, but the name he goes by now is Vakron-Tur. It is a title from the southern oceans and as unlike an elven name as he could take.

"I do not know where he went at first. Some said he went mad, others, that he died. But now I have confirmation that he is continuing on his path of desire toward decimation of all. The confirmation of his return will spread through elven whispers, and all of the woods will know that he is still within our world. He wishes to use the orcs against all who would go against his belief. Once we are done here, I pray you will come with us. We will go to Vueric and search for the secret knowledge the king's city holds. He does not like to admit it, but it was told to the elves long ago that his city held secrets of the Dwemhar. It is there we will find out more of the Black Star and particularly where it is."

Kealin nodded. "If our paths are to be together, it will be so. But I have been clear in my intentions."

That was not the sure answer Ruak wanted, but Kealin could not afford to do anything that took him from actually freeing his brothers and finding out of his sister. He was fighting for them and only them. The world could burn around him, and he would push on to this one goal no matter the stakes in the rest of the lands.

8

SHADOW PLAY

I t had been quite a few hours since they arrived and spoke with the king. Jesia stood on a balcony within the keep. She had changed out of her dirty armor into a fine red silk gown. This wasn't something she expected. She had thought there was a mistake when the attendant brought it to her and insisted she pick one of the several offered. Muera and Krea both had the same reaction. The only time a Rusis woman would have been given such a fine material to wear was if they were being sold to a new master.

Looking out from the balcony, she could see the vast waters of a golden sparkling sea and a red sunset unlike any she had ever witnessed at Cyr. The waves rolled against high cliffs, casting sea foam into the air, and gulls swooped down into the waters below, searching for their evening meal. Muera joined her.

"I did not believe we would end up in this kind of arrangement coming with the others."

Jesia nodded. "Neither did I. This is strange to me. They fight orcs at night and have fine dining the very next night?"

"Seems weak minds do trivial things," Krea muttered. She worked to clean her clothes of their grime. She sat nude with her gifted gown beside her.

"Actually, I was talking with the servants," Muera corrected. "The king's family is one of the last sigil houses in the West. The named houses that once dotted across the continent have all fallen or been absorbed into the Grand Protectorate. House Firda is the last of its kind, an independent lordship, deemed king by what some might call the only rebels of the greater protectorate realm."

"So another enemy of the Grand Protectorate?" Jesia asked.

"It would seem so. It's obvious they resist the idea of an alliance with them. They keep a lot of the old traditions of the crown in place. Lords, ladies, it is a strange thing that such a strong cultural aspect would still be present, but I like it."

"Remember our own, Sister," Krea said. "We Rusis were once the most feared of the races, and now we are mere slaves in the clothes of our soon masters."

She placed her hands on her just-cleaned clothing and used her magic to dry her tunic and leather armor.

"You do not join us at least in custom?" Jesia asked.

"You can keep the fine clothes. I will not play these games. There is a battle coming, and I care little but to prepare. Give you two a second of freedom and you're both falling into the dresses and playing ladies of the court. This isn't a storybook, and we are what we are. Rusis."

She stood up and put her clothes on. Jesia looked to Muera, who was speechless. They both knew that in many ways, Krea made a good point. At that moment, a knock came at the door.

"Ladies of the Rusis?" a voice called out from the other side.

Jesia opened the door to find a servant. He looked her up and down and smiled.

"You do look lovely in those colors, Jesia, it is? Correct?"

"Yes."

"Well, dinner will be served in a matter of moments. I do think your friend Master Brethor is already seated."

"He is not our master," Krea shouted.

The servant was taken aback by Krea's yell. "I meant no disrespect. Slavery is outlawed in the lands of House Firda, but he does not have the title of lord or knight, so that is the most appropriate."

The servant gulped and stared into the room before looking back to Jesia. "I can escort you three, if you like."

Jesia smiled at the obviously nervous man and shrugged. "We know the way to the hall. We will be fine."

The servant bowed and departed.

She shut the door and glared toward Krea. "Can you show an ounce of respect?"

"Sure." Krea pushed past her and opened the door.

"Keep your guard up in this place. These people are too relaxed."

Muera approached Jesia. "Let's go."

Jesia turned and followed them out.

BRETHOR HAD BEEN SITTING down at the table since the first hint of dinner service was mentioned. He and Orolo were given new tunics and cloaks, a gift from the king to go with the polishing of their blades and the face shaves that neither of them had gotten in some time. Brethor had not been this adorned since back home in Elinathrond.

He sipped his wine and looked toward his brother. "So are you done betraying your family?"

Orolo paused and looked around the room. The king had recently departed after first greeting them, finding out one of his other sons had arrived. They were alone for the moment.

"I don't see my actions as betrayal."

"Conspiring with a madman to return one of the greatest vile evils this world has ever dealt with is not an act of good fortune."

"The wizard is not mad. He is a thinking man, and one who knows we must not fall prey to simple men."

"These simple men, as you call them, mean us no harm."

"These men are not whom I worry of, Brother."

.   .   .

FROM THE FAR end of the room, the king entered, a trio of men with him, all in good spirits and kidding with one another. Brethor and Orolo stood as they approached the table.

"Sons, these are some of whom I was telling you about. Brethor and Orolo Srvivnann."

The first man was a man much like Brethor in stature. He wore plated silver armor with the house sigil of a black shark on a blue field in clear view.

"Lord Meask of House Firda, and I welcome you and your companions to our city."

The next two gave shorter handshakes and less than a greeting. With almost forced smiles, Lord Kiras and Lord Ridau took seats opposite of Brethor and Orolo. The king patted the back of Orolo's chair as he looked up at the stairwell.

"And now the Rusis women of Cyr freed from oppression and from what my Rangers say, fierce sorceresses!"

Brethor stood as they approached. He had not seen women such as these and doubted if they were even the same he had traveled with. Jesia led the three around the table to take seats next to him and his brother. Servants were immediately there to tend to their chairs before Brethor had a chance. Both Muera and Jesia smiled and looked at him with an odd glare. Krea sat down and immediately poured a chalice of wine.

Dala joined them now. He was dressed in perfect white, with his jeweled scimitar at his waist. He bowed to the king and took his seat.

From the far end of the hall, a door opened, and the king immediately went that way. "My queen!"

A woman emerged with a large adorned headdress of shells and gold jewels. A bit overdone in Brethor's opinion, but it seemed her attendants were held in much the same way. Though lacking the hair adornments, they all wore fine jewelry.

"My queen," he said again, kissing her hand in a bow. I wish you to meet our guests, Brethor, Orolo, and three women of the Rusis."

"Strange," she said, looking toward the Rusis. "From the description given to us by Vaden, I expected them to have burning flames in their hands at all times."

She laughed, but no one else, save a forced laugh from Lord Kiras, shared her humor. She took her seat at the far end of the table, and the servants immediately went to work, serving a multi-course dinner of salad and fruit, followed by steamed oysters and shrimp. Through the main course of venison and pork, minstrels began to sing, and Brethor sat up as the verses began to reveal more of the city.

"Beside sea and longing lands,
The elven realm does lay.
And with the rocks and shocks and war,
The Dwemhar fell away.
Many men came from afar,
Swords still in our hands.
And upon the stones of ruins long lost,
We built Vueric on the sands.

Long ho
Hold ho
The last house by the sea.
Firda Strong, Firda Great
Shall never bend a knee.

Wakening demons once before,
Threatened sacred lands.
Under shadow of the Black Orc Star,
We lost our upper hand.
Demon rock, of cursed mounts,
Upon the dirt we fought.
Firda ho, remembers all,
Forever wisdom sought.
Long ho
Hold ho
The Dwemhar in our blood,
Firda Strong forever last,
As ancestors knew we would."

As the final course of the meal was delivered, King Firda smiled at the pouring of another long-awaited cup of coffee.

"Be happy, Father," Lord Meask said. "That was the last of the coffee we received from the South. I believe the Grand Protectorate has begun stopping trade ships from the South. Though, perhaps with their vanishing in recent days, our trade routes will return to normal."

"You worry of trade routes when we have orcs in the gateway?" Lord Kiras sneered.

"Yes, dear young brother, for trade is how we supply an army. Tell me, what did you bring to the city? A few man at arms?"

"Five hundred men from the northern border of our realm. Good men. Experienced men. We've been fighting the vampire creatures for the last few years and have no allies since the elves fell back into their woods."

"Except my cavalry, of course," Ridau added. "But good men are in short supply."

"It is an issue here as well," King Firda said. "I have sent messages, but they do not seem to feel the need to reply. Now we have allies who have come to us. Amhe, of Eh-Rin, has sent word that he will support us and alliance against the orcs."

Dala stood. "Good lords and lady, my master is faithful. I have sent word of the king's agreement, and I know we will have at least thirty ships with fighting men headed this way before long. We will do whatever we must to prevent the orcs and their leader from destroying your city."

Lord Meask raised his chalice to Dala's words, and Dala took his seat.

"And of the Grand Protectorate?" Ridau said.

"What of the bastards?" Lord Kiras asked. "They want our throne, our lands, our titles. They will not have it."

"And if the orcs sat upon the throne?"

There was silence for a moment before the king spoke. "That is why we prevent the orcs' continued rise through old allies and not ones who will have our kingdom."

"Dear king," said Brethor, "may I ask a question of your minstrel's song?"

"Go ahead. Interwoven history with music is a great thing."

"You speak of Dwemhar, and Vueric built on ruins. What kind of ruins?"

The king slurped his coffee. "Ruins of a grand design, some that still stand above ground, like the statue before the series of gateways leading here, but most that actually are within the deepest portions of the city lost to time. They are Dwemhar, and well, our best men and women have no clue of what to do with them and haven't in all the years we have been here. We have a large archive here on the palace grounds of what lore we have learned, which is quite substantial, but the doors cannot be forced to get into the deeper regions. What we have has been recovered from random caches of ruins found scattered throughout the mountains."

"Perhaps it is all dust," the queen said. "The Dwemhar are extinct. What bloodline we could trace to them has been diluted for hundreds of years."

"The bigger key is the true evil of these orcs. We had hoped to learn more of this wizard and witch who travel with them," the king said. "But from the captured orcs we did have, they claimed a man was leading them and not the 'Mother' they referred to before."

"It is a man. Two men, actually," said Jesia. "But one

is a wizard and the other is a warrior in black with a mask."

"I know of that man," Lord Meask said. "He is the one spoken of. He first led the orcs. He is a commander."

"These orcs came from nowhere," said Lord Ridau. "We were dealing with the vampires, but then they just came out of the ground."

"Your song," Brethor said. "It is in your song."

"What do you mean?"

"'Under shadow of the Black Orc Star.' It is a reference to the Black Star of Ur. Ur is the demon god of old. They have used magic to draw up the orcs, and it is the Black Star that gives the wizard the power to control them."

The door on the far end of the hall opened, and Ranger Vaden appeared.

He bowed and approached. "King, lords, I have word from the Scions."

"They send their armies?"

"No, the elves still do not march. But they do have knowledge of who does, in fact, lead the orcs. It is an elf, as we feared, one known now as Vakron-Tur. It seems the elves have sent messages to the fringes of the woods. They seem to fear this elf."

"That is a Southern name," Brethor said, "of the lands long lost."

"It seems the only information they are willing to share."

"Did you speak with Ruak himself?"

"No, he and Ivasel and some of the others departed a

few days ago, but he would not say why, and I did not think to ask."

"Well, at least you are a good Ranger," the king teased. "How are our legionary guests fairing?"

"Good, though they still wonder of their freedom to leave."

"They can leave if they wish, but the legatus himself said he wished to fight. I assume he will stick to those words."

Lord Ridau, who at this point had said very little, was staring at Brethor and Orolo.

"Do you want a kiss?" Orolo asked.

Brethor shot him an annoyed look. "Apologies, Lord," he said, turning back to talk to him.

"No, dear man. But I am flattered. I know not the name of Srvivnann in my history of great families. What city are you from?"

"We are of no city of elf or man," Brethor said.

"Then how is it you came to be here and among those of Eh-Rin? I know that Amhe is kind, but he does not allow just anyone into his inner circles."

Lord Meask sat forward in his seat.

"We are of Dwemhar blood, and of a greater purity than most who can claim such a claim."

The king nodded his head. "No wonder you asked of my song. You have the blood of Dwemhar after we thought they were all gone. It shows what we actually know. Perhaps you will find something in the ruins; perhaps there is more hope sitting at this very table than an army?"

"My brother and I would be honored to do what is

necessary to end these vile terrors in the night your people are facing. We wish nothing more but to see Vakron-Tun brought before men and elves to be destroyed for the good of the world."

At this point, Orolo stood so abruptly the others looked around in confusion.

Brethor turned to his brother, but before he could say anything, Orolo raised his hand. "I know your feelings, Brethor. I will not try to convince you of anything. I will assure our family survives this darkness."

Orolo began out, and Krea stood as well. "I will follow him and calm him down. We do not need any more foolhardy decisions."

Brethor went to stand as well but then sat back down with an exhale.

Lord Meask touched his shoulder. "Brothers argue, and more so when they are stressed. It is why we have a dinner such as this in times of darkness that have become so frequent. If we forget what we fight for, we lose a reason to fight in the first place. We have fought the vampires to the north, and now we fight to the south against orcs. Give him some time, and he will relax and be the man he should be when the time comes he is called upon."

Brethor looked to Jesia and then rubbed his hands through his hair.

"He isn't used to this; heck, I'm not used to this. We left our family and journeyed south and got caught up in more than we should, and now we are here. Well, I can say the memory of our home returns to me as well. I do not trust Orolo as I once did. He betrayed me once, and I've struggled to see past that."

"This city is well guarded," said King Firda, "and the Rangers will not let anyone pass the river crossing without reason. It is nearing night as it is. That is when we must be on guard." The king looked up to his sons. "Which is of discussion now. Servants, away with this food."

The servants cleared the table, and another attendant brought up a map.

"Admiral Dala of Eh-Rin, come give your opinions as well."

Brethor leaned over to see a map of Vueric and the river to the south of the city.

"This is a typical nightly discussion of plans for holding our valley lands. As you can see, we have many of the same tactics night after night. Only, we are starting to run out of pieces."

The map itself had worn areas in the same places. The river had seen many incursions, but due to its size and current, it seemed many battles failed. The bridge was another heavily contested area, and from the inscriptions of lost battles and cross hashes, many men had fallen there too. The king opened a box with several black stones. He placed them along the mountains to the south. He took out a few silver arrows and placed them around the river before taking out four black sharks. He placed three in the city and one near the elven woods to the east.

"Our defense has been a steady one," said Lord Ridau, "and my augmented forces are camping in the woods left open after the elves fell back. The fort there is called Eastwatch."

"And to this point, the city itself has been my charge," Meask said. "We have two thousand volunteer city watch manning the walls and our Knights Guard patrolling the outskirts of the city and the inner halls. Our total number sits at five thousand for the protection of the city, including able-bodied man-at-arms who have arrived in the past week."

"Which leaves the River Rangers and some floating sellswords who have taken to securing the river and bridge way," Lord Meask added. He took a slurp from his chalice and sighed. "We hold the river because they haven't brought the numbers they need to get past the lighthouse defenses. Once they breach that place, the river will become much more difficult to defend."

The king smirked. "I know I shouldn't find it amusing, but if we still had the tenth legion, their camp would actually round out our defenses quite nicely."

Meask looked up to his father. "You're not considering?"

"Of course I am not." The king shook his head. "We have Amhe to help us now. Dala, please share more about your forces as of late."

Dala pointed to the southern desert and Amhe's Road. "Amhe will send a large force of five thousand pikemen by land. I believe the army is likely already in route and could've been before we had sent word of your agreement. That is typical of my sultan. The rest will come by ship to the mouth of the river."

"No magic carpet, then, eh?" The king held his gaze

at Dala for some time before the confused admiral shook his head.

"I don't understand your—"

The king cut him off, "Still don't know? Well, then. Five thousand men will be a much-needed augment to our forces. But now that good Brethor is here, I assume there will be more we can do, and Rusis, you may not have numbers, but your powers are no doubt formidable. I ask for your opinion."

Jesia looked to Muera. Until now, they had been ignored, or so it seemed to them. Jesia stood with Muera, following behind her. They looked at the map, and then Jesia glanced at Brethor.

"I do not know much of war plans," Jesia admitted as she looked to the king, "but I think these ruins you speak of and the records of what you have learned could prove useful."

"I would like to see your record hall," Brethor said. "Dwemhar artifacts and ruins can hide many secrets, and aside from dealing with the orcs, we need to know more of the Orc Star itself. There could be something of it in the ruins."

"The rumor is it was lost near Demon Head Peak in the very mountains south of here, but many a man have searched for it to no luck," Meask said.

"How do we not know for sure that the leader of the orcs hasn't gotten it yet?" Muera asked.

"Very unlikely," Ridau said. "The old chronicles said it was like a dark spinning disk that turned the sky black and enraged the orcs into a swarm."

"But we leave nothing to chance," King Firda said.

"This Vakron-Tur is an elf, and in so, he can be killed. If we see him, we will do so, but if he is some powerful wizard as said, we will need magic to help us. Tell us more of your powers, Rusis. I will not insult anyone else with my assumptions of knowledge, but I understand you can cast the elements?"

"Fire, ice, lightning, and some stone," Jesia said. "Though, most of us prefer certain elements to others. We have been considered more formidable for the lack of actually needing a staff, wand, or another channeling device, but I imagine the wizard's magic is of closer level to ours, if not actually much higher."

"We have magical wards too," Muera said. "Defensive spells that can dispel incoming magical attacks."

Ridau smacked his fist on the table. "If we could just get close enough to Vakron-Tur, we could end this."

"Though the Rusis are powerful," Meask said, "he will be surrounded by many orcs, not to mention the black warrior."

"What is one man to all of the Knights Guard, and even the Rangers have good swordsmen. The warrior could not best all of them."

"I have seen him best one of the most skilled swordsmen I had ever seen with not much of an issue at all," Brethor said. "It will take all of us to take him down, and I doubt he will reveal himself until whatever he has planned is well in motion. If we get tied down in a siege of the city, it will get more difficult for us."

"The last thing we want is a siege. Though I won't order our armies forward without a sound plan, I trust that after some time in the ruins, you will discover something. In time, Amhe's forces will arrive, and we will speak with the sultan and move forward. I do not want my people to suffer any longer in fear. For now, we hold our lands and will await your wisdom, descendant of the Dwemhar."

The king smiled with his final words and then stood.

"We are adjourned. I will see you taken to the halls of records and the guards will know of my plans to allow you into the ruins. Though, I am wary of your brother, so I will specify it is you who is allowed in, not him."

The queen stood and looked at Brethor before speaking to her husband. "Is it prudent to allow one and not the other? These are both acquaintances, yet you put the one as more trustworthy by his own statement?"

King Firda nodded. "Of course. The other one will come around in time, but I make one decision now in good faith. Besides, look at our boys. Have we ever known them not to quarrel at some point? It will be fine."

The king and queen departed, leaving the three lords, Brethor, and the Rusis.

"Well, I go to my men," Kiras said, taking an apple. "Seems the best use of my time this far south."

"Yes, yes, go to your men, little brother. Leave the true kingdom saving to us."

"Screw off, Meask."

Meask laughed, as did Brethor.

"Truly, do not worry about your own brother. At one point, we had to convince our father that Kiras wasn't plotting to steal the crown. Assumptions are the worst in almost every family."

"Notice he said almost," Ridau pointed out.

"Come, this way," Meask said.

THEY EXITED the great hall and began down a long corridor. As they walked, Jesia noticed a slight grin between Muera and Ridau that Meask and Brethor had ignored. For a normal man, Ridau wasn't unattractive. He was taller than both of them and didn't have the "regal" air that Meask had. He was the middle brother and, oddly enough, actually was the quietest but had the most mysterious gaze of all of them. He had looked at her once at the table, but her eyes drifted away. Her mind was on Kealin and if he was alive. But his gaze had only drifted over her. He had been staring at Muera from the very start.

Muera giggled and then covered her mouth as Ridau straightened his back to keep composure after a hushed joke. Jesia hadn't seen her fellow Rusis as happy as this in some time. She was very happy to be free of Cyr, but her mind continually went back to Kealin. She missed him even with the little amount of time they had together.

They came to a large white wooden door that was flanked by two candles.

Meask pushed open the door, and a palely lit room greeted them. Large windows lined the upper part of the room, but the last remnants of a purple-hued sunset were giving way to the darkness of night.

"I will get some better candles and torches for reading, but this is it," Meask stated.

Brethor looked around his immediate vicinity and lifted some parchments. "A lot of stuff."

"Yes." Meask laughed. "When you have read what you wish and wish to see the ruins, let my father or me know. My brother and I plan to spend some time throwing arrows downrange in the castle throne room. It's a game we played as kids. Unless you stay in here as long as the sage masters do, then I will see you in the morning!"

Meask turned away, but Ridau remained.

"Um, Lady Muera?" he asked.

"Yes?"

"I had actually wondered if you would like to take a walk with me. I understand if you cannot considering the information we all need, but if you could spare a few moments?"

Muera smiled and walked toward him.

"Good brother! You abandon me so easily?" Meask joked.

"Yes, she is much more interesting than you. Plus, you know I will win at archery anyway. You've always been the better swordsmen."

MEASK DEPARTED, and Muera and Ridau went their own way, leaving Jesia and Brethor to themselves. They began reading through random parchments. Most of what was written down in the common tongue were very rudimentary words. Brethor could read Dwemhar writing, and it was clear the bulk of what was here were poorly translated scratchings from the foyer of the temple. Though, some information was of interest. There was a good deal of rubbish to read through to maybe get to something of actual value.

Brethor walked further into the room and noticed that the shelves he thought ended at the edge of the wall actually wrapped around a small corridor and back around the other side. Jesia joined him, but neither of them could decide if this finding was an exciting one or more of a depressing realization at what horrible task lay ahead.

IT HAD BEEN A FEW HOURS, and both of them began to feel weary. Jesia couldn't actually read what she was seeing, but Brethor had given her a few keywords and their appearance to guide her. As she scanned the first page of a new stack of parchments, she saw one of the words she was looking for.

"Brethor," she said, pointing.

He finished what he was reading and then glanced over before standing and moving his fingers along the next few lines.

"This speaks of Ur, the actual demon lord, or as this reads: *The wretched Itsu father, Ur, demon master, defilers of life.* I knew he was a demon god, but I did not know he was considered the father of the Itsu."

Jesia continued to watch as he moved his finger down the lines of words.

"*The cultures of the world moved against him, and it was the gods of the North who sealed him away. Kel, of the Northern gods, placed eternal bounds on him. But there came from the South a cult, madmen who searched the mountain, ranging from the Iber peninsula after the destruction of the lands to the much further south, all the way to the border of these lands, for any hint of their lord Ur. The elves sent warriors to hunt them down, but none of them returned. The Dwemhar sent their own to find them, and though they found the temple, something was already at work. A portal had been found. A portal leading from within the temple of Ur that could be used to traverse to any active portal in the lands."*

"Active portals?" Jesia asked.

"Um, some Dwemhar cities used a type of whirlpool to traverse to other cities within the world. There is not much known of it, but I have seen inscriptions of such things. A portal can be opened, but it takes an insane amount of magic to open, and they used blood crystals crafted by their own design to power them. It is a magic that frankly is beyond me, but I understand the name to mean it did take blood itself. Franky, my brother understood this level of the Dwemhar technology better than me."

He continued reading and then stopped abruptly.

"The Dwemhar did not abandon this city. They were destroyed from within."

"What do you mean?"

Brethor slammed the book shut and stood. "We must get to the ruins. Come on, we will find Meask."

They exited the hall of records and turned toward the great hall when a scream reverberated from within the keep. Brethor drew his sword and began into a sprint. He entered the great hall and turned toward the doorway. Knights Guard Captain Tiris entered the room from the doorway with a contingent of soldiers as another scream pierced through the hall.

"To your king!" he shouted.

Brethor charged into the open doorway where the queen had emerged from before, and ran up a stairwell that led up to an open balcony. He stammered to a stop as he came upon the queen lying in her own blood with her face disfigured. He looked over the balcony and could see no one. He turned as Jesia closed what was an empty side room.

Captain Tiris followed behind his soldiers as they turned and headed toward the king. Brethor was about to join them when Tiris swung his sword, clanging another blade just to Brethor's left. The captain pulled him out of the way and pushed a black figure to the edge of the railing. It locked a silver blade with Tiris. Jesia opened her hands, summoning a ball of frost before blasting the entity off the balcony. They each ran to the railing as the being fell to the ground and did not move.

"What is that? I didn't even see it when I first walked out here."

"It is dead," the captain said.

They heard the sounds of fighting above them, and they continued further upstairs.

"Upstairs, to the king!"

They ran up the stairwell to reach the king's room. A large four poster bed was splintered from many strikes, and overturned furniture was everywhere. The king was backed into a corner, but it was evident from the many would-be assassins dead on the ground that the king had killed many before now.

The remaining assassins present were pushed to the edge of another balcony. A strange horn call deep and long sounded from within the castle walls. One of them drew a dagger and threw it toward the king, but it landed just to the side of his head. The hooded figure hissed, and then they disappeared over the edge. Brethor and Tiris ran to the railings, but they had vanished. Looking further down, they noticed the one they thought dead was missing.

They turned back to the king, who held the dagger in his hands. He was shaking.

"My king?" Tiris said.

The king stood and pushed himself past everyone, stumbling down the stairwell. He tripped near the last step and rolled against the wall. Tiris attempted to help him, but he swatted him off. He crawled to his wife and began to weep.

"My king," Tiris said, "we must get you to safety."

"If I am not safe in my own damn castle, I won't be safe anywhere you could take me."

A bell began to toll in the distance.

"Orcs have attacked somewhere within the defensive lines," Tiris told Brethor.

At that moment, Lord Meask ran up the stairs and stopped just short of his father. "What happened to Mother?" His face became stricken with grief as tears welled in his eyes.

"Black assassins, shadows unlike anything we've seen yet," Tiris said, "and definitely not orcs."

Meask shook his head, looking over at Jesia and Brethor.

"Where are Muera and my brother?"

Another bell tolled at a much higher rate.

"The castle is breached!"

"You men, stay with the king!" commanded Captain Tiris.

Brethor and Jesia followed Meask and the captain as more Knights Guard came through the main hall.

"Where is the enemy?" Meask shouted.

"They have attacked the ruins in the inner sanctum."

"What?"

The fifty or so men ran down another corridor and down a series of widening stairs to a large area unlike the rest of the keep. In what appeared to be an enormous cave, a massive doorway, larger than any Brethor had ever seen, reached up to the highest levels of the ceiling.

"The door," said Meask. "The door is open."

The guards spread out around the large room. The door that the king mentioned earlier was open, but only a crack. Although, it was enough for a person to fit through.

"My lord!" one of the Knights Guard shouted.

Brethor and Jesia followed him to the edge of a recently collapsed area of the ruins to find both Lord Ridau and Muera. They were both bloodied, but Ridau had a stab wound to his chest and was coughing blood.

Meask called to the guards. "Get the healers, quickly!"

Two men departed.

Jesia knelt down to Muera. "What happened?"

She glanced over to Brethor. "Your brother, he came. There were shadows with him. We saw them in the hallway and followed them. When we saw Orolo opening the door, we confronted them, and then there was a blast, and I don't know what happened. Krea is with them." She began to breathe faster and cough. "It was so nice to talk with the lord. He is very kind. I hope he is not too hurt."

Jesia looked up to see Meask cradling his brother.

Brethor walked to the open doorway and looked into the bleak darkness.

"Master Brethor," the king said behind him.

Brethor turned to see the king, but there was an obvious anger to his stance. "It was my brother, and I will deal with him."

"You deal with your brother," the king crossly stated. "I pray you found something of use to us about these ruins and that you will do what is needed to protect us all. This dagger that killed my wife and was thrown at my head is a blade of that cursed cult of Ur, and it is not my name that is on it, but my city. We have been threatened for the last time. Lord Meask, prepare all of the men of Vueric. I have just received a message that your brother was slain upon the field by the same shadows that took your mother! Lord Kiras has fallen, and he will be the last of my house who will fall to these demons and their shadows. Hear my words, I will send final ravens to every elven king of those cursed woods, and by the gods of the North, if they do not take an orc blood-stained parchment as my sign of need of their armies, we will defeat the orcs by ourselves and then turn every force in our power to bring down their kingdoms."

There was silence in the room. Meask had lowered his head in the hearing of his brother's passing just as the healers arrived for Muera and Lord Ridau.

Brethor went to the stairwell and took two torches.

He bowed to the king as he passed and then handed a torch to Jesia.

"We both have issues in these ruins to deal with. Let's see them dealt with."

9

MOONFALL

The moon had soared above them and returned back toward the distant horizon. Kealin lay on the stone platform with his eyes closed. To others, it may have appeared he was sleeping, but he was not. He took deep breaths and exhaled. He felt his body relaxing, his muscles loosening, and his mind quieting. He could feel the vibrations of the stone twisting beneath him, and the rush of air across his body reminded him of the crisp cold of the Far North.

He kept his eyes closed. He concentrated on those he would soon meet, the Moon Elves. A strange name and one he had never heard before now. There was much he didn't know that he now did. There was another gust of the wind, and the vibrations under his back changed. He opened his eyes to see the gate alight. The moon, just on the edge of the horizon, shot a beam straight through a crystal at the top of the gate. The light gave life to other crystals, and the gateway opened with the sounds of great winds.

The elves around him dropped to their knees. He sat up and then stood. From the opening gate came a white light, as if a living flame that shot out with red fireballs circulating atop the mountain. The balls of fire hit torches on the surrounding peaks, and blue fires burst to life as a deep fog shrouded the surrounding mountain peaks.

Kealin looked ahead, seeing only a trio of female figures. Though each of them wore a sheen silver armor covering their breasts and stomachs, their arms and legs were draped in what appeared actual clouds. The skin he could see glowed with a radiant light. They stepped on the platform Kealin stood upon, and the entire structure began to glow. He could see their faces, if he could call them faces. The center figure had no face, while the left and right had respective images of a face on the left and right sides of their head.

As one spoke, they all opened their mouths and spoke. "Where is the one who ascends, for I am blind and divided by the world?"

Ruak looked up for a moment. "Holy sacrilege, what is that?" he said in a despaired tone.

Kealin was confused but stepped forward.

"Stop, you with the blood of Urlas. You have not been given passage."

He stood still.

"Do you seek to hurt those beyond? Do you not claim allegiance to the god Dimn, a protector of his realm?"

"I protected that palace of winds, yes, but I do not

claim any allegiance to the gods. I search for my family. I am here for my brother."

"The accursed?" the figures questioned. "Did he not come here before, seeking assistance?"

"I do not know."

The figures split apart and surrounded him. His arms were suddenly tight to his side, and he found it hard to breathe.

"He did. He came with the mask. He was injured at some point by an elven blade, the only of such items in the world that can harm the mask itself. He was him for a time, and he begged our help, but already you've come further than him. He was evil. We barred his entry to the realm. Why now must we let you in?"

"I'm going to help my brother."

"It is love that draws you to our high reach as we work tirelessly to secure our brethren to the lands. You work for all elves, then, for we are all brothers and sisters in the great battle of life."

Kealin thought for a moment. He knew the words were not just plainly said for no reason. He would not speak his mind to these beings. "Yes, I honor elves. I work for all elves to protect our realms."

The three figures shifted around him one at a time, moving close behind him and then receding back. At last, after many shifts back and forth, they paused in the dead center of his sight.

His pulse pounded, and he worked to slow his breathing.

"You lie, and we sense it. You are evil. You defy our realm. You are like the one called Vakron-Tur. You are like your brother, and your self-serving desires will not fair well for the knowledge of our kind or the fate of those you care about. The Moon Elves of Risdannia are wise and old and must contain all evil. There are some workings that move against what many would say is evil, but yet some would say is good. None can see the future, for it is shrouded from all, but you come from the Far North. You released Vankou of the imprisoned isle, you laid open the way to the sacred objects of Dimn, and you failed in your guard because of your actions to save those you loved. You must give up yourself to defeat the true evils. You are not ready."

Kealin felt the grip the entities had on him release, but as it did, the three formed to one and floated back up to the gate. The way toward the light began to close. He sprinted across the platform, the open pathway closing as he did. In a flying leap, the last he heard was Ruak.

"Kealin, no!"

Kealin felt his face sucked forward. A bright light turned to a dark orb, spinning around his body and pulling at every inch of his skin. He heard howls and screams, and a searing heat struck his body. Then he saw trees below him. He was falling. In a sudden slam to a stop, he heard only crickets.

Coughing, he sat up. He looked up into the dark sky and noticed not a sign of the moon or stars. Directly above him was a spinning cloud of purples, blues, and reds that reminded him of looking down upon the maelstrom, but instead of flying in the clouds, he looked up.

He glanced around to see the same figure he had spoken with before, only this time, she was not split in three but was whole.

"You have embraced something beyond mere elven lineage," she said. "None of our kind can come here without permission and live. As we tried to destroy you, you resisted. You are immune to such magic."

"The Dwemhar blood in my body is strong, or so I have been told before. What is this place?"

"This is Risdannia, the realm of all magics, the void of the Moon Cullers and those of my kind, the Moon Elves."

"I have been to a few other realms. None had an entrance like that," he said, motioning toward the swirling vortex above them.

"Those realms did not contain such magic as we do here. Walk with me."

He followed the female. She did not make a sound as she walked, and he could see through the skin of her body.

"You question if I am a spirit?"

"It would not surprise me."

"I am a creation of magic, made in the image of the Moon Elves themselves, a vessel for their thoughts, actions, and wishes."

"And what do they wish? Why was I not allowed entry to this place?"

She stopped walking and made a motion with her hands. The trees before them opened up, and Kealin could see down to a great lake. A massive moon sat next to a glowing white orb. There was a single tower that emanated blue lightning into the air, spreading a fine dust that spread toward the vortex high above.

"Magic, a fragile source of so much," she said. "For more ages than that of the gods has magic remained in the world, but evil has shaken the realm of life. It is why I appeared as I did, split, broken, and not as even your companions remember me. We have closed our realm to outsiders, for outsiders seek our secrets."

"I only wish to know of my siblings: my brother and my sister. I must help them."

"Is it the will of any god that spurs you to act?"

"No, I said that."

"Then is it for the elves or Dwemhar that you act?"

"Neither."

"Then you will do whatever you must to reach them, even go against your own kind?"

"Yes."

The figure disappeared, and the view of the lake and tower vanished as Kealin suddenly saw every tree shift around him violently. He drew his blades, not knowing what else to do at that moment. He turned and ran back the way he came, coming to a grove that shifted with a violent wind storm. He could hear nothing but the rushing gusts when a circle of females appeared with him in the center. The winds halted. The sounds of crickets he heard before ceased.

He looked around at the figures and gasped as their eyes opened and he saw only white lights.

"We are the ones who dwell within this realm, Kealin Half-Elf of Urlas, Dwemhar of Old, heir to violence and bloodshed, freer of Vankou and the northern dread. Be that it?"

He was stunned for a moment, but then spoke with a stutter. He was afraid, and more so than he had been before.

"What you have said is true to what I know."

"Why did you and your kind intercede in the events with Dimn?"

"There was a darkness coming, a darkness even Dimn went against. We did what we could to protect the lands. My parents went to the aid of the Scions and from, I thought, the god Kel. A wise man within our realm told us of warnings of shadows, and I went to protect those I care for. That is why I am here. Because I must help them."

"We have seen much. The orcs swell in the mountains and will swarm these lands. The whispers of your name have reached us even before your brother came upon our sacred stone in the mountains. If you wish to free him, you must destroy the one called Vakron-Tur. Then, he will be free of his mask. But there is much in the world, and what has started may not be stopped."

"What do you mean? Do you speak of the North and the one of death?"

"The world is shaking, and the Great Poet, our creator and the author of the words of life, sleeps uneasily. Though, we will do what we have to preserve our world. Horrid evils awaken around us. We are as you and those of Urlas, protected by our realm, but we fear of the lands. Our sight is blinded and our magic is weakened by something else in the world."

"What must I do?" he asked.

The many figures began to fade until only one remained. This was not one of the females he had seen before.

She stared at him. He looked into her eyes and suddenly felt pulled into a starry realm where he floated through the air with the figure moving around him.

"You will play a great part in events to come, but know that for every step you take, another will step against you. The curse of the North is one of death, and it will plague your every action. I show you this to give you hope."

His eyes went black, and for a moment, he saw Alri within a pink crystalline prison.

"Alri!" he shouted.

"She cannot hear you, nor can I tell you where she is. But she is alive. You can find her in your world. There is a place to guide you. A place that the one called Ruak knows of. Tell him you spoke to Etha, and he will tell you of it."

He stared at her.

"Etha? You are the goddess of the elven race. I . . . I . . . don't know what I should say to this."

"Know that even the gods are blinded to what is transpiring. Kel moves to stop whatever evil comes, but his way of war can only get us so far in the schemes of the world. You fought an Itsu Priest within the realm of Dimn and lived. No mere man or elf can do that."

At this point, Kealin noticed he was standing on a rock. The clouds were swirling around him as the goddess hovered before him. He felt his swords brim with energy, the ruinite ore vibrating the hilts in his hands. He slid both of them back into their sheaths.

He took a deep breath as he felt the rock strike a hard surface. He closed his eyes from the impact, and when he opened them, Etha stared into his eyes.

"Do not let us fall into darkness, if your swords can prevent it. We, gods, watch your every move, and we will be with you. Remember all who dwell within the realms."

He watched as Etha floated upward into the reddish sky and then looked around as the fogs receded, and he could see familiar mountaintops. As a strong wind blew the remainder of the shroud, he looked down on Ruak, Ivasel, and Teusk, who were staring upward in amazement.

The great stone he had returned to the realm upon had smashed the very entryway to the realm of Risdannia.

"Kealin?" Teusk asked. "What happened?"

"We saw a golden light ascend toward the heavens and then you," Ivasel said.

Kealin jumped down onto the platform and went to Ruak.

"I was told to tell you I spoke to Etha. I can find my sister, and you know the place."

Teusk looked at Ruak with a confused stare.

Ruak was now red in the face. He was upset but nodded. "For many years, I have known such a thing, but it is not something I have told others. I had a dream when I was but a young child. A starlight ascended to the sky at sunrise, and I floated above the mountains for a time. It is to the east. A vision of our goddess came to me and told me this was my fate. You will find what you seek in the mountains. A tower, hidden in a mountain. It is an old place, and though I know it is not elven, I feel you can learn the way in."

Ruak closed his eyes and began to weep more.

Ivasel was now even more confused than Teusk. "Brother, what is it?"

"That is the last of my fate. At the end of my dream, I died. That is what I face soon, and I fear it."

Kealin embraced him. "You will go with me to this place, and I will show you that death can be faced and beaten. Whatever comes against you in this life, we work for all to preserve all. I will not allow us to fall. Let us get off this mountain."

Kealin led Ruak back down as the other two looked at one another.

"Talking like that, you should join our happy band of Scions," Ivasel said.

Upon reaching the lower level, Elaca ran up to them. "Quite a light show," she said.

"It has been quiet here?" asked Teusk.

"Nothing at all. And now with the rising sun, I feel we have less to worry about. So what of our friend here?"

At that moment, birds deep in the forest took to the air and spread out high in the skies in all directions. A large stone erupted from the ground in their near vicinity and reached higher than the nearest trees.

"The time has finally come," Ivasel said.

The ground trembled, and a large white burst of

lightning shot up into the sky and curved back toward the center of the forest and Fikmark itself.

"An archon must be nearby. If they are calling up the standing stones, the king must have had a change of heart," Teusk said.

He stood away from the others and lifted his staff in the air. A single yellow burst erupted up into the sky and then split into six different streaks.

"A standard alert signal between archons," Ruak said. "Normally to advise others of danger."

Kealin watched within the woods and saw the faint outline of a stag running through the woods. The sun was still coming up, but there was just enough light to see a robed figure riding atop the animal as it emerged from the woods.

Teusk lowered his staff and greeted the elf as she settled her stag mount and approached with haste.

"I saw the warning. Have you enemy nearby?" she asked.

"They were dealt with, but we had made the pilgrimage here to then find the standing stones of Fikmark awakened after our descent," Teusk said. "Has the good king decided to heed our advice?"

"There was a letter received in the twilight hours from Vueric. It was smeared in goblin blood, and the king begged for our aid. King Suvasel and King Rasune of Vumark have called for all forces to march for the city by the sea."

"It took the blood of the orc filth hoarders for my father to finally see the truth?" Ivasel asked.

"It seems he sees the truth, and we are acting with

haste. The vanguard forces have already departed. Once we have the perimeter stones alight, we will depart. If there is no enemy here, I must return to my work."

The elf went back to her stag and turned from them. "Take care on your path back, but do so with haste. We need any warriors we can. The rumors of the orcs are bringing about panic and zeal within the cities."

The archon spurred her stag, and it galloped back into the woods.

"It is finally time," Ivasel said. "My father prepares for the war we've been trying to convince him of. We must get there."

Kealin nodded to Ruak. "You can still go with me if you wish, but I must go to where I may learn of my sister. I'm too close to turn away now."

Ruak reached into his pocket and pulled out a parchment. He had a small amount of ink and a quill for making quick notes, and it would serve him well. Kealin watched as he drew a very simple map.

"To the north, not too far at all from this place. You wind a road that leads into the mountains. Take that and trust your senses to guide you."

Elaca looked to Kealin. "Good luck to you. Those are horrible directions."

"And once you know what you must," Ruak said, pushing the parchment to him, "we will need you south. The Black Star of Ur will not be an easy object to find, and large-scale war will make it even more difficult. It is the only way we can stop Vakron-Tur."

"And I need to kill him," Kealin said.

They embraced.

"Oh, and take this." Ruak gave him the small silver hammer he had used at Lake Traseen to call the water horses. "There is a river to the far south that leads directly to the sea and Vueric itself. From any connecting body of water, only think of what you wish to summon, and strike a stone within the depths. Though you can get fish for food or some other menial water creature, this will allow your friend Tulasiro to come with a certain haste. I will be sure to let the narwhal know that you will be calling for it. Do not forget of us, Kealin of Urlas."

Teusk bowed before him, and Ivasel gave him a half smile. Elaca was already ahead of them and beginning into a run. The others followed suit, and soon he was left below the mountain of the Moon Elves. As the sun rose, he looked to the north and to his map. He now felt strange. He cared for many more lives than he had since he had awoken on the beach following the events at Dimn's temple. Now he had more of whom to worry of.

10

CATACOMBS

Brethor and Jesia had been walking for more than a few hours down a bleak pathway lined with crumbling walls and forgotten passages. Though Brethor seemed like a small child in amazement at times, other moments, Jesia could see the anger in his eyes. She was angry, too, with her fellow Rusis, but Brethor sought blood, and it was painfully obvious that she may see a brother slay another brother.

"We are walking down a street," Brethor told her. "This is part of the old city. Covered in rock at some point, it was literally a city under a city."

"A good way to hide your knowledge."

Brethor stopped and let his torchlight up a collapsed entryway. There was a single sword and a broken shield with the remnants of bones.

"They didn't do it to hide knowledge; it was an attack. By Rusis, or something who worked liked them."

"Rusis?"

They began to walk again.

"The Rusis and the Dwemhar have very different ideas on magic, as you may know. The Rusis are about the outward show of power and control; the Dwemhar were powerful psychics and had technology above that of the rest of the world, but instead of what could have been a perfect alliance, our ancestors decided instead to fight. A pity that such strong races could not rally together."

They came to a sparse region with fewer buildings and a long open-air bridge that stretched over a chasm. They made their way single file across. Jesia looked down to see only a dark outline of a river that ran into more darkness to their left. To the right were massive stone walls. They reached the other side and found two different paths.

Brethor knelt down and looked at the dirt. "This way," he said, turning left.

"You mentioned a portal using magic?"

"Yes, well, the parchment I was reading said that in the final days of the city, their enemy had opened a pathway from their own city to this one. Well, orcs don't have cities, and the parchment was torn, but I saw the name Rinagres. That was the seat of power for all Rusis at one time. It would take a place of magic like that to activate this portal, that is, without blood stones. That is my worry. I do not know for sure, but the description of a bloodstone matches that of the Dwemhar stone that my brother delivered to Vakron-Tur and his mother. It is too much to risk, and now that I know they went here, it confirms my worries."

"But Rinagres was lost. The orcs would not have access like the Rusis. They also lack magic."

"We know too little to know for sure. The clan of Ur has access to many old magics, and I would not have us defending a city from the outside just to have it torn apart from the inside."

Brethor stopped and smelled the air. "Something is burning."

Jesia followed him as he began to run, and they went through several broken-down arches and began an upward climb through the ruins. There were strewn heads of fallen statues and sheer limestone and marble platforms that reached out over the dark abyss. Brethor kept up a steady pace until he came to a lone-standing pillar. Jesia stood behind him. She could see shadows and light from some type of fire just out of view.

Brethor passed her his sword and kept the one he had found on the remains that were well behind them now. She tucked the blade in her belt as he took a glance around the edge and then recoiled back. He looked down at her.

"There are five of the assassins, as well as Krea and Orolo."

"Do you have a plan?"

"I'm thinking of one."

There was a sudden hum in unison. Brethor and Jesia both peeked around the column to see that Orolo was leading some type of enchantment on a large stone circle that was partially lying on its side. His back was turned, and Krea was simply observing.

"Perhaps they do not have the red jewel you spoke of?"

But she soon learned her assumption was wrong. One of the assassins did have a stone, and at the height of pitch in their chant, the stone was tossed into the air. Krea brought her hands up and let an electrical charge strike the stone. The stone began to spin, and several surges of red bolts struck the stone circle.

"Well, here we go," Brethor said.

He stepped out from behind the rock, and Jesia quickly ran to his side.

"Orolo!"

His brother jerked to look at him. "I want to think you've come to join me, dear brother."

"Then you will be mistaken."

Krea put a hand toward them, and Jesia jumped forward, summoning a spinning shield of blue to block the electrical attack that contorted toward them.

"Krea, keep the charge toward the jewel," Orolo commanded. "The Rusis has been very helpful and made our lack of a good power source a small fact. This would have taken longer had she not agreed to help."

"Krea!" Jesia shouted.

She did not respond.

"Krea!"

"What, Jesia?"

"What are you doing? Why are you helping him?"

She raised her eyebrow in response. "We've been used by the cursed race of men for their own toying and manipulating and, on many occasions, pleasure. These men of Vueric are foolhardy to think they can help us, and you are a fool to help them. Men deserve what Orolo's master has planned."

"So the wizard is your master now, Brother?" Brethor asked.

The portal before Orolo began to glow a bright red.

"Brethor, I beg you to see reason. We have spent our lives searching out Dwemhar ruins, and now I have used this knowledge to begin a great campaign for Vakron-Tur! He will march his orcs into Vueric and—"

Jesia was done waiting for her once sister to do anything else, and she cared little for more senseless words. An explosion rocked the ground right next to the portal, throwing Orolo and Krea away from it.

Brethor ran into the black assassins and sliced into two before another two engaged him. The remaining fell, shivering in an icy blast of Rusis magic as Jesia froze him in place. Jesia squatted and looked for an opening in the two Brethor had engaged. As he parried a blade up, she sent another blast toward one of the assassins, landing a weak blast of lightning that threw him off balance. She then she felt a tinge to her right. Krea was up, and her hands glowed red. Jesia braced herself and summoned a ward of water just as a blast of fire struck the ground in front of her. The blast threw her away from Brethor, who had bested the last of the assassins with a slice to his neck, spilling blood into the gray dirt of the ruins.

Orolo began to run from Brethor as Krea turned her attention back to the portal. She had taken the Dwemhar stone. The portal was unsteady and wavering. Jesia ran forward to grab her, but with a blast of magic, she charged the stone gateway and jumped in. Jesia reached the edge and looked into the fading pool. She was gone.

Jesia looked up a climbing path as Orolo and Brethor went back and forth with their blades in a rough duel. Brethor swung his blade like he was a mad beast, with little to no form, and it seemed Orolo was besting him and luring him up the path.

Jesia ran to catch up, feeling her powers recharging. She didn't want to kill Orolo, but she also didn't know what he was trying to do. He betrayed them already, and it was only a guess of what might be worse to come.

BRETHOR TRUDGED UPWARD. His arm had been nicked by the keen blade his brother brandished. It was a Dwemhar blade as well. Sharp beyond that of a normal blade, it took very little pressure to break the skin. It was light too, lighter than the longsword he had used before. Orolo kicked a plume of dust toward him and then kicked him in his chest, throwing him to his back. He sat up to see his laughing brother turn into a large passageway. Jesia pulled him up.

"I will finish him. If he somehow kills me, you can have your turn. But I think we stopped him just in time."

They both ran into the passageway. The corridor was blackened and narrow near the end. Reaching the wall, they looked to their left and right, seeing their right was blocked by debris.

"This way," Brethor motioned, leading them to the left.

Entering a large room, it reminded him of the temple

back in the Mrin swamp with Kealin. There was a large area at the bottom of many stairs, but instead of an altar and a massive bat hiding high above, there were ten of the portals like before. Orolo stood with his sword stabbed into the ground before him.

"Welcome to the start of a grand invasion that will destroy the enemies of magic."

The portals were all spinning a deep red pool that sparked intermittently.

"Orolo, you cannot do this. This is madness. This is beyond any of your games or lies. Stop."

He began down the stairwell when Jesia noticed a hand reaching out of the portal. It was blackened and attached to a beast of a being.

Brethor stopped and shook his head. "Orolo."

Orolo smiled. "They follow my commands here. Just come with me. Speak with Vakron-Tur yourself. You will see that he is not the monster you think."

Brethor turned and began back up the steps.

Jesia lowered her hands and summoned a spell for an ice spike.

"Brethor!" Orolo shouted. "Do not make this mistake."

He turned and looked down to his brother. More of the creatures appeared. They were larger than the orcs before. Grayish-black skin and large eyes stared up at them, forming in ever-growing ranks behind Orolo. He knew he could not get to his brother.

"My only mistake was trusting Amhe enough to bring you here. You are a harbinger of doom and deserve every bit of magic my friend can give you."

He took one signaling glance at Jesia, and she threw her hands forward, sending a spike of frosting ice toward Orolo. He moved just enough for it to strike his arm, and fell to the ground.

"Go!" Brethor shouted.

Scratching and hissing with low-pitched growls echoed through the halls as they began a race back to the bridge way. Brethor knew this was the only place they could slow them down. Down the hills they had just fought their way up, they passed the original portal and to where the massive stone heads led down back into the darkness. Passing under the arches, Brethor turned to see the orcs were gaining on them, but they still had a lead for the moment.

Passing through the lower ruins, Jesia turned, casting bolts of lightning at the ruins to hopefully slow their pursuers. When at last at the bridge way, they ran across and turned back as the orcs began to come into view, closing in on the bridge.

Jesia cast a series of spells at the bridge. The ground smoked and small pieces fell off, but the stone was too strong. Brethor scanned the surroundings and noticed a large pillar. It was partially crumbled and leaning over a series of ropes that were nearing breaking.

The orcs were on the bridge, and with their cruel blades out, they swarmed, knocking one another off the edge but with numbers only growing as they approached. Jesia sent a series of blasts toward the bridge, knocking them back.

"I cannot keep this up," she said.

Brethor jumped on the edge of a pillar and worked

his way to the leaning pillar. After a few more jumps across narrow walkways and near collapsing rubble, he was within sword reach of the ropes. He cut them one after another as the pillar began to pop and crack, leaning toward the bridge.

Jesia was weakening. She had become more accustom to combat than she was before when she attacked the prison in Cyr, but her spells were much less potent at this point in the engagement. When at last a bolt became nothing more than an annoyance, the orcs charged her. She drew her sword to defend herself, parrying blades and slashing claws as she fell further back from the bridge. She knew little of sword play but it seemed enough for these creatures.

At last, a large quake trembled the ground, and the massive pillar and boulders from the cavern above fell into the bridge, plunging the orcs crossing it to their deaths. Brethor made quick time reaching Jesia, and they pushed back the orcs that were in utter shock at the sudden defeat of their fellow beasts. From the other side of the chasm, the orcs wailed in defeat but began firing arrows toward them.

"Let us get out of this forsaken place. We must advise the king of our failure."

11

THE LOOKING CLIFF

K ealin looked up at a bright sun. Though he could see his surroundings, it didn't help much with the rough map Ruak had given him. He followed a path out of the elven woodlands and now walked along a rocky road bordering a mountain range. The way was abandoned, and for many paces, he saw no other travelers. It was a hilly road that seemed to be more hill than straight road in many spots. He was climbing higher with everyone, and in so, could see more of the desolation of the northern woodlands that the elves had spoken of. It was a black wasteland devoid of trees, buildings, or any sign of any form of life. He had not seen a green plant since leaving the region just near Risdannia.

The air was hot coming off the road, and he took the time to find the source of water he could hear bubbling nearby. It was a mountain stream coming from a waterfall he could just make out beyond the jagged teeth of a cliff road.

He filled his water pouch and took a drink, looking up at the road. As he traced the path as far as he could, he spotted a face in the rocks.

Intrigued, he looked at his map and guessed he was somewhat still off from the place he was supposed to be, but remembered what the elf had told him. As simple as it sounded, he didn't really feel anything but he figured he was better off following a barely visible mountain road than continuing down one that was deserted. But he was still undecided.

It had been some time since he had really attempted to focus on his Dwemhar powers. He closed his eyes and took a deep breath. As his mind relaxed, he felt a sudden shudder against him. A flash of light forced him to open his eyes, and he stared toward the waterfall.

With very little debate, he climbed near the waterfall and pulled himself up on a ledge. Hidden behind the falls, was a very narrow path. He had only enough room for the tips of his feet and the edges of his fingertips, but it was a way to a more open path that cut into the rocks he spotted further up. Looking back, he noticed the emblems of stars cut into the rocks that he could not have seen had he not been standing where he was now.

He had found something, and now following a circular pathway cut into the rocks, he snaked up into the rocky reaches of the hidden road. The path was littered with large stones and broken rocks. The gravel filling in some places caused him to slip, and thorny bushes were not a welcoming feeling to someone making their way up. The path narrowed at some points to the degree he could barely find a foothold to keep moving. Whatever this was, he was continually going higher into the sky. Looking up, the clouds made it difficult to see how high he was actually going. But the path continued.

High enough that the river below was nothing more than a string to his point of view, he came to a large solid stone. He placed his hand on it, and a portion of the stone sunk away, forming an eye with a star surrounding it. The stone split down the center, and a passage into the mountain opened.

He stepped in and back in time, in some sense. If Brethor was here, he would have surely not been able to contain himself. This was what Amhe had told him about while smoking in Eh-Rin. It was a hidden Dwemhar structure covered in rock and completely inaccessible to anyone but those with Dwemhar blood. As the stone doors shut behind him, glowing stones lit a large room full of books and maps. A large crystal statue stood at the far side of the passage. It was the image of a man with a hovering light above his hand.

Kealin scanned the room, unsure of where he was. Going to a shelf, he removed a book to find he could not decipher a single word of the text. But he knew what it was.

Dwemhar writing. An entire room of knowledge.

This was a place forgotten in time. Kealin began to walk across the room, and with each step, lines of light appeared on the floor and passageways to the left and right opened up. To his right, there were many bladed weapons of varying length. Their hilts were silver, with emeralds and sapphires in the hilt. To the left, he could see staves with pearl heads. The structure had been untouched since these items were left. He wondered what else he would find in this vault of time.

As he stepped forward, the crystals of a strange device began to spin to life, and he could hear a slight humming sound. It was a cylindrical barred container, if he could describe it. He walked past it and noticed a line of armor against the back wall of the room. It was silver in color, with blue jewels on the shoulders. As he touched it, he felt a twinge in his finger, and his mind seemed to release a fogginess he didn't know was there. He placed his hand on it, and his body brimmed with energy. It was like when he wore the armor of Dimn, but purer and truer to him. He removed his hand and began to feel his normal self, but found it difficult to back away from it.

He looked back at the strange cylinder and noticed mechanical spinning wheels and a strange glowing aura around the device. He walked toward it, and a gate on the side of it opened. Looking up, he could see only darkness, but something pulled him to enter the strange device. He stepped in and noticed he seemed to be floating now. The gate shut, and a sound of sliding metal proceeded a rush of wind and darkness. His feet felt heavy, and he struggled to stand. He grasped the bars to either side and settled himself into a firm grip as flashes and snaps of light gave way to prolonged darkness and then light again. The device had stopped.

An icy wind blew upon him, and he looked out to mountains in the far distance. He was atop a snowy mountain and walking unsteadily from the strange transport that had brought him here. He looked around for why he was brought to this place.

Kealin made a circle and noticed ruins covered in snowfall. It was difficult to see the sky for the thick clouds swirling around him, but as he walked further across the summit, the ground began to tremble, and from the snow came a spinning blue crystal. He shielded his eyes as a bright flash enveloped him, and then felt weak. His eyes saw white for a moment, and then he looked upon the mountain itself, seeing his body on his knees. He floated above himself. His consciousness had left his body. He turned, looking over the mountains, drawn to the east and to a rocky region surrounded by trees. His spirit was floating by some magic of the summit of the mountain.

In a rush of wind, his consciousness flew across the lands, and he looked down at the mountain. His gaze pierced the rocks, and he saw many men and women being tortured by a dark shadow. Their screams of agony were horrendous to him. He then was sucked backward, seeing a large silver mass moving through the valleys. It felt cold to him, and he felt suddenly afraid. He looked around and felt drawn toward a glowing pink light. As he drew closer, he could feel the fires burning in mountains to the east. He looked down at the pink glow, and then at once he saw her. His eyes crossed to hers and she spoke.

"Kealin?"

"Alri!"

His heart thundered in his chest. He could see her as

clear as if she was standing in front of him. But she seemed to be floating and unaware of him.

"Alri! Where are you?"

Her eyes focused on him, and she smiled. The smile faded as she glanced around. "Kealin, no. Do not come . . . here . . ."

"What, why?"

He struggled to look around, but he could see nothing except his sister. He began to see what was glowing pink from before. He noticed she was surrounded by a large pink prism. She was in stasis, suspended over a rocky crevice.

"I can find you. I can find these mountains."

She closed her eyes. "For years I have angered them, ever since we were separated. They will awaken Ur. They will awaken the demon god. I am to do it. But not for Vakron-Tur."

"Who has you, Alri?"

"Beware the one who holds our brother. He is more important than we know. There is so much darkness. I cannot resist much longer. Kealin, the orc, Vakron-Tur, there is . . . you must know . . ."

His vision began to cloud and that of Alri began to fade.

"Alri!"

He could hear her voice, and using all of his energy, he pushed toward where he had seen her.

"Beware . . . kill them . . . the orc . . ."

There was more, but he could not hear it. He floated away from the mountains, taking notes that they were east of a great river. He glanced down the river and could see the Vindas Sea.

It was then, from that very direction, another form appeared. It appeared as a translucent man but seemed to not hold its form into the spirit realm as well as Kealin.

"You are far from those you call friends, Kealin Half-Elf of Urlas."

He knew that voice. He could never forget the sound of the one who laughed as his parents died. It was Vakron-Tur.

The wizard was in similar form as him. An image of consciousness, so he could do no harm to him. Kealin realized this as he tried to draw his blades but could not.

Vakron-Tur pointed at him. "You are Dwemhar and blessed with the higher magics lost to the world. I have studied many lifetimes to be able to ascend to this plane for just a moment. You indeed are a power to behold."

Kealin remained silent.

"The orcs will march, and I will destroy Vueric and all who stand against us, friend."

"I am not a friend of yours."

"Your brother thought that way too." He laughed. "I took a greater risk with him, but in time, his mask will be removed and he will see the truth. I protect him until then."

"You are evil and of the clan of Ur, the demon god and enemy of the world. You bring to life a vile enemy who took ground against our common ancestors. The orcs are an abomination to all."

Vakron-Tur floated next to him, and Kealin wished

more than ever that he could use his blades, but he could not.

"Our ancestors and kin are not my enemy. Man is our enemy. We must destroy them before they come against us. It is coming, a move against us of magic. From the east, I have foreseen a great sadness that will fall upon us all. I will protect us. I will offer alliances with those of the woodlands and anyone who will fight with us. I control the mindless orcs through the power of the Black Star of Ur. They are mine and do as I command. They will not be the scourge they were before."

"I will destroy you and free my brother. You have my sister. Her last words were to kill the orcs. I know she is your prisoner. You seek all of my blood."

"Were they the words she said? You seek your sister, but with every step you take, you are farther from her and cause more death to fall upon those you love. Perhaps you should listen to another for once. I offer you a place by my side, a chance to see the world as I do. I am not your enemy."

"You hold my brother, and I will come for him. I will kill you. By the gods of the North, you will fall."

Vakron-Tur closed his eyes. "I await you, Kealin. I know now that you are like the others. I must burn your world for you to understand. Do not worry. When I find your sister, I will kill those who hold her and offer her a place at my side. If she refuses, she will die. It is a simple life I live and offer others now. Come to me at Demonhead. Your friends, the Scions, know that name."

Kealin felt himself grow angry, and then suddenly,

he opened his eyes to snow, and blood dripping from his nose, staining the snow.

His heart was thudding in his chest, and he was sweating. He drew both of his blades and slammed them into the ground in front of him as he began to weep.

The many words of Vakron-Tur repeated in his mind, and he could not keep the image of his sister, captured and beaten to a person he did not understand, from filling his eyes with tears.

Beware . . . kill them . . . the orc . . .

Those were his sister's words. The last she had said before Vakron-Tur spoke to him. That was his enemy. He knew what he needed to do. His enemy sought to deceive him. He remembered from the teachings of his Blade Master to not fall for a feint, or a blade would pierce his own side. Now in life, he would not let his enemy deceive him. He would drive a blade through his neck.

Kealin took both of his swords and slid them back into their sheaths. He went back to the device and closed the door. It whirred to life again, and he descended back into darkness. He slowed his breathing, taking a deep breath in and a long one out. His heart slowed from the pounding drum in his chest to a soft beat as was normal. He reached the Dwemhar room and stepped out, turning to the armor on the wall. He took the armor and affixed it to himself. A large layered breastplate, shoulder guards, and leg and shin plates. He then walked down the hall to the right and took two separate blades. One was larger than the other, but both were longer than his

Urlas blades. He slung both scabbards on his back. As he began to walk toward the door, the room went dark.

He drew his newly acquired blades and then felt his hands weaken as a burning light appeared before him, wielding two blades in hand as he did.

His first thought was that of Vakron-Tur, but this figure was different.

"You look from the Ascendance Summit as us of old and wear our armor but do not embrace our ways."

"I came here by the will of Etha, Goddess of Elves, and for answers to my questions. I seek my sister."

The burning light spoke again. "You did not get the answers you expected."

Kealin did not know what to say or whom he was speaking to.

"In your heart and mind, you believe your path to be true, but you are cursed by darkness."

The figure reached out and touched his head, and he saw himself standing in a great river. A shroud of black to his left clashed with that of white to his right. High above, he saw the image of a skeletal form absorbing the souls of the black and white that fought.

"What is one more killer to the world but one who troubles the world more? What are truth and false testimony when none know what else is hidden? I wielded blades as you. I fought the Drear demons of the netherworld in the time before the foundations of any Dwemhar, elven, or dwarven hold. You must not go against those who fight now. You do nothing but bring death, for in your haste, you released the one long held.

Let another end this, for you will not be the one to succeed against evils."

"I must save my brother and sister. Who are you to tell me no?"

The light faded, and Kealin stared at what appeared an image of himself for a moment. The man was scarred, torn apart, with two broken blades in his hand.

"The elves called me Riakar, a story you were told as a child. The elf who fought against the demons of old. I tell you now that violence brings upon the world worse curses than you can imagine. I am an ascended Dwemhar, and I speak to you out of desperation. There is killing that is needed sometimes, but I have stepped into your realm to warn you to not follow the path of blood."

"Warn me?"

"You are the one the old gods spoke of, the one who would wake death and end the reign of the wretched Itsu. Before you, the gods could not be killed. Now they can, but there is a greater danger growing. Kealin, you were born of an elven father and a Dwemhar mother. You trained under a master swordsman but rebelled against his teachings for a hero you thought you knew. I was he, but I come to you against those who are ascended to tell you, Kealin, you must not go forward as you think. The world is changing, and in a way that none expected. Embrace the Dwemhar way. Use the powers of your mind to see beyond sword's reach."

"My brother—"

"Your brother is dead. He fell long before that mask, stabbed by the priest of the Itsu. You cannot save him no matter what you think you could do. Embrace the Dwemhar way. I broke my blades to understand this fact. Beware of what you do with blades alone, for they will forsake you in time."

"The Dwemhar were destroyed, Riakar. I had thought you more of a warrior than you are. You were once the destroyer of shadows that established the elven lands.

He turned away from Riakar, "I will do what I must to save my family. I will let no being of evil or supposed good, or god, or wizard named Vakron-Tur, turn me from this path. You waste yourself to remain in this realm to think I will listen to anything but my own understanding. I do not trust others. I will not abandon them to their deaths!"

The room went dark. Kealin dropped the tips of his swords with a clang to the ground. He looked around the room and shook his head before sheathing his swords again. As he approached the doors, a whisper crossed his ear, but he could not make it out. He paused for a moment and turned to look behind him. The room was darkening. As he exited, the lights within the structure darkened completely and the doors closed.

He put his hand against the door and looked up. He pondered the words of Riakar. The elf warrior he had heard stories of as a child had stood before him, warning of his very path. He took in another deep breath and felt his mind awakened like never before. He was focused and ready. Though he felt a worry in his mind, he knew he must not tarry. He would go south to the river and then west to deal with the one who held his brother.

His journey back down to the road was one in a deeper meditation than he expected. Though he wasn't sure if it was the armor and its effect on his psyche or something else, he found his mind bouncing between everything he had seen and heard. He remembered Etha even saying that the gods were blind to what was transpiring. He could only do what he in his own heart felt was right. After traversing back down to the road, he began walking south. He had quickness to his pace, and one that at first, he didn't hear the faint voice calling toward him.

He turned to look down into a small gorge and noticed a figure sitting on a rock. He at first thought to ignore him, but considering how desolate this road had been before and the fact that the figure was literally just sitting there alone, he turned and began down into the gorge.

As he approached the figure, he noticed the man was actually a dwarf but one that oddly carried no weapon. The dwarf had his eyes closed and had a sack with many odd trinkets and vials on it. His beard seemed to flow with the gust of the wind that blew over the rocks.

"I had wondered if they heard me," the dwarf said.

"Who did you hope to hear you? You are alone as best I can see. Why are you here?"

"I prayed to the gods they would help me, and then I saw you. Come, you must be wondering why you are here."

The dwarf jumped to his feet and threw his bag over his shoulder. As the dwarf began further into the gorge,

Kealin turned back toward the direction he was originally walking.

"Come now, dear elf. I need your protection and you need guidance."

Kealin turned and, against his better judgment, jogged to where the dwarf now stood staring into a dark cave. The dwarf had piqued his curiosity.

"Guidance? You do not even know me. And Protection? From what?"

The dwarf threw some dust from his bag onto a stick, and flames burst to life. He began into the cave.

"Everything, dear elf."

The sun was just beginning to set as Kealin followed this abruptly appearing stranger. He descended into darkness.

GATHERING

Since Brethor and Jesia emerged from the depths of the underground ruins, the city was even busier than before. The presence of orcs underneath their very streets was a danger unlike any other, although the fact of it was kept to only the highest of the city watch. The Knights Guard worked to reinforce the walls, and up and down the stretches of outer curtain, spear and arrow caches were replenished. Further out, the lighthouse fort was busy increasing its own defenses. A shipment of dwarf dust had arrived from the northern cities, and Lord Meask oversaw the disbursement to Vaden and the Rangers. The cart was overloaded with many stone jars tightly sealed and surrounded by hay.

"Keep torches far from it. Even though they must be open to the flame to ignite and it would take dragon fire to set it off from within the jars, we do not need any more mishaps," Meask said.

"Ha, I think that was one of those legion lads,

anyway. I will line the outer pike line with the stuff. Trees are getting harder to come by, and keeping the palisade walls up is done almost completely by mud and rock now, which is not the best," Vaden said. "I think the orcs are figuring out another way across the river. At nightfall last night, the woods still stood as always. After the many raids on our outer lines and the tragedies of your brothers and the queen, the forest was bare."

Meask shook his head. "They are preparing. It is why I had wished to receive this dust sooner. Do what we can and do not forget the bridge. I'm counting on the Rangers if the lighthouse falls. You must hold the bridge or assure it can't be used by the enemy."

The Ranger's wife approached. "We will hold the lighthouse. We expect the Knights Guard to hold the plains before the walls. We don't want to be trapped."

"My lady Orta, the Knights Guard will hold the roadway. You have my word."

She slapped his shoulder. "You may be a lord, but I am not a lady. Just ask this one," she joked, smacking her husband now too. "Your highborn ladies can sit on their hands. Us lowborn at least know how to use them."

"That they do," Vaden confirmed.

They all laughed, and Meask turned to Brethor as the Rangers departed.

"Most Rangers used to be deemed criminals by some lords. The men and women of the River Rangers now hold our outer line and have for some time."

"Isn't it amazing what a common enemy will do to those of questionable allegiance?"

"A common enemy who is becoming more common."

He looked toward the sunset. "At nightfall, I expect the orcs will assault us again. It will be another night of fighting, and perhaps more so than we know."

"Did you take some of the dwarf dust to the entrance to the old city ruins?"

"The king will not allow it. He is concerned of detonating an explosive under the city, and I can't blame him, but I'd rather lose part of the city than the whole. It is his order, though. They constructed a defensive line that they are confident will hold. At this time and to my knowledge, no orcs have been spotted, and the ravine that you two destroyed has remained that way."

Meask led him to one of the large towers lining the wall. A lone guard standing beside a large brown door bowed as they approached before knocking three times. The door opened.

"One of our city watch headquarters. I see you lack decent armor."

"I've never been too fond of it, actually."

"Well, at least get yourself some chain mail and neck guard. The orcs love to slash for our heads. You'll be happy to have it when one of their blades cracks swinging against it."

The rows of armor were not the least bit shiny or clean. Blood and tissue even dripped from some, and the men seated around the tables were worn and tired.

"How holds these men, Watch Commander?"

A burly man seated on a back wall spat into his plate as he smoked a large cigar. "By the skin of orc filth, they are tired, but we are ready for the fall of night."

There was an exorbitant cheer, but Brethor could tell they were all weary.

"Is it true the queen and your brothers have fallen?" one of the men asked.

Lord Meask put his hands on his hips. "Such rumors are true. The queen was struck down, followed by my brother Ridau, who was injured. On the eastern woods, my other brother Kiras fell as well, and his body was not recovered. It is a dark time for us all."

"Do we have any more men coming?" another asked.

"Men from the south of Eh-Rin sail and march for our shores. I cannot say of much more, but know that envoys have been sent to the elves."

"The elves retreated!"

"Nevertheless, we call to all of our friends, for if they are against the orcs, we must consider them no matter our pasts."

The lord shook a few hands and then looked down at Brethor's sword. "That's a relic, no doubt."

"A Dwemhar blade. I found it beneath the city."

"When I was a boy, I played on the door. Damn thing is huge. I even climbed to the top once. But of course I couldn't get in. I always wondered what was inside."

Meask helped him latch up his armor and tighten it as needed.

After shaking hands with a few of the men as he wished them good fortune, he led them back out to the city streets. The people were busy moving into the inner parts of the city. Additional palisades were constructed from what wood could be salvaged, and a second line of defense was hastily created within the city center itself.

"Some of our people will flee north, but many do not wish to leave the city itself. If the lines of defense fall, they will die here."

Brethor had nothing to say to the lord's words as they walked between buildings, reaching the main road again. Brethor noticed a man running toward them.

"Lord Meask." It was a member of the city watch. "The legatus of the legions seeks your audience. Riders from the East arrived moments ago bringing news."

"Riders from the East? We have no allies there. Come with me, Brethor. This should be interesting."

JESIA SAT NEXT TO MUERA, who had been sleeping for some time. The healers had done quick work to suture her cuts, and now, after a small sprinkle of Fae dust, Jesia was told she should be fine in some time. The lord Ridau had fared much worse and suffered from broken ribs and bleeding within his abdomen. He was still sweating and took the majority of the healers' time. Jesia was fortunate her friend was well, but the look of heartbrokenness of the king standing alone with only his servants next to him was saddening to her.

Though she had remained with her friend, she had slept for some time. When she fell asleep, the king stood nearby. When she awoke, he hadn't moved. As Muera slept, she stood and went to the king. He looked up solemnly at her, but she didn't speak.

"I had always wished for a daughter, you know. This

one was my youngest, and I love my boys, but a girl is something I never had."

"Some might say girls are more trouble. I attended a girl for a time when I was younger. My master spent many nights away, and when she was three, she was the most rambunctious little one you might ever see. The boy of the house was calmer by her standard."

"They were lucky to have you with them."

"Perhaps, but I was sold from that family to the gladiator master in Cyr. My life took many turns during that time."

King Firda put his hand on her shoulder. "But now you are here. I wish you could've seen this city only a year ago. My people were much happier, our roads cleaner. The very air smelled of sea salt and fresh jasmine in the morning. Now we see this." He made a gesture toward his son. "So much war is in this world now."

A bell rang in the distance, and a man came holding golden armor.

"I told my son no," the king said.

"Lord Meask said you would say that. I am instructed to ignore it by royal decree."

"But I make royal decree."

The man stopped, holding the armor just near King Firda and not too sure what to do.

The king sighed. "Very well, let's get it on. It seems after the attacks, Lord Meask wants even those in the palace wearing some form of armor. Jesia, since you are here and are not quite as useless as some of the ladies of the court, I think I have something you might use with your, um, spells."

The servant continued to help the king affix his armor, and another man girded a sword to his waist. The king uncomfortably shrugged and looked toward his son before motioning for Jesia to follow him.

He walked out of the healing rooms and back into the main throne room. There was a single door behind the throne that he opened and held for her. A stairwell snaked upward, and she followed it up. A torch every few steps gave a little light until they came to a room with glowing bottles on the wall. King Firda took a torch and walked around the somewhat small room, lighting torches. There was a single window that looked out over the city. She noticed that darkness was almost upon them.

"This was the quarters of our court wizard many years ago. She died without any to replace her, but I think you are about the same size she was." He handed her a dark blue hooded robe. "It is said that this increased her magic and made it easier for her to cast. It also has added armor from dragonshark skin built into the shoulders and for your chest and stomach."

"Dragonshark?"

"A carnivorous beast many feel was only legend. But it was indeed real. It once guarded the waters and was a sacred animal to my house. They have not been seen in some time, and armor from them is considered to be almost as rare as a Rusis, so it is fitting for you to have it."

He glanced around the room. "There are other items

here. Potions, books, whatever you find is yours. Darkness is falling, and this night feels darker than most."

As the king departed, she looked out the window. It was quickly becoming very dark, and no moon was on the rise. She slid her head and arms into the robe. It was indeed enchanted and fit almost perfectly. She felt her magic surging through her body. With every breath she took, her fingers tingled, and she could feel the flow of the robe around her body.

There were many potions on the shelves surrounding the room. She knew little of potion making or alchemy in general, but she took what she saw. She knew enough only that the black ones in tiny vials were actually poison. She didn't see a need for those. In the waistband of her armor, there were tiny loops for the bottles. She wondered of the prior owner of her garments but knew there was little time to think much of the dead. Seeing very little else of use to her, she headed back toward Muera. She hoped her friend would awaken soon.

BRETHOR AND MEASK had made it to one of the watch tents near the eastern woods. Eastwatch, or so it had been come to be called by the men, was the other defense line watching the roads that led from the far eastern lands. The camp itself was much less guarded than the lighthouse, but all travelers coming from this direction were stopped and questioned. Aside from a large wooden wall and a gateway on the eastern edge of the woods, a large hilltop provided a good lookout, and the many tents of Rangers and sell-swords led back toward Vueric itself, but was largely undefended, save simple wooden pike lines.

Meask walked into the tent where the man from the East sat with a cup of wine.

As Brethor followed, he nearly ran into the back of Meask, who had stopped just after walking into the tent.

"Who allowed this man to remain in the tent?"

Brethor noticed the man he was speaking of. The man wore white robes and was quite old.

"He is an old man," one of the Knights Guard said. "He was tired from his journey and requested a drink."

"We do not share wine with his kind."

Meask slapped the cup from his hand. "Did your people not clearly understand that House Firda wants nothing to do with the Grand Protectorate?"

The man reached down and picked up the cup. "The tenth legion did, and clearly we question when one of our legatus goes missing. Your army was not available to assist Legatus Iruis?"

The legatus walked into the room.

"Did you send for this man?" Meask asked him.

"I did not, my lord. I have professed my loyalty to your house and saw my legion as deserters."

"Your legion was not permitted into the city. Forced to camp along the river, they were attacked nightly until finally, they broke camp," the old man said. "I would leave, too, if treated as such!"

Meask poured himself wine and offered a glass to Brethor, which he took. "My entire land is attacked nightly. Your men were camped between our outer defenses and the wall of the city. Hardly a horrible place to be. I cannot contain a legion of men inside the city walls. Would you have me place them in the beds of my people?"

"A better fate, I'd say. From your words and able bodies, then I know something of your numbers available to defend. And you speak of your land. Does that mean you are king and the late King Firda has fallen?"

"It is my land because it is my family's. The king is alive and well and cares little to speak to the Grand Protectorate."

The man in robes gave a smug smile. "I have not come to speak but to tell. The Grand Protectorate knows of the vile orcs. Though we are not allies, we are sending ten legions to support the eradication of this enemy."

"I will not allow ten legions to march into this valley! What you mention is an act of war on our lordship."

The man laughed. "You have an act of war every night from your enemy, and every night they encroach on your land. The Grand Protectorate has arms, fighting men, and weapons to aid you. Perhaps we can work out a tribute that you can pay, and you can retain your lordship. It is an offer not likely offered by the elves. Am I correct?"

"Our alliances are our own," Meask stated. "Keep your men. If we fall, you will need them to guard your own holdings. The city of Vueric does not need or want help from your empire. You speak words of alliance and what would be camaraderie, but I know not of a single house of men that has remained once your people became involved."

"Then perhaps you should take heed to your own words, Lord Meask. The Grand Protectorate did not keep control of so many by backing down. The men march and are commanded by our most skilled general legatus. When the orcs swarm your city, you will wish you had his merciful hand to aid you." The old man stood. "Legatus Iruis, I expect you will return to the East with me. No sense in you dying here."

Iruis threw his blade at the man's feet. "My allegiance is with these people. I have lost many defending this ground, and it would be a disrespect to abandon their memory. In time, I feel the men here will open up to the Protectorate, but I care little of that at the moment."

Meask glared at him, and Brethor couldn't decide if the lord respected or was more annoyed by the legatus.

"So be it, Legatus."

The man, who had still not introduced himself, pushed aside the Ranger standing near him and began to walk out.

"Old man," Meask said. "I know your kind is not much for regal respect, but which name should I give to the king to advise him of your presence here?"

"I have no name of importance to you. My kind watches over all men, and it is clear you are more concerned of House Firda. You are not privy to my name."

The man walked outside, and Brethor and Meask followed. As Brethor looked out of the tent, the man was already on a horse, and with an accompaniment of legionnaires, they rode away. A Ranger drew his bow and looked to Meask.

"No, let them go. If they have ten legions anywhere close, I would not want a war with them."

Iruis stood next to them now. "Ten legions is close to fifty thousand men and supporting auxiliaries. A welcome ally, but I understand the threat to your king."

Meask turned to Iruis. "I respect that you stand with my men here, but you know your masters may treat you as a traitor?"

"They already see it that way. I lost my legion and stand with someone that resists them. My legion were cowards, obedient as dogs but to the wrong master. I care little of their thoughts of me. I pledge allegiance to House Firda, as do my remaining men."

He knelt before the lord.

Meask placed his hand on his shoulder. "And I accept it. I will send word for you to have access to the city as you need. You and your men."

"Thank you, but for now, I will depart for the lighthouse fortress, not the city. We have found ourselves in good company there."

The legatus mounted a horse and left the camp in quick order.

"We will return to the city for now," Meask said. "My father will find the news of the Grand Protectorate interesting, and I wish to check on my brother."

"I am curious of the Rusis, too," Brethor said.

"If only we could get the allies we wished for and could convince the Grand Protectorate to leave us alone," Meask commented. "We sent envoys to the Gray

Scourge, dragon-riding sell-swords of the South. We got no response from them. I guess orcs aren't something they wish to deal with."

"I didn't think the quarry mattered to sell-swords, only price."

"Perhaps."

As they began to mount nearby horses to quicken their pace back to the city, the darkened sky was split by lightning. The fields before the camp swayed with a gust of wind coming from the southern mountains. The earth quaked, and a fog ran over the river, shrouding it.

"Rangers! To the palisades!"

The camp churned with activity, and Meask drew his blade, leaving his mount.

"Perhaps we will wait," he said.

Brethor drew his blade as well, not sure if it would be orcs or assassins who attacked them. From their position on an elevated hill, they looked down to the ramparts and wooden gateway.

The ground not too far out from them rippled with movement. The smashed grasslands gave little cover to hundreds of hunched orcs just in sight of the Rangers. A flurry of arrows flew into the darkness, and snarling and yelps of pain followed.

Another stout command followed. "Release!"

From an area behind the walls to their right, catapults flung stones over them and into the swarming line.

A beast of a sort roared in the darkness. Only its outline was visible, but it was charging the gate. The ground trembled and shook, and Meask sheathed his sword. A spear lay against a weapon rack nearby. As

Brethor watched the shadowy form grow larger, the lord grasped the spear and pulled a shield from one of his men. The shield itself was large, with the sigil of his house upon it.

"Go, send word to the city watch to prepare for an attack."

The man scampered to run away as he headed to deliver the message.

The Rangers released several flaming arrows into the mounted beast that approached. Its tusked face became evident as the massive bull-like creature smashed into the gate, breaking partially through on the first strike.

One ram.

Two rams.

Three rams.

The gate began to falter. A barrage of spears flew over the ramparts, and Rangers fell at every turn. With a final smash, the gateway broke and fell. A Ranger jumped onto the beast from above but was thrown into a tree, turning the ground into a bloody mess. Meask moved forward with his shield and spear as the creature roared and was spurred into a run. He knelt down with his spear, aiming for the vitals of the creature. The impact of the creature upon the lord was violent and threw him backward, splintering the spear, but the creature tumbled, overthrowing the orc rider atop it.

Brethor ran forward, driving his Dwemhar blade into the creature, pinning it to the ground. When he looked up, Meask was already up, and with a thrust of his sword, he killed the creature.

"Forward! Hold our line!" rang out over the sounds of battle.

The rest of the camp was moving to the breaking walls swarming with orcs. These were much larger than the orcs at the lighthouse, and wore quite a bit more armor. Though it was not of the best quality, it deflected random arrows and poorly swung blades. As a group of swordsmen slammed into the opening of the gateway, more Rangers formed on the hilltop, sending a rain of arrows over the wall. The catapults fired, and the men stabbed and slashed as orcs' shields battered the ones of men.

A flaming arrow shot up near the lighthouse, and a thundering sound followed.

Meask pushed himself from the battle line and ran up the hill. Brethor followed and looked over toward the wall. Large fires erupted across the fields, lighting the darkness, revealing the ground covered in orcs. From the sea, it seemed the Eh-Rin ship had moved closer to Vueric and was firing into the orcs on the shore. With a loud horn call, the defenders on the city walls released their own volleys.

"They attack us on all fronts," said Brethor.

"This is more than the nights before. They've never hit us this hard before."

The palisades began to shift, the wooden timbers splitting and the wall leaning toward the camp. Orcs clamored over the top, stabbing and biting the Rangers atop it. Men fled the battle line, and it became difficult to see any defenders in the mass of orcs.

"Eastwatch has fallen, send word! Eastwatch has fallen!" a man shouted out.

"Eastwatch holds as long as I live," Meask shouted.

Brethor picked up a shield and stood with Meask in front of the Rangers atop the hill. The orcs pushed up the green grasses, slipping and falling over one another as a constant plinking of arrows slapped into their faces and bodies. The edge of the camp going back toward the city was overwhelmed. Orcs climbed the hill. Where the catapults were on the other side of the camp, a man lit pitch on fire, sacrificing himself and burning the orcs surrounding him.

Lightning flashed again, and it seemed the many orcs cowered for a moment as another blast of white shook the sky.

The orcs were nearly upon the last defenders of Eastwatch when the trees rustled with a barrage of silver spears that came arching from behind them and falling with deadly accuracy into the orcs. Brethor turned to see elves at full sprint emerging from the trees and charging down into the orcs. Another white blast followed, and an arc of energy shot into the sky, lighting up the fields and stunning the orcs. Stag riders emerged from the lower woods, charging into the orc line and enveloping them. The orcs that could see stretching from the river turned from the approaching stags and fled as elven archons cast flames along a line in the field, forming an abrasive barrier to the attackers. The orcs at Eastwatch retreated, and another elven battle line ran for the southern wall of the city. The orcs there were already retreating.

A host of elves approached Meask from the woods. One was taller than the rest and had a long silver spear.

Meask knelt as the man approached.

"Lord Meask, it does seem you are in need of allies. The elves of Vumark come to your aid as the acting vanguard force. King Suvasel and I bring our armies to disperse these aggressors. Though early, I think I came exactly when needed."

"King Rasune." Meask smiled. "Your aid saved us this night."

A loud horn sounded from the fields, and the elven forces halted, forming a line within the fields. The orcs continued to flee, and over the clamor, shouts of victory roared from the city walls and the lighthouse.

"The orcs retreat! The orcs retreat!" men said.

"Orcs?" Rasune asked. "What orcs? These are goblins."

"These are not orcs?" Brethor asked.

"Of course not. They swarm like ants to a carcass. They overwhelm with numbers and hop about, slashing wildly. Orcs have at least some fighting form. They are more than a rabid mob."

"It seems our classification was wrong," Meask said.

"They are not the Drear Orcs we fear, but troubling in their own regard. If these are alive, so will be the ones we seek. Goblins are the slaves of orcs. They are fodder in battle. They will attack again. Vakron-Tur has been hitting your defenses to test them. He found a weakness here and will return. But we are ready for them."

· · ·

MEN WENT ABOUT, looking for injured, as archons worked to heal those directly before them. The elven vanguard forces went through the field, killing stragglers and patrolling the river.

Meask walked with King Rasune through his forward camp just within the trees north of Eastwatch.

"The Fikmarkian forces will be here by dawn. They, and the rest of my forces, augment the defenders of the valley by approximately six thousand swords. The wars against the demon men have had many casualties."

"We thank you for your support but fear we have been so concentrated on defending that we have little knowledge of how to stop them."

"The Orc Star," he said, taking a drink. "It is how Vakron-Tur controls them and bends their will to his. I believe he has it at least. It hasn't been revealed. We may still have time. Before the construction of Vueric, there was a tower in the mountains above this valley, a place the demon god, Ur, called Demonhead. It is there we will find him."

"The southern mountains are not approachable. A legion of Grand Protectorate men assaulted that position, chasing the witch woman, and very few of them returned."

"Well, that is your first folly, trusting those wretched excuses of life consumers with anything beyond betrayal. At least your father has resisted their aid and assistance. We must keep true to the old vows. The elves have worked with House Firda for many years. Though, with so many enemies, it has been difficult to protect the woods as we used to."

He turned to Brethor. "I do not know you."

"Brethor Srvivnann of Elinathrond."

The elf king gave a peculiar look to him that even Meask noticed. "Far from your home. What brings you here?"

"At the moment, a desire to help this lord and his people. I have an affinity for Dwemhar cultural items."

"An odd fact to be plainly stated among the common company."

An elf brought a parchment to the king. He read it to himself and then stood.

"Very well, inform your father that we will hold this ground and send scouts in the southern mountains. At dawn, we will augment all positions with the remaining elven forces and then make a push south. Your people will not spend another morning waking to the sound of goblin voices or orc clamor at their doorsteps, and their wretched bodies will never foul our woods."

As Meask and Brethor exited the tent and returned to Eastwatch, Dala and many warriors of Eh-Rin arrived at the hilltop.

"I bring men to add to the guard. I received word that the land army of Eh-Rin is marching north along the coast. We soon will have all we need to defend your grand city."

"Thank you, Admiral Dala," Meask said. "Speak with the remaining Rangers and determine where your men can best assist." He looked to Brethor. "Now, back to check on my brother and the Rusis, before any other attacks come this night."

. . .

JOURNEYING WITH HASTE, Brethor and Meask had made it to the front gates of Vueric when a messenger from the lighthouse bound for the king caught the lord's eye. He motioned for the man to come to him and read the parchment. He looked to Brethor in slight confusion.

"The Drean, they too send ships. They expect to be here tomorrow near high noon. We just received a message from Cyr advising us of their approach."

A passing young Eh-Rin warrior overheard the conversation. "The Drean are not friends. We must not trust them."

Brethor went to speak but then noticed a single blue flame growing atop the southern mountains. It was near one of the peaks of a three-pronged summit.

Meask had not taken notice. "Well, lad, against our enemy, we will accept whatever friends we can, within reason. Their alliance is unexpected but the Drean have never had bad blood with the houses of men."

"With respect, Lord," the soldier replied, "we of Eh-Rin cannot trust them. I must warn those of my people. You should be wary of those who would profit from your destruction."

The soldier departed, and Meask saw that Brethor was watching something else.

Brethor noticed fogs rolling off the mountains. The dark night made it difficult, but the brightening blue fire cast light onto the fields. The elves along the river began to form up. From the mountains, goblins began to descend and swarm the riverbanks. A glowing light of a green color appeared in the mountains, and in a whirl-wind of black ash, it rose up and then sat down on the closest edge of the bridge to the lighthouse. A man appeared, holding a staff, but did not move.

Those at the lighthouse took notice, and at least three Rangers seemed to take aim. The figure pointed the staff toward them, and the area they were standing was torn apart by a gust of wind and the sounds of snapping logs.

"That must be him," Meask said in a hushed voice. He turned to a nearby man of the city watch. "Deliver my words to the king. I go to speak with our enemy."

13

DARK TRUTH

Kealin followed the dwarf with a careful watch through the strange cave. The rocks in many areas glowed a soft red, and while some areas had clear-cut walkways, others had small pools and slippery slopes. The journey into the caves was a silent one, and the dwarf had only stopped once before they came to an old wooden walkway that he would've missed had the dwarf not stopped.

"Now we cross here, and then to a door we will go!"

The sudden exuberance of the dwarf, whom he had not even gotten a name from, further perplexed him.

The walkway went over a deep ravine, but at the far end looking to his right, he could see some type of light.

"Dwarf, what is your name?"

"Well, dwarf is a good one, but Wualu will work too."

"A strange name for a dwarf."

Wualu turned to him. "And just how many fine dwarves do you know?"

"No fine ones or even amicable ones. Just dead ones. Though I did find one I did like, he is dead now too."

The dwarf gulped and began walking again.

"And how many legionnaires do you know? Good friends of yours?"

"I know of one, a legatus, but I really don't have an opinion of the man. I've killed many of their kind too."

Wualu made it to a door and opened it just enough to peer in before slowly opening it fully. He tiptoed out and looked around. Kealin kept his hand on his blades and followed, finding a pile of dead dwarves just on the other side. Wualu shut the door, and the wall looked as if no door at all existed. They had been traveling through a secret passage and now stood in a massive corridor that led further down into the mountain.

"Well, I hope you do not wish me dead, not just yet, at least. Plenty of killing done already, and I don't care to fight."

"A dwarf who doesn't fight? A strange thing."

"And why is it strange?"

"I've never met one who didn't have an axe tucked away somewhere just waiting to split open the head of someone."

"Dwarves have many professions. Some fight, some mine, others, well, we are different."

They began to walk, and Kealin followed just behind Wualu. Aside from dead dwarves, there were many fallen legionnaires lining the hallway. Sprung traps in the ceiling filled with rotting corpses created a stench in the confined passage that stirred even Kealin's stomach. The dwarf broke into a short verse.

"Oh, what putrid hall
where dead man waller in their fall!"

"Are you a poet?" Kealin asked.

"Ha! Enough for the mead halls, maybe. And no, wrong."

As they walked onto level ground, the side of the passage opened up to that of a massive ravine and the night sky in the distance. A waterfall fell through towering ruins into a deep pool that was out of sight and far below them. Some large torches still burned but were reduced to embers. Whitish stone that made up the structures he could see had been partially blackened by fires. There was no one else here.

"Lucky so far, no legionnaires. Before, there had been plenty of them. They came really quickly. They wanted to talk, and we did not. You do not tell them no. They make you think you can, and then . . . well, the rest is written on the walls."

As he said that, they passed the body of an armored dwarf with a spear pinning his bloodied form to the rock.

"Many good dwarves died. Good children too."

"So you're saying the Grand Protectorate did all of this?"

"They did. They and their dragons. But dragons cannot fight in our inner halls, but their legions can."

They continued walking and came to a large sealed door. There was a keyhole to one side where Wualu placed a silver key and turned a half rotation before walking to a pillar to the left of the door. He pushed in a block, and a crystal appeared in the door. He placed one hand on the crystal, and with the other, he finished opening the lock.

"Good that this door stands, a good sign. Even with a key, you must have dwarf blood running through your veins to open it. Very good the door is still shut. There may be hope still. Tell me of the orcs I hear the animals speak of."

He pushed the door open leaving it that way.

"Do you wish me to close it?"

"It does not matter. Come and tell me of the orcs."

Kealin went ahead and shut it. Getting followed by the enemy was not his idea of wise.

As they walked toward a distant door flanked by torches and a large brazier above it, he looked around at many odd alchemical devices and crafted potions.

"The orcs return to the mountains south of Vueric. An elf wizard and follower of the god Ur used Dwemhar blood to resurrect the orc armies sealed away by the elves."

"Ha! By the elves, go ahead, tell me more."

"You act like I'm supposed to know something, yet won't tell me what you know?"

"You, dear elf, did not ask, and you assume you know what is true based off someone you have just met? I know you are not from these regions. You do not act it nor look it. Now, go on, please. Tell me of the destruction of the orcs."

"They were bested by the elves, Dwemhar, and Rusis warriors, or some combination of those, anyway. They were sealed in the mountains to never awake."

"Well, the last part is true. Sure, there was a lot of

fighting, but it was dwarven ingenuity that defeated the masses! Our god Throka and the god of war, Kel, played a large part in the downfall of the orcs."

They came to another door that was simpler than ones before it. He opened it, revealing a large circular room. Kealin noticed that part of the room was lit by torches, but on the far right, it was darkened and many torches were out. As Wualu walked in, he slowed his pace and then ran toward the center of the room. He dropped to the ground at a pedestal.

He slammed his fist into the ground over and over and let out a sorrowful scream.

"What is it?" Kealin asked. He looked around at the room, trying to discern what could've been here to cause such an emotional outburst in the dwarf, but could see no sign of the cause.

"The book, it had the rites, the spells, the formulas. How did they get in here?"

He looked over to the darkened walls and leaned forward, further squinting. Scurrying over to the blackened wall, he paused for a moment and then slipped into a small opening. Kealin knelt down to look in and pulled away some of the loose rocks. He could barely fit and squirmed just to force himself in. Upon reaching the other side, he found Wualu lying on the body of a dwarf next to a long line of slain dwarves. This one seemed different, though. This one had gold bracelets and seemed to be less brutish than the other ones. It was a female. She seemed to be missing one of her hands, but the dwarf didn't seem to notice that.

Wualu sobbed and then looked to the other dwarves.

They were chained together, and each had slashes to their necks.

"They enslaved my brothers. They required my family to force open this way. These walls? See how jagged they are? They forced my family to mine this passage so their filthy hands could take what they came for! And now, and now . . . my wife joins the dead. Have you ever lost one you loved? Do you know what these wars that so many of you charge into cause? Death.

"They are all dead. This city was once a jewel. Michranok on the Lake. It was a center of knowledge. A place of relative peace. The bastards came in here with a ruse of friendship. They sought the true bane of the orcs, and they have the book. The sacred text that none save the grand alchemist should hold. It was the dwarves who defeated the orcs, but not with axe blade and sword, but the sciences of earth and flower and spirit. It was a dark spell, but it worked. It sapped them of life. Sure, the war helped kill many of them, but it was our actions here and the knowledge kept here that secured the end of that war. Now men have it. The bastards have it. We must all fear the Grand Protectorate."

Wualu paused and now noticed the severed hand. This meant something to him, it seemed to Kealin. Wualu stood up, looked around, and then went back to the crawlspace. Kealin worked to follow him, taking a last glance at the slain dwarves before climbing back through. As he entered the room with the pedestal, he followed the glimpse he managed to get of Wualu as he hurried to another door. They went down a snaking long hallway lit by glowing stones until he came to a bridge, which was right above the river itself. There was another door, one like before with a crystal. This was a lone tower away from the rest of the city. He glanced down to see the severed hand from Wualu's wife dropped onto the ground before the door. Entering the room, he found the dwarf on his knees, staring upward at empty shelves.

"They took them all. All of the mixtures and of the dangerous secrets of our research here. I had brought you to protect me from them, but it seems it doesn't matter. You worry of the orcs, and I tell you they are foul creatures and deserve death, but I cannot tell you what this means. You cannot trust them. You cannot trust any but your own. There is a war coming, and suffering and no matter of bloodshed will stop it. I tell you, warrior elf, they are true evil. Not the evil you face that is black and darkened and of the dead brought back by Dwemhar blood, but the evil that smiles as they drive a blade in your back. They destroy you from within."

The dwarf paused and seemed to fumble something in his hand. Kealin could not see what it was, but as he stepped forward, the dwarf rose his hand and was holding a glowing stone.

"Have you guessed it, elf? Have you guessed who I am?"

Kealin thought, trying to find the right description or words that could make sense of the past few moments. "A studier of sciences of the earth? The Grand Alchemist?"

He had heard Wualu say it before. Given his knowledge of the place and the details, it made sense to him.

The dwarf laughed again. "Ha, I am the bane of us

all. That is all I am. I may had been what you said once, but that was only until I let a greater evil take what I was so foolish to create. But nothing else matters now. Do you know the way out, dear elf?"

"I know the way. We can get out the way we came easily enough."

The dwarf lifted his hand. In his grasp was a glowing stone that was growing in incandescence with every passing second. It began to squeal.

"Take the river, dear elf. THE RIVER, NOW!"

Kealin turned and ran, leaping through the open doorway and over the edge of the path he had taken straight into the rapids. A moment later, a quaking fiery blast shuddered the very walls as he was sucked by the current. The river twisted and turned before dropping further and further. He could hear the sound of falls and was then pulled under just before he felt himself flying through the air. He landed into a deep pool. It was a massive lake on the outside of Michranok. Hitting his knee on submerged ruins, he scrambled to the surface and pulled himself onto a ruined arch that was lying in the water. He turned to look at the rocky falls he had emerged from and noticed rocks were scraping and hurling off the side as the entire cave system seemed to be giving way.

He pushed himself up and began to run, leaping from rock to ruin and back eventually to rocky ground as he sprinted away from the dwarf's explosive destruction.

The rubble came to rest as giant pieces fell into the lake. He exhaled, looking up the mountains and the river that spilled from the higher points of the ruins of the city.

Kealin looked back, thankful he had escaped and confused as to what had actually happened. The dwarves had been betrayed by the Grand Protectorate, and not only was something of immense power stolen, but every dwarf was slaughtered.

His knee was sore, but he limped quickly to the water's edge, grabbing the hammer that Ruak had given him. He tapped a rock underwater and waited. The lake before him was still until a rumble shook from beneath its surface. The water began to swirl and then flash just under the surface. A moment later, the narwhal Tulasiro broke the surface with his boat in tow.

"It is good to see you, my friend."

The narwhal nodded, and her frosty crown chilled the water as Kealin sat down in the boat. As Tulasiro pulled them away from land's edge and toward the Great Isira River, Kealin prepared himself. They would proceed toward Vueric, and Kealin would free his brother no matter the cost.

14

ALL SHADOWS FALL

J esia had been awoken by one of the servants coming into the palace. She had fallen asleep with her head on Muera, but the increased commotion in the room had forced her to sit up and quickly piece together what was going on.

"You will ride for the northern cape, get him to the safety of Revas, and then continue to heal him there."

The king gave strict orders to a servant and a host of the Knights Guard.

"What is wrong?" Jesia asked.

"He has not awoken, and I'm going to send him away from here. I've already lost one son; I will not lose this one when he cannot even defend himself." He turned back to the Knights Guard. "Take the lost gate from the lower city. You have twenty men. You will not stop until you reach the city of Revas unless by personal decree of House Firda, my decree. House Firda will not fall today, and I will make sure of this."

Ridau began to stir. He attempted to raise his hand off the table.

"Give him more of the soothing balm. He must not stay here, and if he awakens, he will refuse."

The servant hesitated, and at the same moment, the doors of the hall opened. Captain Tiris came in with a large host.

"My king, the vanguard of the elven army arrived within the last half hour. We also have word of more vessels of Eh-Rin and that the Drean are sailing here as well. The enemy is swelling along the Isira at this very moment. We have also spotted orcs gathering in the ruins of the old city.

"Then we must act quickly! Send for the dwarven dust. If not all of it was sent to the lighthouse, we will sacrifice part of the city. I did not see it coming to this, but if we must do that, we will. We must keep them out of Vueric."

"I will personally see to it," Tiris said.

As the Knights Guard carried Lord Ridau from the stone table, Muera awoke and sat up.

"Muera!" Jesia said, touching her arm.

"Where is he going?"

"Who?"

"The lord Ridau."

Jesia shook her head. "He is still ill. He is to go to safety. The orcs are growing in numbers."

"He will be safe here, as we all are. Those of Eh-Rin are coming."

"He is a lord of House Firda, and the king has

spoken. Muera, you only just met this man. Keep your mind where it should be."

"I am no servant of yours, Jesia. My mind is where it wishes to be for the first time in my life. The first ounce of normalcy. I didn't want to be some warrior slave. No one has ever asked me what I wanted. This was my first taste of normalcy and to hear at least kind words come from a man who had nothing to gain or demand from saying them. No one has judged you with your solemn-ness over Kealin and the way you continually cradled that baby. How would you be if that baby, whom you took to protecting for the few days you were around it, was suddenly threatened?"

Jesia stared at Muera and forced her mind from the thoughts of Kealin and his infant brother. She couldn't think of them now. "Muera, we are Rusis. This city is under attack, and if you care anything for that lord, you will help defend this city and his home and his father."

Muera had tears fill in her eyes, and then she grimaced a smile. "I will do what I must. He will go and be healed and return to his city in time."

She threw her feet off the table and unsteadily stood.

The king was already leading the host toward the door of the hall, and Muera and Jesia followed. Outside, they looked toward the lighthouse and the many lights across the field. They could see the burning fire in the mountains and wondered what it meant.

"You may as well come," Meask told Brethor. "I

guess my place will be here and not in the palace for now."

Brethor mounted a horse with the lord and began a rapid trot toward the bridge way. A small group of Knights Guard rode with them, but they all stopped short of the bridge.

More elven horns called, and they looked back to see a large contingent of elven banners emerging from the woods. They marched into the field but stopped approximately half a league from the river. Their shields flashed out as archons in their ranks held their staves aloft with burning fire at their tips. Brethor looked back toward Vueric to see King Rasune approaching on a stag.

"Well, I guess we will attempt a negotiation," Meask said.

Meask and Rasune took the lead as they walked across the bridge. The wizard known as Vakron-Tur stood alone in the center of the bridge. He wore silver armor with a gray cloak that furled behind him. His staff glowed white, and a small twisting cyclone sat atop it. He had orange flames that surrounded a clawed black hand as his personal sigil.

"Good kings of the western lands. It is a fair night to converse of our plans for conquest."

Rasune dismounted from his stag. "You were an elf once, but no more will I believe it. You have the mark of the demon god on your chest, and you bring war to our woods, and the vile orcs live again because of your evil."

Vakron-Tur shook his head. "I have tried to explain myself to others to no avail, but I will attempt again. I move to save us. The orcs may have been our enemy, but

I can control them. I will use them to crush men, and in so, save us. There have been visions from the god Ur given to his sacred clan. We must not be blinded by hate in this hour. We must see the truth."

"The truth is seen," Lord Meask said. "Ur is not a god we speak of. He is evil and the father of the Itsu. I have read my history. My great house and the elves of the Vumark Woods will destroy your evil and any that come against the sanctity of our kingdoms."

"Young boy, you may be wise and of many years by your standard, but by my own, you are still a suckling calf. Your kind will be who destroys all of magic. I have seen it. I have seen the truth."

"Seen the truth? You are no god, no seer, no wise man of a hidden cave as the stories say," Rasune said. "You are a plague to our world where already we fight demon men and vampires. Where the northern woods of our most vast elven lands are nothing more than craters, and yet you bring this to our other border?"

"Speak with the dwarves of Michranok of my words."

"You know they had an unfortunate travesty with their mining. Delving too deep into the earth cost them their lives," Meask said.

"Dwarves? Dying from doing exactly what they do? Have you been behind the sealed doors of their sacred places? Have you seen what tragedy happened there? What source of your information has told you of some accident? Your own spies? Who do you trust who cannot be bought with the promises of a *grand* kind?"

"I understand your emphasis, but the Grand Protectorate knows their place. They wouldn't dare assault

House Firda. They wish to keep peace and coerce us with their sly words into giving our kingship away. They want the allegiance of our people."

Vakron-Tur twisted his staff in hand. "Trusting those men is the single worst thing you can do. They no doubt offered you assistance against me. You should be wary of any army that marches into this valley. My army follows my command, and I wish to protect elves, dwarves, and all manner of warriors of magic. I do not want to fight you this day. I say we draw up an alliance, an agreement. I will lead my forces to the east with the combined armies of House Firda and the Greater Varmark Woods. We will crush the legions of our enemy, and then I will return to the south and reclaim the old kingdoms of Ur. The orcs will not trouble you or your people. I did not take the son-rite of the Matriarch to join her, but I have destroyed the old clan of Ur. Their evil was the first that I eliminated. I then convinced the Matriarch that she did not need their power. I supported her and did what was necessary to secure power, but we all make sacrifices. I sacrificed my very soul to wield the power of the Orc Star. I am them, and they are me. A new power of magic holds the Five Staves of Ur. We will bear the hardships with all of magic kind."

More horns called, and drums played a thunderous beat. A line formation from the woods north of the river emerged, bearing the symbols of King Suvasel and his Fikmarkian elves. The host took a position in front of the other elves, taking the ground just before the Isira. Another host of stags followed the army and came to the bridge. King Rasune went to bow to Suvasel, but the elf king drew his blade, *Vank-Rus*, as he approached Vakron-Tur.

"You bring *Orc Biter* here? Well, I was just speaking to your alliance of such matters," Vakron-Tur said.

"Your words are empty. The Fikmarkian are here to return you and your army to the mountain graves."

"High King, I seek a parlay this day, not bloodshed."

"By the gods of the North, silence, you filth of an elf."

Vakron-Tur stepped back as Suvasel pointed his blade at his head.

"You must see beyond yourself and your beliefs," Vakron-Tur said. "We must fight together against the coming evil."

"There will not be darkness upon my woods beyond what has already fallen. We have fought under the sky of the Great Poet, with the blessing of Etha upon our backs and the blood of Kel rushing through our veins as we draw blades against the bastard creation of the bastard god. Orcs will no longer breathe past sunrise this day."

Rasune stepped beside Suvasel and drew his blade. "This is the way it is. By sunrise, your summonings will be put down. Your clan and you may be given mercy, but these demons must be put down."

Vakron-Tur bowed his head and sighed. "I tried. May all histories remember that I tried. You say by sunrise? There will not be a sunrise for any of you."

A surge of wind struck the host from behind Vakron-Tur, and he thrust his staff at Rasune's chest. A white blast pierced the elf king's armor, blasting him apart and throwing the entire host to their backs. Suvasel was the first up and ran for the wizard. Vakron-Tur shook his head, and then in another blast of wind, he lifted himself from the bridge and landed beyond his orcs.

Brethor pushed himself up and grasped his sword as Meask crawled to King Rasune. The blast of magic had torn his chest apart. Blood ran from his broken body.

Suvasel stood on the edge of the bridge. "Fikmarkian elves, release!"

The elves near the river released a volley of arrows, striking into the orc and goblin lines.

The elf king went to the other elves along the bridge.

"Send word that King Rasune has been murdered by our enemy. I now command all forces of the Fikmark and Vumark lands until the completion of this engagement. Command Archons to turn that mountain to a burning light and send stag forces to the eastern flank. We must contain and hold them until dawn."

Suvasel turned to Meask. "At dawn, we assault the mountain. We will kill that wizard. Hold this bridge until then." Suvasel looked back to the city. "I sent my son and the Scions to confer with your king of our plans."

"You had no intent to parlay?" Meask questioned the king.

"I know the way this ends, good lord. We must destroy them. I may be rash in my workings, but your mother and brother were murdered. I would expect any ally of mine to enact revenge with harsh haste. We of Fikmark are with you and House Firda."

The elf king embraced Meask and then went to his stag, spurring his mount away from the bridge.

On the other side of the bridge, the lighthouse fort was fully engaged with the goblins nearest them.

Flaming arrows flew out from every defender as the enemy swarmed the palisades.

"We will take command of the fortress. We must hold the path. Vaden and the legatus need any men we can muster."

They rode across the bridgeway as plinking arrows struck the shields of the Knights Guard that rode on either side of them. They came to the gateway, and a man above noticed them.

"Open up for the lord Meask!"

As the door opened, the mountains shook. The blue fire burning high in the peaks shot into the air, and a dark structure began to rise into the sky. The archons within the elven army fired out, arching blasts of fire high into the cloud cover that split off as they burst into white streaks, peppering the mountains and lighting their ash-colored rocks. The orcs emerged from the darkness with large spears and filed down toward the river.

Meask and Brethor entered the fort where Vaden met them.

"Negotiations failed, I assume?"

Meask didn't entertain his sarcasm and instead went toward one of the stairwells leading to the wall.

Even from a distance, Brethor could see the difference between the goblins they had been fighting and these Drear Orcs that the archon fire made clearly visible. They were larger, and had weapons that could take a man off a horse or push back a shield wall. The goblins were pushed into the water, and a series of explosions shook the bases of the mountains, sending rocks hurling toward the elven lines. From caverns hidden behind the rocky walls emerged wooden structures. The orcs used the tusked creatures Brethor had seen at Eastwatch to pull the structures down the embankment and into the rivers. As soon as they were in the river, the creatures' bonds were cut, and ten of them stood on the bank, facing the Fikmarkian elves.

The orcs had built massive bridges, and now they charged across them as the tusked creatures rammed the elven line. Many of the creatures died, but others broke into the ranks, and a flurry of arrows did not stop them.

The concentration seemed to be on the elven lines, but more of the orcs and goblin forces were moving toward the fort. Brethor stood with many good men and women among the Rangers. The legatus and his men had taken up bows and filled into the battle line on the walls. Dala and some of those of Eh-Rin did what they could to reinforce the actual walls. For now, they were holding. Vaden came to Brethor and smiled at him.

"It is good you come to fight with us. It is a crazy time, but my love and I have found it fitting to announce she is with child. I will have a son, I know it! Nearly better than that, the men now seem overeager to keep this ground. A bit of happiness in light of darkness can do much to lighten the burden of death."

Brethor smiled back but felt his comment an odd one. He couldn't imagine the feeling of fighting for the life of one's unborn child. He looked down at the orcs clawing and scratching at the fort as the mother-to-be directed men to fire into the hell below. The battle was only beginning.

. . .

JESIA AND MUERA STOOD OUTSIDE, watching the events of the dark morning unfold. The city had begun to ring the bells throughout, and though the orcs had not reached the walls, they did everything they could do to prepare the city, as many of the townspeople moved to the inner part of the city.

The host with Lord Ridau had departed, and now the king spoke with leaders of the town watch and Captain Tiris, who never made it to the lighthouse to inquire of the dwarven dust.

"Use whatever we can to block those ruins. Have the town watch take burning oil to the hallway. We will melt the way into the structure if we must."

"This rock will not melt with simple oil, my king. Dragon fire could do it, but we do not seem to have dragons!"

"Some people have fled, my king. Women and children have left the city and headed north."

"The darkness and clamor of battle has taken them. We must wait for sunrise. That will be the turning point. The orcs will fall back."

At the moment, the gateways leading to the inner keep opened, and a group of elves walked in.

Two of them stepped forward and bowed to the king. "King Firda of Vueric, we are the Scions of Starfall. I am Ruak, and with me is the son of King Suvasel, Ivasel of Fikmark. We are here to assist you as needed and advise you of the battle plans."

"Well, our city is prepared, elf. Though we have a small issue within, if you would like to assist us there. I do know of you from speaking to our Rangers. Your kind has done well to assist us for so long."

"We are happy that the rest of our peoples have finally decided to come help. At morning, the elven forces will assault the mountains and end this fighting. We must hold until then. Now of your issue. Lead us to it," Ivasel said.

The king took them into the main hall and down the hallway leading to the excavation site and the entrance to the Dwemhar ruins. The massive doors were now wide open, and from even a good distance, one could see the ruins and buildings of the old Dwemhar city.

One of the Knights Guard approached Captain Tiris. "We have taken down a few stragglers who tried our defenses, but they have not made a major push. They construct a crossing, but if we approach, their arrows keep us from getting too close. We have fallen back to the doorway."

"Can you still not shut the doors?"

"The mechanisms are beyond us, and it will not budge. It must be tied to the magic in the ruins themselves. They've actually opened more, obviously."

"What are your thoughts, King Firda?" Ruak asked.

"We must seal this off. Block this path."

"A strange place, here under your city," the archon said.

"It is a Dwemhar ruin," Jesia mentioned.

"Our friend Teusk enjoys his histories," Ruak said. "But we will keep at task for now. My scions and I will push forward and attempt to destroy the crossing. I knew orcs to be industrious, but these must have been massive tunnels to go so far under the city from the other side of the river."

"The bridge way was destroyed by me and my friend Brethor. His brother activated portals within the structure."

"Activated? Another one of Dwemhar blood?" Teusk asked.

"Another one? What do you mean?" Jesia asked.

"We parted ways with a half-elf named Kealin not too long ago."

"He lives?"

Ruak smiled. "Very much so. He searches for his sister, but I believe he is coming this way soon. You are the Rusis he mentioned, and your friend and his brother were the ones of Dwemhar blood. Our world is getting smaller, or so it seems."

"They are both Rusis," Teusk said, pointing toward Muera and Jesia. "I did not believe it possible in my life to see another Rusis, but I am honored."

Jesia and Muera both smiled.

"Then, good king, if you can part with some of your men, we will go into the ruins and destroy the crossing they are building. After that, we will figure out a way to close this off."

"I had hoped we could somehow destroy part of the walls or rock and close it off."

"Not likely, possible. Dwemhar structures like this have rock denser than mere magic can destroy."

Teusk pointed his staff and sent a blast of fire above the opening. The rock merely smoked, and pieces of dust fell.

"Once we secure this way and buy the armies more time, if Vakron-Tur is not destroyed, we will hopefully find the source of his power."

"The Orc Star?" asked the king.

"Yes, with dawn, our forces will have the advantage, and we will move upon them," Ruak told him.

Captain Tiris pointed to some of his men and some of the town guard. They joined the Scions. In total, they had a small group of twenty.

"We will secure the crossing, good king."

Jesia and Muera went with them. The archon smiled again. "Hard for any Rusis to turn down a fight. I see you wear the armor of the archmage of Vueric."

As they passed through the gateway, the Knights Guard lifted their shields, and Elaca set an arrow to her bow.

"I do, but only recently. A gift from the king."

"She was a friend of mine, many years ago. It is good that her armor was not lost to time. It will protect you, I assure you. Her death was a dark one, and one I do not care to think of right now."

15

BLOODBATH

Brethor parried a pike head forced between him and Meask. The orcs had managed to climb partially up the walls, but Vaden had yet to give the order to detonate the remaining dwarven dust he had in the field.

"We must wait until we have no choice!" he shouted again as he came alongside them with his blade. An orc reached on top of the battlement, and Meask stabbed its wrist, piercing through bone and flesh. The creature hung for a moment before it fell, leaving its shredded hand on the wall.

Vaden reached down and picked it up. He sneered and threw it from the wall.

"Perhaps sooner than I planned. We *should* give them a little shock."

The orcs had directed more of their goblins to swarm near the edge of the water, and now they climbed up the battlements on the edge of the wall. Rangers on the lighthouse aimed their bows that way. Volley after volley flew from that position until a rock hurled from the hordes in the fields, smashing into the side of the lighthouse. A large portion of brickwork crumbled, but it still stood, for now.

The orc had one catapult in the field, and more were moving in from the caves in the mountains.

"Now! Blow the bastards!"

The Rangers worked to release the log already in position as the catapult released another rock. The log began to roll. Aflame and spinning fast, it made the descent down the wooden railings toward the wall. The catapulted rock smashed into the top of the wall, and the entire structure holding the log buckled, sending the rock into part of the palisade. Rangers were crushed under its burning weight as goblins rushed the opening.

"Hold the wall!" Meask shouted.

Brethor and Vaden moved with Meask from the wall to the courtyard as the Rangers of the river valley, the few men Meask had brought, and the legatus and his legionnaires fought to hold the opening. Dawn was approaching, and they all waited for the sun's light to strike their orc and goblin foes.

Brethor paused, looking across the ocean. He could see the ships of Eh-Rin approaching the coastline. Far down the roadway, a white shroud moved in unison toward them, and something, like hundreds of large birds, covered the sky, moving quickly through the morning clouds.

Brethor worked his way down. The goblins that had pushed past the defensive line did their typical jumping and hacking, but his Dwemhar blade pierced their bodies easily. His armor was bulky to him, but his enemy seemed to like to grab him as much as actually fight, as many had their blades knocked from their hands in the swordplay that they clearly were not as skilled in. One clawed at him, and he punched it off. Thrusting his sword into its body, he thought, for a moment, that a single large bird shot over the top of the battlements. There was a flash in the corner of his eye, and the sound of a rush of wind.

Dala looked up as two more passed over the light-house, and then began to smile. "My brethren come!"

Flaming balls began to fly into the orcs on the other side of the wall as more and more of the strange entities flew over them. The orcs began to fall to confusion as they were confronted by a new enemy.

Meask and Brethor went up to the battlements again, fighting their way to clear them as the morning sky of orange and red was crowned with what could only be described as golden carpets flying through the air. The forces of Eh-Rin rode atop enchanted rugs of some kind, dropping high from the sky, wielding small staves that they used to shoot fire into the enemy. The orcs were pushed away from the fort as more of them made strafing runs just along the wall, casting burning mud onto the wood. The orcs fell back or were struck down in their confusion.

As their new allies encouraged the defenders, Vaden was not celebrating. He had fought off the orcs near the opening in the wall, but now, he was on his knees in the mud.

Meask went to him but did not touch him as he saw why he had paused.

The large tree that was meant to set off the dwarf dust had struck several Rangers as it tumbled to the ground. He held the hands of one of them, his love, whom Brethor had seen just after they arrived but never knew. She was quivering. Her pelvic and stomach had been crushed, and most of her body was burned. Her life was fading. She coughed blood and winced as she tried to move her hand closer to Vaden.

"Rest now, my love. You and our little one."

Lady Orta closed her eyes, and he slid a dagger into her throat. She coughed but then quickly faded.

He stood and sheathed his knife. A moment later, the dwarf dust exploded from one of the Eh-Rin carpet riders. The ground trembled, and Vaden reached down, picking up a second weapon, an abandoned orc axe.

"Vaden, of the Rangers, where do you go?"

"To return this axe to the enemy and then to join my wife."

The Ranger disappeared through the gap in the wall, leaving the lighthouse and disappearing into fire and smoke.

The ships of Eh-Rin had landed along the coastline opposite the lighthouse and disembarked. The lightly armored swordsmen moved forward to the aid of the elves as more orcs moved both against the elven army and that of the lighthouse. It was the heavy Eh-Rin pikemen from the road who sought to push back and reclaim the land between the lighthouse and the mountains. As they met the orc lines, the porcupine-like protruding spears were nearly impossible for the orcs to break through. On the edges of the phalanx, the carpet riders shot fireballs, blocking the path of any orcs that might have tried to flank them.

The sun was rising, and the orcs were slowing. The sunlight was affecting them even in this small amount.

Brethor had taken to shooting a bow, considering the orcs were now more concentrated on the Eh-Rin forces. Meask met with Dala and other Eh-Rin men who had come down the bridge. But Brethor noticed something of the blue fire and the tower in the mountains. It had turned black and gold, and the wizard Vakron-Tur hovered above it. The fire above the tower glowed brightly, and then a spark flew out from atop it and over the valley. A black object grew in immense size above the battlefield, and clouds began to roll out from it. The strange object began to turn, and Brethor's skin suddenly was cold. The sky became dark, and any hint of the morning was chased away by black clouds that stretched in all directions. A blast of wind struck downward into the elven armies, and they were thrown asunder. Deep horns bellowed from the mountains, and trolls and another wave of orcs charged across the river, crossing into the dazed elves, breaking their lines.

"It is the Orc Star of Ur," Meask said. "Light will not return to us, and now I truly fear of our peoples."

The hope brought by morning had faded.

THE HOST within the underground city was not even halfway to the bridge. They were attacked twice, but in each time, it had taken little to put their enemy into despair and inspire them to flee. They moved very slowly, and Teusk constantly kept himself in front of Jesia.

"You have potions," he said to her. "Taken from the archmage's belongings?"

"The king said it was okay."

He nodded. "Of course, but do you know of them?"

"I had never had the opportunity to learn, but I—"

"The reddish ones will invigorate your magic. You will not tire as quickly, and if you are tired, you will feel better. The bluish ones help with water breathing, and the white ones, for health."

"Thank for . . . for that information."

He smiled. "If only I could teach more. I know what they've done to Rusis, especially further west. These men of this house are strong and honorable. Be lucky we have them, and do not judge all men against the ones you have known."

"We have been treated well here, dear elf," Muera said.

"Good, I would be surprised to hear otherwise."

Ruak, who before had been leading, drifted back to Jesia. "How much further to the bridge?"

"A good while," she said, "and when Brethor and I came here, we weren't dealing with orcs."

An arrow plunged into the ground just in front of Jesia, and Teusk shot a blast of magic into the air above them that burst to blind those firing at them. It had worked before, but this time, another barrage came and flew straight into the men in the front. Many of the men of House Firda fell.

Elaca pulled back on her bow and released a few arrows in quick succession, dropping the front line of orcs and goblins that approached.

The Rusis and the archon ran to the front, and several blasts of magic sent fire and ice into the approaching enemy. Ruak and Ivasel stood with the rest of House Firda behind them. The orcs fell over and over. A large smoldering pile of them began to build as a mix of melted ice magic, charred skin, and blood began to run away from the pile. But something moved over them, the wind changed, and then a loud sound turned the non-magic wielding warriors to look behind them.

It was a swordsman. The black swordsman. The one mentioned many times in rumor and fewer times by actual survivors. Ruak looked at his face and saw the mask, the one Kealin had mentioned. This was his brother.

"Elaca!"

The elf turned and fired her bow. The red glowing arrow struck the armor of the swordsman, and the arrow splintered. Men of the House Firda charged toward him, but in one fell swoop, he waylaid each of them, shattering their armor and leaving a pile of bleeding corpses.

Ruak and Ivasel charged forward, bringing their blades up in a leap before attempting to cut into the man's head. He parried Ivasel and pushed forward into Ruak, catching the elf's blade in the crux of his armor and snapping it. They were no match for him, and it seemed that his power had increased since Kealin had faced him.

"Rusis, Teusk! We must flee!" Ivasel shouted.

Ruak jumped from another swing of Kealin's brother's sword as an arrow struck the side of his neck with a bouncing graze off his armor. Elaca had climbed onto a building, and now the black warrior moved toward her.

Jesia sent a blast of ice against another orc and then grabbed Muera's arm as they began to run back toward the doorway. Teusk followed and ran up to the swordsmen, grabbing his armor and ripping him off the building he had partially leaped into. He pushed his staff against his knee, and with a blast of magic, shattered the armor protecting his leg.

A rush of orcs and goblins swarmed around him, and he turned to attacking those as he fell back toward the other.

Elaca ran along the top of the buildings, firing arrows behind her until she jumped and was struck by an arrow herself.

"Elaca!" Ruak shouted. He went running up to a building to climb to her when the masked warrior stood and his eyes flashed a bright red. He threw a block of crumbled building toward Ruak, collapsing the structure he was about to climb up.

Teusk and Jesia fired several blasts of magic at the warrior, but orcs took the brunt of the attacks, leaving the warrior free to climb onto the building. Elaca drew her bow and fired an arrow at the approaching enemy, but the arrow did nothing. Ruak watched in horror as the warrior pulled her by her feet into the air and drove his blade into her back. He then threw her body against the far side of the road they stood on.

"We must run, now!" Ivasel said.

In the time it took them to get to this place along the road in the ruins, their sprint back to the doorway seemed to be the fastest Jesia had ever run. They did not stop to fight. They did not stop to check if they were still being pursued. The clamor of the orcs behind them and the rhythmic pounding of war drums and whizzes of missing arrows reminded them of why they ran.

They soon saw the doorway and the solemn defense that stood there. As they came through the opening of the doors, the archon turned and shot an ear-deafening blast straight up, causing several large stones to fall down behind them. The orcs slowed for a moment, giving them time to get beyond the makeshift wall.

"What happened?" the king asked.

"We failed and they are coming."

Several arrows flew into them at that moment, one scratching the king on his leg but only causing him to topple for a second. He was lucky the shot had missed.

"Get the king into the keep!" Captain Tiris shouted.

The scions fell back with the king, and the captain of the Knights Guard watched as the orcs tore apart the barricade and slew the men defending it. He barred the door leading into the keep and pointed.

"Go! Into the throne room!"

The guards assigned to the inner hall ran toward them, and the king was pushed into their center. The door they had locked was forced open just as the main door leading to the hall was barred. The Knights Guard formed a shield wall at the door.

Captain Tiris looked toward one of his men. "You, go signal the bell towers. Give the warning that the keep is overwhelmed. Take the king and get him out of here and to one of the main towers. He will be safer there."

"The Scions stand with you, Tiris," Ruak said. He drew a dagger.

Tiris tossed him his sword before going to the wall and lifting another from a mount.

"No, protect my king. Get him to elven lands, if you must, but get him to safety. I will hold them here as long as I can."

The king drew his blade. "I will not cower behind my guards. I will stand with you here."

"With my respect, King, I am to guard you, and you have fought many battles. This is not the one you will die in. Let me defend the keep."

Jesia noticed that seemed enough for the king to reluctantly agree. They began out of the keep as fast as they could run. The doors opened to the outside and a still-dark sky.

"It is supposed to be morning now," Ivasel said, looking around.

"I know why." Ruak pointed toward the valley.

"The Orc Star. Darkness has come and light will not return to us," Teusk said.

"A bleak outlook for such a man as yourself," Muera said.

"The Orc Star was what we fear. There will be no break in the fighting. We must destroy Vakron-Tur."

"We must survive this first," the king said. He went to the wall leading out of the inner keep and looked out as the others joined him. The mountains were alight in fire from Eh-Rin carpet riders and archons in the field. The valley was one large massacre with no uniformity that any could notice. The ships of Eh-Rin fired their crystals into the mountains, sending purple and blue sparks up into the peaks, but all they could see was the vast numbers of the Drear Orcs still emerging from the caves.

"I dare ask," King Firda said, "how many orcs were buried in those mountains?"

"It took ten kingdoms of elves and over four hundred thousand to push them out of the North. We also had dwarven, Rusis, and Dwemhar allies. Dragons destroyed many of them, but I care not to think how many were actually sealed away. We must destroy the wizard. That is all we can do. We cannot win this through fighting the orcs into submission. It is clear now that Vakron-Tur wields the Black Orc Star of Ur."

The Knights Guard who had been instructed to get the king to safety attempted to pull his king from the wall.

The king shook the man off of him.

"I heard your orders, but I will stay here. This is my protected city, and I will remain here as long as I may. You have a new order. Remain by my side and see your captain's wishes followed."

They could hear shouting from the keep. There were crashes and clanging sounds. Those in the court-yard spread out against the back edge. Jesia stood with her hands out. She took one of the red potions and took a swig before passing the remaining half to Muera. She then grabbed another one and offered it to Teusk.

"No, thank you. I had quite enough to drink before I arrived. I would much rather you hold it for me."

The king held his sword out next to Ruak and Ivasel.

Jesia noticed the statues that lined either side of the doorway seemed darker than before. Their blades of white stood out now, and as the clouds swirled above them, it seemed there was a strange presence suddenly upon all that stood in preparation for battle.

"Gods of the North," began King Firda, "hear my prayers. Let not the city of Vueric fall without your hands here to protect it."

The doorway of the keep was thrown open, and a bloodied body flew out, rolling just before the stairs. The masked warrior approached, his sword held high as the person pushed himself up.

"Let not the members of House Firda continue to bleed."

The body was that of Captain Tiris, and as he rolled over, he drew a dagger only to have the masked warrior cleave into him, splattering blood across the stonework of the courtyard.

"Let not the filth of the demon god defile our sacred grounds."

The orcs swarmed out of the doorway and lined up beside the masked warrior.

"Do not forsake us in this final hour."

With those last words, the many statues beyond the line of the masked warrior and the orcs moved in unison, their white blades plunging deep into the orcs before them. The masked man was caught off guard and stumbled forward as a second wave of orcs poured through the doors.

The eagle statues were alive and defending the faithful servant of Kel, King Firda, as he had prayed. The remaining defenders fought to hold their ground as the masked warrior fought the holy statues of Kel.

Jesia and Muera cast their spells next to Teusk, who frankly was casting much more powerful and effective spells. A blast of fire shot up and over the front orcs, throwing back the second and third line in an explosion. He spun his staff, and a flash of energy shredded four orcs where they stood.

The eagle statues slashed and sliced, but the masked warrior parried and jumped from their strikes, taking down one after the other. They were massive, strong, but were beaten by this terror. The orcs began to avoid the courtyard and instead went for the gateway and the path of teeth, the layered defense meant to protect from the outside. One of the orcs turned a switch, and the gates opened. The way to the city was open. People began to scream and flee as the orcs filled into the city.

"Alert the armies in the fields," shouted the king. "Let them know the city is in trouble!"

Teusk lifted his staff and sent a massive spark into the air, sending a crackling flare raining over the city. It was just as the one outside Risdannia, only much larger.

"That is all I can do, King Firda. The archons will see it but I fear they will not have warriors in the field to spare."

He took to a knee and held his staff with both hands.

Jesia noticed a wall formed out of the air that shot out from him and blasted the orcs back. The Scions and the men of House Firda charged forward with renewed strength for the moment. Jesia cast a series of bolts, bouncing with the open doorway, throwing more of the attackers back, and then joined Muera next to the archon. She gave him one of the potions, which he took and chugged.

"See?" he said out of breath and sweating. "I knew it was good to wait."

Ivasel and Ruak pushed into the doorway and fought to hold off more reinforcements for the moment. The masked warrior had taken down most of the eagle statues, and now the last two dueled him to the far right of the door.

Ruak pulled the inner doors of the halls closed, and both Ivasel and him shoved spears and swords into the handles to close it off for the moment. Almost immediately, the orcs began ramming the door.

They fell back, the other remaining warriors forming a half circle around the king that moved slowly to the open gateway and the screams of those in the city below. The masked warrior roared as he walked around the corner. His eyes were white and his voice shrill.

"He wears armor crafted with the magic of the demon god. He is more protected than I daresay any of us," Ruak said.

The orcs from below heard the call of their master and came running back up the road. The king moved forward, attempting to strike the warrior, but he was thrown back into the courtyard. He landed in a roll, sliding across the stone ground. His sword was out of reach, and he held his hand up to the blackness approaching.

They all ran forward. A series of spells struck his back, but it was the thrusting blade of the near-dead Knights Guard captain that caught the masked warrior's attention. With his last bit of strength, through choking blood, he drove the blade into the warrior's lower leg, causing him to fall to his knee before swinging his arm around and smashing Tiris across the face. Blood and teeth flew against the side of the keep, and the masked warrior followed again with his blade, smashing the man into the ground. It seemed he noticed that the doors to the keep were barricaded and turned his attention to that as the others picked up the king. Though the masked warrior had been injured by Teusk before and now the fallen captain had pierced that same leg, neither injury seemed to slow him.

"I AM OKAY," the king said. "I am just sore. We cannot continue to fight this here."

"Is there another way out of this level?" Ruak asked.

"No."

The orcs swarmed from the lower level, and now the door was unsealed and they were surrounded again. The masked warrior stepped out again into the courtyard. It was the Scions, the Rusis, and only a handful of the king's men who remained.

"We fought well," said Ivasel, "but there comes a time when even the gods cannot help us."

A blast of blinding light struck the masked warrior, and he was forced to the ground. Another blast of blue lightning cut into the orcs, and the sound of a roaring storm was above them. Jesia looked up to see the most radiant golden glow. She shielded her eyes and was forced to the ground with the others as a gusting wind struck the confined walls of the keep, shooting dust up in a plume around them. A loud whirring, almost melodic sound, drowned out the screaming orcs and just before them, something appeared in the shroud of dust. The blinding light was overwhelming, but Jesia heard a voice that was comforting.

"You have done well, Rusis. Now, let us go from this place."

She looked up to see Amhe standing before a magnificent golden object. Glowing runes ran up its side, and crystals lined its bottom. The Scions were as amazed as she was but spent no time in climbing into the inside of this metallic beast. King Firda embraced the sultan.

"The flying carpet. I had wondered."

"We stabilized the energy required, finally. It took us some time after you and I found it in the cave system."

Jesia walked up a walkway of sorts that led into the strange object and found herself confused by what she saw.

It was a large circular room with a ceiling that stretched up taller than twenty men. A large silver ball of what appeared to be some kind of liquid was electrified by two staves held by those she knew as the Sanguine monks in Eh-Rin. She felt her stomach suddenly shift, and the whirring increased. Amhe stood from a deck that overlooked a window. They were now high above the city.

"The Sanguine monks discovered that energy fed directly into the metal pool would spin and create the power to stabilize our flight. The crystals we had used before only lasted so long, but once enough energy was used, we managed to return the machine back to its old self."

"You saved us, Sultan," Firda told him. "I did not believe my own jokes of you bringing the carpet, but you did."

"Well, our carpets were here before me. They've been cutting a line through the orc to open up the mountain, but it was a decent journey to where we left this device. I can hardly call this a carpet, given that it is not made of cloth! What reason did we have for naming it something so foolish?"

Firda smiled. "We were younger then."

"Indeed we were, but I say let's keep aging and not let this long night end our lives."

The elves were as frightened as was Muera, and though they floated through the air with no change other than the initial lift off the ground, they were too afraid to move. As they moved forward, the loud sounds the machine made changed to that of a defined musical hum both ominous and deeply peaceful at the same time.

"So when we get out of this demon," said Ruak. "I will buy you a drink, dear sultan, wherever you want one in whatever place you want it. Just know we are staying on the ground. We can get out of this, right?"

The sultan laughed. "Yes, we can. The two monks who power it work in unison to fly us to where we wish to go. One operates the crystal weapons, and the other moves us through the air. It has taken them many months to get this far in the controls with meditation. A Dwemhar weapon such as this is not the easiest to master."

"They operate it as Dwemhar? How? They are not Dwemhar," said Teusk.

"As one of the arcane arts of magic studies to be like Rusis in some ways, the Sanguine monks have worked for many ages to be as the ones we called Dwemhar. We must accept the blessing given to us and work together as all races did so many years ago. Although, I do question, dear Firda, what possessed you to contact the Drean?"

"I did not. They claimed they wished to help us and sent ships."

Jesia noticed that the two rulers stared at one another in a concerning way before looking back out toward the battle.

She wondered not only of Brethor and Lord Meask but also of Kealin. He was supposedly coming. She hoped he would get here in time.

As they came onto the shoreline, the battle north of the river was moving away from the shore as the orcs gained ground, pushing the elven forces north. Whatever plan that had been made by King Suvasel had well failed now, and though the forces of Eh-Rin and the carpet riders had done well to carve into the flow of orcs from the caves, they, too, were only doing so much.

The flying ship came to rest on the ground before

the landing area of the Eh-Rin fleet. The door to the ground opened, and the elves and the Rusis departed. The moment they made it to the ground, Ivasel and Ruak both vomited. The ride in Amhe's machine had been too much for them. Jesia looked back up to the king and the sultan.

"We will support from above and help clear the path to the mountains!"

The doorway shut, and the crystals began to spin as the golden craft lifted off. Waves of energy rolled around it, and the outside shifted as the mechanics moved the machine into the air as they flew up higher.

"Wheels within wheels," said Teusk.

"What?" Jesia asked.

"The Dwemhar machines of legend, described by one as 'something of wheels within encircling wheels and radiant light-like music.' To see such a thing in my time almost makes my life complete."

Amhe's machine roared over them to the cheer of the Eh-Rin forces. It ran first along the river, sending a blasting bolt of energy along it, tearing apart the bridges before ascending up the mountain with several blasts, causing avalanches of rocks. The carpets rallied around it, and the entire mountain became alight in small fires as they shot flames upon it.

"Across the bridge, Scions!" Ruak said.

As they ran across the bridge, the waters that ran under it was thick with the bodies of orcs, goblins, and elves. Along the shores, the dead stacked up, and the stench from the many burning bodies was horrid. The doorway to the lighthouse fortress was thrown open, and as they entered, they noticed a long line of Eh-Rin spearmen now held the opening in the palisade walls. Jesia looked around, curious of those she had seen before when she came in. She did not see Vaden or many remaining Rangers. She noticed a few dead legionnaires on the ground. As she scanned, she at last saw a face she did recognize—Brethor. He was sitting on the ground and covered in mud and orc blood. He sipped water and looked as disheveled as the rest of them.

He smiled as he saw her and Muera.

"You decided to join the fight down here. That's okay. I just swore I saw a flying metal pot land across the bridge. I think I'm a bit too wearied to be fighting at the moment."

"It was a Dwemhar machine. The sultan Amhe is here."

"Well, good. At least I know we are both a bit crazy."

They shared an almost forced laugh. "How is the city fairing?"

"It is overrun with orcs."

"Overrun?" another voice said. It was Lord Meask. "My father and brother?"

"Your brother was sent to the northern cape to be protected. He was still unconscious. Your father is in the metal machine over the mountains. But the city is lost. They attacked from beneath, and it is only a matter of time before the forces from there proceed across the field."

A sudden gust struck the fortress, and above the mountain, a massive cyclone formed as Amhe's machine moved over the tower. The many carpet riders attacking began to move away and deeper into the valley as others were caught in the twisting wind and thrown to their deaths. The tornado moved just over Amhe's machine, and it whirred loudly as it attempted to push up through the clouds. A bolt of blue energy shot down into the tower, and the entire structure began to vibrate, and the lightning tore into it.

The tornado was now unable to reach the machine, but Vakron-Tur moved it to the river, pulling up the fragments of the broken orc bridges in its grasps. The tornado moved along the river, at last dropping them near the bridge. The orcs not pushed aside by the remaining pike line of Eh-Rin went for the roughly constructed bridge, charging straight across and into the few Eh-Rin defenders near the ships.

The tornado then moved into the phalanx of Eh-Rin, tearing apart the formation and throwing men and spears in every direction. When at last it dissipated, the orcs had many openings to attack, and very quickly the forces against the orcs were falling apart.

"We must fight our way into the mountain!" said Ruak. "We must push up toward that tower!"

Meask raised his sword. "Rangers, Knights Guard, and all who can fight, charge into them! Force them back into their caves!"

16

LOST

The river path had been a long one. Tulasiro thundered forward for many hours, and though Kealin knew it should be dawn, he had also seen the veil of darkness that took the land. The clouds flashed with lightning, and he took it as an omen of what was to come. He worried for the Scions and was ready to end Vakron-Tur's reign. If he could only get there.

Rolling fields were on either side of him, and fairy lights danced along the riverbanks. He passed into a wooded region and began to smell the distinct stench of burning flesh. As they came to a clearing in the river, he could see plumes of smoke rising up beyond hills ahead. He then spotted lights to his right. It was the elven army, he assumed, but he could not be sure. It was too dark, and the many lines of torchlight were too far away to accurately discern.

The river current was faster here. As Tulasiro pulled

them into deepening waters, the path opened up. The rocky shoals on either side began to pass faster than before, and they flew down a small waterfall. The impact on the lower level forced Kealin to grasp the railing on either side, as there was another drop and another. The river widened and began to turn around the mountains.

It was then he could see it. The tower in the mountains and a beam of lightning erupting from above tearing apart the bricks and stones that it was constructed of. He looked down from the mountain and could see the waste of the battlegrounds. There were torchlights ahead and the opening to the mountain caves. He spotted goblins and orcs, along with several trolls, at the water's edge. He drew his blades, slashing a goblin that was closest to him on the bank. There was a lighthouse further down the river, but it seemed the path was blocked by wreckage from the orc bridge crossings that were thrown against the main bridge earlier. To his right, he saw nothing but chaos, and he looked to his left to find another cave and a wave of orcs charging into warriors of Eh-Rin.

Some type of fire flew over him, and a series of blasts struck near the bridge from the lighthouse fort. Looking north of the bridge, he saw that the orcs were overwhelming the ships of Eh-Rin, and many of the ships were burning. Blasts of lightning thundered up and down the shore, but many orcs were now swarming over the bridge.

Near the fort itself, he spotted several people running into the attacking orcs.

"Tulasiro, escape this river!"

The narwhal pounded the water and dove just under the surface. From the crown of Meredaas, a blast of wind struck the bridge, blowing off several orcs as the narwhal leaped from the water, pulling the boat over the edge of the bridge. Kealin timed his jump and landed with both Dwemhar blades spinning on the bridge.

The orcs screamed and scampered to avoid his singing swords that in the presence of battle turned a bright white. Hundreds of orcs now swarmed the bridge way, and he heard a battle cry behind him.

Men of Eh-Rin moved forward, jabbing their spears into the approaching fiends as Muera and Jesia sent blasts of fire into the orcs. The orcs fled the bridge way as Teusk slammed his staff in the ground casting a bright flash into the air. Teusk then saw Kealin and shook his head in disbelief.

"Good friend Kealin, indeed you came to join us!"

"I did."

He spotted Jesia in her silver armor and cloak. Her face was blackened with soot and orc blood, but she smiled, and he felt a stir in his chest.

"You are well?" he asked.

"I am, but more than once I feared you dead."

Kealin smiled. "Not yet. Where is my baby brother?"

"He is guarded by the Sanguine monks in Eh-Rin."

"That is good." He then turned and looked back to the tower and the bridgeway behind him. "Has there been a warrior in black? One with a mask?"

Teusk nodded his head. "In Vueric, he led the assault that claimed the life of Elaca as well as countless others.

Amhe saved us at the last possible moment, but I expect he will return to the field soon."

The archon sent a massive blast of energy into the bridge, and several rows of orcs fell back as pikemen of Eh-Rin pushed across the bridge.

"Some have moved up into a mountain path," Teusk continued. "I will stay behind to hold this bridge, and the pikemen will hold the path open to the mountaintop. The rest of them, including Ruak, Ivasel, and your friend Brethor, have gone up to face Vakron-Tur."

"Then I must join them," Kealin said.

He and Jesia began to walk away. Muera and Teusk remained at the bridge.

"I will stay with the archon," Muera said. "End the fighting, Jesia."

The two of them smiled, and then Kealin and Jesia began to run, pushing past the pike line fighting the orcs to a narrow path that was barely visible, save the path of bloody orcs that lay strewn going up the mountain.

As THEY ASCENDED THE PATHWAY, the blue lightning from the clouds ceased and the tower began to crumble. The whirring sounds increased, and Kealin watched as Amhe's machine dropped below the cloud line for a moment.

"What is that?"

"A Dwemhar machine," Jesia said. "The king of Vueric and Sultan Amhe are aboard it. You would not believe me if I told you how it felt to fly above the battlefield."

He had never seen such a sight, but he pushed his pace as they reached a much wider stairwell leading upward. He could hear the clang of metal and the shouts of men.

As they made it to an upper-level platform of ruins built into the rocks, he saw the others beating several orcs into the ground. Brethor glanced toward them as they approached and then immediately came toward him.

They embraced.

"I seemed to have gotten myself into a bit of battle," Brethor said. "Did you learn of your sister? Did you find her?"

He shook his head. "Not yet, but I feel like I know which way we must go. I must save my other brother first. He is a prisoner of Vakron-Tur, a warrior in a mask."

"Your brother is here, Kealin," Ruak said. "We have dealt with him plenty already."

Meask stabbed his blade into a still-struggling orc and surveyed around them. Dala looked up the path and shook orc filth from his scimitar. Meask went to Kealin.

As he came closer, he pointed his sword out. "Kealin, I assume. I hope you can fight. We have much we must do and it will not be easy. We move towards the summit."

"Let's go," Kealin said.

The warriors moved up another stairwell flanked with multiple burning basins of blue fire, and to a large opening in the rocks. There was a gateway built into the rocky chasm. Meask attempted to open it, but it wouldn't budge. Ruak smacked it with his blade.

"Let me," Brethor said.

The gate glowed gold and then opened.

"Dwemhar ruins, up here?" Meask asked.

"This very tower could've been Dwemhar at some time. It has taken quite a beating from Amhe's machine so far, and normal stone could not have done that."

The path turned to one that could only fit single file for most of the journey. When at last they came to an opening, they ran down several widening stairwells and to a large open basin flanked by mountain peaks, with only a single path to the large tower. The black and gold flames atop it were more evidently unnatural this close. They saw no sign of the wizard. Walking to the base of the tower, they looked down upon the battle plains. The elven army was concentrated on the eastern side of the valley, with hills to their back and the woods to their side. The orcs were encroaching quickly, and the trees that lined the northern region of the river were burning. The orcs had completely taken the lower valley and still swarmed the bridge. Blasts of magic were evident from even this high up, and the ships of Eh-Rin turned to trying to rescue their own who were in the burning ships along the shore. Further out at sea, white glowing ships approached. It was the Drean.

"More of our allies come," Meask said. "We must end this evil."

There were two doors leading into the tower. He pushed open the door, which surprised both Brethor and Kealin. He turned to them and pointed out to the valley.

"Our men fight for us; our friends fight for us. Wherever this evil is, we must find him. Follow me and let us end this shadow."

Meask turned and then gasped. A blade pierced through his helmet, and he quivered before falling to the ground. His killer emerged.

Kealin ran before the rest of them as Orolo and Krea appeared. The Rusis outstretched both of her hands and a blue wave of ice erupted from the tower. Jesia summoned a ward around her and Brethor. The icy spikes struck it and disintegrated.

Kealin took a spike to the hand but pulled it out. He tightened grip on his swords and moved up to the doorway just as a blast of wind threw them all far away from the tower.

He was on his back. He looked up to see the spinning spiked object high in the clouds. The fires atop the tower seemed to be sending a wisping magic field toward it, creating the darkness over the lands. He grimaced as Vakron-Tur came into view above them.

"Well, have we decided to at last see the truth of events, or are there plans for unfriendly happenings?"

"You have murdered one of the last lords of House Firda," Brethor said.

"As I will destroy any who stand in the way of the truth. I am your last hope, and even now, the elven army is crumbling. There is still time to stop this. We can stop the killing. I must only will it."

He looked to Kealin. "Your Dwemhar blades are not meant to draw my blood, for I am not the true enemy."

Kealin pointed one of the blades toward him. "I've come for my brother."

"He is well." Vakron-Tur smiled. "He has taken Vueric and returns to my side as we speak."

"Taslun will no longer be your prisoner."

"No, he will not. The moment his brother joins me, he will see the truth as well. I think he already is understanding. It is not too difficult once you drop assumptions of old."

"Do not be stupid, Brethor," Orolo said. "I have worked to this end, and I know it is right. Father would know this is the right path. Even now you know we guard a city meant for any and all of magic. Others have seen a coming doom. It is why we protect Elinathrond. Vakron-Tur knows we can prevent it."

"Orolo, our family is one of honor, not senseless bloodshed. Thousands have died this black night in the wake of what you know to be right."

Dala shouted and threw a dust high into the air. It flashed and glowed a bright red.

"In moments, the carpets of Eh-Rin arrive to assist us. You cannot escape, not one of you."

Vakron-Tur laughed. "Foolish desert rat, they will be the first to die, and because of you, Dala, admiral of the Eh-Rin. I will inscribe in the new history to be written." He lifted his staff. "I proclaim this day a day of tragedy for all of magic. When elves, Rusis, and Dwemhar descendants failed to see the light of the gods and came against their own salvation. You of little faith in the true path, I will go upon the world and will save those I can before the ultimate tragedy befalls us."

"You are foolish to believe you will succeed," Kealin said. "We have many allies. The Drean bring their fleet; the elves bring more to aid. I saw their forces marching in the darkness of the night from the east. The West will sing songs in remembrance of those lost, and I will drive my blade through your heart."

"You are truly foolish, Kealin of Urlas. I assure you no army of elves come, and you should know yourself, the Drean would never side with Eh-Rin."

Carpet riders flew over the top of the mountain, and blasts of fire erupted upon the tower. Krea had cast a ward, protecting them, but a moment later, Kealin was upon Vakron-Tur, and they began a duel as the others charged Orolo.

Jesia shot a blast of lightning, bouncing up to Krea, who cowered behind a ward. Ivasel and Brethor met blades with Orolo, who moved between them in a sword dance unlike Brethor had seen him do before.

"Kealin's brother taught me well in what little time we had. Perhaps you should have trained up as well."

Orolo parried Brethor and then punched Ivasel in the face, staggering him. Ruak jumped forward and slashed a near miss toward Orolo's head. His over-judging swing caused him to stumble past. At this point, Dala, took to the sky on a carpet. Though he sought to help the others directly, it seemed orcs scampered up the mountain path. He flew with the other carpet riders down into the gully, turning the entire path to flame to protect those on the summit.

Brethor crossed blades, locking his guard against his brother's. "I do not understand you, Brother. We have done so much together. Why now? Why betray your own blood?"

Orolo broke the hold and parried his brother's blade upward before driving the pommel of his own blade into his head. Brethor fell to the ground as Orolo ran upon him, putting his blade to his chest.

"The Srvivnanns have vowed to protect all as stewards of Elinathrond. The founders foresaw disaster, and I work to avoid it."

Ivasel came behind him and slashed across his back. Orolo stumbled forward, and Brethor rolled over on top of him. He punched his face over and over, at last smacking his gauntlet into the side of his head.

"Good," said Ruak. "If one more person speaks of a disaster this night, I'm going to smack them over and over too!"

A blast of wind struck the plateau, the area they fought upon, and Kealin and Vakron-Tur brought the battle directly beside them. Vakron sent deafening gusts over Kealin's head, and the half-elf used both Dwemhar blades to funnel the blast over his head before swinging for his leg. His blade missed, and Kealin spun to the side, slashing at his cape as the wizard struck the ground with an explosion of rock throwing Kealin, Brethor, and Ivasel away from him.

Jesia and Krea were still locked in a stalemate, but Krea had forced Jesia into a counter-ward by moving away from her, thus weakening the effect of the spell. Jesia focused her magic through her fingertips, envisioning a storm in her mind as her fingertips burned from failing to break the attack for so long. Her electricity turned white and she intensified the surges, wrapping it around the ward Krea held.

It was then whirring returned, and Amhe's machine flew above them. The crystals lining its base electrified the air, and a blast struck the tower. In a crumbling avalanche of debris, both the Rusis jumped away from the collapsing structure as the arcane pyre atop it tumbled onto the ground. A thick plume of dust covered all that fought atop the summit, and the very sky seemed to vibrate above them.

Kealin sat up and noticed the ruins of the tower had split down the middle of the summit. He couldn't see anyone else. Jumping onto the ruins, he ran to the edge and watched as Amhe's machine returned to the lower valley to fight. It was then he spotted another standing near the summit. It was Taslun. He held a large spear that dripped with red blood.

A blast of icy magic stuck near Kealin, and he looked to see Krea coming directly toward him. Jesia appeared as well, but Krea turned and sent a blast of fire toward her. She was upon Kealin and about to cast her spell when the spear struck center chest. She fell, grasping the spear. She began to seize, and then released her grip. The Rusis was dead.

Kealin looked toward his brother. "Taslun?"

Vakron-Tur appeared near the middle of the fallen ruins. "You may have succeeded in destroying my tower, but you cannot escape, and the power of Ur is great. His star still shadows all, and my claim remains on your brother. He wishes to kill you himself."

Taslun drew his blade and ran toward Kealin. As his

brother charged, he jumped to the side and twisted his blade in a half-circle, attempting to deflect his brother's blade. Jesia arose from the rubble to see Vakron-Tur observing the duel with his staff crossed. She took one of the vials to enrich her magic and then noticed both Ivasel and Ruak running behind the wizard. He turned, sending a blast of magic that they both dove from. She ran toward him and, with every ounce of magic she had, sent a blast of lightning into his back, pulling him into the ground with her powers. Her fingers burned. Her body shook. But she did all she could to hold the wizard down. She twisted her spell into a weave of bolts forcing it into the ground completely enveloping Vakron-Tur in the snare.

Kealin brought his Dwemhar blades down upon Taslun, attempting to force his brother back. Taslun laughed, and his sword became a fiery red. Kealin's blades seemed to react by shining white. He felt his body surge with energy, and he pushed forward. They swung their blades, and one of Kealin's shattered in the magical force his brother produced. He fell to the ground, dropping his other sword. His brother lunged towards him but he rolled just out of immediate reach.

He thought of his father and how easy he had bested Taslun. He wished his father was here now. Pushing himself up, Kealin drew his Urlas blades, but he knew that was not enough. He felt himself back in their woodland home. He remembered his brother. He remembered the man he was. He also remembered that he had nearly beaten him in every occasion. He wondered if it was possible now. But he had been going about this wrong. Defeating his brother was not his intent this night.

He ran for the edge of a boulder and climbed upward. His brother followed, although much slower. The hours of battle had likely weakened his brother, and his armor was heavy even without the enchantments and wards placed on it by dark magic.

Kealin made his way up the rocks and came to a bare hill. He turned, seeing Taslun moving up at an increasing rate. He sheathed his swords. As his brother came to the edge, he charged him and dove forward, driving his shoulder into Taslun's armor. They tumbled partially off the side of the mountain, and Kealin grabbed at the edge of the rocks, scraping and sliding as he did. Taslun had landed on a lower level than he had, and was already working to make his way back up.

He had a small amount of time. Kealin pulled himself in a quick climb back to the summit.

JESIA'S POWER WAS HOLDING. But the wizard would not be beaten. Suddenly, Jesia could feel winds wrapping around her. The twisting force took her feet, and she fought to hold her ground as the very air around her rushed against her magics. Vakron-Tur stood as her power was distilled around his own. He walked toward her, slapping her with his staff, and then leaped on top of her. He smiled and pointed his staff at her chest. She grabbed the head of the wizard's weapon and pushed it to the side as a blast of wind turned the stone near her to dust. He forced the staff to her chest again, and she grimaced, but he had became distracted. At that moment, Kealin jumped upon the staff, driving his blades into Vakron-Tur's chest, piercing his armor.

The wizard stumbled, coughing blood and falling backward. Kealin lunged forward, his blades pointed at his adversary. Vakron-Tur attempted to push his staff toward the half-elf. He parried it aside and slashed over and over, tearing the edge of the wizard's armor and breaking what protection remained from the wizard's body. He tore into his flesh, splitting it into several swathes, splashing bloody flesh on the summit of Demonhead. Vakron-Tur fell to the ground, and Kealin drove his blades into either of his arms, pinning them.

The wizard coughed and wept as he lay on his back. Ruak and Ivasel joined Jesia and Kealin above Vakron-Tur.

Horns began to sound in the distance. Strange horns. Not elven or House Firda, or those of Eh-Rin.

"I die, and so will we all in time."

"You murdered my mother and father. You were sentenced to a death by my blades. I told you of your fate."

Vakron-Tur coughed again, blood pouring from his mouth. He gargled on it as he forced a smile. "And I tried ... to warn you ... of yours ..."

A blast of blackness shot up around them. They staggered back from Vakron-Tur as his body was devoured in flames. A face appeared in the smoke. "I speak through the realms, through the blackness of my star. Not worthy was he to hold the Black Star of Ur."

The ground began to tremble, and a white light shot

out from the spiraling clouds above. A white fiery mass appeared where Vakron-Tur had set the device, and the fire descended before them. Hovering in air, the multi-pronged black and sheen device known as the Black Star of Ur was before them. From a center sheen black stone, a face appeared.

"Who will command them? The creation of my holiness?" the ghostly face said.

Before anyone else could do anything, Ruak stabbed his elven blade into its stone center. The Black Star of Ur shattered, and a deep gust blew upon them that blackened with the image of the unholy face and then moved to the south in a blazing fire of gold and black.

The summit became eerily still.

"It is done," said Ruak. "The Black Star of Ur is destroyed. The shroud of its shadow will fade but it will take time. Vakron-Tur has been destroyed. The orc will fall back with the coming sun and then soon afterward, their life forces will fade from existence once again."

Dala brought his carpet to land and bowed before them. "Great warriors, all of Eh-Rin respect your acts this dark night."

Brethor searched around for Orolo. He looked where he had left him but found nothing but rubble.

"Orolo! Orolo!"

But there was no response.

Kealin went to Jesia and looked over to Krea. "I am sorry—your friend."

She closed her eyes and buried her face into his chest. "She made her choice."

"Brother!" Brethor cried out.

Ruak and Ivasel began to help him when he slowly fell to his knees. Kealin and Jesia ran toward where Brethor stood. He held his brother's hand that was the only part of him visible from beneath the pillars of the fallen tower.

Brethor wept as he placed his other hand on the rock that covered Orolo. "I will tell Father of our deeds, the ones we did together. I will tell him of how we fought the evils of this world until your end."

KEALIN LOOKED down at the ground in sorrow for Brethor. He then looked over to where the entrance to the summit was and saw a figure approaching.

Brethor and the others lifted their swords up. Kealin did not. The black armored figure dropped his sword as Kealin began to approach him. Taslun reached up to the mask that veiled his face and pulled it off before falling into his younger brother's arms.

"Taslun! I have freed you," Kealin said.

His brother embraced him and then looked at him with tear-filled eyes.

"I have done so much. I have done so much that none could forgive me. I am free of that mask, and I thank you, but there is so much pain that I feel. I killed our mother and father. I killed children of men and elves."

"It doesn't matter now. You are free, free to do what you decide to do. Alri is lost; we must find her. She is to the east. She is held among the sounds of torturous screams. We must go as soon as we can. Alri needs us."

Horns called again. Taslun immediately went

toward the cliff, followed by the others. Looking down into the valley, the orcs were still everywhere but no longer moved forward with purpose.

On the hills on the east of the valley, a grand army had arrived. Their numbers were vast, and their formations like blocks of sheen metal.

"The legions of the Grand Protectorate. They have come to fight against the orcs," Ivasel said.

"No," said Taslun. "That is what Vakron-Tur revealed to me before this battle. It is what he foresaw. They, Kealin, hold our sister. They have used many ways to manipulate the world to their own desires. The Torturers, they created many travesties. They are a true evil. They are followers of the Itsu ways, the same as that priest we fought many years ago."

Roars filled the air, and on the horizon to the east, gray dragons appeared just as sunlight finally broke through the thick haze.

"The Gray Scourge," said Ruak. "They are the ones who had been searching near Risdannia."

The elven army was forming on the lower fields as the orcs began to flee toward the river crossings at the bridge.

"Dala!" said Ivasel. "Take me to my father on your carpet. I must get to him to warn him."

Dala and Ivasel both sat on his carpet, and they took off in a hurried flight into the valley. The dragons passed before them and began down toward the river ford and the bridge where the last of the defenders fought.

.   .   .

TEUSK AND MUERA had pushed the orcs back, and now they stood nearly on the other side of the bridge. They were both weary and struggled to keep their stances.

"We need to go back. We need to fall back to the fortress! Find more men of Eh-Rin," Teusk said, winded and sweating.

Another wave of orcs approached, and they began to back step to find more orcs on the opposite side of the bridge. The Rusis reached down and took a sword before running with the archon to nearly the middle of the bridge. They took stances back to back.

Muera heard a roar in the wind. A blast of fire engulfed them as Teusk lifted his staff. The elf casted a white ward just in time, blocking the flames. He grabbed Muera's hand. She felt her power faltering as the ward above them grew in size and solidified for a moment. The fire rolled around the edges of the sphere. Teusk's staff trembled, and Muera watched as the ward began to fail.

Teusk shouted out, "I cannot hold this much longer!"

Muera concentrated, working with the archon and pushing the ward back off as the elf's body trembled and he began to weaken. When at last the flames receded, Teusk collapsed.

She looked up as a dragon flapped over them, and then spotted another dragon burning the fortress around the lighthouse. Men of Eh-Rin who were still alive screamed as they were engulfed in the red dragon fire that splashed the stoneworks.

Teusk pushed his staff toward her. "Be from this

bridge; be from this place. Our friends still fight upon the mountain, but it seems the Orc Star is no more," he said, pointing to the sky. "Get to them."

His eyes closed, and he fell lifeless, sapped of his own life force from the outburst of magic required to hold the ward.

She looked around. Fires burned around her but had avoided the many barrels holding the dwarven dust on the bridge. The ward must have been just large enough. She looked toward the fortress and saw that dragon fire blocked her path. She looked back toward Vueric and saw only orcs.

Taking the staff in hand, she began to run toward the orcs. She swung her sword and staff, knocking back the first orcs she met before holding the staff out and blasting a ball of fire into them to clear the way. She was getting weaker with every cast.

As she jumped over two orcs, she felt several sharp pricks in her back, and she stumbled, falling onto the surface of the bridge. A dragon swooped over her, and she felt her back, feeling the poisoned spines it fired from its tail. The poison was already working, and her strength was gone. She looked up; the orcs had turned their attention down the road. She could hear approaching hooves but struggled to see who it was. A man approached. He fought the orcs, slashing and cutting into their bodies. There were others with him, but they fell around him as he made it to her. She looked up and saw the symbol of House Firda, the shark on the blue field.

The dragon swooped around, and the figure dropped

down beside her on the bridge as it sent a single ball of fire screaming toward them. It exploded, and the figure held the ground, shielding them both and deflecting the blast into the bridge itself.

The dragon took to the sky and left them. The figure dropped his shield and picked her up.

"I came. I came to fight, and I came to find you."

It was Lord Ridau.

She reached up, touching his face as he held her in his arms.

"You were sick. Your father sent you away. How are you here?"

He pulled her close, and she could feel his heart pounding beneath his armor.

"I awoke on the road north and ordered my men back to the city. I still was injured, but we happened upon fairies fleeing the dread of the orcs. I was healed. I rode for the city but found it overran, but I could see the lighthouse still stood. I came to find any who still fought, and I found you. Let me get you to my horse."

She felt very dizzy, and it was becoming hard for her to breathe. He began to lift her up. She glanced around, seeing the now exposed barrels of dwarven dust and the flames that licked the fine powder.

"Ridau," she spoke.

He looked down at her as a flash overtook them both.

"The Gray Scourge seems to be attacking the orcs. They have cleared those that surrounded the lighthouse," said Ruak.

Jesia dropped her glance to the ground. "Teusk and Muera defended the bridge."

His expression of slight happiness quickly changed as he realized the fact that more of their friends had died.

The dragons began to burn the edges of the valley, forming an encircling ring of fire. Amhe's machine flew out of the flames and hovered near the remains of the fleet of Eh-Rin as Drean ships approached.

Kealin watched from above as the elven army fell back toward the approaching forces of the Grand Protectorate.

DALA FLEW ABOVE THE ELVES. Ivasel searched for a sign of his father and at last made out his father's armor surrounded by that of the Vumark elves. He leaped off the carpet to the surprise of his father, who took note as Dala flew back out of the valley. The two royal guards with his father bowed to him and he noticed they each were bleeding profusely. His own father had many new slashes and breaks in his armor.

"Son! You have survived the hellish night! Men have come, but we must pray it is not too late. I have come to welcome any who may fight these dreaded beasts. For many hours, I feel I have only seen bloody orcs, goblins, and elves. You have defeated Vakron-Tur, then. The orcs flee! A wondrous day that these wretches are too late to partake in the glory of. The kingdoms of Fikmark and Vumark endure!"

Ivasel grabbed his father by the shoulder. "The men,

I fear they do not come as allies. We must move into the woods. We must move behind the protection of our borders!"

The king and his son looked around at the battered soldiers around them. They had fought a long time in increasingly worsening conditions and were now weary beyond fighting much more.

"They would not move against us like this. They did not know we would not succeed against the orcs."

"That is what I'm saying, Father. Vakron-Tur warned us. He wasn't the evil against us. He has never been."

A series of drums began to roll upon the hilltops, and a single loud horn bellowed. The sky blackened with the release of arrows and spears in a deadly shower that struck down the last of the royalty of the elf kingdom of Fikmark.

As HORNS BLEW AGAIN, the legions of the Grand Protectorate charged forward into the forces of the elves. Kealin looked down in horror. The dragon riders began attacking the carpets of Eh-Rin, and Amhe's machine moved over the valley. In a blast of energy, it began to strike down dragon after dragon as other dragonriders attempted to attack him.

Taslun looked to Kealin. "The legions are using this valley to destroy all. We must use their blindness against them."

"What can we do?" Kealin asked.

"You and your friends must escape. Go south and

then to the river east. Go toward Alri, if you wish, she can still be saved. But know I cannot go with you."

He begin to walk away with a slight limp. Jesia handed him a healing potion which he drank and then grimaced as his leg began to rapidly heal.

Kealin glared at him. "Taslun! I am your brother. Your actions here do not sentence you to die!"

"I am not your brother. Your brother, by that name, died upon the steps of Dimn's palace. I ceased being Taslun at that moment. I consider it an honor to die with Calak before the gates than to live on as a shell of what I was. Let me do what one thing I can to enact revenge upon them and do good for the evil I am responsible for."

"I . . . I can't just let you go alone." He went to embrace his brother, but he was stopped.

Taslun gripped Kealin's shoulders as he stared into his eyes. "There are mages to the south, Kealin, mages who know of Alri. They know more than even Vakron-Tur. We were going after Alri after this battle. I understood, even beyond the power of the mask, the purpose of what Vakron-Tur was doing. The Grand Protectorate is a vast and powerful force. I know what our parents searched for and why they came so far south after the Northern kingdoms of the elves were destroyed."

"They were called by the Scions of Starfall. Ruak told me himself."

"The Blades of Urlas, yes. But there was something greater at work. It is the rumor Dimn abandoned us for. A weapon that can kill a god. Seek the mages to the south; they are waiting for one of our blood. There is so much I wish I was able to tell you, but there isn't time.

Vakron-Tur was only a pawn, dear brother. My blood is not as strong in our mother's ancestry as yours. Go. You will need allies, and I will assure the Grand Protectorate will be blinded to your escape. I do still have an army."

He began to walk back toward his sword.

"The orcs are burning in the valley below," said Ruak.

"Not all of them, Ruak. I also have men of shadow, trained in the blade as myself and Kealin. We will attack the back line of the legions. I will seek redemption as I slay as many of them as I can."

"You cannot control them as Vakron-Tur. The Black Star of Ur was destroyed."

"Orcs follow the strong," he said, reaching for his sword and mask. "I wore this mask to lead them then. They will follow me again."

He put on the mask, and his eyes flashed red.

Kealin approached his brother, kneeling before him. He drew out his brother's Urlas blade. Taslun dropped his other and took his old sword in hand.

Taslun spoke to him in the deepened voice from beyond the mask. "A good blade is a welcome friend. Kealin, do not weep for this body to die. Go with your true brothers, the ones who have stayed with you and were true to the cause of all in an honorable form. I go to finally join Calak and Mother and Father."

With those words, Taslun descended down the path, leaving Kealin on his knees.

Jesia touched him on his back, and he stood to embrace her. He wept but looked up to Brethor and Ruak.

No words were spoken, for none needed to be. The amount of loss heavy upon each of them would make any trivial talk insulting.

Kealin ended the long embrace and jogged over to the edge of the cliff, refusing to look down into the valley. He picked up the remaining Dwemhar blade and slid it into the empty spot left from his brother's sword. He held back the tears. He had seen enough death.

He climbed onto the rocks as the others followed him. He didn't know where they would go, but he knew returning off the mountain on the north side was too risky. They began working down large rocks that made up the outer edge of the summit as they went south.

He looked over. Still able to see the sea, he noticed the Drean ships had destroyed Eh-Rin's fleet. He saw a flash and spotted Amhe's machine. The dragons followed just behind it, flames blowing out of it in multiple places. There was a blue flash, and Amhe's machine fell in a burning mass to the sea.

Kealin closed his eyes and shook his head. He then felt a sharp pain in his head. He saw the Glacial Seas, the maelstrom, and then the tower of ice. He spotted Vankou rocking and playing his organ and laughing. He then saw Val's face, aboard the dwarven vessel. Val shook his head and reached out, but his neck was still severed, and he died. Vankou then came into full view, and all his eyes could see was the one of death. He then saw Eh-Rin, and a shadow descended upon it. He heard his baby brother's cry, and he screamed out.

"No!"

The next thing he knew, Brethor and Ruak had him by his arms as he dangled off the side of the mountain.

"Kealin! Hold on!" Brethor said.

They dragged him up and waited for him to catch his breath staring at him in confusion.

"My brother in Eh-Rin. We cannot leave him."

Brethor grabbed him by the shoulders. "The Sanguine monks are beyond even those of Eh-Rin. They will keep him safe. We must have faith. We must get to Alri and try to reverse whatever we can of the evil done this day. Leave your brother to the ones who can protect him better than you."

Kealin was torn, unsure of what to feel, to believe, or to trust. He wanted to reach Alri. He still could see the mountain she was at. He wanted to go to his brother, but doing what he sought had done little good up until this moment. He stared at Brethor and gave what little bit of a quick smile he could. On his feet again, they followed the stone edge until they came to another hidden stair-well in the southernmost place they could safely reach.

Brethor had no doubt that these were Dwemhar ruins. He could feel the vibration under the rock, but upon finding another gate with ruins above it, he knew it to be true.

Kealin pushed his hand on it, and it turned to gold before opening. They hurried down the stairwell that descended into a dense forest surrounded by mountains. Kealin looked up, seeing a twilight sky in the distance. The shadow of the Orc Star had all but completely faded, and now he moved toward the light.

17

FIRES OF THE FALLEN

Dala had been forced down, and his carpet lay tattered along the beach near Vueric. He looked upon the mighty ships of Eh-Rin and the havoc caused by the forces of the Drean.

He stepped over the bodies of his fallen brothers, tripping over an orc carcass and pushing himself up to see the smoke-filled sky above. Everything and everyone he knew were burning. He made it up to the roadway and ducked down behind a trio of slain horses as another dragon made a scorching pass.

So much had changed so quickly.

He turned over to lay his back against the corpse, when suddenly, multiple Drean men were upon him.

"Dala!" one of them said. "The grand vizier would love to speak with you. I would suggest we take your ship"—he laughed—"but most of them are already sunk."

Dala thrust his sword up, but a scimitar cut into his hand, severing it from his body. He screamed and rolled on the shore as his arm squirted blood. He was bound with a rope, and a rope was tied to his bleeding arm.

"Don't want you to die too soon," one of them said.

They dragged him to a nearby ship and tossed him in before beginning a rocky journey out to an awaiting vessel.

The water was thick with blood and burning wood. He was taken to a pristine vessel that had likely stayed far away from any actual battles until it was deemed safe.

Before he could even sit up, a firm grasp took hold of him and threw him against a large barrel. There were shared laughs and then a staunch command to stop from a deep voice.

Dala glanced up through blurry vision to see a man squatting down to him. "Your empire has fallen, and now I, Vizier of the Drean, have command of the seas across the Vindas Sea. We will burn your precious city of Eh-Rin, and know we will enjoy all of the pleasures to be had in doing so."

"Kill me," Dala said.

"Oh no, there is no quick death for you. You will watch." He laughed. "We have no other person of your army to do so. You and your carpets. That was hilarious. Has no one told you that carpets are for walking on, not flying?"

There was another shared laugh among the crew.

"How much did the Grand Protectorate pay you?"

"Enough. But to burn your fleet, there was no payment needed. They will support our claim to these waters, and that is enough."

Dala winced in pain at his severed arm, but as the vizier turned his back, the admiral of the burning fleet of Eh-Rin drew a hidden dagger from his gauntlet. He stood and charged, but the vizier turned and slashed him with a large blade.

"Shame you will die so soon now. Eh-Rin will likely be a beautiful sight when it is made to burn brighter than the desert sun."

Dala's eyes faded, and he saw no more.

THE LEGATUS IRUIS had fallen along the stretch of beach near the Eh-Rin fleet. Knocked unconscious in the fight to hold the bridge, he had survived the explosion that destroyed the bridge itself. He heard sounds first, and then he thought he should already be dead. He awoke and looked up to see camels surrounding him. He tried to see whom it was, but was forced into the sand.

"This is the one. They said to grab him if we saw him. He will fetch us a nice bounty from the general."

A sack was put over Iruis' head, and he could only hear the sound of trotting camels. He could tell from the smell he moved through burning lands but could not guess where he was going. It was some time later, he was pulled from the camel and dragged on the ground.

"Let me see this traitor," a voice said.

Iruis shielded his eyes as a torch was held just near his face. "This is him."

As he was pulled up to his knees, he could see he was in a Grand Protectorate camp. Walking beside him was the old man from the Eastwatch camp. The one who had spoken of ten legions to Lord Meask. The hands holding him threw him on the ground, and he looked up to see two boots directly in front of him.

"Get up!"

He pushed himself to his knees and then stood shakily as he wobbled and struggled to stand. The man staring back at him was one he did not recognize. It was a general, by the armor he wore and the insignia of an eagle brooch on his cape.

"Behold the glory of the Grand Protectorate," the man said with an outstretched motioning to the west of him.

Iruis looked out, seeing the grand devastation of the battlefield. There was no one left alive in the piles and piles of dead that stretched across the entire valley. The city of Vueric was aflame from dragon fire. The lighthouse was nothing more than a crumbling mass beside the broken bridge that was covered in bodies that had washed downstream. The vast legions had spread out through the valley, and many headed north into the elven woods. Above them, the sun finally pierced through in long rays giving more light to the horrid sight.

"Behold the beginning of our new world, a world you betrayed, a betrayal that will be dealt with."

He punched him in the stomach, and Iruis fell to the ground.

Hands grasped him again as he was taken to large pyres built atop the hill. He was dragged along the set logs and tied to a pole. There were others there. They were elves, but none he knew. They were some of the survivors who were not as lucky to have died a quick death as many did on the field of battle.

"Enough is enough waiting," the general said. "I held off the burnings, looking for the betrayer, and we found him."

Iruis looked down at the logs beneath his feet and then looked up. Something was happening.

Multiple legionnaires fell dead along the outer edge of the camp as shadows moved along the perimeter.

"Legions, rally!"

Horns began to sound in rapid bursts, and Iruis looked to the south to see a mass of orcs and a man in black armor charging toward them.

Legionnaires began to fall into formation from all areas of the camp, and the approach of the orcs and the warrior in black slowed until the fighting bogged down just outside the range from where the shadow warriors were. The elves next to him suddenly had their throats slit as a flash of shadow gave final deaths to the ones captured. The shadow came before him, and then a spear was thrust up into the shadow. It took the form of a bleeding man before a legionnaire stabbed it repeatedly.

The general fell back, pushing the old man back as well.

Iruis watched as the warrior in black broke through the legionnaires and charged the general. A line of legionnaires rushed forward with throwing spears, and the warrior was struck multiple times. Other shadow warriors moved in sporadic flashes, barely visible, but the general caught one after the other with the edge of his blade, dropping them before the masked warrior.

The last of the orcs were pushed back, and the general laughed as the many would-be assassins struggled to still strike him. Legionnaires came alongside the general, awaiting the order to end their lives. The old man raised his hand.

"Let us not kill these ones just yet. My friends and I, well, we might have a use for such keepers of death as these. Bind them."

The general gave the order, and the shadow men were bound. What magic they used was lost, as they appeared now as normal men. The mask on the warrior fell off and crumbled as the bleeding man died.

The general went to him. "Good there was only one of you. I'm not ready for the afterlife, friend."

He then turned to Iruis and picked up a torch from a nearby brazier.

"Oh, but you, traitor, you are ready for your burning. By order of the Grand Protectorate, I sentence you to death by fire."

He lit the pyre, and Iruis felt the flames lick his legs and then felt a searing heat as his eyes were blinded and his body burned.

It was many hours since the events at Demonhead. The realization of all that transpired was heavy upon them, but they each tried not to show it to the others. They came to a river, and each took long drinks as faeries flew around them. Kealin held out his hand, and the fairy sat on his finger before then twisting and turning up and down his entire body. He felt renewed, but shuddered at the pain in his chest.

"It will not fade from any of you, what travesties that have happened."

The voice was sudden and seemed to speak from within the woods itself. Each of them heard it.

They looked around, looking for the source and holding their hands on their weapons. Jesia summoned a ball of fire that quickly extinguished in her hand. She looked at Kealin with a confused look and drew her sword.

"There is no need, survivors. The five have foreseen. The five know. Come to the five. Sacred truth to you we'll show."

Kealin looked deep into the woods and saw a single figure who appeared only as a shadow. He closed his eyes and in his mind he saw Alri in the prism as before in his vision.

"This way," he told the others.

Thank you for reading! If you enjoyed these books, please consider leaving a review of the set! The final trilogy is available on pre-order now and is releasing very soon! Join my mailing list to get a notification:

Mailing list: https://www. subscribepage.com/rogueelfofurlas

Shadow of the Orc Star is one of the darkest of my novels. The sudden deaths of multiple characters across the battlefield in a short time served to show the horror to come with the true enemy of those of magic, the Grand Protectorate of Men. Modeled after the Roman Empire in many ways, the Grand Protectorate tries first to have you "surrender" your crown and then if you do not submit, they take control or destroy you completely. In this case, the arrival of the orcs and Vakron-Tur served to served as a catalyst for the actions taken by the Legions.

Vakron-Tur and the other option.

Death could have been avoided. At least, death of so many of the characters as happened in this final book of the Songs of Shadow trilogy. While there had been raids and small conflicts, the brute force of the orcs were held at bay. The conversation on the bridge was the last chance. Vakron-Tur was the villain that could had been the hero, from a certain point of view (cue Obi-Wan.)

Had an agreement been struck, orcs and elves would have marched East, with most of the elves never needing to go to war themselves. The race of men would have been struck down and while there would have no doubt been protest by some inner circles, Vakron-Tur would have pushed through to the capital cities of the race of men and could have ended the war to come.

But he's dead. The orcs are gone. Alri is still missing. There is a deeper secret here and Kealin is about to discover the truth of all that has moved beyond his sight. The other option, the other path that all could have taken is no longer a choice.

Ruak? Isn't Ruak in the Stormborn Saga? Why is he not working with the King?!

As I showed a bit of here, Ruak and King Suvasel had a falling out. Yes, this is the same Ruak who held the line defending against the waves of vampires with Evurn and Aeveam of Stormborn Saga, the forward hand of the King and the hero who went on to fight in the great war with the Rangers of Taria. But don't worry, Ruak is better not being under the rule of the King. But even that has a bit of a twist. You'll see in the upcoming trilogy!

"Killing Cliches"

I chose to kill several characters and I do feel somewhat bad about it. BUT, we can blame one of my soundtrack songs... Personally, my favorite was the Lord of House Firda attempting to save the Rusis on the bridge. A "knight in shining armor" saving his "love" though by deflecting the dragon fire, he set off the Dwarven Dust and in turn caused an explosion...

Is everyone dead? Really?

Death is a finicky thing in this world. I think you'll start wondering this a bit more when you come across the very first new character coming up in the next boxset. Necromancer's Curse is quite a story. :)

The Legend of Zelda References

I had a few in this book. From the fairy in "The Lost Woods" Kealin found himself in at the beginning to the "Water Temple" of Lake Traseen. Did you catch anymore? Let me know!

My Writing Playlist

There were many songs that I listened to while writing this but one stood out. I kept it on repeat, listening to different versions and loops, all while writing the book that would find eighteen of twenty-three characters either dead or missing by the end. You'll see which one I'm talking about and if you're familiar with Game of Thrones, you'll understand... (at least it was a battle and NOT a wedding.)

Shadow of the Orc Star Playlist

1. Rains of Castamere (various versions but I preferred the one by Srod Almenara. This is the rock/metal version.)

2. Black Blade, Archangel, Victory, Nero, Aura -Two Steps From Hell (all tracks listed here for simplicity)

3. Alesia - Eluveitie

Hello,

If you're new to my writing and have gotten this far, thank you! Book one is one of my oldest titles and while I worked to clean it up, it wasn't a full "rewrite" but I did my best to improve on what was already there. I'm actually writing the sequel series to these boxsets right now.

Why did you do two box sets of your Half-Elf Chronicles series?

I did two because between three and four there is a shift in the tone of the story. While books one, two, and three we see a more desperate Kealin searching and grabbing for any chance of hope in his siblings, the second trilogy reveals and then takes a "wrathful" dive into a true reckoning upon the world. I'm excited for you to read this next trilogy!

This was a dark story.

It was. I get that real life is dark, too. As a reader, a story with a tone like this can be depressing but I promise it improves. :) My profession before I was writing full time was a first hand look into some of the darkest parts of the civilian world. I was a full-time Paramedic working in EMS. I've seen and witnessed many things and one truth I can pull from my nearly ten years on a truck was that life and death rarely makes any sense but at least here, in this fictional world, some of this death will and I think you'll be surprised!

I hope to see you at the end of the next boxset after the final book, The Last Dwemhar. Don't worry, the next boxset will have more bonus stuff like this one... and even Tulasiro going up against a sea monster... just for good measure. :)

May the lights of Wura guide you,

Jeremy

The World of the Dwemhar

If you would like to know about new releases, specials on other books, and get insider information before anyone else, head to my website and join my mailing list!

www.authorjtwilliams.com

STORMBORN SAGA
Stormborn
Mage Soul
Elf Bane
Stormborn Saga Trilogy
Ranger's Fury (Ranger Trilogy #1)
Black Moon (Ranger's Revenge #2)
Aieclo (Ranger's Revenge #3)
Epochs (Clockmaster's Shroud #1)
Shards of Etha (Clockmaster's Shroud #2)
Shadow Cry (Clockmaster's Shroud #3)

HALF-ELF CHRONICLES
Half-Bloods Rising
Seer of Lost Sands
Shadow of the Orc Star
Necromancer's Curse
Wrath of the Half-Elves
The Last Dwemhar

ROGUES OF MAGIC
Rogues of Magic Trilogy

LOST TALES OF THE REALMS
Ranger's Folly (Ranger's Revenge Trilogy Prequel)
The Dwarven Guardian
A Stranger's Quest
Wizard Trials

All books listed here are within the same world. For further information, please head to my website!

www.authorjtwilliams.com

ABOUT J.T. WILLIAMS

USA TODAY BESTSELLING author J.T. Williams writes both epic fantasy, inspired by the likes of Tolkien, Salvatore, and Brooks, along with darker sword and sorcery, fueled by countless hours playing Elder Scrolls, The Legend of Zelda, and many other fantasy RPG/ MMORPGs. When he isn't writing, he wages war in his backyard with his children having make-believe battles against the orcs invading from next door. He is married and has five little orc slayers.

As a longtime lover of fantasy and the surreal, he hopes you enjoy his contributions to the world of fantasy and magic.

www.authorjtwilliams.com